Khrist...

Dear Re:

We at Berkley invite you to enjoy ~~Kristen Granger's~~ exciting trilogy of glorious romances set in Charleston, South Carolina, during the Revolutionary War in 1780–1781. The Charleston Women are three beautiful, brave, and thoroughly memorable cousins who face the war in vastly different ways and who fall in love with heroic men who will delight you as soon as you meet them.

Each heroine is featured in her own book, but her cousins appear in her story so you never lose sight of these very special women. Noelle Arledge confronts Indians and Redcoats *(Crimson Sunrise)*; Erin Banning embarks on dangerous supply runs to aid Patriot soldiers *(Midnight Star)*; and Lilly Arledge must follow her heart and her own beliefs despite pressure from her Loyalist father *(Carolina Moon)*.

Their adventures, bravery, and romantic spirit will give you hours of reading pleasure you won't want to end. Each romance stands on its own, but together they form an unforgettable trilogy about love and courage in the midst of America's fight for independence on the coast of South Carolina.

Happy reading!

Judith Stern

Judith Stern
Senior Editor
The Berkley Publishing Group

MIDNIGHT STAR

KRISTIE KNIGHT

DIAMOND BOOKS, NEW YORK

MIDNIGHT STAR

A Diamond Book / published by arrangement with
the author

PRINTING HISTORY
Diamond edition / July 1991

ISBN: 1-55773-537-9

Diamond Books are published by The Berkley Publishing Group,
200 Madison Avenue, New York, New York 10016.
The name "DIAMOND" and its logo are trademarks
belonging to Charter Communications, Inc.

PRINTED IN THE UNITED STATES OF AMERICA

10 9 8 7 6 5 4 3 2 1

For Michael Ashley Sproles,
my son,
who never lets me down;
who taught me the real meaning of life;
whose birth made a woman of a little girl;
and who is my very best friend.
I love you.

For my dear baby sister,
Joyce Knott,
who listens and laughs and loves without judging.
I apologize for kicking you out of bed
when we were so very young.
Nobody ever had a better sister.
Nobody ever had a better friend.
I love you.

CHAPTER
1

December 25, 1780
Charleston, South Carolina

UNEASINESS KEPT ERIN BANNING AWAKE. FOR HOURS she had tossed and turned until she could stand no more. Sleep usually came easily to her—but not tonight. Where could Papa be? she wondered. Rising from her bed, she slipped into a wrapper and peeked out the window, knowing she would see nothing to relieve her apprehension. After pitching another log onto the fire, she curled up on the divan and tucked her feet beneath her to keep them warm.

Her father, Arlen Banning, should have been home last night, and Erin worried about him. The British patrols that were so prevalent around Charleston could have caught him and shipped him off to St. Augustine without her ever finding out. Erin felt that something awful had happened, but outside her bedroom her manner had to remain confident or the whole household would be in grave danger.

"Why did this horrible war ever start?" she whispered aloud, then clapped her hands over her mouth and glanced around.

Sleeping across the hall, Walter Martin, Colonel Balfour's civilian assistant, compounded her problems. Life in a city under siege was difficult enough without having a British official billeted in her house—particularly since her

1

father ran a supply route that provided necessities to the Continental Army.

The bells of St. Michael's broke the silence. One, two, three . . . five times. Too early for most people to be about. Erin glanced around. Something was wrong. Papa had promised to be home in time for Christmas. He never broke a promise to her, and today was Christmas Day.

A clatter startled her as she worried about her father. Listening intently, she waited to see if she heard the sound again. Unable to identify the single noise, she went to the window and looked out again. She could see nothing.

The sound had come from her backyard. Erin left her room, hurried noiselessly along the dark passageway, descended the servants' staircase, and paused at the back door. With the sliver of a moon veiled by thick clouds, nothing of the yard was visible when she peeked through the lace curtains.

Biting her lip, she waited, wondering what she should do. She knew it couldn't be her father; he wouldn't make so much noise.

Her eyes finally adjusted to the darkness, and she saw a shape moving from the carriage house toward the piazza. Whoever was there had found the wooden bucket that Toby used to water Arlen Banning's horse. As the figure neared, she discovered that two men were stumbling along together, barely able to walk.

Unable to stand the tension any longer, she opened the door and stepped outside. One man seemed to be almost dragging the other along, and she hurried down the steps to help.

"Thank God we're here!" a male voice said, heavy with anxiety. "Help me get him into the house. If anyone sees him, we're all bound for the prison ships."

Erin stared in stunned disbelief. The stranger was dragging her father! Dark clots stained the left side of her father's face, and Erin was so shocked she couldn't move.

"Don't just stand there! Help me." The whispered pleas became urgent.

Taking her father's arm, Erin helped the strange man drag him to the piazza. For a moment, questions bombarded her mind. What had happened? Who did this? Would Papa die? Nothing coherent or useful came to her.

The shock wore off a little, and she motioned to the door. "This way."

She held the door open, and they went quickly inside. Noticing the scent of spices, she absently wondered what kind of Christmas they would have if her father was injured as badly as he appeared to be. The man supporting her father was tall, but she couldn't see his face. Erin knew he was staring at her and felt the color rise in her cheeks. No man other than her father had ever seen her in a dressing gown.

"We . . . we'll use the servants' staircase," she explained and pointed the way. She paused only long enough to take a candle, then moved forward. "Some of the servants may be up already, so go quietly. Our day starts early."

"Lead the way." The man shifted Arlen Banning's weight slightly to get a better grip, adjusted a leather satchel on his shoulder, and moved as quietly as possible down the dark hallway.

With every step up the staircase, Erin cringed as she felt her father recoil with pain. The smell of blood caused her stomach to turn, but she never wavered in her assistance. Terrified, she struggled on and tried to ignore the bitter gall rising in her throat. Questions tumbled in her mind, but she refused to voice them until she knew he was out of sight. Fortunately, his room was at the rear of the house near the servants' stairs.

When they reached the top of the steps, she paused. "Wait here."

Tiptoeing down the corridor, she prayed that Walter Martin still slept. Outside his door, she stopped and listened. Soft snores greeted her, so she returned to her father's side.

For once Erin was glad her father snored so loudly that her parents had been forced to sleep in separate rooms.

Waking her mother with the news of Arlen Banning's injury would be disastrous—and that could be postponed for now.

Always a featherhead, her mother, Vevila Banning, would surely swoon at the sight of blood and screech at the top of her lungs about Arlen Banning's injury. For some time now Erin had expected her mother to die of grief, but somehow Vevila Banning lived on, although she seldom made any pretense of knowing what was going on around her. Erin knew that their safety depended on secrecy. Her mother never could keep secrets.

Fear for her family assailed Erin as they reached her father's room, but she opened the door without hesitating, and they hurried inside. Leaving the stranger to support her father's weight, she closed the door quickly.

Throwing back the bedclothes with one hand, she motioned with the other for the man to bring her father forward. Erin allowed Arlen to fall back on the pillows while she removed his muddy shoes. Blood caked one side of his head, shoulder, and left leg. The fabric of his shirt had hardened around the shoulder wound, while the woolen breeches formed a crusty circle around the injury to his leg. A shiver racked his deathly still body. "We'll need a fire. He's freezing."

"So am I, miss. Here, Arlen insisted that I give this to you. We were almost killed trying to salvage it."

Bowie Gallagher handed the leather satchel to her and waited while the young woman hurried around the room and lit several candles. This had been a long night, too long, and he felt the exhaustion seep through his muscles and bones until they threatened to give way. In the golden glow of candlelight the room came to life. For the first time he noticed the slight stature of his hostess. Nearly a foot shorter than he, she'd nonetheless upheld her part of Arlen's weight when they brought him upstairs.

When she turned to face the stranger, he was taken aback. Pulled severely away from her face, her auburn hair hung in a single braid across her shoulder like a spike of flame on the soft white of her dressing gown. Looking closer, he saw that her square face betrayed a strength most Charleston women worked hard to hide. He sensed that this young woman would never be so petty as to hide her inner strength.

She strode to the mantel and lit the candles over the hearth. Extending her other hand to point to the fireplace, she turned to him. "Can you light the fire? I've got to send Nero for the doctor."

He took the kindling from her hand and felt the impact of the scent of rosewater and her penetrating eyes and found himself unable to look away. Deep green, they sparkled with the reflection of the candle she carried in her other hand. Her skin was creamy, and the fine planes of her face were highlighted by a hint of pink on her cheeks. Bowie found that he could hardly speak. "Miss . . ."

"Banning. Erin Banning," she supplied, looking up into his eyes. Color crept into her cheeks under his penetrating gaze, and she broke the silence. "I am Arlen Banning's daughter."

"Oh, yes. Arlen speaks of you often." Bowie stared for a moment and then realized how foolish he must look. "I'm Bowie Gallagher, your father's partner. I'd be delighted to start the fire."

"Pleased to meet you, Mr. Gallagher. Papa has mentioned you as well." Erin watched as he arranged the kindling and then placed a sizable log on top. More than a little curious, she shifted the leather satchel to her other hand, but she hadn't time to look inside now, nor did she wish to do so in view of this man.

For the past year she'd wondered about this phantom partner of her father's, but she understood the need for secrecy. In these uncertain times few people could be trusted, and Papa always avoided public contact with Mr. Gallagher. He had spoken enthusiastically of his partner's daring, but had never mentioned his name or described him to Erin. Mr. Gallagher's broad shoulders, snugly covered by his coat, tapered to a narrow waist, and she found herself wondering how he looked without the garment. She soon found out.

He removed his damp jacket and hung it over the back of a chair by the fire. He walked back to Arlen's side and looked down.

Feeling a bit flustered, Erin jerked into action. "I'll send Nero for Dr. Rutledge."

Erin hastened as quietly as possible up the servants' stairs to the third floor, taking two or three at a time. She wanted to send Nero on his way before questioning Mr. Gallagher about her father's injuries. Reaching the slaves' quarters, she gasped for breath before striding to the second door. She listened quietly, hoping to hear sounds that would indicate Nero was awake. She heard nothing.

"Not a good day to oversleep, Nero," she muttered and tapped lightly on the door.

As she was about to knock a second time, the door flew open, and Nero appeared completely dressed. "Yes'm, Miss Erin?"

Erin sighed with relief and silently thanked the Lord. "Nero, Father's been injured. Hurry to Dr. Rutledge's. You'll have to go around the long way to Tradd Street to keep from waking Widow Jenkins's dogs. You know it won't do for you to be caught. And be careful when you come back. We don't want to awaken Mr. Martin if we don't have to."

"What I say if anybody ask where I'm goin' this early?" Nero asked as he pulled on his cloak.

"Tell them you're headed for the fish market," she answered without thinking. "No, no. That won't do. Anybody with a pea for a brain would know that Toby would do that. Uh, tell them you're . . . Why, tell them you're going for the doctor. Everybody in Charleston knows how ill Mother is. Tell the truth."

"Yes'm. Don't you worry none. I bring back Dr. Rutledge lickety-split. An' I sure ain't gonna go near them dogs," he answered as he donned his black hat.

Nero followed Erin down the stairs and exited through

the back door. She watched him go down the steps and called, "Nero, please be careful and hurry."

Erin watched until he was out of sight, then went to the kitchen to look in the satchel. She pulled out a jar of preserves and a duck. Papa had promised her a duckling for Christmas dinner! Grinning, she raced back upstairs. She found Bowie tucking her father in bed. "Is he conscious?"

"Off and on. I removed his clothing to make him more comfortable. The injuries to his head and shoulder aren't as bad as his leg. There's a bullet lodged in the leg, and he cut his head when he fell against a sharp stick. It looks like a second bullet passed through his upper arm." Bowie gazed at the concern in her face. From the things Arlen had told him, Erin Banning was a fearless, spirited young woman. He hoped it was true. She would need courage during the next few days.

"What happened, Mr. Gallagher?" Erin could refrain from asking no longer. She sat on the edge of her father's bed and took his hand in hers. It was cold, too cold. She jumped up. "Just a minute. I'll get him some more covers. He's still freezing."

"Can you bring me a blanket, too?" Bowie glanced at her as he rubbed his hands together over the fire. "You look as if you may need . . . uh, I mean, it's too cold for that . . . you need something warmer to wear."

Erin gazed at him for a moment, not understanding what he meant. She wasn't the least bit cold. Then she looked down. She'd forgotten that she was wearing her wrapper. "Oh, I apologize. I never thought . . . I mean, I'll be right back."

Erin hurried to her room and took a few minutes to pull on a suitable dress and shawl before collecting several quilts from the armoire.

Wondering if Mr. Gallagher had been shocked by her attire, she squared her shoulders and strode into her father's room. She had neither the time nor the inclination to be embarrassed about appearing in her dressing gown. It was, after all, still the middle of the night. "Here, Mr. Gallagher. Wrap up in this."

Bowie took a quilt from her and draped it around himself. The chill he'd gotten from hiding for several days on damp ground beneath bushes and in the rushes at the edge of streams made him feel as though he'd never be warm again. He glanced at Arlen as Erin spread two more quilts over him. The man's skin was gray.

Bowie shook his head and wondered if his partner would die. "My thanks, Miss Banning. I'm freezing."

"Sit by the fire to get warm. I'll take care of Papa." Erin ran back down the servants' stairs to get the kettle of water left simmering on the back coals and returned quickly. She hadn't time to awaken the other servants. After hanging the kettle over the fire to keep it warm until the doctor arrived, she cast a furtive glance at Bowie Gallagher. He wasn't handsome in the sense of the foppish men she knew here in Charleston, but his strong profile silhouetted in the firelight intrigued her.

When he caught her staring, he raised his eyebrows questioningly. "Have I done something wrong?"

Erin thought quickly. What could she answer? "No, you were going to tell me what happened."

"Oh, yes. Some British soldiers ambushed us," Bowie answered and tugged the quilt closer around his shoulders. He felt foolish sitting here with this lovely young woman while he looked like an Indian squaw, but he was too cold to care. "I think it was blind luck on the part of the Tories, but I can't be sure. Someone could have informed them of our whereabouts."

"But who? No one knows about the supply route." Erin dipped a cloth in the hot water. Wringing it out carefully, she winced at the sting of the scalding water and looked up at her guest. He was clearly concerned both for her father and for their business—and for the Patriot cause as well. Luckily he cared for her father. Otherwise, Arlen Banning might have been left to die by the wayside. Tears stung her eyes as she considered losing her father to the British. "You have my undying gratitude, Mr. Gallagher."

"Bowie. Call me Bowie." He leaned forward in the chair. "I'm afraid we're going to become acquainted rather quickly because of this incident."

"What do you mean?" Erin asked, letting the steaming water drizzle through her fingers into the kettle as she wrung out the cloth again. Watching Bowie, she crossed to her father's bed and began to bathe his face with the cloth. He hadn't moved since they'd placed him on the bed. "I don't understand."

"Well, I'll have to stay here in Charleston for a few days until I can find someone to take Arlen's place." Bowie unwrapped himself and walked over to Arlen's bed. He tried to think of something else, something that would allow him to forget that his very best friend, his partner, a man who was more than a father to him, might die while he stood there. "Can you trust this doctor that you sent for?"

Erin gazed at him before answering. "I trust him with my life. It's Dr. Rutledge. Do you know him?"

"I know of him." He came closer to Erin. When she gazed up at him, he whispered, "Arlen told me you have a British official billeted here."

"Yes," she murmured. For the past few minutes, as she raced up and down the stairs, she'd hoped that Walter was still asleep, but he would soon be up, if he hadn't already risen. She couldn't risk having him see her father in his present condition. "We'll have to be very quiet. I'll have to find a way to tell Mama about this without upsetting her. She isn't well, you know."

"I understand. Your father said he hadn't told her about the nature of our business venture. Will that be a problem?" Bowie turned his back to the fire and watched her working with her father. By the time the doctor arrived, she would have most of the blood washed away.

Erin stopped and turned to look at Bowie. How could she tell a stranger that if her mother knew something, all of Charleston would know it? Keeping secrets had never been one of Vevila Banning's strong points. "It may be. I suppose I could lie to her."

"To your mother? Surely she will notice Arlen's injuries. What does he tell her when he leaves?" Bowie asked, stepping away from the crackling fire.

Erin concentrated on his questions. "Papa always tells her he's away on plantation business. As for his injuries, she will notice them, but I can very easily tell her he fell from a horse or something."

"I see. He also tells the British soldiers he's on plantation business." Bowie nodded and grinned. "It's a good thing she's as gullible as they are."

With a twinkle in her eye Erin returned his smile. "I wouldn't go that far, but she's quite gullible. Walter Martin probably suspects something, but he never mentions it because he eats better here than he could anywhere else. Walter brings us food, and Papa smuggles in hams and fresh fish."

"That helps me to understand your boarder a little better." Bowie looked at her, again struck by the courage she needed to live in such a dangerous situation. "Now, how are we going to explain me to Walter?"

Erin's mouth fell open, and she stared in disbelief at Bowie's words. "You can't be meaning to present yourself at breakfast, can you? Walter is willing to ignore certain things, but I don't think he'd risk his post over you."

Bowie nodded his understanding. He needed to come and go freely, but he couldn't put the Banning family in further danger by openly showing himself to Balfour's assistant. "I suppose you're right. Is there a place in this house where Walter never goes? I have a place to stay, but I can't get there for a few days. And I'd like to be able to consult with Arlen about the route. You know, I've never actually been up the supply route."

"I understand. Hmmm. Let me think about that." Erin considered the situation and cast a worried glance at her father. "I probably can hide you in here for today. Tonight I can help you get away."

"Thank you, Miss Banning." Bowie smiled, thinking that he'd have the day to get acquainted with this fascinating woman. The idea intrigued him, but his work was too vital for him to remain any longer than was absolutely necessary. "If you recall, I've been riding all night and—"

"Forgive me, Mr. Gallagher." Erin tilted her head and gazed into his eyes. "Mr. Martin has the run of the house—except the sleeping rooms. I'll take you to my room, where you may sleep safely for the day."

Bowie suddenly felt his spirits lift. "I understand some of the officers billeted here in town really enjoy life. They throw elaborate parties and dances while the townspeople starve." He considered the situation and shook his head.

"What's that, Mr. Gallagher?" Erin gazed at him. His light brown hair framed a strong face and bright blue eyes. He stood almost a foot taller than she, but his powerful presence, more than his height, seemed to dwarf her. "Can I help?"

Bowie considered her offer. Spending time with Erin Banning, using the excuse of working for the cause, seemed to him an appealing notion. Thinking quickly, he opened his mouth to speak but closed it without uttering a word.

A noise from the street distracted them. Bowie glanced at her as if to seek a place to hide immediately. "Who do you suppose that is?"

"It's probably Dr. Rutledge. I can't imagine why they're making so much noise." Erin glanced around the room and then at Bowie, who seemed reluctant to be found in the Banning home at this hour. "I told you Dr. Rutledge can be trusted. Stay here. I'll let him in."

Thankful that Dr. Rutledge hadn't tarried, Erin raced out the door, grabbed her shawl from her room, and tiptoed down the stairs. Outside, the streets were still quiet; the citizens of Charleston had not yet arisen.

Dr. Rutledge's carriage stood at the end of the walkway. Nero carried the doctor's bag, and the two men moved quickly toward the steps.

Erin drew her shawl closer and gazed over their heads

for a moment. The sun was rising over the bay. Glorious shades of scarlet, pink, and lavender blended to produce a spectacular sunrise. A few puffy clouds drifted lazily over the Ashley River; the day would be cold but splendid.

As the physician approached, she smiled and extended her hands in greeting. "Thank you for coming, Dr. Rutledge."

"You know I'm always available when you need me." Dr. Rutledge took her hands and clasped them for a moment. "I'm sorry about the noise, but I felt that my being quiet would cause speculation we can ill afford. People are accustomed to my habits and see my carriage here too often to question my comings and goings."

"I'm sure you're right, but every sound echoes in my head like a cannon," Erin explained. "It seems that the quieter I try to be, the more noise I make."

"Is Arlen conscious?"

Erin shook her head. Her father had regained consciousness briefly, but not when she was present. "No. But Bowie . . . Mr. Gallagher said he was conscious for a few moments. I fear he's lost a great deal of blood."

"Take me to your father, Erin, my dear. We can talk later."

Erin nodded and removed her hands from his grasp. Nero followed the two of them up the stairs, but Dr. Rutledge stopped the servant at the door to Arlen Banning's room. "Thank you, Nero. I'll take this from here."

As Nero sauntered back to the staircase, Erin opened the door and led Dr. Rutledge into the room. Bowie sat by the fireplace and nodded when Dr. Rutledge closed the door and followed her to the bed.

The doctor glanced at Arlen Banning and opened his black leather case. After taking his coat off, he said to Erin, "Please bring the light closer. Where is that confounded boarder of yours?"

Erin moved the candelabrum to the side of the bed. "I haven't heard him stirring. He had rather a late night last night."

"Thank the gods for that." Dr. Rutledge opened each of Arlen's eyes briefly and looked at them. He examined the cut on his patient's head, then turned to Erin. "Good job, my dear. I need you to work with me. You make a good nurse."

"Will he be all right?" Hoping to see some sign of recovery, she gazed at her father's limp body.

"Can't say, my dear, can't say." Dr. Rutledge continued his examination and finally turned to her. "The leg wound is serious." He continued probing the ragged bullet hole until he found the ball and removed it. "I'm amazed he survived this long. He's lost a lot of blood. He'll have to be handled carefully during the next day or so if he's to recover."

Stunned, Erin could only stare. Her mouth opened, but nothing came out. Dr. Rutledge was saying that Papa might die. Feeling suddenly cold and alone, she looked at her father. He was too young to die, too vital. Suddenly she was struggling to hold back tears.

She'd known his condition was serious from the moment she saw the injury, but to have Dr. Rutledge confirm it aloud was something for which she wasn't prepared. She watched as Dr. Rutledge sewed up the leg and then bandaged both wounds. Erin felt the strong touch of a hand on her shoulder and turned to see whose it was. Bowie slid his arm around her and held her straight when she wished she could faint to black out the possibilities. But she needed to be strong and had never fainted in her life.

The comfort of Bowie's arm around her helped a little. She realized he was suffering, too, but nobody felt the way she did. Erin Banning had always been Papa's little girl.

"Erin, my dear." Dr. Rutledge patted her arm. "Your father is going to need you during the next few days. You must care for him yourself during this critical period."

Lifting her gaze to his, Erin tried to smile. "Then, you think he may not . . . that he may . . . live?"

Dr. Rutledge nodded. "He's tough. It'll take more than the British to kill him, I believe. Although his condition is quite serious, I think he'll make it with the proper care."

"Anything, I'll do anything." Erin's smile widened with hope. "Just tell me what to do."

"Sir, I'll be glad to help if I may," Bowie put in, tightening his grip on Erin's shoulders slightly. He wasn't about to let Arlen die without a fight.

"Oh! I wasn't thinking clearly," Erin apologized hastily, feeling better now that Dr. Rutledge had given her some hope for her father's recovery. "Dr. Rutledge, allow me to introduce my father's partner, Bowie Gallagher."

"Ah, I thought you were the daring Mr. Gallagher." Dr. Rutledge extended his hand and clapped Bowie on the shoulder. "Arlen has spoken of you often. Delighted to meet you."

"You can't imagine how happy I am to meet you, sir. I thought Arlen would die before I could get him here," Bowie admitted and looked down at Erin. "This young lady is quite a bit like her father, don't you think?"

Dr. Rutledge laughed. "More than Arlen would ever have wanted. And I imagine poor Vevila wishes Erin had taken after the Teagues rather than the Bannings. She does look a bit like her mother, though, with that auburn hair."

Bowie glanced at Erin. In the soft candlelight her hair appeared to be tinged with gold. "Her mother must be a beautiful woman."

"Quite handsome, quite," Dr. Rutledge agreed. He picked up his black bag and turned to Erin. "My dear, I'll stop by again late this afternoon. If Arlen wakes up, give him a few sips of beef broth. Needs to build up his blood. Don't try to force too much down him, though. Might make him sick."

Erin thought the two men had forgotten she was there. They had talked over her head as if she were invisible, but she felt almost giddy with the knowledge that her father had a chance to live. "I'll do my best."

"Are you staying in Charleston, son?" Dr. Rutledge asked Bowie when he stopped at the door.

"Yes, sir. I need to find someone to fill in for Arlen." Bowie didn't move his arm but let it continue to rest comfortingly around Erin's shoulders. At first he had comforted her, but now her nearness and the wonderful scent of roses lifted his spirits.

The next few days might prove interesting, he thought and hugged her a little closer. Earlier, when he'd asked where he could remain out of sight, he'd intended the question to be innocent. But when she offered him her room, his mind had drifted toward a purpose far different from hiding out for a few days.

Erin Banning intrigued him. As Dr. Rutledge had observed, she was remarkably like Arlen. Her courage and strength seemed as great as Arlen's, and Bowie wondered how living with a woman with such fortitude would be.

Beginning to feel a bit embarrassed by the strong arm around her shoulders, Erin glanced up at Bowie. He stared down at her in such an intense way that she blushed.

When she turned to speak to Dr. Rutledge again, he was gone. She would have followed him, but Arlen stirred and her attention immediately focused on him. She broke free of Bowie's embrace and ran to her father's side. Watery eyes met hers, and a wan smile teased at the corners of Arlen's mouth, but speech was impossible. "I'll get you something to drink, Papa."

Erin raced down the stairs as if fleeing for her life. At the bottom of the curved staircase she paused to catch her breath. She realized that she had no choice but to let Bowie stay, but she wondered how long she could endure those clear blue questioning eyes without wilting where she stood.

"No time to think about him," she muttered and turned toward the kitchen. As she whirled around, she found herself face to face with Walter Martin. "Mr. Martin, I . . . I didn't realize you were up. I'm sorry if we awakened you."

"No, I've been up for quite some time. I awoke early. Some noise outside startled me." Walter eyed her closely.

"Yes, I had to send for Dr. Rutledge," Erin admitted, hoping that Walter hadn't been awakened by the noise of Bowie bringing her father home.

"The noise that awakened me occurred before Dr. Rutledge arrived," Walter remarked and leaned against the railing at the bottom of the stairs. "Something in back of the house, I believe."

Erin felt the strain of trying to act calm when her heart had almost stopped, but she shrugged noncommittally. "Cats or dogs, I suppose. Or perhaps Papa's return. If you'll excuse me, I need to hurry into the kitchen to warm some broth."

Hurrying past him, Erin felt his eyes on her but didn't turn around. If he knew something, there was nothing she could do about it now. If he didn't, she might let information slip if she continued to talk to him. Anyhow, she could do nothing now but wait. Her father couldn't be moved, and Bowie couldn't leave now that the sun had risen.

Once in the kitchen, she closed the door and leaned on it for a minute. Nero had stoked the fire, and she found a bowl of leftover beef soup. She ladled out some and put it in a pot over the fire. Several moments crept by as she watched the pot in silence.

Her thoughts drifted to her father's partner. Bowie Gallagher was different from the other men she'd met, and Erin found that she liked that difference very much.

CHAPTER
2

THE SOUND OF HORSES ON THE STREET PULLED ERIN from her thoughts as fear rose in her for a moment, but the riders passed by without stopping. By this time the broth was bubbling and rolling in the heavy black pot. Exercising great caution, she lifted the pot from its hanging position, carried it to the table, and ladled a small bowl of the fragrant soup for her father.

After a moment she dipped a second bowl of soup for Bowie. He had to be ravenous by now. She found some leftover biscuits and placed them on a plate with generous scoops of butter and blackberry jam. She could eat later, after she took care of her father.

Erin placed all the food on a tray, poured a glass of milk for herself and Bowie, and headed for her father's room. Briefly she wondered what she would tell Walter Martin if she met him on the stair, but decided that she would point out that her ill father always ate in his room and that she was going to join him for breakfast since his condition had worsened during the night.

She encountered no one on the staircase, however, and hurried down the hallway to her father's room. Juggling the tray precariously, she managed to open the door and step inside without being seen. Without hesitating, Erin strode to her father's bed and placed the tray on a table nearby. She glanced at Bowie and whispered, "Any change?"

Bowie shook his head. The fragrant smell of the soup reached him, and for the first time in many hours he felt

17

pangs of hunger, and his mouth watered. He gazed hungrily at the extra bowl and hoped she'd brought it for him.

"Mr. Gallagher—"

"Bowie," he corrected and eagerly watched her lift a bowl of soup. His tongue traced his lips while he studied the changes in her face as she first grimaced and then smiled.

"Bowie," she conceded and moved toward him, her skirts swaying gently as she walked. "Would you like some soup? It's not much, but—"

"I'm so hungry I could eat a saddled horse." Bowie smiled and raised an eyebrow thoughtfully. "Well, maybe I'd take the saddle off first, but I'd sure like to have some of that soup."

Erin grinned and nodded, wondering if he'd eaten since the ambush. She placed the bowl on a bed tray and handed it to him with a spoon and napkin. "Im sorry I can't invite you downstairs for breakfast, but I'm sure you understand. Walter Martin is already up and wandering about. I ran into him downstairs."

Desperately trying to appear nonchalant, Bowie sipped the soup with as good manners as his mother could have wished, though he wanted to tilt the bowl and slurp down the delicious contents. He watched her over his spoon as she picked up a small plate of biscuits and a glass of milk. He paused and smiled. "This is good. Do you think Walter heard our noise or noticed anything strange?"

Erin placed the milk and biscuits on the bed tray and hesitated. Her father seemed to be sleeping, and she was reluctant to awaken him, though he needed the nourishment. "Yes. I think he heard some of the commotion. I assured him that my father had returned ill from the plantation and that I had sent for Dr. Rutledge."

"Did he believe you?" Bowie asked the question carefully, wondering what they would do if Walter didn't believe her. Bowie didn't want to alarm Erin, but as he ate his soup, he imagined British soldiers converging on the house. He eyed her thoughtfully. She didn't appear to be the type of woman who would frighten easily, and he felt sure she could handle

Walter Martin in any situation—but perhaps not after the stress of this morning.

"And why shouldn't he believe me?" Erin gazed at Bowie for a few seconds and then turned to her duties. Her father appeared to be waking up. "Here, Papa, have a bit of broth."

With Arlen awake, Bowie forgot the discussion. He watched as Erin touched the spoon to his partner's lips. With a weak hand Arlen pushed her away and whispered, "Bowie."

Before Erin could answer, Bowie sprang to his feet, almost overturning the bed tray. "Here I am." He placed the tray on the floor by the fireplace and strode across the room.

Sighing, Erin smiled at her father. "Papa, you're home and safe."

Arlen glanced around, apparently startled that Bowie had managed to bring him safely home. "Thank God. Bowie . . . son, I . . ." His voice trailed off, and again unconsciousness claimed him.

Erin felt the tears press against the insides of her eyelids, but she refused to cry. Son. Papa called Bowie "son." Her father seemed more interested in his business partner than her. No doubt Bowie had become the son her Papa always wanted. Though she tried, she couldn't fill that void. For a moment anger touched Erin, and she stared at Bowie but realized the situation wasn't his fault.

Then she noticed the anguished look on Bowie's face and never doubted that the feeling between the two men was mutual. Bowie loved her father as much as her father apparently loved Bowie. Feeling a little excluded, she moved to the fireplace and watched. Papa loved her, she reasoned, he always had, but now he had a son—or someone close enough to call his son. "I'm sure Papa was trying to thank you for what you've done, Mr. . . . Bowie." She swallowed deeply and smiled. She wanted to express her gratitude, as well as her father's and a simple thank you wouldn't be sufficient. But what could she say? "I think he's very fond of you."

A little surprised by her statement, Bowie nodded and

then looked at her. "As I am of him. He's done a lot for me in the past few years. Through him I began to realize that I couldn't ride the fence in this war. My mother and father . . ."

Erin saw a wince of pain cross his face. "You don't have to explain anything to me," she said. "I understand."

"Understand? No, you can't. Nobody can." Bowie closed his eyes briefly and remembered the agony of listening to his parents screaming at each other, of his father slapping his mother, and he shuddered. "Freedom and independence are two things a man has to fight for, no matter what else happens. Nothing can stand in the way."

Erin glanced at her father, who seemed to be sleeping soundly in spite of the conversation. She felt that Bowie needed this catharsis, the telling of a story that still gnawed at his heart. "I doubt if he'll want to eat anything right away. Please go on with your story if you like."

"I think I've said enough." He tried to smile and cocked his head to one side. "Don't want to bore you until you fall asleep, too."

Bowie felt that something had changed in her attitude, something he couldn't discern. He shrugged, returned to his chair, and picked up the tray. For a few minutes he ate in silence while Erin moved the stoneware bowl that contained broth for her father to the edge of the fireplace to keep warm in case Arlen should awaken again. "We haven't settled the issue of where I'm to stay for today."

"You'll remain here, of course." Erin looked at him thoughtfully, although she wished he would find someplace else to stay. What could she do with him for the next few hours? He had business that must be attended to since Papa was ill. "How may I help you, Bowie? I want very much to make a contribution to the Partisans' efforts."

He considered her for a moment. He thought about her courage again and grinned. "Well, I'll need information. Nothing too difficult to obtain. Nothing that will endanger your life."

"What kind of information?" she asked, feeling eager to

help. This was one way she could repay the British for their horrible treatment of her friends—and especially her father. "Tell me what to do."

"As I said earlier, I understand that the British give parties and dances here in Charleston in some of the fine homes they've confiscated. Have you ever attended one?" He wondered if he should inquire about her social status. For all he knew, she could be engaged to be married. His gaze fell to her hand, but he saw no ring. When he looked at her face again, he was surprised by the angry flush.

"I'll have you know I don't socialize with the dirty scoundrels any more than I must to preserve our residence and freedom. I may have one of them billeted in my home, but that doesn't mean I lick their boots like some of the girls in town who seem to have forgotten—"

"Hold on," he interrupted, holding his hands up as a defense against her verbal barrage. "I just asked. I didn't intend to start the siege of Charleston all over again."

Erin calmed down a little. After all, he did need to know about her habits if she were to be useful to him at all. More calmly she continued, "I see the men who attend the infrequent dinner parties given by my boarder. I don't attend those outside this house."

"Perhaps you should. Is there any way you can finagle an invitation to some other parties? You can listen for information that will help us considerably." Bowie felt the rise of excitement tense his brow, and he tried to relax. If he could get advance notice of the British shipments and rob them, he could replace the supplies lost in the recent ambush.

"I'm not sure. I don't really see that I could learn anything of value to you while I seemed to enjoy myself at a Tory party." Erin settled more comfortably in the wooden rocking chair and held her cold hands up to the fire. The idea of spying intrigued her, but she doubted whether she could overhear anything significant at a party.

Bowie thought for a minute and sipped his milk. "Do you have any friends who are Tories?"

Again, Erin felt her anger rise. Was he testing her? "I find your line of questioning an embarrassment in this house, particularly in light of the fact that you know my father so well, Mr. Gallagher. I'd expect that of the British, but not of you. My father has long been a valuable asset to the Patriot cause, and his injuries are evidence of his loyalty. Furthermore, I—"

"Whoa, don't get upset again. You're like a hound on the trail of a coon. I'm trying to find a way you can be helpful without endangering yourself or anyone else." Bowie frowned. What he really needed was somebody to drive the supply wagons. He could hardly continue to slip in and out of Charleston by boat to procure supplies from the Bahamas and drive the supply wagons himself. "If only you were a man."

"I beg your pardon." Erin truly became irritated with him this time. Within a few minutes he'd all but called her a Tory and followed up by wishing she were a man. Indignant, she hopped to her feet and glared at him. "How dare you? First you accuse me of being a Tory, and then—"

"Hold it," he interrupted and flinched away as she came closer, as if to strike him. "I apologize for all my shortcomings, but we've got to find a way to make this supply route work, or the Patriot cause will be severely hampered. I haven't the time to play a chivalrous knight in shining armor to avoid hurting your sensibilities."

"How would my being a man help? Would you hand me a musket and powder and put me in the woods to shoot stray British soldiers?" Erin found his excuse barely acceptable, but sat down again. Nobody who knew her ever doubted her word. She glared at Bowie, hoping he'd leave.

Bowie chuckled softly. What a feisty wench she is, he thought. "No. I'd hand you the reins of a wagon and put you on the supply road. As it is, I can use you to obtain—"

"Drive a wagon?" she repeated and jumped to her feet again. "I can drive Papa's wagons. I went with him on many trips before the war. Just ask him."

Bowie glanced at the unconscious man on the bed. "At the moment—"

"Not now, you goose. When he regains consciousness." Erin almost danced around the room, anticipating the joy of playing a role in winning this war—not to mention the elation resulting from the freedom of the trail. Now she could make a difference. Allowing the possibility to buoy her spirits until she felt the room couldn't contain her, Erin began her campaign to convince Bowie that choosing her for the task would be his most prudent course of action. "I could do it easily."

"Impossible. Even if you are capable of driving a wagon, the rigors of being on the route in this day and time would be impossible for you to overcome," Bowie began and watched her animated face change to anger—which always made her eyes sparkle. She gets mad quicker than a wet settin' hen, he decided and resolved to proceed cautiously. "Erin, there's a war going on all around you. There are other things you can do. Things that won't endanger your life."

"You need me. You just said you did." Erin felt disappointed, as if her lungs were collapsing, and closed her eyes regretfully. "Why can't I do it?"

"For the love of a sailing ship," he muttered and met her eyes. "You're a woman!"

"And what difference should that make? You need a driver. I can drive. You need someone who knows the routes. I know the routes. You need someone you can trust," she declared and paused to suck in a boosting breath before continuing. "You can trust me. There's nobody else you can turn to."

"Not so fast, Miss Eager-to-Get-Herself-Killed-Pioneer. I have friends, too. Somebody can take over Arlen's job until he recovers." Bowie tried to hide his grin but couldn't quite conceal it. He liked this woman's spunk, though she obviously overrated her abilities. Maybe Arlen had taken her on some of his trips, but she was far too feminine to handle the rough trail she'd have to follow and the awful conditions that were inherent in driving the trails. It might take him a few days, but he'd find someone to drive the wagons. He'd have to. "You need to be here where it's safe. Besides, who will care for Arlen if you go?"

Color sprang to Erin's cheeks. "How dare you insinuate that I'm unable to . . . to . . . that you'd consider somebody else when I already know the routes and . . . an outsider . . . how can he be assured of safety along the way? The people at the safety points know me . . . I'm the only choice you have."

Bowie bit his lip to keep from laughing. He'd be willing to bet she could almost persevere against the British Army, but he wasn't willing to wager with her life. "The answer is no. I'm not going to have your blood, as well as your father's, on my hands. No. End of discussion."

"You have no right to—"

"Shhh!" Bowie cocked his head to one side. He moved silently across the deep green carpet and pressed his ear to the door. Someone had just walked down the hallway. He glanced back at Erin.

Standing nervously in the dimly lit room, she watched him with surprise. The sun had risen, and light filtered through the separations in the heavy draperies. With clenched fists she stood unmoving until he returned to the hearth.

He came close and whispered, "I heard someone outside. Could it be Martin?"

"I don't know. Should I go and see?" Erin felt the color drain from her face. In her fit of anger she'd almost shouted at Bowie. Though he deserved it, she didn't intend to jeopardize their safety by arguing loudly enough for Walter to hear.

Bowie thought about it for a few seconds. "No, I don't think so. If you do and it was Martin, he may wonder why you were listening at the door so intently."

"True. What, then?" she asked, her voice low, and settled back in her rocker.

"Wait and see what happens." Bowie sat, hoping that the listener had been a servant.

"The discussion about my taking the next load of goods up the wagon road isn't over. We'll postpone it until we find out what's going on," Erin stated and crossed her arms. She could be as stubborn as he was. Papa probably would say I'm worse, she acknowledged and cast a furtive glance at the bed.

If she could somehow convince Bowie that she was his only choice for the job of taking the supplies to the South Carolina Irregulars, who would take care of Papa? Nero could do it. He was as smart as anyone in Charleston, though he sometimes tried to hide his intelligence. Her mama would be more of a hindrance than a help. A new thought occurred to her. Erin decided to take her parents to Bluffwood. Having her mother remain in Charleston had always been a danger, especially since her fall. Unconscious for days, she'd been unable to think clearly when she'd awakened and lacked power of concentration, even that of a toddler. They'd be much safer at Bluffwood.

Pleased with the new ideas forming in her mind, she smiled at Bowie. She'd wait until this latest crisis had passed before informing him of her plan. If Papa and Mama were at Bluffwood, she'd have a logical reason for going in and out of Charleston.

Bowie decided he'd better go easy on Erin for a while. He'd been pretty rough with his refusal of her offer, but he'd done it for her own good. "Now, to solve the problem at hand. Can you say I'm a cousin or something? If Walter goes out today, I could present myself when he returns."

Erin thought about it. Feeling generous after her decision to drive the wagon in spite of Bowie's disagreement with her plan, she smiled and nodded. "It sounds like a perfect plan."

"Can we get me some clothes? It's not likely I'd turn up without clothing. I have a couple of things, but not much." Bowie stroked his chin thoughtfully.

"Maybe we could say a band of Patriots attacked you,"

Erin offered. "That would work well. Walter would be delighted to hear that. He'd ask lots of questions, though. We need to plan for that."

Bowie nodded. "That might work. I could always claim to be a planter who was burned out by the Patriots. I think this is a fine idea. Now tell me about your family."

"Well, there's my cousin Noelle Arledge, who lives in upstate South Carolina. You could say you lived near her. Her father, Charles, died earlier this year. Her mother's been dead for years." Erin began thinking of little tidbits that only close family would know. "And there's my uncle Jonathan and cousin Lilly Arledge. They live here in Charleston over on King Street."

Bowie considered the information a moment and then shook his head slightly. "That could present a problem. What if I run into your uncle or cousin when Walter is around?"

"I suppose that could be dangerous. Walter knows Uncle Jonathan." Erin felt deflated. Her idea would have worked so well except for her Tory uncle. "I know. You can be from the Teague side of the family. My mother's family."

"That sounds good." Bowie nodded and continued, "I suppose your uncle Jonathan doesn't know the Teagues too well."

"Not very. Everybody in the Teague family looks down on Uncle Jonathan, so he avoids them whenever possible. They're a haughty bunch of intellectuals who always considered him beneath them. You know the kind, all brains and no common sense." Erin thought about her uncle and grimaced. "He's such a staunch Tory that nobody really wants much to do with him."

"Tory, eh? That may be the answer to another problem of ours." Bowie grinned and slapped his knee. "That's great. We'll use him."

"Use him? How?" Erin didn't like the idea of involving Uncle Jonathan in her business. She didn't even want to be around him. He had always been just a little too friendly to suit her.

Bowie considered the situation. If her uncle Jonathan were such a Loyalist, then he would be useful, more than Erin imagined. She was such an innocent. Her realm of knowledge was limited to her immediate surroundings, but Bowie could use her influence with Uncle Jonathan to obtain information.

"Bowie, what are you thinking? I'm sure Uncle Jonathan won't help us. He's . . . well, he's in Balfour's pocket." Erin hated to admit that she had a relative who was not only a Loyalist, but also an arrogant opportunist at that. He'd never hesitate to turn his family over to Balfour if it would enhance his position with the British.

"Can you get invited to a party at his house? I'm sure he must entertain some of the British officers," Bowie suggested, hoping she'd see the sense of his plan. "We could eavesdrop on their conversation. Our visiting there could certainly better our chances of gaining information."

"We? I couldn't take you. He'd be suspicious right away." Erin thought desperately of a way to convince Bowie that his plan would never work. Nothing seemed to come to mind except the danger he'd be placing himself in. "Impossible. I hate to go over there. Uncle Jonathan always asks too many probing questions, and I'm afraid I'd accidentally let something slip about Papa."

"Look, we've—" Bowie began, but stopped and listened. He heard the sound outside the door again.

An alarmed look passed over Erin's face, and she jumped to her feet. "Quick. Into the armoire."

Bowie glanced around and headed for the large piece of furniture. He pulled the door open, paused to shove aside some clothes, then climbed inside.

Erin was closing the door when she heard the door to her father's room open. Turning, she glanced at the room to see if there were any signs of Bowie's presence. *His coat!* She picked it up and tossed it behind the bed as her mother stepped into the room.

"Erin, dear, whatever are you doing in—" Vevila Banning spotted her husband lying bandaged in the bed, and panic creased her forehead. "Arlen! What happened? Erin—"

Running to meet her mother, Erin almost stumbled on the rug as she tried to keep her mother from collapsing on the injured man. "Mama, stop. Papa's going to be all right."

"What happened? Oh, my dear Arlen. What shall become of us?" Vevila clung to Erin and swayed back and forth as if she were about to faint.

"Mama, get a hold of yourself," Erin commanded. "You're not helping Papa. Besides, you'll wake him."

"I want to wake him. I want to talk to him." Vevila started toward the bed, but Erin held her firm.

"Papa needs his rest." Erin glanced at her father. He stirred slightly beneath the heavy quilts but didn't open his eyes. "Dr. Rutledge said so."

Vevila Banning gazed at her daughter. "He's been here already this morning? Why, the sun's barely up. Did you offer him some breakfast?"

"He was here early. Right after Papa got home." Erin rolled her eyes at her mother's silly questions. "I didn't offer him breakfast because I forgot. Besides, it was really too early."

"Erin, your lack of manners appalls me. To think that he'll go about Charleston, telling everyone that you didn't even offer him breakfast after he came so early. We're disgraced." Vevila's shoulders sagged, and she moved to the rocker Erin had sat in earlier. "We'll never be able to show our faces again."

Marveling at how easily her mother's attention had been diverted from Arlen Banning, Erin stepped to her mother's side. "Mama, he won't say anything. We're not disgraced. Why don't you go back to your room and lie down? I'll have Tupper bring you some warm milk and biscuits."

Vevila looked up through her tears and smiled wanly. "Would you, dear? That would be nice. I doubt whether I can come down for dinner, even though it's Christmas. I feel rather unwell."

"Yes, of course, Mama. I'll take care of everything." Erin

helped her mother to her feet and walked to the door. "Can you make it on your own?"

Wobbling slightly, Vevila patted Erin's arm. "You're such a dear girl. Your papa seems to be sleeping, so I won't disturb him. I'll try to manage alone. You go on and take care of my breakfast."

Erin stood at the door and watched until her mother disappeared into her room. Then she returned to help Bowie out of the armoire. "It's all right now."

"It's really stuffy in there." Bowie extricated himself from among the coats and stepped back into the room. He rubbed his stiff neck thoughtfully. "Next time I'll hide under the bed."

"Sorry. It's all I could think of so quickly." She watched as Bowie's nose wrinkled up and he sneezed. "Bless you."

"Thank you. I need it." Bowie touched a handkerchief to his nose and smiled. "Apparently those coats aren't worn much."

"I'll have Tupper air them today." Erin glanced back at her father. "Well, maybe next week."

"Perhaps you'd better see to your mother's breakfast before she returns," Bowie suggested and returned to his chair. "I believe my soup is cold."

"I'll get you some more while I'm downstairs. Maybe I'll bring up the soup kettle. I could always say that I want it handy in case Papa wakes." Erin smiled and hurried out the door.

Downstairs, she found Tupper pouring hotcake mixture on the griddle. "Oh, that looks good. When some of them are done, I'll take them up to Papa's room for his breakfast and mine. You take some to Mama."

While Tupper finished the hotcakes, Erin poured milk and coffee for two. She didn't like to deceive the servants, but Bowie needed food. A well-fed man is a happy man, her granny always said. He might be more amenable to her plan after he ate. She placed the beverages on a tray and took two plates of steaming hotcakes from the table with a small pitcher of syrup. "Thanks, Tupper. Don't forget Mama."

Without waiting for Tupper to answer, Erin dashed from the room and headed up the stairs. She met Walter coming down. "Oh, hello."

"Hello, again." He looked down at the tray. "Breakfast for two?"

"Papa and me." Erin tried to cross her fingers but found it difficult to hold the tray at the same time. "Oh, do you plan to be here for dinner?"

Walter gazed down at her for a moment before answering. "Is something special going on?"

Erin grimaced. "Not really. We usually have a big Christmas dinner, but with Papa sick and Mama, too, I suppose I'll be dining alone." She pursed her lips thoughtfully. "Maybe I could have Christmas dinner with my cousin Lilly. If you're not planning to be here, of course."

"Well, I've been asked to dine with Colonel Balfour," Walter said and smiled. "But if you want me to—"

"That's fine. I'm sorry to rush off, but Papa's hotcakes are getting cold." Erin flashed Walter a smile and hurried past him.

Shaking with fear that he'd follow her, she managed to balance the tray on one hand and open the door with the other. After casting a quick glance at the stairwell to determine if he was watching her, she continued into her father's room. Before she took two steps, she heard the front door open and close.

Bowie leapt to his feet. "I heard you talking to a man. Walter?"

"Yes." Erin put the tray down on the table between the two chairs by the fire. "I thought you'd like some fresh hotcakes. Tupper makes them better than anybody in the world."

Bowie tore into the thick cakes. His stomach was screaming for food, and his head had begun to hurt. "These are delicious."

Erin nodded and cut into her own hotcakes. "I lied to Tupper. I told her those were for Papa. She looked at me like I was crazy but didn't say anything."

"Can you trust her?" Bowie asked and took a sip of coffee. The hot liquid warmed every part of his body. He glanced at Erin. He imagined her in her own home one day. She was level-headed and could probably be counted on in any emergency.

"Of course I can trust Topper." Erin watched him eat. She knew nothing about him, except that he was a sailor and her father's partner. His manners were those of a well-to-do planter's son, but she couldn't understand how he became a sailor. He knew nothing about her. He had no way of knowing how determined she could be when she wanted something. Erin wanted to drive that wagon so badly she could hardly sit still.

"Something wrong?" he asked, a forkful of hotcakes dripping syrup poised halfway to his mouth.

"Wrong? No. Nothing. I was just thinking." Erin took another bite of her breakfast and eyed him thoughtfully. "Bowie."

"Yes?"

She took a deep breath as she tried to look stern and uncompromising. "I intend to drive the next shipment of goods to the South Carolina Irregulars."

Bowie almost dropped his plate. "You what!"

Smiling with the feeling of release, she pronounced her words very carefully, working hard to imply that the decision had been made and could not be changed. "I intend to drive the next wagonload of goods in my father's stead. There's nothing you can do about it."

"Like hell there's not."

CHAPTER
3

ERIN DIDN'T ARGUE WITH BOWIE'S DECLARATION THAT there *was* something he could do to prevent her from driving the next wagonload of goods. Winning him over wouldn't be easy, but she knew she could outlast him in any argument.

Now that Walter had left the house and Bowie had eaten, Erin wondered what to do next. She glanced at Bowie and realized that he was near exhaustion. "Would you like to sleep now?"

"If you don't mind." Bowie rose. He hated to leave her, but his tired mind kept him from thinking clearly, and he was afraid he'd do something rash. "Will you awaken me if I sleep too late? I want to get out as soon as possible after midnight."

Erin nodded. She wanted him out as soon after midnight as possible, too. He was going to be sleeping in her bed, and that might make matters difficult. "Come with me."

Leading the way, Erin took him to her room. A quick glance showed her nightgown draped over the divan, but other than that the room looked neat and inviting. The fire had long since gone out, so she turned to Bowie. "Would you like a fire?"

Shaking his head, Bowie gazed at her. "I don't think I'll notice."

"Well, I'll leave you to rest." Erin turned toward the door but stopped before opening it. "Walter's room is just across the hall, so please don't barge into the hallway without checking first. In fact, you'd better wait until I come for you."

"And if you don't come?" Bowie asked and leaned on the bed gently. He glanced at the feather mattress with delight. After several days of sleeping on the cold ground, the soft comfort would be welcome.

Blushing, Erin sighed. "I'll check on you periodically. I'll try to disturb you as little as possible, but if I don't come in here occasionally, someone might become suspicious."

"I'll be as quiet as possible." Bowie folded his cloak and laid it across the divan. He noticed the soft linen gown casually tossed there and smiled. He knew that when she'd changed earlier, she hadn't planned for him to be sleeping in here.

Erin's gaze followed his eyes, and her blush deepened. Trying to appear composed, she strode across the room, picked up the nightgown, and tucked it into the chest of drawers. "I'll have to keep Tupper from cleaning in here today. She'd never be the same again if she found you in my bed."

Thinking that he might never be the same again after sleeping in her bed, Bowie merely nodded. He watched the door close behind her, then removed the rest of his clothes. He found fresh water in the pitcher and did his best to remove some of the worst dirt from the trail. If her maid would be surprised to find him in Erin's bed, what would she think of dirty sheets?

He shivered and threw back the bedclothes, grimacing at the soft blue velvet bedhangings. The room was attractive— for a girl, but definitely not for the likes of him.

Briefly he wondered if he would be safe. Falling asleep when a British official roomed across the hall sounded like a foolhardy idea, but Bowie was too tired to look for another place now. He also wanted to talk to Arlen after he slept off the effects of their arduous journey.

A difficult task lay ahead, and Bowie needed to rest, too. Finding a replacement for Arlen was his highest priority now, and so he lay down.

The mattress puffed up around him as he settled into the bed and pulled up the covers. He glanced around, wondering about the bright young woman who lived in this room. Already a witness to her intelligence and strength, he found himself intrigued by her. How would she react to a kiss? Had she ever been kissed? Bowie's lips parted, as if in anticipation of the moment when their lips would meet, and he smiled.

"Some day, Erin, my dear, I'll find out how you react to kisses," he mumbled and fell asleep.

Erin moved quietly about the house. She checked on her father and found him awake. "Papa, how do you feel?"

"Like every cannon in this hellish war landed on my leg." He tried to sit up but fell back in pain.

"Now, be careful. Dr. Rutledge says you're in poor condition." Erin hurried to his side and placed a second pillow behind him so he could sit easier. "If you're too rambunctious, you'll cause your wounds to bleed again."

Arlen looked around the room. "Where's Bowie? He didn't leave, did he?"

"No, Papa," she answered as she pulled her rocking chair close. "I put him in my bed."

Eyeing her sharply, Arlen grinned. "A fine lad, don't you think?"

"I'm eternally grateful to him for saving your life, if that's what you mean." Erin averted her eyes. Spotting the soup kettle, she jumped up. "Would you like a little soup? I've kept it hot for you."

"I suppose you'll insist." Arlen shook his head good-naturedly. "Well, bring it on."

Erin ladled a little of the steaming mixture into a bowl and brought it to the bedside. "Here, I'll feed you."

"Nonsense." Arlen took the spoon and began to eat. "Do you like Bowie?"

Blushing, Erin didn't answer for a moment. She didn't know exactly what he wanted her to say, but she felt instinctively that he was matchmaking. "I's sure he's a very nice person."

"You know what I mean. Do *you* like him personally?" Arlen put down the spoon.

"I hardly know him. Now, eat." Erin wanted to change the subject but couldn't think of anything intelligent to say. "Are you warm enough?"

"Yes, yes. When can I see him?"

"As soon as he's awake." Erin stood up. "I'll go get you a cup of coffee—or would you prefer a glass of milk?"

"Neither. Stay where you are," he instructed and tried to place the bowl on the table beside the bed.

Erin took the bowl. "You didn't eat enough. Dr. Rutledge says you need to eat plenty of meat and meat broth to help replace all the blood you lost."

"A pox on the good doctor." Arlen pulled the covers up and shivered. "Perhaps you'd better add a log to the fire."

Glad for the opportunity to escape her father's watchful eye, Erin almost ran across the room. She, too, was chilly. The temperature seemed to have dropped several degrees since Bowie left the room.

After placing two split logs on the fire, she located her shawl and pulled it about her shoulders to ward off a case of the shivers. With her father still awake, she felt she couldn't leave the room unless it was necessary. "Mama came in earlier."

"I'm sorry to hear that," Arlen admitted and shook his head gently. "Was she upset?"

Erin grinned wickedly. For once in her life she was happy that her mother had the common sense of a peahen. "Terribly upset. I forgot to ask Dr. Rutledge to breakfast, and Mama thinks we'll be outcasts from now on."

Arlen smiled wanly. "Delighted to hear it."

"She was quite concerned about your health, at first, but when she found out that Dr. Rutledge had been here and gone without being offered food, she nearly fainted." Erin settled back into the rocker and began to rock gently. "I sent her back to bed. She's been napping ever since. You know her—when something distressing happens, she likes to sleep. Tupper took hotcakes up a while ago, and Mama barely touched them. I suppose I should peek into her room to see if she's asleep."

"Good idea, but don't go now." Arlen reached for Erin's hand and patted it. "I'm sorry about ruining your Christmas, daughter."

Erin smiled. This would be one of the most wonderful Christmases ever since her father hadn't been killed in the ambush. "It would be more joyful if the war weren't still going on and if the British would leave Charleston."

"That it would," he agreed, "that it would. But that isn't to be the case this year, and I'm glad I have you to depend on. You and Bowie. Without the two of you this could be a catastrophe."

Erin grinned sheepishly. Her father's words made every moment of terror worth the trouble. A plan was forming in her mind. "Papa, I think you'd recuperate better at Bluffwood. You know what a green goose Mama is. If she finds out you've been shot, all of Charleston will know before the next sunset."

Arlen appeared to be considering her words. "I suppose you're right, but I can't leave until I find out if Bowie can locate another driver we can trust."

"Papa," she said slowly, knowing she'd have to approach her father carefully. He'd be more reasonable than Bowie but wouldn't like the idea of her driving the wagon. "Finding someone trustworthy is going to be difficult enough, but who can you find who knows the route?"

"That's a problem." Arlen rubbed his chin thoughtfully. "I don't know. We'll just have to do the best we can."

"And you know how suspicious the men at the safety points are." Erin shook her head, gently commiserating with her father's predicament.

"Quite so. This is a dilemma, that's for certain." Arlen exhaled heavily. "Such problems. Confound the damn . . . pardon me, daughter, the British for their musketballs."

"I suppose . . ." Erin began and tilted her head as if she

were concentrating. "I suppose that I could fill in until you're well enough to resume your duties."

"What?" Arlen raised up abruptly but fell back with a groan of pain. "Have you taken leave of your senses? Has your mother's Teague mentality finally seized your brain? She had little sense even before her fall. . . . That's the most absurd notion I ever heard."

Erin let him rave for a few minutes. He berated her for her harebrained suggestion, moved on to the lack of dependable help, considered the crisis, and then glared at her. All the while she sat quietly with her hands in her lap and listened like a dutiful daughter.

"If you were a son, I'd have difficulty enough allowing you to take such a risk," Arlen continued, "but your mother would have me skinned alive if I sent you off alone on such a journey."

Nodding gently, she smiled and then appeared to be considering another plan. "Of course, she'd never have to know. We wouldn't tell her any more than we tell her about your trips."

"Out of the question." Arlen crossed his arms with finality and grimaced in pain. "Have you been tippling in my good brandy?"

"You know I can't abide that stuff," Erin retorted. "If you and Mama were at Bluffwood, she'd never know where I was. You've used that excuse for quite a while."

"Certainly, but I'm a man," Arlen replied, considered the question, and continued. "A grown man used to the rigors of the trail."

Erin made a final plea. "Papa, think about this." She wanted to do this more than anything she'd ever tried before. Women were barred from helping in this horrible war, but she wanted to help—to get even for the death of her friends and the destruction of her beautiful Charleston. "I know the routes as well as you. I know the safety points and the men who mind them. Why, before you closed down your regular supply route before the war, I was your constant companion. When you reactivated it to supply our fighting men with ammunition, clothing, and food, I felt that we were doing something worthwhile. I can continue for you. If you and Mama are at Bluffwood, I'll have an excuse to come and go."

"No. Absolutely not under any circumstances." Arlen appeared to have made up his mind. He shifted restlessly on the pillows and smiled. "You are too dear to me, Erin. How could I send you into the face of almost certain death? It's dangerous for a man familiar with the rigors of the trail and the British deviltry. But for you, no. Never."

"Posh. You know the risk is minimal after you leave the outskirts of Charleston." Erin felt her irritation begin to rise and fought to keep it from her voice. If she sounded impertinent, her father would dismiss her arguments as the ramblings of a child. She needed to sound disciplined and logical. "Papa, you know that our men desperately need supplies. How can you deny them? You know that Bowie can search Charleston until the Ashley and Cooper rivers dry up and find nobody as qualified as I am—if he finds anyone at all."

"I can't deny that our men need these supplies," Arlen agreed. "God knows their lives are lean enough without their supply routes being cut off. But, Erin, even if all the things you say are true, what kind of father would send his only daughter . . . would allow his only child to undertake such a mission?"

"A Patriot," she answered simply. Her father was a Patriot through and through. To indicate that to do less than whatever was in his power to do would point toward a weakness that Arlen Banning could never embrace. Her two words summed up their whole argument. She had nothing left to say, and neither did her father.

Arlen Banning's anguished look touched her heart. She knew how much her father loved her and felt guilty over her childish—if momentary—jealousy of Bowie. Tilting her chin slightly, she watched her father.

Wrangling with the decision he must make, he simply stared at his hands. She knew his thoughts as well as if she could read them or as if he said them aloud. Although he'd always been a planter and a gentleman of the first water, the feel of the leather reins in his hands symbolized a freedom that he found no place else. To use his skill and knowledge to support a cause he loved as much as life itself came easily to him. To sacrifice his only child to that same cause tore at his heart as much as if he'd be the one to take her life.

"Erin, I can't do it," he said finally with a sigh. "To die myself for this glorious cause is a price I'm more than willing to pay, but your life is priceless to me. I'd remain under British dominance for the rest of my life or live in that stinking rat-infested prison in St. Augustine for my remaining days to keep you safe."

Erin's mouth hung open. She'd thought she'd won. With a last effort she inhaled deeply and moved to the edge of the bed. She caressed his brow and kissed his lips softly. "But, Papa, I am not willing to live under that domination. I, too, am willing to give my life to end British rule in America."

"Then, praise God you will never be called upon to forfeit your life. I cannot allow you to do so." He smiled and patted her hand lightly, then took it in both of his and held it to his heart. "This is the proudest moment in my life. Had I a son, I would have worked diligently to instill the Patriotism so evident in you. I shall not allow it to be quieted by the musketball of a British maggot."

"Papa," she began but realized that their discussion had tired him tremendously. "Sleep now, Papa. We'll talk later."

Erin sat and rocked quietly for a few minutes until her father's soft snores assured her he was asleep. Wondering what she could say to convince him that she intended to take his place, she lay her head on the edge of the bed and succumbed to the lure of sleep.

A noise startled her. Erin sat up and glanced around. She couldn't have slept for long. A glance assured her that her father hadn't stirred. Almost certain that Walter Martin had guessed something was wrong, she suspected he had returned to investigate. Rising as quietly as possible, she prepared herself to meet whatever challenge awaited her.

Padding softly to the door, she inhaled deeply and promised to make a role for herself in this war. The life she led, encumbered with the burden of living in a city under siege— the uncertainty of a savage war, the forced sociability with the enemy, the loss of her youth and freedom—dictated that she must do something other than smile prettily at her boarder and the British soldiers she encountered everywhere she went. Had the war not begun, she would have been invited to numerous parties and soirees since her introduction into society last year. Instead, she'd been compelled to settle for a small dinner party with no real follow-up visits or invitations.

She'd witnessed the violation of her city, the disruption of a sweet and gentle society, the barbaric treatment of her friends and neighbors, the death and injury to thousands of young men—too many things to forgive easily. As she pressed her ear to the door, Erin Banning made up her mind. Neither her father nor Bowie Gallagher could prevent her from doing her part to end this war.

She listened intently for several seconds before opening the door. Glancing up and down the corridor, she discovered Walter opening his door. "Hello. Back already?"

"Yes. Since this is a holiday, I have no duties." Walter looked appraisingly at Erin. "Your choice of a gown for the celebration of Christmas is . . . interesting."

Erin felt the sting of color in her cheeks. When she'd pulled on this rag of a gown early this morning, she hadn't anticipated seeing anyone except Bowie—and that in the darkness of her father's room. She'd expected to change into a suitable day dress but hadn't had the time. Now she could hardly parade herself, for the sake of vanity, into the room where Bowie slept.

"Thank you." She decided that his remark bordered on sarcastic, and for that reason she refused to acknowledge or answer it further. She left him standing at his door and started down the servants' stair. Once out of sight she hesitated until she heard his door close before continuing on her errand. Somebody had to make sure the household ran as smoothly as possible—as if nothing were wrong.

Erin hurried through her instructions for Tupper, Toby, Nero, and 'Lasses. They knew exactly what to do. All of them had been with the Bannings for years, and their routine seldom changed—until the war. They'd spent most of the winter at the Bannings' plantation and sought the cool of the city during the summer season, to avoid mosquitoes and fevers, taking the house servants with them.

After she spoke with the servants, she rushed back up the stairs because she didn't want to leave her father alone too long and wanted to check on her mother. Even though it was Christmas Day, she still had to see to her chores.

Time moved slowly. Erin sat at her father's side for the remainder of the day. When darkness began to fall, she knew she would have to awaken Bowie. If Walter saw her in the same gown, he'd know something was wrong.

Before going to her room, she found 'Lasses and asked her to bring up a fresh pitcher of water. Bowie would probably want to bathe before coming to see her father. After hesitating for the briefest moment, Erin summoned her courage and entered the room, not risking a knock for fear of disturbing Walter.

She found Bowie sitting up in bed and motioned for him to be silent. When she heard 'Lasses approach, Erin opened the door slightly and took the pitcher. Assured that 'Lasses had gone, Erin closed the door, put the pitcher on the table, and said to Bowie, "I'm glad you're awake. I hope you don't mind if I select a gown for dinner. I really need to change."

"How can I object? This is your room." Bowie patted the quilt around him and watched Erin cross to the armoire.

The gown she had worn all day was of simple navy serge, durable, warm, and tattered as Walter had so pointedly indicated. When she closed the door of the armoire, she draped a blue gown over her arm and stepped through the door that led to what he supposed was her morning room.

"I won't disturb you further. My morning room has a door to the hallway," she whispered and closed the door behind her.

Bowie flung back the covers and got up, stretching the kinks from his muscles. At the sound of the door opening again, he jumped back into bed and jerked the quilts up to his chin. "Yes?"

"Sorry to disturb you again. Supper will be about eight. Walter is going out, so we'll be dining alone." Erin smiled and closed the door again. She felt sure he'd been out of bed, and for some reason that knowledge cheered her. After all, he'd seen her in her wrapper this morning, and it didn't hurt to give him back some of his own treatment.

Hurrying, she removed the serviceable dress she wore when she had work to do and pulled on the gown of sapphire silk her father had given to her last winter. She didn't know where he had found such lovely fabric, but she didn't care. She and 'Lasses had worked for several weeks making the dress.

With no real parties to attend, she had never worn the gown. But this evening she wanted to look special. This Christmas Day had been somber enough, and she wanted to sparkle even though there were no real festivities to dress for. She brushed her long hair briskly and pulled it into a neat chignon at the base of her neck. A few wispy curls sprang free and softened the effect of her severe hairstyle.

She waited until she heard Walter's door close. Under no circumstances did she want him to see her so dressed up for what she'd told him earlier would be supper alone. Walter had never made any advances to her, but she'd seen him watching her and didn't want to risk having him change his mind about dining out.

While she lingered, awaiting his departure, she patted rosewater on her neck and wrists. She told herself that this was a part of her ritual but found herself thinking of Bowie as she did it and wondering if he liked the scent of roses.

Standing abruptly, she scolded herself for thinking such a thing and shook her head.

Erin didn't oppose falling in love, but when she did, it wouldn't be with the likes of Bowie Gallagher. She wanted someone stable, someone who would share his life with her, someone who would always come back—not a daredevil sea captain like Bowie. Although she admired his derring-do, she didn't feel he would make a good husband.

Feeling the chill of the room, she wished Walter would hurry and leave. She positioned herself at the window so she could watch for his departure. He must be waiting for her to come downstairs, she surmised. Besides being hungry and cold, Erin didn't like being cooped up in her morning room when supper was waiting. A light tap on the door between her bedroom and the morning room startled her.

She hurried to answer before Walter heard. Since she hadn't noticed the noise of his departure, she assumed he was still downstairs. When she opened the door, she found Bowie dressed in fresh clothes. His breeches were well cut but showed no particular stylishness. A white shirt, plain stockings, and blue frock coat completed his attire.

"My, how lovely you look," he whispered. "Did Walter leave?"

"I don't think so. I've been listening and watching for signs of his departure but have been disappointed so far." Erin couldn't help noticing Bowie's broad shoulders and narrow waist and decided that anything at all would look good on him. Pretending to be busy, she strode across the room and straightened a picture that didn't need straightening.

"Maybe he's waiting for you." Bowie watched her fluttering about like a nervous peahen and decided that she didn't like being closeted with him in the small morning room. "Why don't you go and see?"

"I'm afraid if he sees me dressed for supper, he'll decide to stay," she explained, feeling a trifle silly for her fears. What if he did change his mind about going out? Bowie would simply have to eat in here. "Well, I can't remain up here for the evening without arousing suspicion, so I'll go and see what's keeping him. Wait here."

Erin scurried out into the hall and down the stairs. Bracing herself for the possibility of a confrontation, she walked sedately into the parlor. Walter stood with his elbow propped on the mantel, and Erin wanted to groan aloud. "Oh, hello. I didn't expect you to be here still."

"I waited purposely for you. Ever since you told me you would be dining alone, I've felt terribly guilty." Walter turned and smiled at her. "Colonel Balfour has graciously invited you to join us for the evening's festivities."

Feeling the weight of the world settle on her shoulders, Erin lowered herself onto her favorite chair. What reason could she give him for turning down his "gracious" offer? She'd have to think of something quickly. "Oh, Walter, how kind of you to think of me. I don't know quite what to say."

Grinning, he moved to her side and patted her shoulder in a brotherly fashion. "Think nothing of it. Let it not be said that the British have no feelings."

Fighting her temper, Erin looked up at him and smiled, though she wanted to slap him for his remark. If the British had feelings, they would leave Charleston, she thought. "You are kindness personified, but I'm afraid I can't accept."

The grin faded from his face. "Why not? You're dressed beautifully. You've nothing to keep you here."

"But I have." She ignored his oblique reference to her earlier attire and latched onto his last remark. "I must feed Papa, and I don't want to leave Mama on Christmas Day. She's feeling quite ill, and I may have to call for Dr. Rutledge again. You know, she's never been well since her fall."

Walter grimaced but nodded in agreement. "I hoped you'd allow the servants to care for your parents this evening."

Erin hung her head like a woman turning down an invitation she really wanted to accept. When she met his eyes again, she offered a sliver of a smile. "On Christmas? My . . . My parents may be gone before next Christmas. How would

I feel if I'd left them with servants on their last Christmas? Oh, it's unthinkable."

She knotted her hand into a small fist and put it to her mouth as if to bite back tears. Lowering her head slowly for effect, she sagged back in the chair and sighed. "I . . . I dressed in this silly old dress because it's Papa's favorite."

"And well it should be." Walter perked up. "As I said, it's lovely."

"You're so kind." Erin raised her gaze to his. "Please, don't delay any longer. I'm sure Colonel Balfour is awaiting your arrival."

"Quite. Well, I'm off." Walter started toward the door but then turned back. "I suppose I could offer my apologies to Colonel Balfour and—"

Erin leapt to her feet. "Nonsense. This is a celebration. You can't afford to offend the colonel on Christmas. How would it look? You might lose your post."

"You're correct as usual," Walter conceded and returned to the door. "Good night, Miss Banning. Merry Christmas."

"Thank you for your offer." She sighed again and fluttered her eyelashes. "Merry Christmas to you. Give my regrets to Colonel Balfour and thank him for the invitation."

"Certainly."

Erin fell back into the chair. How close she had come to having to eat alone with Walter, as she'd done many times since he had taken up his post. He ate his noon meal at the office or at the tearoom but came home almost every night.

The smell of Christmas spices, sweets, and evergreen did much to overcome her fears. Walter would probably be home early, but she and Bowie could eat a quiet meal without fear of being disturbed. She sprang from her chair and hurried up the stairs like a squirrel with a choice nut. As she raised her hand to knock on her morning room door, it opened.

"Did he leave?" Bowie whispered. "I heard the front door close."

Erin nodded. "He left, but I don't know how long he'll be gone."

Bowie extended his arm and smiled. "Miss Banning, may I escort you to supper?"

Batting her lashes and pursing her lips in a flirtatious manner, she took his arm. "Why, I'd be delighted, Mr. Gallagher."

They walked down the stairs to the parlor. Erin tugged on the bellpull and then crossed to her chair near the fire. "I hope he stays away long enough for us to have a pleasant evening."

"Does he usually stay out late?" Bowie strolled to the bay window and peered out into the night.

Oyster Point seemed deserted. Apparently everyone in Charleston was sitting down to Christmas Day supper, whether it be a feast or meager repast. The British could besiege the city, but they couldn't defeat the spirit of this day nor the spirit of Charleston's people. The South Carolinians would find a way to win this war, and when they did, the British would limp back to England spouting lies about their defeat.

Erin watched Bowie. She couldn't tell what he was thinking, but she believed his mind was elsewhere. Though she'd begun to look forward to dining with him, if he intended to remain stoically silent, the evening would be difficult. She studied his profile. His straight nose was just the right length between deep-set blue eyes almost the color of her gown. High cheekbones accentuated the strong planes of his face and, with his square chin, presented a visage of strength that pleased her.

Finding her heart hammering in her chest, Erin turned to stare at the fire. What did Bowie Gallagher have that the few other men she knew didn't? Why did looking at him affect her in ways she never recognized before? She turned to look at him again and found him watching her.

"Miss Erin," came a soft feminine voice behind them.

Thankful for the interruption, she averted her eyes to the doorway. "Yes, 'Lasses?"

"Supper ready." The spry older woman grinned and danced away, singing a Christmas carol.

"Miss Banning, shall we go in?" Bowie held out his arm again.

When she crooked her arm in his, Bowie couldn't contain his grin. He felt like the owner of the largest, fastest, most beautiful sailing vessel on the high seas. Erin Banning caught at something in him he didn't know he had, and he couldn't yet define it. But he knew he felt grand when she smiled at him and felt awful when she scowled.

Tonight would be a night of smiles.

CHAPTER 4

ERIN PLACED HER NAPKIN IN HER LAP AND SMILED across the table at Bowie. The act seemed so normal that she could almost forget the war that raged outside and too close to her home. "I hope you like oysters."

"I love them. Living around the coast, you either like them or starve to death." Bowie savored the delicious flavor of the steamed shellfish for a moment and then sipped his wine. As he studied her across the rim of the crystal wineglass, he wanted to shut out reality completely for this one evening, to pretend that nothing abnormal was occurring while they ate. "This is a fine wine. Where did you get it?"

"Papa still has a few bottles left." Erin felt a surge of pride as she sipped the excellent vintage. Even during a siege she set a fine table. Her trapdoor in the stable had saved much of their food and wine. Sometimes she felt a little guilty about having good food while others in Charleston had so little, but her ingenuity had saved the day when the Patriots made a house-to-house search for food during the siege. She shuddered to think what would have happened to them if she hadn't realized that with the exceedingly hot temperatures, the masses of meat and other foods brought into Charleston to feed the troops would spoil. But she didn't want to think about that now. "This is one of his favorites. I'm sending a glass up to him with his supper. Bowie, about the wagon route, I—"

"Wait. Don't talk about the war. Tonight . . ." he said

and hesitated. "For tonight, well, let's pretend the war doesn't exist."

Erin sighed with relief. She felt the same as Bowie about discussing the war at supper, but she had believed he'd be more comfortable talking about subjects most people talked about these days, and everyone's favorite topic of conversation seemed to be the war.

Reveling in the remainder of his glass of wine, Bowie watched Erin eat daintily. She ate tiny bites and continually dabbed at the corners of her mouth with her napkin. So used to the poor manners of his crew, Bowie enjoyed her feminine demeanor. "This is a wonderful supper."

"Thank you," Erin said with pride.

Tupper served the duck with Queen Anne's lace jelly, yams, rice, and orange sauce. For a moment both of them ate in silence, content to savor the fine supper.

"I'm surprised that you have so much food." Bowie wiped his mouth and hoped he didn't look like an idiot as he dug into his duckling again.

"I have a secret hiding place for some of the food we keep, but you smuggled in the duck." Erin grinned and raised her eyebrows with an air of mystery. "It was in Papa's satchel."

"You mean that the satchel he refused to leave behind contained our supper and nothing more?" Bowie asked, incredulous that Arlen had risked his life over a duck. "The way he clung to it, I assumed it contained papers that assured the end of the war."

"No. It contained a few other items." Erin picked at her oysters. If Bowie felt that the duck wasn't worth bringing, then what would he think of the letter from Cousin Noelle and the jar of blackberry jam she sent as a Christmas gift? "My cousin sent the jam."

Bowie laughed and shook his head. "Well, I'd have to say that jam was worth the effort. It was mighty good. After a meal like this, you may never be rid of me." Bowie pushed back from the table.

"Just a moment, Mr. Gallagher," Erin called and rang a dainty little silver bell. With a glint of mischief in her eyes, she laughed and gazed at him over the candles and holly decorating the table. "Aren't you joining me for dessert?"

Bowie sank back into his chair. "Dessert?"

"Yes. Tupper makes the best flummery in the world." Erin signaled to Tupper when she entered the room.

"Flummery, eh? Well," he said and patted his stomach, "I believe I can make room for that. Nobody loves a flummery better than I do."

Erin nodded. She loved that treat, too. For a moment she watched as he spooned the porridge-like dessert, but she couldn't wait for long. Her taste buds were begging to be satisfied.

After supper they walked back into the parlor. Erin poured a glass of brandy for Bowie and handed him a cigar.

"I'll take the brandy and save the cigar for later. Bowie tucked the cigar in his pocket and sipped his brandy as he moved toward the fireplace to smell the fresh evergreens artfully placed on the mantel. He motioned to the harpsichord by the window. "Do you play?"

"Yes, although I don't think I play well." Erin walked to the instrument. "Do you play?"

"No. Not at all." Bowie hastened to pull the seat away from the harpsichord. The scent of her cologne surrounded him, and he leaned over a bit until his lips almost touched her hair. Shaking his head to regain his composure, he whispered, "Would you play for me?"

"Yes, if you wish." Erin sat and poised her fingers over the keys. Hesitating for a moment while she decided what to play, she inhaled deeply.

From the moment she touched the keys, Bowie felt the magnetism of her style. She was a skilled musician and played with a passion he'd seldom seen before. Without doubt she could have become a professional in a theater if she wanted.

Her depth of concentration allowed him to watch her closely. With each difficult passage her lips pursed or her brow furrowed, but she played flawlessly the pieces of Bach, Haydn, and Mozart. After the more formal pieces she played a series of Christmas carols: "The Holly and the Ivy," "The Coventry Carol," and the lilting French song, "Pat-a-Pan." Erin's fingers romped over the keyboard with the more rollicking tunes and caressed them during the more moving pieces.

A tiny foot peeked from beneath her silk gown, and Bowie noticed it keeping time. From there his gaze took in the graceful curve of her full skirt and the gentle swell of her bosom. Feeling an unexpected surge of desire, Bowie fought to keep his attention on the music but failed. At times he hummed or sang along, but he didn't want to distract her. Deep inside he discovered that he really wanted to sweep her off the chair and whisk her up the curved staircase to her bedroom. Instead, he focused on her long, delicate fingers as they caressed each key.

Erin heard the grandfather clock toll in the hallway. "Oh, my, I've let the time slip away." She rose from her chair and looked at Bowie. His dazed expression told her that his thoughts were elsewhere.

"Bowie, I think we should be leaving the parlor. Walter could return at any moment." Erin blew out the candles in the candelabrum on the harpsichord. "Bowie?"

Somewhat abashed, he jumped to his feet and strode to her side. "I've never heard such a moving performance."

Erin felt a blush creeping into her cheeks. "You're too kind. My teacher was always quite critical."

"Then he must have been tone deaf. You play magnificently." Bowie touched her arm. "I'm impressed."

"Thank you. Perhaps it is you who is tone deaf," she suggested and laughed.

"I'm wounded that you think such a thing. Why, people say I sing pretty well, so I have some knowledge of these things." Bowie hoped he didn't sound boastful, but he wanted to emphasize that he wasn't the average listener.

"Did I hear you humming while I played? Maybe some evening you can sing for me. I'll be glad to accompany you." Erin looked at him with renewed interest. His voice, a deep bass, would be beautiful, but tonight wasn't the night for a concert. "We must go upstairs, or Walter will find us here dallying about the harpsichord like two geese around a corn mill."

"That wouldn't do at all." Bowie held out his arm, and she tucked hers into the crook of his. "I'd just as soon not have to chance meeting him."

"We're prepared if we're forced to explain your presence, but Walter isn't as pea-brained as I sometimes like to think." Erin hurried along, wishing Bowie would speed up a little. She hadn't meant to play so long, but she found such peace while playing the lovely carols. "Don't you think we need to move a bit faster?"

"And have him catch us rushing up the stairs like birds after a beetle? He'd most assuredly become suspicious then." Bowie patted her hand reassuringly. "I, too, prefer to avoid him altogether if possible."

As they reached the top of the stairs, the front door opened. Glad for the curving staircase, they hurried into Erin's bedroom, which was the door closest to the stairs. She pushed him past the bed and indicated that he should lie down. "Walter must have heard us," she whispered. "Hide here. I'll change quickly."

Without hesitating to see if Bowie had obeyed, she slipped off her gown, all the while marveling at her bravado. War made women do strange things, she mused. Taking her wrapper in her arms, she moved toward the door. As she reached the door, she slipped it on and secured the fasteners. Listening intently for a moment, she at last heard the sound of Walter's boots on the stairs and bolted into action.

Erin opened the door and stepped into the corridor as Walter stepped onto the second-floor landing. "Oh," she gasped and drew her wrapper more closely about her as if his presence surprised her. "I didn't hear you come in."

Walter smiled lopsidedly and swaggered forward slightly, almost toppling back down the stairs before he found firm footing. "Good evening, Miss Banning. You're looking lovely as ever."

Feeling the color drain from her face, she tried to smile.

A drunken British official might present problems she hadn't considered. "Thank you, Mr. Martin. I was just on my way to check on Papa. Will you excuse me?"

"Had a little eggnog. Great drink. Have you had any?" Walter asked, slurring his words and leaning against the railing.

"No. I'm afraid I had a quiet meal, practiced my harpsichord, then came up to go to bed." Erin eyed him carefully to gauge his reaction to her lies. "I really must see to Papa."

"After you do that, why not have a drink with me? A little brandy . . . never hurt anybody." Walter nodded toward his room. "Many . . . women find it . . . comforting on a cold night."

"Really, Mr. Martin. You're overcome with drink already. How dare you suggest that I . . ." Erin let her voice dwindle into silence and glared at him with her most aristocratic stare while crossing her arms.

Walter ignored her objection and continued. "After all, Miss Banning . . . Erin . . . I've been here for some time and—"

"Good night, Mr. Martin." Erin swept past him to her father's door. She hesitated long enough to cast a withering glance over her shoulder and then went in.

"Papa?" she called lightly, hoping he hadn't heard the altercation between Walter and her in the hallway. Disturbing her father would make her feel guilty, especially when he'd been so ill-used already by the British—

"Erin? Come in, daughter. Where's—"

"Mama?" she supplied quickly, closing the door abruptly so Walter wouldn't hear if her father mentioned Bowie. "Mama's in her room. Still not feeling well." Erin ran lightly to her father's side and whispered. "Walter's just arrived, and he's drunk."

"He didn't—"

"I can handle him. Don't worry." Erin kissed her father's forehead. There was no need to worry him. "Merry Christmas, Papa. I'm sorry you couldn't come to table. Bowie and I had a lovely time."

"I heard you playing the harpsichord. Wonderful thing. Like the music of the angels on Christmas." Arlen patted his daughter's head fondly and whispered, "Where's Bowie now?"

Erin giggled. "In my bedroom. I had to push him in there to keep Walter from seeing him. He's hiding under the bed. I really need to get the lock fixed on my bedroom door soon."

"Now, there's a sight I'd like to see—Bowie Gallagher hiding under your bed!" Arlen chuckled and then coughed. "Believe I'm coming down with something. When I feel better, I'll see to your lock."

"Don't you worry about anything but getting well. Dr. Rutledge will stop by in the morning." Erin rose. "I'll check on you again during the night. Well, I'd better rescue Bowie."

"Good night, my dear."

"'Night Papa." Erin kissed him again and scooted out. She tiptoed down the hall and into her room. She looked about for Bowie but didn't see him. Wondering where he could be, she decided he must have gone into her morning room to wait until Walter had gone to bed. That was fine with her. She felt too tired to look for him. All the players in this daring charade had slept during the day except her.

Shrugging, Erin took the pins out of her hair and let it tumble over her shoulders. She brushed it briskly, gazed at her reflection in the mirror, and then toyed with the curls, arranging them on her shoulders. When she looked up again, she saw Bowie standing behind her.

"You're lovely," he whispered and reached out to touch the waist-length hair.

Color sprang to her cheeks as Erin stood and walked away from him. She edged around the bed and glanced out the window. She didn't quite know how to handle a situation like this. Wearing nothing but her dressing gown over her petticoats put her at a distinct disadvantage. "You're very kind, sir, but I fear you're teasing me," she said in a low voice. Staring down at the harbor, she continued,

"When I was a little girl, Papa told me that the Ashley River and the Cooper River met at Charleston and formed the Atlantic Ocean. Lots of people tell their children that."

Bowie shrugged. "Seems I heard something about that, too."

"And some even go so far as to say the abbreviation *B.C.* refers to 'before Charleston' instead of 'Before Christ.'" Erin looked back at him. "A little conceited, don't you think?"

Ignoring her question, Bowie strode closer to her. "You really are beautiful. No matter what you're wearing."

"Now I know you're teasing me. With my hair awry and without the lovely gown, I'm as plain as hen's feathers." Erin felt her heart pounding inside her chest. Nobody had ever told her she was really beautiful. Bowie sounded serious, but she couldn't allow the conversation to remain on her appearance: they had too much to do and too little time to do it.

"On the contrary. I'm quite serious." Bowie followed her to the window and put his arm around her shoulder. Looking down into her eyes, he marveled at the depth of green that held him captive. Brushing her thickly curled auburn hair away from her face, he tilted her chin until her lips were very near his.

The desire to kiss her had been growing ever since he'd met her, but he hadn't allowed himself to think about it until now. He lowered his mouth to hers and barely brushed her soft lips before drawing back. No matter how badly he wanted to kiss her, he didn't want to frighten her or make her angry with him.

"Mr. Gallagher, this is quite improper—"

"It certainly is." Bowie kissed her again, this time savoring the sweetness of her mouth, lingering over the dewy softness that invited him in spite of her words. He drew her against his body and enfolded her in his embrace, mentally willing the moment to last forever. Within less than a day she'd wriggled her way into his heart in a manner he never considered possible.

Erin couldn't breathe and didn't care. She'd never been kissed, really kissed, by a man who knew how to tantalize her so expertly, and this moment was exquisite. She tentatively encircled his neck with her hands and leaned against him, feeling the hard muscles of his body respond with a quiver. Her body trembled in his arms, and she felt that she would fall if he let her go.

A clatter in the hall startled them, and they jumped apart. Erin felt the panic rise in her. No servant would enter without knocking. As the door began to open, Bowie almost dived beneath the bed, leaving her standing at the window with her chest heaving.

Erin stared at the slowly opening door. "Who's there?"

"Walter," came the reply, and he stepped into the room.

She glanced down and saw that Bowie wasn't fully under the bed. Striding briskly across the room, she glared at Walter. "How dare you enter my room without my permission, Mr. Martin! You may live here, but my room is not yours to enter without invitation."

"Ah, but it is." Walter slumped against the door, closing it behind him, and watched her closely. "You see, in the eyes of the British, this is my house. It was given to me."

"I'm sure that's true, but I'm not a part of your perfidious bargain, and I'm not about to become your . . . your kept woman." Erin glanced around. She had nothing to use as a weapon except the poker on the hearth. Even as she spotted it, she knew she couldn't use it without being sent to jail. Killing a representative of the British government—even in self-defense—would be tantamount to treason, and now, more than ever, she needed to remain free. The Patriots needed the supplies she'd deliver in a few weeks. "Leave now, Mr. Martin, before I completely lose my temper."

"Call me Walter. We can be friends." Walter stumbled forward and almost tripped over the stool at her dressing table.

"Mr. Martin, if you expect us to be friends, you must leave immediately. Let me get Nero to help you to bed." The bellpull probably would bring Tupper or 'Lasses, but

Walter stood between her and the cord, making the possibility of rescue by that means less than hopeful. The look in Walter's eyes frightened her, and she feared that Bowie would make his presence known if Walter pursued her further. The memory of Bowie's recent caress lingered on her lips, and color dappled her cheeks.

"I don't want that old cuss to put me to bed, but you can do it," Walter suggested. "Come on. We don't even have to cross the hall. You have a great big bed here."

Feeling close to screaming from the tension, Erin watched him cross the rug and collapse upon the bed. She made use of his lapse of attention and jerked on the bellpull. "Someone will be here shortly to escort you to bed, Mr. Martin. I'll see you at breakfast, when I hope you'll be sober enough to make your apologies."

Erin ran across the soft carpet and into her morning room. She slammed the door behind her and secured the lock as quickly as possible, hoping all the while that Walter wouldn't search her room. Dear God, let him go away or pass out! She listened for a moment and then remembered the door to the hall. Without hesitating she raced over and locked it.

Feeling more secure, she listened at each door in turn for an indication that Walter was attempting to come after her but heard nothing. She opened the hall door and peered out. Tupper was standing outside Erin's bedroom door and was about to knock.

"Tupper. Run and get Nero and Toby. Quick!" Erin exclaimed in a loud whisper. "Run!"

Without waiting for an explanation, Tupper ran down the stairs. From her door Erin could hear the old woman rousing the two slaves. "Hurry yo'sef on up there. Miss Erin want you faster'n a striped haint."

Erin returned to the door of her room and listened. She heard nothing but didn't want to chance opening it to Walter's renewed assault. By the time she reached the hallway again, Toby and Nero were topping the stairs.

"What is it, Miss Erin?" Nero asked, glancing about to see what had caused such a commotion.

Embarrassed a little, she nodded toward her bedroom. "Mr. Martin, drunk with Christmas eggnog, forced his way into my room. I believe he's passed out on the bed. He came home drunk, and, well, he wanted to . . ."

The lines of Nero's face hardened into a frown. "I'll kill that scoundrel. You jes' wait here."

"No, Nero," she answered and touched his arm. "We can't afford to harm a British official. I just want you to move him from my bed to his."

Nero nodded warily and opened the door. Toby edged inside. From her vantage point behind them, Erin could see Walter still lying on the bed. Bowie was nowhere to be seen, and she silently thanked God. Walter's presence had been difficult enough for her to speak about, but to try to explain *two* men's appearance in her bedroom in one evening was a task she heartily wanted to avoid if possible. 'Lasses would hear of it and preach to Erin all night about the pitfalls and torments that awaited loose women.

When the two servants left with Walter's limp form, Erin hurried into her morning room and opened the door that passed through to her bedroom. Surveying the room, she called softly, "Bowie?"

His head appeared above the edge of the mattress and he grinned. "You're getting all kinds of Christmas night visitors. This room is as busy as Charleston during race week."

Erin ignored his reference to Charleston's reputation for drawing huge crowds for the opening of the horse racing tracks in February. She remembered his kiss instead. Feeling the tint of color creep into her cheeks again, she busied herself straightening the rug where Walter's feet had rumpled the edge. "That was as close to disaster as I wish to come in my home."

Bowie stood and watched her as she lit some candles on the mantel and fiddled with the evergreens and ribbons. He walked over and threw another log on the fire. Wanting desperately to sweep her into his arms and off to bed, he held his emotions in tight control. Now, he realized, was not the time to make love to her. He was too new to her—and this was too soon after Walter's befuddled attempts. "Erin, as soon as we're sure Walter isn't likely to come stumbling back in, I want to speak to Arlen for a moment, and then I'll leave. We'll give Walter a few more minutes, and then you can see if your father is awake."

"Are you going to leave? I thought . . ." Erin's voice trailed off as she remembered that he told her he had a place to stay for the days he must be in Charleston. Briefly she wondered where it was but put her mind to more useful thought. "Will you be available for Papa if he needs you?"

"I'll be around for several days. Until after the New Year begins. After that, I don't know." Trying to keep his hands busy, Bowie stoked the fire, then turned to face her. "I'll be back."

"What if he needs you before you return?" Erin asked and held her hands to the warming fire. "How can I find you?"

Bowie considered the question for a moment. "We'll have to arrange some kind of signal. I'll try to pass by several times during the next few days."

Erin nodded her head in agreement and considered what kind of sign she could use to attract his attention. An idea came to her. "If it's at night, I'll put two candles in the front window by the harpsichord."

"That's good. What about during the day?" Bowie asked and sat on the divan to watch her pace back and forth in front of the fireplace.

"Well, I suppose I could place a basket of holly by the door on the piazza. But people might become suspicious if I put it out and take it back in arbitrarily."

"It's a good idea, though. What about ribbon? Do you have some different colors of ribbon you can use?" Bowie glanced around. Everything in the room was neat and orderly. Why couldn't she be like other girls he knew and leave her ribbons and geegaws lying around?

"Of course." Erin almost ran to her dressing table. Pulling out the drawers, she said, "I have several colors. Red, green, blue, yellow, pink—"

"Hold on. We only need two." Bowie laughed and moved closer to her side. He reached into the drawer and removed a lovely red velvet length of ribbon. "Can you fashion a bow out of this?"

"Certainly. I'll put the basket outside tonight with the red ribbon. If I need you for anything, I'll change the ribbon to green." Erin started arranging the red ribbon into a fluffy bow. When she finished, she looked up at Bowie and grinned. "See? Such a wonderful holiday color. Nobody will notice."

Bowie smiled as she hurried into her morning room and took a neat workbasket from a table. When she returned, she dumped the embroidery floss into a drawer and held up the small basket. "Maybe I should put it on the table be-tween the rocking chairs on the piazza. It's so small you may not notice it by the door."

"I'll see it, but if you put it on the table it'll be easier for me," Bowie agreed and glanced out the window. The time must be nearing midnight, and he must leave soon. Below, South Bay looked deserted.

Erin gathered the evergreens and holly from her mantel and more from her morning room. Quickly she arranged the greenery in the basket and secured the red bow to the handle. "See? It looks beautiful. Stay here. I'll put this on the piazza and check to see if Papa is awake."

Tiptoeing out the door, Erin glanced at Walter's door. Not wanting to risk being caught, she scurried lightly down the stairs and opened the front door. Pulling her wrapper close to keep out the cutting wind, she looked up and down the street. When she saw no one coming, she stepped over to the table and placed the basket in the middle.

She hurried back up the stairs and into her father's room. The fire burned low, and there was little light. Her father seemed to be sleeping, but she knew he wanted to see Bowie almost as badly as Bowie wanted to see her father. She crept to his bedside and shook him gently. "Papa? Papa, wake up. Bowie's about to leave, and he wants to talk to you before he does."

"Send him in," Arlen murmured sleepily and smiled a lopsided smile at his daughter.

Erin ran lightly back to her room, but before she opened the door, she crossed the hall to listen at Walter's door. For several minutes she stood there with her ear to the heavy wooden door. She could hear Walter snoring as she hurried back to her room. When she opened her door, Bowie was nowhere to be seen. She called his name and waited. The top of his head appeared on the other side of her bed. "Were you sleeping?" she teased.

"Hardly. I heard someone in the hall and couldn't risk having Walter charge in to find me, so I hid again." Bowie stood up and straightened his clothes. "I feel like a criminal."

"You are," she whispered and laughed. "You're becoming quite familiar with the underside of my bed."

Bowie gazed at her for a moment, memorizing the delightful twinkle of eyes that seemed as green as the holly boughs she'd taken to the piazza. "I'd like to become more familiar with the top of your bed."

For a moment Erin didn't know how to answer him. His smile thrilled her, and the tiny lines radiating from his eyes told her that his expression was genuine and not manufactured like Walter's were so often, but she didn't exactly understand his response. "Well, perhaps you'll get more rest where you're going."

"Perhaps," Bowie agreed and moved around the bed closer to her.

Without pausing to ask permission, he slipped his arms around her and touched his lips to hers. For a moment he savored the feeling of her body against his and the scent of rosewater that surrounded her like the soft mist that rises over the Ashley River early on spring mornings when the sun first caresses the water. He wanted to remember the kiss, the innocence of her response, the desire that surged through him and tightened his loins.

He touched her hair, drawing the length of bouncy curls
through his fingers and then winding the soft strands in his
fists to pull her lips close again. This time their kiss was
yearning and insistent, as if both of them realized that this
tender moment, this sweet and warm interlude of their lives,
would disappear the second their lips parted. Bowie reluctantly withdrew, taking time to gaze into her eyes to see if
she felt the same chill that beset him.

Grappling with her emotions, Erin lifted her chin and
stared at him. Did their kiss stir him as it had her? Would
he return to fulfill the promise his lips made during that
fleeting moment when the rivers stilled around her?

"Take me to see Arlen," he whispered finally against her
hair. "The time has come for me to go."

She left his embrace and opened the door a bit to peek
out. The hallway and stairwell were empty, and she stepped
out to look more closely. Waving to him to follow, she crept
along the landing to her father's room and entered as
quickly as possible. Bowie came right behind her. He closed
the door while she moved to her father's bed.

Arlen gazed up at her. "Erin? Let me see him privately
for a few moments."

"Yes, Papa," Erin whispered and fluffed his pillow a little.

Erin strode away from the bed. Sitting in her rocking
chair by the embers, she listened as they talked quietly. As
she suspected, they were discussing who would drive the
next supply wagon. Neither seemed to have any ideas, but
Erin did. Without doubt she'd be holding the reins of the
animals pulling the wagon. I just need to find a way of convincing them I'm the right person, she thought.

"I'll look around. I've got a place to stay here in town
that won't bring suspicion on you," Bowie whispered in
conclusion and grinned. "Erin and I have arranged a signal.
If you need me, just tell her and she'll let me know."

"You're not endangering my daughter, are you?" Arlen
asked, raising himself slightly on one elbow. "I'll not have
it."

Bowie nodded quickly. "No. No, of course not. I couldn't

do that. I . . . it's out of the question, but we need to keep in touch. This war won't wait for your leg to heal."

Erin's shoulders sagged as she sighed with disappointment. If the two of them agreed that she couldn't do the job, then her task would prove much more difficult. Jutting out her chin, she glared at the two men across the room. They thought the British were hard to deal with. Well, they hadn't yet come across anybody as determined and stubborn as Erin Edana Banning—but they would, and soon.

CHAPTER
5

MORNING FOUND ERIN WAITING BY THE HEARTH IN HER sitting room. Her fire seemed cold with Bowie gone, but Erin's frustration made the coals seem even colder. She felt bound to her room because Walter had gone downstairs earlier and hadn't left yet. She felt sure he would be staying home since he'd been so drunk on Christmas Day.

Erin thought about the past two days. They had been the most exciting days of her life—even more exciting than those days last April when the siege of Charleston had begun.

At first Erin had amused herself like many of the other ladies of Charleston by climbing out onto the roof of the piazza to watch the fighting. In the early morning hours the sight was a thrilling one. Balls of crimson flame shot through the air like hundreds of meteors converging in a spectacular display for the Charlestonians.

As beautiful as the spectacle was, Erin felt guilty for allowing herself to be entertained by such devastation. Houses all around were stained with black streaks from the acrid smoke, and roofs were charred and open where the fireballs ate into the wood before the inhabitants could douse the flames.

Even the Banning house hadn't escaped. While Erin had sat watching the battle, a fireball landed on the roof near her. For a few seconds she couldn't act, couldn't think. Finally she'd removed her wrapper and beat the flames down until the roof barely smoldered. Then she scrambled through the window and brought back the pitcher of fresh water 'Lasses had left for Erin's toilet. Choosing carefully, she'd poured it on the smoking wood until the fire went out completely. Though the event had shocked her, it hadn't frightened her enough to send her screeching through the window or clambering to leave Charleston as many other women had.

Her mother knew nothing of the fire on the roof. If she went out occasionally, she might have noticed, but Vevila Banning never ventured past the front door. For that Erin was exceedingly grateful. Her mother would never understand the changes taking place in her beautiful city, for Erin hardly understood them herself. Each day she prayed that the Patriots would free Charleston from occupation, but while she prayed she also acknowledged that if so many soldiers were busy here, then the cause of the Partisans was the better for it.

Her thoughts turned to Bowie. Yesterday her world had been secure—even in an occupied city. Her routine varied little, but she kept busy enough to amuse herself. Today her mind refused to concentrate on her everyday activities. When she stoked the fire, she pictured Bowie doing the same thing. When she ate her hotcakes, she remembered Bowie wolfing down his. As she played her harpsichord, she recalled his enjoyment while listening to her.

Shaking her head to clear the visions, Erin peeked in on her father. Dr. Rutledge had stopped by early and remarked that her nursing seemed to be effective. To Erin, there was too little she could do. Changing bandages, applying liniment, and feeding her father was something a servant could do, especially when supply wagons were stopped for want of a driver—and she could take over.

'Lasses can change bandages and feed Papa, Erin thought and punched the padded brocade arm of her chair. She wanted to become involved in the process of winning the war, and it appeared that she was as helpless as her wounded father. Jumping to her feet, she grimaced and wondered why men were so stubborn and why they couldn't see the answer to their problems when the solution was so obvious to her.

Erin began to pace. She didn't doubt that she could find a way to convince Bowie and her father of the sense of using her to drive the supply wagons, but what could she do meanwhile? A smile tickled the corners of her mouth and spread to her eyes. Bowie had mentioned that she could obtain information for him. He'd suggested that she should attend her uncle's party and eavesdrop on some of the British soldiers. She could do that without a single problem. Men considered women stupid and helpless, so she would be the perfect person to coax information from the opposition.

But how could she attend Uncle Jonathan's party without him becoming suspicious? She'd always made it clear that she didn't like his close association with the British, and now she'd have to find a way to indicate that her feelings had changed. One way was to appear at the Arledge house with a British escort.

Erin ran into her room and almost tore off the serge dress that Walter had found so distasteful. She surveyed her dresses and selected a gown designed to dazzle her uncle. Though she'd already turned down the invitation to his party, she hoped he'd ask her again out of courtesy. Everybody in Charleston knows that Uncle Jonathan can't resist a pretty girl, she thought. Though she seldom thought about her appearance, Erin knew she was prettier than many of the girls she saw on the streets. She wanted to emphasize that for her own purposes.

Slipping a white chintz gown with pale blue stripes over her head, she wondered about her hair. She hadn't time to waste dressing it as she normally would, so she drew it into a chignon and allowed some wisps of hair to soften the impression. Finally she fastened a sprig of blue flowers to a ribbon and tied it around her neck. Taking her lace fan and handkerchief, she hurried out the door and down the stairs.

She glanced into the parlor. Walter sat on the sofa, staring at the fire when she walked in smiling. She hoped he would think she'd changed her mind about him. His presence at

Uncle Jonathan's would help her cause considerably. "Good afternoon, Mr. Martin. It's a lovely day, isn't it?"

"Lovely?" He gazed up at her and then sprang to his feet. A grimace appeared briefly before he managed a smile in return. "Quite, Miss Banning. And speaking of lovely, I believe you're the fairest lady in all of Charleston."

"Oh, Mr. Martin," she gushed and fluttered her fan as she'd seen so many young ladies do when they wanted to impress a man. Silently she prayed he wouldn't see through her charade. "How you go on. You're teasing me now, aren't you? I'm sure you've met plenty of pretty girls."

"Well, yes, of course, but may I say that there is none lovelier than you at this moment," Walter reiterated and stepped closer. "Were you going out?"

"Oh, yes. I wanted to visit my cousin Lilly Arledge." Erin batted her eyelashes at him and sat on the edge of the nearest chair. She glanced toward the window and pursed her lips thoughtfully. "I declare, I hate to go alone, but I haven't seen her in ages."

"Alone? You're going alone?" Walter asked and settled across from her with a puzzled look on his face, as if he couldn't believe she was paying this much attention to him. "You really shouldn't go out alone. There are so many . . . well, a great deal could happen to an innocent young lady."

Erin shook her head sadly, hoping his expression didn't mean he was becoming suspicious. "I'm afraid I have no choice. You know how ill Mama and Papa are. And I've been nursing Papa since he came down with that gout, and now he's growing so cross I think he's getting worse. I simply have to get away for a while."

She dabbed at the corners of her eyes with her lace handkerchief and hung her head while she sniffed as she watched him covertly. He jumped to his feet and then plunged to one knee in front of her.

"Why, Miss Banning, I'd be delighted to accompany you. Please allow me to do so. I'd be so honored," he babbled, taking her hand solicitously.

"Oh, Mr. Martin, would you?" Erin batted her eyelashes again and flashed him a smile. "You are kindness itself."

Walter uttered something about finding his cloak and rushed from the room. Erin sagged back into the chair. "I don't know how some women do it," she muttered. She rose and went to find Tupper to tell the servant of her plans.

When Walter returned, Erin was standing by the front door, beaming up at him. He looked a little sick, and Erin almost giggled. She knew he was feeling miserable after imbibing so much eggnog and punch. "I must admit I'm delighted for your company, Mr. Martin."

"I'm happy to be of service, Miss Banning."

Without further conversation, they left. The Arledge household was several streets away from the Banning house, but Erin didn't mind the walk. She always loved strolling through Charleston and felt particularly happy about it today. With one victory behind her, she knew that her goal would be easily reached.

The brisk wind ruffled her satin skirt, and Erin enjoyed the bracingly cool air as they walked past several houses with black scars across their piazzas or roofs, reminding her of the battle for Charleston last April. Walter pointed out several things he found of interest about the city, but Erin hardly heard him. She nodded and smiled to make him think she agreed with his assessment of damage done during the spring siege that resulted in the occupation.

Passing several shops on Queen Street, Erin waved and called out to friends and acquaintances. When they reached the intersection of Queen and King, she directed Walter to the Arledge residence three houses from the intersection.

From that moment Erin's heart fluttered. The housekeeper informed them that Jonathan and his daughter, Lilly Arledge, were home and conducted Erin and Walter to the parlor. She despised her uncle and had hoped he wouldn't be home. She'd rather have worked her plan on Lilly. While Erin waited, she heard Jonathan berating a slave for her ineptitude. When the angry voice quieted, Erin steeled herself for her uncle's probing questions.

"Erin, my dear, what has happened? Are my dear relatives worse? Has someone died?" Jonathan Arledge burst into the room, questions flowing from his mouth like the Ashley River after a spring rain. When he saw Walter, he stopped and stared.

To cover the awkward moment, Erin rose and tried to answer his questions without arousing his suspicions. "Uncle Jonathan, it's nice to see you. I hope you had a happy Christmas. My father has been seized by a particularly bad case of the gout, and Mama is about the same as always."

"Shame about your mama. A beautiful woman, she is." Jonathan moved closer to his niece and kissed her cheek.

To keep from flinching, Erin stiffened herself and accepted the caress. "Uncle Jonathan, I'd like you to meet our boarder, Mr. Martin. Walter Martin of Colonel Balfour's office. Walter, my uncle, Jonathan Arledge."

"Quite pleased to make your acquaintance, young man." Jonathan grinned and opened his arms wide as if to take in the expanse of the room. "Please make yourself comfortable in my humble home."

"It is an honor to meet you, sir. I've heard a great deal about you," Walter answered.

Erin bit her lower lip to keep from laughing. The two men were posturing and gesturing like actors in a stage play. She sat back on the sofa and listened to them talk for a few minutes.

Finally Jonathan turned to her again and eyed her suspiciously. "And what brings you here, my dear?"

"I've come to call, Uncle Jonathan. It is Christmas, you know." Erin hoped her face didn't flame with color because of the lie she told. "Your housekeeper told me that Lilly was—"

"Erin!" Lilly Arledge exclaimed as she swept through the door. "Oh, Erin, how good to see you."

Erin jumped up and hugged her cousin. Though they were politically divided by the war, Erin still loved Lilly a great deal. To her left, she could see Jonathan grimace. Walter rose and waited to be introduced, but Erin was too delighted to see her cousin at the moment. "Lilly, how lovely you look."

"Papa, may we be excused . . . Oh, I must apologize. I didn't realize we had other company." Lilly tried to smile. "I'm Lilly Arledge."

"Lilly, this is Walter Martin, Colonel Balfour's assistant," Jonathan explained. "He's boarding at the Banning house. Mr. Martin, allow me to present my daughter, Lilly."

Walter still stood quietly by his chair. "Delighted to meet you, Miss Arledge."

"Welcome to our home, Mr. Martin. Have you been in Charleston for long?" Lilly asked, assuming the role of hostess. She moved to a vacant chair and sat daintily, crossing her hands in her lap.

Erin suppressed a groan. Though she loved her cousin a great deal, this extreme deference to a British official would test any love she had. Inwardly Erin wanted to screech that Walter Martin was the enemy; outwardly she smiled sweetly.

She wondered how Bowie would handle this situation. He'd probably charge up to Walter and start a fight. Erin was glad Bowie wasn't here to see her simpering face and ladylike manners with the enemy, although she secretly thought he'd commend her performance.

Never mind him, she chided herself. With three Tories in the room she needed to keep her wits about her or she'd give away her plan. She grinned at Lilly. "Did you have a happy Christmas?"

"I suppose we did. We had several guests for supper." Lilly smoothed her skirt and eyed Erin carefully. "What did you do? Are your parents feeling better?"

"I . . . Mama and Papa ate upstairs in their rooms. Both of them are unwell." Erin hoped that her evasion of the question would satisfy Lilly. Apparently the answer was satisfactory because Lilly nodded sympathetically.

"I'm so sorry. You could have had supper with us. Our

guests would have welcomed the sight of a pretty girl like you." Lilly rose and touched Erin's shoulder. "Would you like to see my new gown? Papa had it made for a party we're giving to celebrate the coming of the New Year."

Erin perked up. This party sounded like the perfect opportunity to obtain information that would be of use to Bowie. "I'd love to see the gown."

"Papa, Erin and I are going to run up and look at my new dress. Will you and Mr. Martin excuse us?" Lilly watched her father nervously, as if she expected him to roar at her.

Erin, too, turned to Jonathan Arledge. His fits of temper were legendary in the family, and she didn't particularly want to risk being the object of his vile humor, so she remained silent. For a few seconds he looked as if he would explode like one of those fireballs the British had used to bring Charleston to her knees, but he didn't. Perhaps he didn't want to tarnish the impression he made on Walter.

"Yes, yes, go on." He waved his hand and glanced at them before returning his attention to Walter. "You were saying?"

Lilly led the way, although Erin could have found her room easily because they used to play together when they were children—long before the war ripped the city into factions. Lilly's room was pleasant. Decorated in various shades of yellow, its cheery glow made Erin feel at home, reminding her of the old days when life seemed so easy and fun. She and Lilly had made a thousand plans here: balls they would attend, their coming out, what kinds of men they would marry, what kinds of homes they would have—all the dreams little girls have, many of which no longer could come true.

For a moment Erin became sad for the things she'd never have, the dreams that never could be fulfilled, but grew sadder when she thought of the other results of this horrible war. Many boys who had grown up with her and Lilly were dead or disfigured or disabled—a price far more precious than the frivolities denied to her by the war.

She lifted her head and jutted out her chin. Well, Erin Banning would do something to make a difference; she would in spite of everyone who tried to deny her that right. Looking at Lilly, Erin suddenly felt sorry for her cousin. Her mother had died when Lilly was born, leaving Lilly to the care of housekeepers and servants. Jonathan cared little about the bringing up of a daughter and often made Lilly aware of her low status in his life.

Erin knew that since Lilly had grown into a woman, her value had changed in Jonathan's eyes. No longer a gangly girl who craved love, Lilly's beauty couldn't be denied and offered him a way of luring British officials to his home. Jonathan used his daughter as bait, much like a fisherman might. With a lovely daughter in the house, many soldiers tried to get invitations to supper or to parties, making Jonathan a popular man with the British. Being in constant demand lined his pockets well.

Hate flashed in Erin's heart, but she fought with it and finally smiled at her hostess. "My, but this room is prettier than I remembered."

"I like it. It's my . . . well, my refuge. Papa has so many guests that I . . . I escape when I can." Lilly blushed and looked away. She hurried to the closet and found the dress in question.

"Oh, it's lovely." Erin fingered the embroidered silk and felt a rush of envy. She held it against her and looked in the mirror. Something didn't seem right. The bodice was cut very low, much lower than the current style. She glanced at Lilly and realized what was happening. Jonathan dictated the fashion in the Arledge house. To attract more of the British soldiers, he dressed Lilly in nearly indecent gowns.

But Erin couldn't deny its beauty. The gown was more beautiful than anything she'd ever owned or hoped to own. Though the Banning household ran smoothly, thanks mainly to her father's illicit business and Walter's contributions, fabric was hard to obtain, especially as fine as this. "I'm sure you'll look lovely wearing this."

Lilly groaned and sat. "But for what? Papa brings home

all these men and wants me to . . . to be nice to them. I mean, he doesn't insist that I . . . well, he wants me to be popular, as popular as you always were." Her head and shoulders dropped, and she fiddled with her skirt. "Oh, Erin, what shall I do? I'm afraid Papa is going to . . . that he'll make me . . . Oh, what can I do?"

Erin sat down and put her arms around her cousin. What could she do? Lilly was his child, still under the age of consent. Fighting the tears that pooled in her eyes, Erin hugged Lilly and whispered, "If he ever tries to make you do something that . . . that you feel is wrong, come to me. I'll find a way to hide you somewhere."

All the way home Erin bristled with anger. Her uncle was trying to use Lilly like the women down by the wharves who attracted men with their gaudy clothing and painted faces. Though she'd always disliked Uncle Jonathan, now she felt a seething, roiling hate that almost soured her stomach. "How dare he?"

"Pardon?" Walter asked, looking down at her.

"Uh, nothing," Erin replied quickly, hoping that Walter couldn't guess her thoughts. "I don't feel very well, that's all."

"My goodness. Should we send Toby for Dr. Rutledge?" Walter stopped and peered into her eyes. "Hmmm, your eyes are a bit red. I guess you could be coming down with something."

Red eyes. If he only knew that she was seeing red with those red eyes. But she couldn't afford to let him know her thoughts. Before they'd left the Arledge household, Uncle Jonathan had invited both of them to his New Year's party, and that, at least, was the one thing she achieved today.

Excitement raced through Erin's body as she walked up the steps to the Arledge house. From inside, music and raucous laughter filtered through to her, and she smiled a secret smile of triumph. Careful, she scolded herself, you can't count a victory until you've won the battle. Even so, she felt the thrilling sense of doing something positive toward ending the war.

During the past few days, she'd seen Bowie only once. Erin had been sitting in the garden, seeking a moment's respite from all the day-to-day problems of the household and her nursing duties. The breeze off the harbor ruffled her shawl as she stared at the stately live oaks, and she fell into a dream-like state. Her thoughts drifted to Bowie Gallagher, and she sighed. His cocky smile seemed to haunt her these days.

As if conjured up by her thoughts, he appeared on the walkway several feet away. "Bowie!" she exclaimed, jumping to her feet. "What are you doing here?"

"I came to see you." He glanced around as if to ascertain whether they were alone.

"Is there some problem?" Erin asked, settling back down on the stone bench and arranging her dress modestly. She willed her pulse to stop racing and tried to look normal.

"Uh, no." Bowie gazed at her. He'd been unable to get her out of his thoughts. He realized that he'd made a mistake. By coming here, he'd simply reinforced whatever magical hold she had on him. "I just . . . How's Arlen?"

Erin stared at him. He seemed so flustered, when he was usually so calm and unruffled. "Getting better."

Bowie stepped closer. He could smell her scent, the lovely soft fragrance of roses that always clung to her, and it nearly drove him mad. "I, uh, well, I guess I'd better be on my way. I've lots of things to do."

Watching him back away, Erin wondered what had happened. He'd seemed happy to see her and then didn't even stay to chat. As he walked backwards, he tripped over the bricks edging the walkway and fell into a clump of rose bushes.

"Damnation!" he exclaimed, trying to extricate himself from his thorny bed.

Erin jumped up, making an attempt to stifle her giggles, and hurried to help him. "Oh, dear me, I hope you aren't hurt."

Feeling foolish, Bowie regained his feet with Erin's help. "Thank you. I don't know what . . . this is certainly . . . I'm embarrassed to have . . . "

He glanced down at her. Erin's upturned face was just inches from his, and he wanted to kiss her again, felt compelled to kiss her. Bowie leaned down, placed his arms around her, and drew her into his embrace. For a moment he relished her soft femininity as she allowed him to hold her. He could wait no longer. His lips found hers hungrily, as a starved man seeks bread, and she responded by opening her mouth to his.

Bowie felt warm all over. He pulled her further into his embrace, knowing that he should run as fast as he could. "Erin," he whispered against her hair. "Sweet Erin."

Regaining his senses, Bowie drew back and gazed at her. He stepped back and almost fell into the rose bushes again. "Got to go. I mean . . . I'll see you soon. Goodbye."

Erin hugged herself and sat back down. Bowie Gallagher was certainly a mystery man.

Now breathing deeply, she knocked at the door and waited. For once she was glad the weather was warm enough for her to walk here comfortably. Walter had asked her to come with him, but she'd declined. His disappointment was evident, but she didn't want to appear to be with someone; she wanted to be free to dance and talk to every soldier and British official present. Ordinarily, young ladies didn't attend parties unescorted, but since this one was at her cousin's house, Erin didn't mind flouting convention. A servant opened the door, and she strolled in as if she hadn't a care in the world—even though inside she felt the tremors of anticipation fighting to gain control of her.

She found Lilly quickly and hugged her. "How lovely you are, Lilly." Erin tried not to stare at the deeply cut bodice of Lilly's dress; it revealed much more than a lady's clothing should.

She had worked hard on her own dress for this party. She'd taken one of her gowns and reworked it a little, adding ribbons and sprigs of artificial flowers. Then she'd embroidered a border on the deep ruffle of the dress and sleeves until it looked nearly as stylish as Lilly's, while remaining in good taste. The square bodice was embroidered and fit snugly over her full breasts and tapered to a narrow waist emphasized by the emerald-green silk.

"Erin, please have some punch. It's delicious." Lilly signaled for a servant, who brought a tray of punch.

"Thank you, Lilly. I must admit I'm thirsty." Erin sipped her punch and looked around the room at the vast number of soldiers. There was a wealth of information out there if she could find a way to obtain it.

"Oh, Erin, I want to introduce you to some of my friends." Lilly tugged on Erin's arm and led her to a group of young officers chatting by the hearth.

"Gentlemen, I have a surprise for you," Lilly announced as they approached. "My cousin, Erin Banning, I'd like you to meet Captain Gregory Saunders, Captain William Fuller, and Lieutenant Dwight Thomas. Gentlemen, Miss Banning."

The three officers immediately clustered around the two women and began to talk. Erin felt a surge of pleasure. Since the beginning of the war she'd had little enough male attention, but more, she understood that these three men would be the key to her successful mission.

"Would you like to dance, Miss Banning?" Captain Gregory Saunders smiled eagerly.

"Thank you, Captain. I'd be honored." Erin allowed him to lead her to the dance floor.

For the next several minutes they danced, talked, and laughed. Erin had been prepared to hate all the British soldiers she met here this evening, but she found that Captain Saunders was an easy man to like. She kept reminding herself that he was the enemy, but that did little good. She danced with Captain Fuller and then Lieutenant Thomas before she returned to the hearth where Lilly was laughing with another young man.

"Miss Banning, may I have this dance?" a deep masculine voice said from behind her.

For a moment before she turned to answer, she thought the voice sounded familiar—but she knew it couldn't possibly be Bowie's. He wouldn't dare enter this house when it was filled with British officers—not even the daring sea captain was that foolhardy. Determined to accept any invitation, she pirouetted gaily around and felt the smile leave her face. The foppish man standing before her dressed in pink satin breeches, pink and white striped frock coat adorned with golden acorns, a brocade jacket decorated with sequins, and striped stockings, seemed as out of place as Bowie Gallagher would have.

Erin forced a smile, glanced at the two watch chatelaines that decorated his waist and tried to keep from giggling. "Well, I've just . . ."

Her voice dwindled off as she looked up at the man's face. Surprise stifled the giggle that had threatened, and with astonished glee she realized she was talking to none other than Bowie Gallagher. "Uh, I'd be delighted, Mr. . . ."

"Farthingale. Chauncey Farthingale at your service." His face contorted into a snobbish smirk as he gazed at her. "Mr. Arledge and I have become quite friendly. You see, he has need of my services and . . . but why am I prattling on so when I can see you are dying to dance the minuet with me?"

With a baffled stare she murmured, "Certainly, Mr. Farthingale. I can think of nothing I'd rather do."

CHAPTER
6

To GIGGLE AND LAUGH LIKE A GIRL OF TEN WOULD BE calamitous, but Erin almost did. Bowie presented such a priggish picture that she could hardly contain herself, much less dance and maintain the demeanor expected of her. But somehow she managed, though Bowie did nothing to help.

"I say, Miss Banning," he continued, using a thick British accent that made even some of the soldiers turn to stare. "This is quite the thing, isn't it? Although we're here in the colonies, away from the civilized world, we have some measure of comfort in knowing that Charleston still belongs to the king. So true, so true."

"So true," she mimicked and gnawed on her lip to keep from embarrassing both of them. She realized that his ridiculous attire and demeanor were a disguise that allowed him to move freely about Charleston without appearing to be a threat to anyone. "How fortunate you found us. Have you been in Charleston for very long?"

"Oh, my dear girl, simply ages," he answered and pointed his toe primly before posturing and posing for effect. "Simply ages, I have. I'm quite put out that we haven't met before, for we could have become such good friends, you and I. I assume you keep yourself hidden within the confines of your home, or I would have seen you."

Erin rolled her eyes and turned smartly to the beat of the music, though she could hardly believe what she was hearing. "As you may know, my parents are ill, and I stay at home to nurse them, so I know so few new people in town."

"How unfortunate. Perhaps I could call sometime in the future to pay my respects, although I wouldn't dream of disturbing your dear parents," he rejoined and bowed gracefully. "I can't tell you how much I've enjoyed our little dance. Would you think me terribly forward if I ask for another dance later in the evening? We do dance frightfully well together, don't you think, my dear?"

"Yes, I'll dance with you again. I, too, have been quite amused during our time together this evening." Playing along with his charade, Erin batted her eyes playfully and allowed him to escort her from the dance floor to where Lilly and the British officers were standing and watching the dancers.

"Oh, Erin," Lilly called as her cousin came closer. "I see you've been dancing with the elegant Mr. Farthingale."

"Such an interesting man," Erin answered and gazed at her cousin. "He's quite a charmer."

Lilly stared at Erin as if she'd said something ridiculous or embarrassing. "Yes," Lilly drawled in a puzzled voice. "He certainly is."

Erin didn't explain her opinion further. If Lilly thought him silly, then he must have been here several times for her to get to know him so well. When? she wondered. It didn't really matter. Bowie must have had a good reason for making friends with Jonathan. Erin would have to trust Bowie and go along with him. He must be trying to obtain information, much as she was.

"Miss Arledge, you've been a bad chit to keep your lovely cousin a secret from me," Chauncey Farthingale scolded and shook his head. "Such a naughty girl you are. Miss Banning is quite the charming young lady, isn't she? She dances simply divinely, and her gossip is exceedingly amusing."

"I do apologize for not introducing you to her. I never thought that you would become such fast friends." Lilly glanced at Erin through narrowed eyes, as if she were wondering what her cousin could have said to interest such a prissy man. "I presume you have introduced yourselves."

"Oh, yes." Erin glanced at Bowie, hoping he'd go away.

She could sense the discomfort of the soldiers around such a sissy of a man. They were unlikely to let any valuable information slip around another man—even if that man were Chauncey Farthingale. She wanted the officers at ease or they would never feel free to discuss troop movements, battles, or other items that might be of interest to Erin.

"Oh, we're quite the thing now, old friends, I should venture." Bowie struck a pose and gazed at the soldiers. "Such honorable men. In the service of their king. I'm humbled by your presence, as is all of Charleston, I'm sure."

All three of the officers mumbled something but didn't attempt to enter the conversation. Finally Captain Saunders asked Erin to dance, and she agreed.

After their dance was over, Captain Saunders invited her to the piazza for some fresh air. Since the night was warmer than most December nights, she agreed, thinking that if he liked her enough he might try to impress her with his knowledge and allow some information to slip.

She was wrong about Captain Saunders. A pleasant man, he strolled with her across the piazza and down the brick steps into the garden. As they wandered among the palmettos and palms, he talked of his home in England and how much he missed it.

"The weather is finer here, though," he acknowledged and glanced at the sky. "Such beautiful skies, so little fog, not so much rain."

"We do have nice weather." Erin tried to think of a way to question him about his part in the war without sounding too inquisitive. "What do you do here?"

Gregory Saunders looked down at her. "What do you mean?"

"I mean, are you here permanently or do you go in and out?" She hoped the darkness covered her blush. This wasn't as easy as she'd expected it to be.

"I'm here most of the time," he replied without elaborating.

Erin decided that she'd get no information from him. "I think we'd better get back. Lilly will be searching for us."

Once they reached the group, Erin wondered how she could talk with the other soldiers without traipsing through the garden with them. After a while someone would suspect her of being less than a lady if she took every man with whom she danced to the garden.

She danced once with Walter and introduced him to the group gathered by the hearth. He seemed to be quite shy when meeting Bowie, or Chauncey, as he called himself. Erin lacked the time to waste on Walter, for she could eavesdrop on him at home. She didn't know why it hadn't occurred to her before, but she could easily bring in tea and cakes while he had guests instead of leaving that task to 'Lasses. Dismissing Walter from her mind, she resolved to do that in the future.

"Miss Banning, will you sit with me at supper?" Captain Fuller asked eagerly while they danced.

"I'd be delighted, sir," she answered. Would he be more open about his job? Would the information she could obtain from him be helpful?

Erin felt the frustration rising in her as he bowed, she curtsied, and they left the dance floor. She refused to give up so easily. If these three soldiers wouldn't or couldn't provide her with information, then she'd just have to find someone who could.

Supper proved to be delicious. Since nothing else seemed to be going right, Erin immersed herself in her meal. Bowie sat on one side of her and Captain William Fuller on the other. While Bowie conversed with a pale young woman Erin didn't know, she listened to Captain Fuller.

"Miss Banning, I believe you're the prettiest girl in Charleston," he said and smiled down at her. "I'm glad you agreed to have supper with me. Miss Arledge seems to prefer Captain Saunders, and, well, sometimes I feel left out."

"A man like you? You're so . . ." Erin tried to think of something that would make him feel good enough to loosen his tongue. "You're such a leader, such a brave soldier."

William Fuller grinned. "Well, I wouldn't say that, Miss Banning. But I do my job well."

Aha, she thought. Here was her opportunity to get him talking about his work. "What do you do, Captain Fuller?"

"Please, call me William," he replied and puffed out his chest.

"What do you do . . . William?" she asked breathlessly and fluttered her eyelashes at him as she touched his arm. "Is your work quite dangerous?"

"Well, Miss Banning," he began and glanced around as if to see who might be listening to their conversation. "I'm not in much danger as a rule, although I'm occasionally in the direct line of fire. Why, just two weeks ago I was on my way north to take some clothing to our army when we were almost spotted by some rebs. I could have been killed if they'd seen me."

"Oh, how awful!" she exclaimed and clapped her fingers over her mouth in horror. "My dear Captain Fuller, you weren't . . . I mean, you didn't . . . Oh, I just can't think it. How horrible for you. Do you have to go into the wilds outside Charleston often?"

"Well, I'm occasionally called upon to do so. I'll probably be taking another shipment in two weeks." He beamed at her, seemingly proud that someone thought him important. "It's a dangerous job. That scoundrel Francis Marion, the outlaw they call the Swamp Fox, is always lurking around. He could be anywhere, ready to attack."

"Oh, I'm horrified. You'll be most careful, won't you?" Once again she placed her hand on his arm and fluttered her eyelashes. "I'll be so afraid until I know you're safe. Will you be gone for very long?"

"No. I believe our next trip will take a mere week at the most." He glanced around at the other diners, pausing when he saw Captain Saunders with Lilly. Suddenly turning, he grabbed Erin's hand and held it tightly. "Will you honestly be worried about me?"

"Most assuredly. I'll be unable to sleep a moment while you're in danger." Erin looked around to see if anyone had been listening. The most logical person to be eavesdropping was Bowie, and he was engrossed in conversation with the girl next to him. "Will I see you again before you leave?"

William Fuller's eyes brightened, and he nodded his head. "We leave on Monday week after next. May I call on you before then? I mean, would your family agree to allowing me to call?"

Erin's heart sang. Now she had something concrete. With William so enamored of her, she could obtain information from him fairly easily. "Oh, I'm sure they'd be delighted, although I'm taking my parents to our plantation. I'm afraid they're both quite ill and need the solitude of the country to get well."

"Yes, city life can be so awfully bad on one's health," he agreed. "Perhaps after you return I could call on you."

"I'm sure that would be nice," Erin replied and sipped her wine. She could hardly wait to get home, to begin formulating her plans. Before she left here, she needed to tell Bowie that he should come by later so they could discuss the information she'd gleaned from Captain Fuller.

After supper they moved back into the parlor and ballroom. Erin fought to contain her glee. At least she could make a difference; she possessed information that might help the Partisans in their effort to beat the oppressive enemy. Her happiness turned to tension before long as she considered the ramifications of her new knowledge.

"Dear, Lilly, I'm afraid I must go," she told her cousin and hugged her close. "I've been away from Mama and Papa far too long."

"I'm so sorry. Please give them our regards and a kiss from me." Lilly walked with Erin toward the door.

Erin really hated to leave Lilly alone with all those British soldiers, but she couldn't stay any longer without giving herself away. Besides, she wanted to go before Walter discovered she was leaving and tried to accompany her. He was deeply engrossed in conversation with Gregory Saunders.

Erin smiled fondly at her cousin. Over Lilly's shoulder Erin saw Chauncey approach. She could hardly keep from laughing as he strolled across the floor. "Give my regards to the gentlemen and to Uncle Jonathan."

"Do you plan to walk alone?" Lilly asked as she helped Erin into her cloak. Noticing Chauncey, Lilly added, "Here's Chauncey. We can't let Erin walk home alone, can we?"

"May the gods forbid," Chauncey said, tilting his head to one side. "I'll escort this lovely child to her home if she will agree."

"Mr. Farthingale, I appreciate your offer, but I must decline." Erin fought to maintain her composure. "I just can't take advantage of your kindness."

"Nonsense, you goose. I refuse to allow you to walk the streets of this city alone at such an indecent hour." He wagged his finger at her as if she were a naughty child. "I would indeed be remiss if I let you go alone and some harm befell you. What sort of gentleman would allow—"

"You're so kind, Mr. Farthingale," she interrupted and rolled her eyes at Lilly. "But I'm sure you have other things to do."

"Nonsense. You just heard Miss Arledge say you can't walk home alone."

"No, Erin, really. Mr. Farthingale is quite acceptable as an escort, I'm sure." Lilly smiled reassuringly at her cousin. "He's a real gentleman."

Finally Erin gave in. If she continued to try to dissuade Chauncey from walking with her, she'd look suspicious to Lilly and anyone else who might overhear her. "I'd be delighted for you to escort me to my home if it won't delay you from your plans for the remainder of the evening."

"On the contrary," he quipped. "I plan to be sleeping early tonight. I have a task that requires that I rise early tomorrow."

"Well, good night, Lilly." Erin hugged her cousin again and whispered, "Remember, if Uncle Jonathan asks you to do anything . . . anything you don't feel is proper, come to me. I'll hide you until we can send you somewhere safe."

Lilly grasped Erin's hands and sighed. "Thank you, Erin, thank you for everything. I love you."

"I love you, too, Lilly. Season's greetings to you." Erin reluctantly removed her hands from Lilly's and hurried out the door with Bowie right behind her.

"What was that about?" Bowie asked when he closed the wrought-iron gate at the street.

"My uncle . . . he makes Lilly . . . did you notice her dress?" Erin finally asked, feeling slightly foolish for being unable to articulate the words she wanted to say.

"Oh, yes. I noticed, as did every man there. Why would she wear such provocative clothing?" Bowie held his arm out, and Erin looped her hand through the crook of his elbow.

"My uncle forces her to do so. Lilly doesn't like it, but he pays for her clothing, and the seamstress does what he asks," Erin explained and loved her father all the more for his kindness and undeniable generosity. "I fear he'll barter her away for favors from some British officer."

"I don't doubt your assessment." Bowie slowed as they reached the Battery. "What will she do?"

"I've told her to come to me. I'll send her to Cousin Noelle in the Ninety-Six District." Erin pulled her cloak closer against the rising wind coming from the river. She glanced up at Bowie's profile. "And what of you, Mr. Farthingale? You must have been busy for the past few days. I never expected to see you at Uncle Jonathan's party—particularly dressed as you are and with your foppish manner."

Bowie laughed. "That, my dear Miss Banning, is a demeanor I adopt to keep the soldiers away. If they feel I'm as priggish as I appear, then they don't watch me too closely."

"Ah, I see. Therefore you can come and go as you please without arousing their suspicions." Erin grinned at the cleverness of his scheme and turned to look more closely at him. "I must say, you could fool even your mother."

"I thank you for your compliment. My disguise saves me a great deal of explanation," Bowie admitted and stopped.

As Erin stared, the moon broke through the clouds. Across the water the moon's reflection shimmered like candlelight on a satin ballgown. Erin gazed at Bowie, wondering why he paused. After a moment he cupped her chin in his hand and kissed her gently.

"I've missed you these past few days, Miss Banning." Bowie gazed down into her eyes, now shadowed and dark because of the dim light filtering through the clouds.

"You're teasing me again, Mr. Farthingale," she countered, feeling a chill race up and down her spine. "I think you're funning me. Anyone could see that your attention was elsewhere during supper."

For a few seconds Bowie didn't understand what she meant. All evening long he'd been forced to stand aside and watch her dance and flirt with those British soldiers while he amused himself elsewhere. And during supper he'd chatted idly with some feather-headed twit who knew nothing about everything while Erin and William Fuller were involved in a quiet conversation that excluded everyone else.

"If you will recall, Miss Banning, you ignored me entirely during supper and most of the evening. You danced with every officer there, more than once, and even went into the garden with one of them." Bowie felt a little jealous although he didn't really know why. He'd never been jealous of any woman before, and he didn't intend to become possessive now, not of Erin Banning nor of any other woman.

Erin blushed. He'd noticed her fervent conversation with William. She felt a little flattered by his attention and lifted her head to look at him better. Is he jealous? she wondered. No, he couldn't be. He'd barely known her a week and hadn't shown any tendency toward that emotion. He hadn't even been particularly attentive since he'd left on Christmas night after his talk with her father.

But he'd kissed her. Her lips were branded forever by his kisses, some sweet and gentle, others fiery with passion and desire.

Erin could hardly breathe. Despite the cold night air, a warmth suffused her body, and she felt tingly all over. Could this be the result of a single kiss? she wondered, but decided that she should think about business now and kissing later.

She wanted to tell him what she'd learned during dinner, but they were too vulnerable. Bushes and shrubs lined the street, providing plenty of places for someone to hide. She'd wait.

Bowie gazed down at her and felt a swelling sensation in his chest. He couldn't read her eyes, but her response to his kiss had said enough for him—for now. His feelings were too new—and too precious—to define at the moment. There would be time later to think about kissing.

He longed to ask her why she'd changed her mind about going to the Arledge party. Her face had seemed so intense while she pretended to have fun. Could she have taken his suggestion to eavesdrop on the British seriously? He realized that she must have and looked around.

The place was too public to discuss her reasons for going to the party. Bowie refused to endanger her life by speaking where passersby could hear them. He'd wait until tomorrow and call on her as Chauncey had said he would. For a few seconds they said nothing and didn't move. Finally he took her arm, and they walked the rest of the distance to her house in silence.

When they reached the gate outside her house, he paused again. "I'll see you soon, Erin."

His lips found hers, and she eagerly accepted his kiss. Leaning against him, she felt the air whoosh out of her lungs and thought her feet would leave the ground from the sheer weightlessness of her body. She slid her arms around his neck, returning his embrace and abandoning all rational thought.

When he pulled away, she whispered, "Good night, Mr. Farthingale," and ran into the house. She stopped long enough to speak to her father and look in on her mother before hurrying to her own room.

Bowie stood watching long after the door closed. His heart pounded in his chest and threatened to break his rib cage with its ferocity. In a few minutes he turned and strode back down South Bay, whistling as he walked, but then he stopped. He needed to talk to her. Tomorrow might be too late if she had really been eavesdropping. There was no telling what she would do if she'd learned anything she considered significant.

He'd sensed an excitement in her that made him aware that she might have learned something important. He returned to the Banning house and started up the walk. Hesitating before he walked up the steps to the piazza, he thought about Walter Martin. Could he have returned? Bowie and Erin had stood down by Oyster Point for several minutes—plenty of time for Walter to arrive.

Bowie slid behind a bush while he considered his options.

Tonight had been fun. With Erin there to witness his little charade, the entire event became a game he wouldn't have missed for all the king's gold and guns. Erin had mentioned the twit who sat at his right at dinner. True enough, he'd talked almost exclusively to her all evening, but it was to cover his anger at Erin for accepting the British officer's invitation to sit with him during supper. Bowie cursed under his breath. Given a few more minutes, she would have been his own companion for the evening instead of Fuller's. Damn the forward officer for his speedy invitation. But his mind was wandering. He needed to concentrate on the problem at hand.

Erin brushed her hair thoughtfully and then stopped abruptly. After Bowie had kissed her, she'd forgotten to tell him about the shipment William had spoken about during supper! Pulling on her dressing gown as she ran, Erin scurried down the stairs with a fresh green ribbon to tie on the basket of holly resting on the table on the piazza. For a moment she thought Bowie must be right about her. She'd forgotten her first mission because of a kiss. Then she told herself she was being too severe with herself—she was already correcting her lapse.

She hoped Bowie would see the basket early tomorrow because they needed to begin making plans for ambushing the British shipment of goods William had mentioned. On the piazza she hesitated and gazed across Oyster Point. Thoughtfully arranging the ribbon on the basket, she recalled Bowie's kiss.

She'd been kissed before but never the way Bowie kissed her, and she had never felt as she did tonight. Her heart still pounded, and her fingers fluttered with nervous energy. Erin knew she'd have a difficult time falling asleep with her vivid memories of Bowie's kiss and her first foray into the world of spying.

Spying. Erin thought it was funny that she hadn't called what she'd done spying until now. She had not spied in the classic sense of sneaking up to the window of a building where secret plans were being laid, but she had committed an act of spying nonetheless. She knew she could go to jail as a spy but pushed the thought aside. She simply couldn't worry about that when her help could possibly shorten the war or make some poor soldiers more comfortable and better armed.

A sound coming from the jasmine bushes in front of the house startled her, and Erin moved into the shadows of the piazza. She hadn't considered that someone might be about, walking the streets or hiding in her front yard. For a moment she toyed with the idea of running for the front door, but she feared that whoever was in the yard could reach the door before she did.

Trembling, she gazed into the depths of darkness that lined the yard by the fence. She stiffened her spine and stared at the point from which the sound had come. Sensing rather than seeing a movement, she focused her eyes on a spot that seemed to be lighter than the shadows around the bushes. She wondered what to do. Someone definitely was hiding there, watching her as she'd daydreamed. Could it be a British soldier, someone who'd overheard her conversation with William and guessed her plot?

The silence wore on. Erin stared and knew someone was looking back. Who would give up and move first? The wind rustled through the trees, rattling the fronds of the palmettos. Cold air ruffled the hem of her wrapper, and she pulled it closer about her.

"Erin," she heard from the darkness.

"Who's there?" she replied in a low voice, shivery with the cold.

"Chauncey Farthingale," came the reply.

Stifling a giggle, Erin wondered what to do. Should she risk inviting him inside? A gust of wind helped her decide. When she glanced up and down the street and saw no other people out, she waved frantically. "Hurry."

While he took the steps three at the time, she raced for the door. It would never do for Walter to find her dressed in her wrapper while entertaining Chauncey Farthingale. Once inside, she closed the door behind them. "Let's go to my morning room. I think we'll be safe there."

They hurried up the stairs, down the hall, and into her morning room. A chill suffused the air, and Bowie laid a log on the smoldering coals. "What were you doing out on the piazza at this hour?"

"Why were you hiding among my Carolina jasmine bushes?" she countered. Shivering, she moved closer to the fire, although it gave little warmth. "I was trying to send you a message."

"What kind of message?"

"Don't you remember our code? I was to change the ribbon on the basket to green if I needed you for anything." Erin glared at him, wondering if she'd misjudged him. He didn't seem like the sort of man who would forget something as important as that.

"No, I mean what is your message?" Bowie rubbed his hands together briskly. "It's getting colder outside. I didn't realize it when we left the Arledges'."

"I know. I learned something—"

"Shhh!" he warned and listened carefully. "I think I heard the front door open."

"Walter's home," she guessed and glanced about. "Come with me."

She all but dragged Bowie into her bedroom and shut the

door, wondering if Walter would try to come into her room tonight. After his behavior on Christmas night, she couldn't really predict what he might do. Walter seemed even more taken with her since she'd tricked him into taking her to Lilly's that day. Her flirtatious manner had achieved her goal, but now she was suffering the consequences. "Get under the bed again."

"This is getting a little tiresome, don't you think?" Bowie asked as he flattened himself on the floor and slid underneath her bed.

Erin made sure he couldn't be seen, then flung off her wrapper and jumped into bed. If Walter decided to come into her room tonight, he'd find her already asleep—or at least pretending to be asleep—and leave her alone.

When she heard the stairs creak, she felt a tingle of anticipation, much as men must feel before a great battle, she thought. She considered what would happen if Walter found Bowie hiding under her bed. More than likely, the entire city of Charleston would hear of it, and she would be forever disgraced. Erin didn't really care too much about her reputation, but she didn't want to face the questions that were sure to be asked of her, nor did she want to face the bawdy remarks that would result from a sullied reputation. Still, she could face anything she had to face—she hoped.

Time seemed to stand still as she waited for Walter to reach the landing. Finally she heard his footsteps, then heard them outside her door. With a sense of foreboding, Erin cursed herself for not having the lock repaired. She would simply have to deal with him if he entered.

Erin thought of Bowie lying under the bed. He must be freezing down there, but she could hardly remedy the situation now. Realizing she was grinding her teeth together, she tried to relax. Then the door opened slightly, and she felt the tension twist through her muscles like a strong cord until they were knotted with pain.

The urge to fling back the covers and scream for help grew strong, but she resisted it. She also fought the desire to find something heavy and bounce it off the head of this pompous jackass. How dare he enter her room without knocking?

With her eyes closed, she couldn't tell what Walter was doing, but she knew he hadn't left the room. As still as a wooden doll, she lay in her bed silently willing him to go away. She could deal with him, but she didn't want him to find Bowie.

Bowie lay there staring at the ropes and mattress that kept him separated from Erin. He could almost feel the tension in the way she lay, in the way her body didn't move. He considered slipping from under the bed and taking Walter by surprise. The lout didn't deserve to die like a man, but like the whoreson he was, sneaking into a lady's room without being invited.

Bowie knew that Walter had never been invited into Erin's bedroom before. She was too strong and moral to succumb to an Englishman's advances—especially those of Walter Martin.

Erin tried to concentrate on anything besides Walter. She almost wished that Bowie, hidden under her bed, would slam Walter's foot with a hammer. What a surprise that would be for the amorous Mr. Martin!

With that thought Erin wanted to clamp her hands over her mouth to keep from laughing out loud. The image of Walter dancing and leaping about on one foot was a funny one indeed.

Erin decided to concentrate on the problem at hand. She had to outlast Walter's stare. Either Walter had become enamored of Erin during the past few days, or he suspected that something strange was happening in the Banning household.

Bowie shifted uncomfortably. He couldn't afford to jeopardize the safety of his friends, so he considered ways to escape without being caught. He wondered if Walter would believe that Erin was having an illicit affair with Chauncey Farthingale, but decided not.

Erin prayed that Walter would leave. He seemed to have been standing beside the bed for a lifetime, and her body was aching from the strain on her muscles. By the time he backed slowly away from the bed, she was near to screaming from frustration.

She heard the door close but was afraid to open her eyes for fear that Walter was trying to trick her into betraying the fact that she wasn't really asleep. For several seconds she lay there unmoving. Then she heard his door open and close. She leapt from the bed, her thoughts intent on safety. She tried the lock, but it wouldn't catch no matter how she fiddled with it.

Bowie slid from under the bed and sat down. "What did you want to tell me?"

Erin clapped her hands against her breast and shook her head slightly as she tried to quell her fears. "I thought he would never leave! I talked all during supper with William. If you'd been paying attention to me instead of that whey-faced chit, you might have heard something interesting."

"What? What?" Bowie wanted to shake her. "This is no time to be catty."

"Well, it seems that William is attached to a unit that transports supplies to the British troops on the field," she whispered triumphantly.

"So? Most of the soldiers here in Charleston are connected with supplying their troops in some capacity." Bowie was intrigued by her information and thought that William might be a good source for her to cultivate. If he knew her better, then he could begin to trust her enough to confide other more meaningful details.

"That's not all, silly goose. You don't think I'd risk freezing my feet to change that silly bow if I just wanted to tell you something as insignificant as that, do you?" she asked, feeling a little peeved with Bowie for misunderstanding her point.

"I apologize. Go on with your story." Bowie lay back against the pillow and looked at her profile. Her nose was slightly turned up, quite pretty, and her cheekbones were high and pronounced enough to add character to an otherwise beautiful face.

"Are you listening?"

"What? Oh, yes." He couldn't imagine that she'd said something of interest that he'd missed while looking at her pretty nose, but evidently she had.

"Well, William told me that he's going to leave Charleston on Monday week after next to take some goods toward North Carolina." Erin eyed him to make sure he caught the import of her knowledge.

"He told you that?" Bowie sat up straight and gazed at her. Would a man divulge secrets that might earn him a court-martial simply because the listener had a lovely face and figure? Sure, he concluded. Men had done so for much less.

"Yes. I was afraid someone would hear him, but apparently everyone else was caught up in their own conversations and paying no attention to us." Erin felt elated. She'd discovered something important. Now Bowie would have to let her drive one of the supply wagons. He had no one else to do it.

Bowie looked at her thoughtfully. She could be quite valuable here if she were willing to continue seeing those soldiers she'd met tonight. Very likely, they considered her to be a Loyalist and wouldn't think that speaking in front of her would be a breach of loyalty to King George.

"Damn, it's too bad we don't have somebody to lead the wagons. This could be a real opportunity." Bowie felt frustration roil up in him. He worked so hard to maintain the supply routes—he made so many trips in and out of Charleston that he'd be caught soon. This information could save him several trips, but in reality amounted to nothing since he had no driver.

"I'm going," Erin announced. "Somebody has to. You haven't found anybody yet. Papa certainly can't go. You find a way to ambush those supply wagons, and I'll be waiting at the appointed spot to take over."

"Balderdash. You're not going, and that's final," Bowie

almost bellowed. Frowning, he glanced at the door. "I hope Walter is asleep."

"I hope so, too. You ought to be ashamed," Erin scolded and glared at him. "I'm going—and *that's* final. You can't stop me."

CHAPTER
7

Erin inhaled deeply of the brisk invigorating salt air. She couldn't recall ever feeling so delighted to make the trip to Bluffwood. With her entourage in tow, she boarded the Banning skiff and set sail. It took her a few minutes to settle her mother, who gazed warily at the Spanish moss hanging from the live oaks as if they were haunted. But Arlen Banning rested easily in his deck chair and watched Erin closely.

Knowing that he wanted to speak to her, Erin tried to avoid being alone with him. He'd been against her plan to drive one of the teams from the start and bellowed more than once that he couldn't understand why Bowie gave in.

Well, Erin was past that point now, though Arlen still caught her off-guard occasionally and voiced his concerns. A sadness had overtaken her father from the moment she told him of her plan. He'd have to wait and see her success, she reasoned.

Both her parents fell asleep during the trip up the Cooper River to Bluffwood. Glad for the quiet, Erin mentally covered the entire route she would take to deliver her supplies. She could drive that road in her sleep, but now she grew concerned about it—not scared, but worried.

Erin knew that Bowie had left Charleston to gather his men. She wondered where he was now and what he was doing. In two days he would attack the British wagons after they left Charleston. What would he do with the men guarding the wagons? Would he have to kill them?

Her thoughts returned to her own journey. Automatically watching the direction they took when they veered off the Cooper River and onto a narrow tributary, Erin tried not to think about killing and death. She liked William, the young officer she'd met at Lilly's, even though he was a little silly. He'd trusted her enough to tell her a military secret, and she'd answered that trust by betraying him. Maybe Bowie would recognize poor William and treat him kindly.

Bluffwood finally came into view, and the skiff glided to a stop at their dock. Away from the main routes, this plantation seemed so quiet and peaceful when compared to the others Erin had visited. On the more traveled routes, guests who were making their way to or from Charleston would stop and expect the plantation owners to offer their hospitality for a night or two, complicating the housekeeping requirements considerably.

Erin leapt from the skiff and rang the bell hanging on the dock. Several servants came running from all directions to see who rang the bell. When they saw Erin standing on the wooden dock, some of them shouted with happiness. After a few moments of welcoming conversation, they began to unload all the trunks and bags the Bannings had brought from Charleston.

"I do declare, Miss Erin, you gets purtier ever time I sees you," declared Annabell, the housekeeper. "When is you gonna settle down and get married?"

Erin laughed. Annabell asked that question every time she saw Erin. "One of these days—when I find a man as honest and noble as Papa who has less of a belly and more of a twinkle in his eye."

"That's a tall order, Missy. That's a mighty tall order." Annabell took Vevila Banning's arm and led her up the path toward the main house.

The rest of the group followed closely behind. Toby and Nero placed Arlen on a narrow wagon that used to belong to Erin's little pony, Babette. Laughing at the sight of her father in the little cart, Erin took her small bag and trod along with them.

Bluffwood smelled of beeswax and fresh candles. The
Banning home in Charleston couldn't afford to buy candles,
so the ones they burned came from here. After tucking her
parents away in their beds, Erin set about checking on everything else. She discussed meals for her parents, house-
cleaning, planting for the spring, and so many problems that
her head ached by the end of the day.

Annabell provided a delicious supper of wild turkey with
yams, greens, and rice. She told Erin about the British soldiers who came through looking for food. They took all the
chickens, hogs, rice, and flour they could find, but thanks
to Erin's hiding places, much of the food had been saved.

Erin urged Annabell to use the thick growth in the woods
to hide more food. The situation wouldn't improve soon,
so she told them to make adequate preparations, especially
now that there were extra mouths to feed with the Bannings
in residence.

The days passed slowly at Bluffwood. Erin fluctuated between worrying about Bowie and anticipating her own journey. The waiting made her quite anxious.

During the days that followed, Erin found secure hiding
places and helped the servants store casks of rice, molasses,
and flour. She also moved some of her family's treasures to
safer places. With Tarleton on the rampage, pillaging and
burning plantations, nobody knew where he would raid
next.

Looking back on the night when Erin announced that she
would be driving the wagon, Bowie felt foolish. If he'd had
a choice, he would have forbidden it, but he had no real
choice. He couldn't take the supplies up the route himself
because he didn't know the checkpoints, nor did he know
the men who would be accepting the goods.

He'd searched until the day he had to leave but found
no one capable of taking Arlen's place. Arlen had raised the
very dickens, indicating that his condition was improving
steadily, but he finally agreed to let Erin go. Her plan was
sound, and she was probably less suspect than a man would

be, although that didn't necessarily make Bowie—or Arlen—like the situation any better.

Bowie drew his horse farther back into the cover of the woods. He and his men had been waiting for most of the day since Erin couldn't find out exactly when the British supplies were going to leave Charleston. He glanced at his assistant, Sidney Sterne. More a sailor than an outlaw, Sidney looked out of place on the big stallion Bowie had provided.

"Say, boss, you don't think they got wind of an ambush, do you?" Sidney asked and rose in his saddle to peer down the road. "I ain't seen nothing that looked like a British dog since we tapped that lookout on the noggin."

Bowie had been thinking much the same thing, but he couldn't afford to get lax. "Quiet. They'll be along."

"It's getting dark, and me backside's getting cold," Sidney grumbled more quietly. "I don't fancy sleeping on this big brute."

"If you don't keep quiet, I'm going to feed you to him." Bowie glared through the growing darkness at his friend. Sidney had been Bowie's friend and confidant for a long time. They'd sailed around the world together and were as close as two friends could be.

"Harrumph," Sidney grunted. "At least I'd be warm in this steed's gullet."

"You'd be warm in hell, too, and if you keep chattering like a schoolgirl, I'll make sure you get there soon. Or the British will hear you and send you on your way," Bowie whispered. He peered down the lonely road, wondering why the British were so late.

"If they hear anything a'tall, it'll be me teeth chattering," Sidney muttered and buried his face in his cloak for a few moments. "I swear me breath's a-freezin' on me mustache. Ain't a fit day for dogs nor weasels."

Cold drizzle began to fall as they settled down to wait. Bowie pulled the collar of his cloak higher around his neck and nestled down into it as much as he could and still see the road. Instinctively he knew that something must have happened or the supply wagons would have been here by now, but he couldn't risk backtracking to look. They might walk straight into an ambush themselves.

"I can see the death notice now, sir. Men found frozen in woods. That's us, frozen as hard as them icebergs in the North Sea, we'll be. No thawin' us out till summer," Sidney complained good-naturedly.

Bowie knew he couldn't prevent his assistant from making remarks about their situation; Sidney never shut up, at least not while he was awake. Letting the murmur of Sidney's voice flow over him, Bowie turned his thoughts to Erin again. "The devil take her for talking me into this," he muttered.

"The devil take who, sir?" Sidney asked and raised his eyebrows slightly as he gazed at Bowie's shocked face.

"Sorry, I didn't realize I spoke aloud. Forget what I said." Knowing he must keep his mind on the ambush to come, Bowie peered down the rutted clay road and listened carefully, raising his hand against further conversation. He motioned slightly across the way to Phillip Hunter, Arlen's assistant, who came along to help in the capture of the British supplies.

Anxiety bore down on Bowie as he glanced at the dozen men gathered with him in the dim light of the forest and hoped that the British force would be small enough for the rebel band to engage. He felt sure they could defeat an equal number of soldiers, and perhaps a superior number if not too great. His problem was to determine how many were too many. Was the risk of battle worth the bounty captured? Was the possible death of one man, one friend, enough to let the troops pass without knowing of the existence of the raiding party?

At sea Bowie never questioned his own decisions; they were made almost automatically, and his orders were always obeyed to the letter. On land would his men react as they did at sea? He couldn't know and really shouldn't ask it of them. They'd signed on as sailors, spirited, fighting, blockade runners whose abilities were legendary at sea, but what of their prowess on land?

The time had come to find out. Someone was coming up the road, and Bowie became more alert. Soldiers! He watched and counted the leading troops as they rode by in their green cloaks. Disgust ran through him as he recognized some of his former friends clad in the green of the Tory guard. He fought his first instinct—to charge into the midst of them and begin the fray—and waited to see if the odds were in his favor.

Laughing and talking, the advance guards didn't seem to be aware that they were being watched, and Bowie knew he and his men could take the Tories by surprise. Still he waited. If the greenbacks were far enough ahead of the wagons, then Bowie and his men could attack the wagons and be far gone before the guards knew of the strike.

Beside him Sidney patted his horse to calm him. A single whicker could alert the British troops of a presence in the surrounding woods and obliterate the surprise of Bowie's raid. Bits of conversation reached Bowie's ears, and he listened keenly.

"What was the problem?" asked one man who slumped a little in his saddle.

"I don't know. Something about needing all their men to converge with Tarleton. Something going on, that's for sure," a second man complained. "Hellfire, we ain't supposed to be guarding no supply wagons."

"Where are they, anyhow?" The first man peered over his shoulder and squinted. "Them wagons're slower than a tick suckin' blood out of a dog."

"Well, we aren't waiting on them. We've got to catch Tarleton, too," one officer shouted to the others. "That red-headed bastard ain't waiting on us, and if we get too far behind, we could be defeated by a group of innkeepers' daughters."

Bowie couldn't suppress a grin. These Tories, though eager to find favor with the British, were a careless lot. They left the supply wagon troops to fend for themselves, while these greenbacks hurried off to impress Tarleton.

Settling back to await the arrival of the dawdling supply wagons, Bowie winked at Sidney, who shivered in return. He had heard everything Bowie heard and now seemed more content to wait.

With the wind at his back Bowie snuggled down farther into the shelter of his cloak. The cold drizzle changed into sleet. The South Carolina soil did occasionally freeze, but snow rarely fell in Charleston. Bowie wondered if the Lord was giving him a sign, trying to tell him that this wasn't the time to raid the British supply shipments.

Erin paced back and forth in front of the fire, stopping now and then to rub her hands together to stimulate the circulation. Sleet pelted the piazza, and already the trees were laden with ice. Driving the wagon up the supply route looked even less inviting than it had during the rain this afternoon.

All day she'd gathered the items she considered necessary for this trip. Her warmest clothing was packed and ready to go. While she didn't expect to have a chance to change clothes often, she did want a clean dress or two in case she needed them. Along with her clothes, she'd tucked in a pistol, powder, and several balls and cloths, hoping she'd only have to use the weapon for game. In her spare boots she'd placed a dagger for good measure. Once she started off, she'd move the dagger to the boots she wore.

In addition to her warmest woolen cloak, Erin packed a heavy beaver fur cloak, hat, and muff. With the sleet beginning to form patterns on the dead grass, she knew that winter would be at its fiercest when Bowie came for her. Eager to be gone, she changed her route and began to pace from the fireplace in the parlor to the window. When she reached the window, she peered out in dismay at the thickening sleet; when she returned to the fireplace, she rubbed her hands together briskly.

"Miss Erin, you gonna wear a hole in that there carpet

if'n you don't stop that pacing. You is worse than any expectin' daddy I ever seed." 'Lasses watched Erin's face and grinned. "I sho hope you got some warm clothes for us to wear. Me and Nero already freezin', and we ain't even started yet."

Erin smiled to reassure her servant. "Yes, yes. I've got lots of warm clothing. Fur cloaks and rugs to cover our legs and to lie under at night. We'll be warm enough." She hoped she sounded convincing, because with the chill wind whistling through the cracks around the windows, she wasn't sure herself. "I really wish you didn't have to go, but not even I am willing to go chasing about the countryside with a bunch of men and no chaperon."

"You jes' try and leave me here. If you goes, I goes." 'Lasses scowled at Erin. "Supper's ready. Is you gonna carry yours whilst you walks back and forth between the fire and the window, or is you gonna set down and eat like a lady?"

Catching the slight reprimand, Erin grinned. "I'll come to the table."

Time seemed to stop for Bowie in the moments after dusk. His face felt frozen in an expression of frustration, while his body trembled with the cold. Even Sidney hadn't spoken for some time.

"Sir, do you think we're a-waiting on a ship that ain't never gonna come in?" Sidney finally asked through the darkness.

"Ship or wagon, it looks like we're wasting our time," Bowie conceded, wishing he was sitting in the cabin of his ship in some tropical port. "We'll wait a while longer. I doubt if they're likely to be traveling much later than—"

A screeching sound reached Bowie's ears, and he perked up in the saddle. After a few seconds passed, he recognized the noise as that of a wagon wheel straining against its axle. Still waiting, Bowie heard voices, the whickers and neighs of horses, the steady plod of oxen and mules, the creak of wooden wheels on frozen clay.

Glancing in Sidney's direction, Bowie wondered if he'd
imagined the noises. He could detect no sign of movement,
other than the sleet's steady deluge. The slippery ground
would make fighting more difficult, especially if the wagons
were well guarded.

Bowie's plan had been that if the wagons passed during
the day, he would signal to the men whether to engage the
enemy or let them pass. In the absence of enough light to
see his sign, his men were to assess the odds and make the
decision individually. If one man saw fit to charge, the others would follow. Bowie hoped he didn't have a lot of war-
starved men who would fight regardless of the size of the
opposing force.

Squinting to see better, Bowie dusted the ice crystals from
his eyelashes and peered into the darkness. Against the
growing white landscape, he could dimly see shapes moving
past. He could hardly determine whether the shadowy out-
lines were of men mounted on horses, or of men riding in
wagons.

Never one to sit idly and watch opportunity pass him by,
Bowie handed his reins to Sidney and dismounted. Creeping
along and taking great care to remain hidden, Bowie
crawled to the edge of the road and gazed at the passing
force. He counted four wagons, each with a driver and assistant. There were no mounted troops accompanying the
wagon train. In his elation Bowie almost sang out his decree,
"Charge, men!"

Sidney reached Bowie's position and held the horse
steady. Bowie pulled himself into the saddle while galloping
into the fray. Nervous energy seemed to flow through the
men, making the roundup of drivers an easy task. Bowie lit
a lantern and stared at the motley group. Tattered, cold, and
hungry, the men had given in quickly to avoid being killed.
Bowie swung down from his horse and approached the men,
who appeared afraid.

"Sir, don't kill us. We didn't want this job. We was captured at the Waxhaws when that bas— Beggin' yer pardon,
sir, when Tarleton came through back in May," one man

explained. "We didn't want nothin' to do with them. God, it was awful sir. Men tryin' to surrender was run through with bayonets. I never seen such a slaughter."

Bowie knew of the incident, one that had helped give Tarleton his nicknames—"Bloody Tarleton" and "Bastard Tarleton," which was a play on his name, Banastre Tarleton. Nodding, Bowie said, "You men have nothing to fear from us. Were all of you captured at the Waxhaws?"

Some said yes, some no. Two were captured during the siege of Charleston. All had sworn allegiance to King George and vowed never to take up arms against him again, and were now put to work for him.

Looking at the driver who assumed the position of spokesman for the ragtag group, Bowie asked, "What would you like to do now, gentlemen?"

The man glanced around at the rest of the group and grinned. "Well, sir, m'name's Porter, Jimbo, eh, James Porter and I'd like to join up with you if'n you'll gimme a gun and a horse."

A chorus of "me, too's" resounded through the glade where they were standing in the ice and sleet. An idea came to Bowie. "Gentlemen, I have a job for you. You've been assigned to this wagon train. Do you know the routes? I mean, are you familiar with the sentries who send you in the right direction . . . for the Patriots, that is."

Almost in unison the men shook their heads negatively. "Sir, we was supposed to be ridin' along with them greenbacks, but they left us shore as I'm a'standin' here chawin' the fat with you," Jimbo admitted, scratching his head thoughtfully. "I reckon they was more interested in warmin' their backsides at Tarleton's fire than in pokin' along with us."

"It's a good thing for us they were, Jimbo," Bowie reminded the man and laughed. "Come with me. I think we can find us a fire where we can get something to eat and make a few plans." He turned to Arlen's assistant, who seemed to recognize Jimbo. "Phillip, do you know this man?"

"Oh, yes, sir," Phillip answered readily. "Mr. Banning and me run into him ever now and again."

"Can he be trusted?" Bowie asked.

"As much as you trust Mr. Banning, sir."

Bowie nodded. "Phillip, how long will it take us to get to Bluffwood?"

"I'd reckon about two hours, sir, considering the weather." Phillip looked around and shook his head. "Don't show any signs of letting up."

"Well, let's hide these wagons where we planned and head for Bluffwood." Bowie remounted. "You new men, drive your wagons behind me. Phillip, you and your men bring up the rear and cover our tracks. Sidney, you and your men come with me."

Bowie led the drivers to the appointed place. He saw to the hiding of the wagons under a pile of dead branches and bushes before heading toward Bluffwood with Sidney, Jimbo, and three others.

Erin finished her supper and meandered back to the parlor. She would have gone upstairs but knew that she couldn't sleep or even relax until she heard something about Bowie. He had been due at Bluffwood hours ago, and she was growing anxious about him and his men.

This venture was dangerous to say the least; Erin would blame herself if Bowie died as a result of her spying. For all she knew, the information could have been a plan to draw the Patriots into a battle they couldn't win. She strode to the window and peered into the darkness that glistened like starlight where the ice froze on the skeletal branches of the trees and shrubs.

In the transformation of Bluffwood into an icy fairyland, the chances of Bowie's arrival lessened, and Erin flopped into her favorite chair to ponder the situation. They were scheduled to leave early in the morning for the encampment where the supplies were being kept. When the sleet turned to snow, she began to worry that she'd be snowed in by morning, and Bowie would be a frozen part of the forest.

"Miss Erin, you can't do nothin' tonight," 'Lasses called gently from the arched doorway. "Either he gonna be fine or he ain't."

Erin sighed and tried to smile. "I know, 'Lasses, but I can't rest, and I certainly can't sleep without knowing. I feel as if this is all my fault. If I hadn't insisted on taking Papa's place, he wouldn't be out on the trail tonight in this terrible weather."

"Missy, they ain't nothin' you can do to change what's done. And you can't be no different from what you is." 'Lasses stepped inside the room and placed her hand on Erin's shoulder to comfort her. "Why don't you lie down for a while, chile?"

"You go on up." Erin lay her cheek against 'Lasses's hand. The slave had always been available with good advice or a kind word when Erin needed it the most. "I'll wake you if I hear anything."

"Good night, baby." 'Lasses patted Erin's shoulder one last time and headed up the stairs.

Erin watched 'Lasses go, leaving a candle burning in the vestibule. Silence settled over the household, and Erin returned to her vigil. The candles in the parlor burned brightly but did little to chase away the darkness forming in her heart.

Hours later a sound coming from the direction of the river startled her. Erin's blood raced. Could it be Bowie, or was it Tarleton? It could be one as easily as the other, she decided. Anyone would be drawn to the light on a night like this.

Hovering between her fear and the urge to run into the yard to watch who came up the hill, Erin peered through the window, straining to see. If it's Tarleton, the door won't matter, she mused, and scrambled to her feet. By the time she reached the front door, she could see several figures plodding slowly toward the house.

She thought Bowie planned to come alone, and this looked like a small group, probably four or five men. Inhaling deeply, Erin flung the door open and stepped onto the

piazza. Whoever came across the yard was bound to be cold
and hungry, and Erin could ill afford to turn anybody away
because of the task she'd set for herself in this war.

A creak on the stairs behind her startled her, and Erin
jerked around. Nero and 'Lasses were creeping down the
stairs, and Nero carried Arlen Banning's Brown Bess musket. Erin grinned and returned her attention to the front
yard, praying that it was Bowie and his men who were riding closer to her piazza.

" 'Lasses, go put another log on the fire in the parlor and
heat up a kettle of soup. Maybe you'd better put on a kettle
of water in case someone is injured," Erin added.

With Nero behind her Erin felt braver and ventured onto
the piazza. As her eyes adjusted to the darkness, she could
see the riders individually now. Their coats weren't red, but
she couldn't tell if they were the green of Tarleton's men.
From the way the men sagged in the saddle, she could tell
they were desperately tired.

"Nero, can you see any of them well enough to recognize
them?" she asked, peering into the group as they approached.

"No'm. I can't see nothin' but a bunch of folks with ice
on they clothes," Nero answered, staring at the riders.

Erin stepped to the edge of the piazza and took the musket from Nero. She could shoot as well as he, and she
wanted to be in control in case something went wrong. Aiming at the man riding in front, she called, "Halt or I'll
shoot."

Bowie grinned. By heaven's gates she was a spunky
woman! "Don't shoot, Erin. We're friendly."

"Bowie? Is that you?" Erin felt the relief softening her
tense muscles as she began to relax. Then, remembering that
he had planned to come alone, she yelled, "Who's with
you?"

"My own men and one other Patriot we recaptured from
the British." They rode almost to the piazza, and he dismounted. "Put that blasted musket away before you hurt
yourself and someone else in the meantime."

Erin lowered the firearm slowly. She watched as Bowie and the others tried to walk up the icy steps with some semblance of dignity.

"If we take off our boots and stockings, may we come in and warm ourselves by your fire?" Bowie asked, keeping his eye on the musket. Though she'd pointed it away from him, she didn't seem to trust him. With his last spurt of energy he reached the piazza and took her in his arms, spinning her around gleefully. "Now, Nero, take that musket. Erin, is there anybody who can give us some food?"

Feeling a little more secure, Erin grinned as he stood her down on the piazza floor. "I've already sent 'Lasses to put the soup kettle on. Is anybody injured? Why are you so late? What happened?"

"Whoa, one question at a time. And before I answer, let us come in," Bowie insisted wearily.

"Come on, all of you," Erin called and waved at them. "Oh, but try to be quiet until we get in. Papa is sleeping just overhead."

The men dismounted, tied their horses to a rail out on the driveway, and slowly climbed the steps. At the top they removed their boots and stockings, leaving them by the front door, and filed past her.

"Good evenin', Missy," said one man as he paused before entering the vestibule.

"Erin Banning, this is Jimbo Porter. He and his men were driving the wagon trains for the British," Bowie explained and walked with Erin into the house. "Most of them were captured at the Waxhaws last May, and the rest were caught during the siege of Charleston."

Inside the house the men were forming a semicircle in front of the fireplace. They sat with their feet and hands extended like little children. Nero and 'Lasses came from the kitchen with a kettle of soup, several spoons, and bowls. 'Lasses ladled soup for each man before returning to the kitchen, leaving the half-empty kettle behind.

While they ate, the men related their story to Erin. First

laughing, then almost in tears, she listened carefully to each man as he spoke.

Bowie watched her as she encouraged the men to talk about their time in prison, about the horrible conditions, the inhumane treatment. He saw her reach out to comfort one man who told of seeing his entire family slain, even the baby. Seeing her in this capacity, Bowie realized that Erin was a special kind of person, one who felt the agony of others more acutely than most women ever would, especially when the men were as bedraggled and stinking as these were.

He leaned back, enjoying the feeling of warmth in his belly, and observed her moving through the men, refilling their cups of milk or ladling more soup into their bowls. She advanced gracefully among them, smiling and chatting as if she were their protector. With her quiet charm she enchanted the men, and they were soon gazing at her with adoring eyes.

Bowie felt a stab of jealousy. Erin Banning possessed a special quality rare in women her age, rare in people altogether. He sensed that she'd be successful at whatever adventure life sent her way.

CHAPTER
8

TELLING HER MOTHER GOODBYE WASN'T EASY FOR ERIN. She lied and said she was going back to Charleston. Vevila didn't like the idea, but with her short attention span she didn't dwell on the matter.

Saying goodbye to her father made her more emotional. Erin knew her father was aware of the danger and importance of her journey and felt guilty for allowing her to go, particularly in view of the nasty weather, though the sleet had stopped during the night and the temperature was rising. When Arlen discovered that Erin carried a dueling pistol in each of his boots that she wore over her own, he railed at her for almost ten minutes. If she drew her weapon, he warned her, most men wouldn't hesitate to shoot even a woman.

Looking back over her shoulder as they rode away from Bluffwood, Erin felt tears sting her eyes. Something of her youth died in that moment, but something else was born.

For years she'd considered herself an adult, but she realized now that her idea of adulthood was a game. Now she stepped fully from that nebulous state between childhood and adulthood, leaving the gay young girl behind while the woman rode into the future. Erin experienced mixed feelings: she felt elated with freedom, thrilled at the prospect of doing something for the cause—and scared to death.

Bowie rode beside Erin as Bluffwood passed from sight. Watching her carefully, he noticed that she held her chin high and proud, that she looked back only once. Until the early hours of morning, he'd tried to convince her to abandon this project. He worried that she didn't truly understand the risks involved for herself and for her little band of followers.

He couldn't blame Jimbo and the men for following her. From the moment she'd invited them into her home, fed them, listened to their stories, laughed with some, and cried with others, they were sworn to defend her in any situation and to follow her wherever she chose to go. Bowie suspected that few leaders could claim such respect and loyalty from their men.

They rode along the riverbank for the first hour. Erin contented herself with listening to the rushing water as it tumbled over fallen branches and smooth rocks. All around her the ice crackled, limbs snapped, and chunks of ice fell and shattered on the rocks while she watched and rode in silence. She and Bowie had argued again before leaving, but she had prevailed.

Jimbo, elated to be free to fight for his beliefs, caught up with Bowie and Erin. He chattered easily about his family, his farm, and his old granddaddy, who first cleared the land in the Ninety-Six District.

Erin perked up. "My cousin lives in the Ninety-Six District. Where exactly do you hail from?"

"Well, Missy, I doubt your cousin lives anywhere near where I come from. You see," he explained, removing his fur cap to expose his balding head, "my folks live way up close to the frontier. Up around the Tyger River."

Smiling broadly, Erin nodded. "That's where my cousin lives. Do you by chance know of the Arledges from Tyger Rest?"

"Arledge? Well, as sure as this ground's hard, I do." Jimbo pulled his hat back over his head and grinned. "I know them purty well if the facts be known. If'n you go up from my place about three miles on the Tyger River, you'd come upon the Arledge place. Out close to John Brook's place."

Erin nodded. She'd heard of John Brooks when her cousin, Noelle Arledge, and her friend, Captain Drake Hastings, had come last fall after her father died and the house was partially burned. She told Jimbo what Noelle had said. "And the final setback came when John Brooks and his sister were killed by the Cherokee. Ash Meadow was burned to the ground."

Jimbo hung his head and shook it slightly. "Them was real nice folks. Had a nice place, too. It's a shame and a disgrace that them bloody British had to go stirrin' up them Injuns again."

Erin gazed at him and smiled. "That's why we're going to defeat them soundly. You and I—all of us—," she said, gesturing to take in the entire band of men, "are going to help run the British out of South Carolina for good."

"That we'll do, Missy." Jimbo moved back with his men and began telling them of John Brooks's fate.

Amid the grumble of men who knew the Brooks family, the sentiment became clear. In addition to having their own personal reasons for defeating the British, they now had the blood of good friends to avenge.

The trail became more difficult to follow as they neared the place where the wagons were hidden. Bowie raised his hand to stop the procession. "I think we should go on ahead and scout the area first to make sure the British didn't discover our hiding place. Sidney, come with me. You men can light a fire to keep warm. I doubt if any of the British are close enough to distinguish between this fire and one from a cabin fireplace."

The two men left their horses tethered to low-hanging pine boughs and continued on foot. The remainder of the group dismounted, brought water from the creek, searched for dry brush, and started a campfire. The fire popped and crackled cheerfully as Erin put a kettle of stew over the logs to heat their noon meal.

Several men stamped about, apparently trying to return

the blood flow to their cold hands and feet. Jimbo stationed a couple of men as lookouts and sat by Erin. "Miss Banning, why are you doing this?"

"Doing what, Jimbo?" she asked and stirred the thick stew with a wooden spoon.

"Going out into the wilds like this. A purty lady like yourself needs to be at home, taking care of herself, making purty little geegaws to go on her dress." Jimbo poked at the fire with a stick, and sparks billowed upward. "I didn't want to say nothin' in front of Bowie, but I think he's right. This is too dangerous for you."

Erin thought about his question. So Bowie had told Jimbo about their argument. She knew Bowie and Jimbo were right, but she was right, too. Her quest would render warmth and comfort to a lot of soldiers who could find help from nobody else. "Jimbo, I'm just another American who's doing her part to help our fighting men. I don't think any officer would let me carry a gun into battle, but no one can stop me from bringing supplies that may mean the difference between winning a battle and losing one, or between living and dying for a lot of the men."

"I know you're right about that, but why you? Why not some strong buck?" Jimbo asked and stared at her with eyes as brown as the best coffee in South Carolina.

She tried to think of a way to explain her reasons, but men never seemed to understand her. "Jimbo, you're taking a risk, too. You've sworn never to take up arms against King George again. What will happen if you're caught?"

Jimbo considered her question and rubbed his chin thoughtfully. "Well, they'd probably ship me off to some godforsaken prison in St. Augustine to feed me to the rats. But I'm a man. I can't just sit around and watch my country being overrun by them damned Englishmen."

"Neither can I, Jimbo. Neither can I." Erin motioned to 'Lasses, who'd been pouring coffee for the men. "Here, I think this stew's as ready as it's ever going to be. Will you serve it?"

"Yas'm, I will." 'Lasses took a cloth and lifted the kettle

from the fire. With her pewter ladle she filled the bowls of every man and then two more for herself and Erin. "Missy, how long you think Mr. Bowie gonna be gone?"

"I don't really know, 'Lasses." Erin gazed into the depths of trees ahead, not knowing how far Bowie and Sidney would have to travel before they came to the hiding place. "We'll wait and see."

Erin wondered if Bowie had reached the spot where the wagons were hidden. The wind ruffled the curls around her face, and she pulled her fur cap lower over her forehead as she sipped her black coffee. The bitter brew warmed her as she gulped it down and stared ahead. She felt a little guilty sitting here safely while Bowie risked his life making sure their captured goods were still where they'd left them.

She wanted to keep the stew hot for Bowie and Sidney, but she set the men to cleaning up everything else. Each man washed his bowl, spoon, and cup in the icy creek water before returning them to 'Lasses to be stored until their next meal. Nero hovered about, looking after Erin as if she were still a child who needed his "mothering."

Talking to Jimbo relaxed Erin. These men were all accustomed to the hardships of the trail and living outdoors. She, 'Lasses, and Nero would benefit from the experience of the others. Erin understood the reasons Bowie recruited the men to help with the journey. Her knowledge of the checkpoints and the men who manned them made her a vital part of the group. But the men could compensate for her lack of experience on the trail.

Feeling good about her part in this adventure, she stirred the stew absently until she heard the low tone of a birdcall that didn't sound exactly right to her. She glanced around her and noticed that the men were alert and had stopped whatever they were doing.

Somebody approached and signaled, she thought. That has to be why everyone is so vigilant all of a sudden. Waiting, she expected Bowie and Sidney to come barging into the camp, but whoever was out there didn't appear. For a long moment she held her breath, wondering if the sound could have emanated from a British instead of American voice. Praying that it hadn't, she forced herself to breathe normally and continued to scan the woods for Bowie's familiar face.

Judging from the actions of the men around her, Erin's attitude was shared. Two men sitting on the ground near her picked up stones. Several others wrapped their fingers around broken tree branches. If Bowie was out there, why didn't he show himself?

Unbidden, Bowie's image obliterated her surroundings, and she found herself thinking only of him. A smile teased the corners of her mouth into a grin as she recalled his kisses, and she wondered if he would kiss her again before he left her in the morning. Something deep inside her warmed as she recalled his lips on hers, his body pressed against her, willing her to respond to him.

She respected Bowie, perhaps more than any man besides her father. Bowie's courage, his honor, his dedication to the cause generated a pride in her, for her father had found Bowie and helped him to see the value of serving the Partisans. The man that was like a son to her father was beginning to mean far more to Erin than just a friend, far more.

In the woods Bowie peered across the vast expanse of loblolly pines and sighed. The British unit seemed to be hurrying north, and he didn't want to attract their attention. Staring at them, he searched for a familiar face but found none. Either the soldiers had missed Erin's motley group, or they had killed them all.

Cursing under his breath, he wondered how he could have ever viewed the British side as just. Bowie's family was divided. His mother was a staunch Patriot and his father a steadfast Loyalist; Bowie had found ways to appease both parents until Arlen came along. Arlen had pressed Bowie to look into his heart and serve the cause that meant more to him. Ever since then Bowie had sailed from tropical port to tropical port, bringing goods needed by the Americans and slipping through the British ships blockading Charles-

ton Harbor. It was a painful choice—as a result, his father
had disowned him.

Homesickness touched Bowie as he recalled the gentle
breezes blowing off the surf at Edisto Glade, his parents'
plantation on Edisto Island. He hadn't been there in more
than four years. One night he'd docked at the family wharf
and surreptitiously made his way to the house, hoping to
see his mother for a few minutes. Looking through the windows, he'd seen her with his father, and she wore a sad expression on her face. Although Bowie had waited for several
hours, his father never left her alone.

Sadly Bowie had sailed out of the inlet, never to return
again. Though he desperately wanted to see his mother, to
talk to her, to hold her once again in his arms, he couldn't
stand the pain of watching her and being unable to visit with
her. Since then, his ship, the *Midnight Star,* had become his
home and at times meant more to him than anything else
in his life.

From his vantage point Bowie saw that the soldiers had
passed without noticing his position. Sidney signaled that
the way was clear, and they moved on. Bowie had to restrain
himself to keep from crashing through the woods like a boar
to find out if Erin and her men were dead or alive. He didn't
know whether other soldiers would be traveling along the
same route as the first, but he didn't want to attract any notice to himself.

Erin held her breath. From somewhere in the distance
the sound of a snapping twig caught everyone's attention,
and almost simultaneously they all looked to a point in the
woods a few yards past a large deadfall. After a moment
Erin spotted someone moving out there, stealthily spying
on the group.

Moving as slowly and deliberately as possible, she slid her
hand down into her right boot and grasped the butt of the
pistol. As she did, she prayed that she was sitting in a way
that prevented whoever watched them from seeing her remove the gun and cock it.

She fingered the smooth wood of the weapon and slid it between the folds of her skirt as she waited for the men watching to make a move. Her lungs burned, and her chest felt as though it would burst if she didn't breathe, but she dared not risk any motion for fear of attracting attention to herself.

Bowie watched the camp for a few more moments. Everyone had seemed to be acting normally, but something had alerted them. He wondered if their demeanor was meant to be a signal to him. Could British troops have discovered the little band and substituted some of their members? He tried hard to make out the faces of the men. He spotted Jimbo easily and then Phillip Hunter, Arlen's assistant.

Nudging Sidney, he whispered, "Do you think something's wrong?"

"I don't know. Seems like they're awfully jittery," Sidney admitted and continued observing the group.

"Look, I'm going to walk into the camp. You keep an eye on everyone. If anything suspicious happens, start firing, and I'll do the same." Bowie got to his knees and smiled at his friend and assistant. "I don't relish the thought of dying like a landlubber."

"I'll cover yer backside like a tight pair of breeches," Sidney whispered, cocking his pistols and his musket.

Bowie crawled through some of the dense underbrush toward the camp. From there he could smell the stew he saw Erin stirring on the fire. Something looked wrong, really wrong. She was stirring the pot with her left hand.

He knew that he'd never find out what had happened unless he stood and presented himself to the group. Inhaling deeply, he rose and stepped into the clearing, taking short steps that would allow him to dive back for cover if someone started to shoot.

Out of the corner of her eye Erin saw a man stand and start walking toward them. Turning her head slowly, she gazed at his hands to see if he carried a pistol or musket.

Emptyhanded, the man moved ever closer to them. Satisfied that he wasn't a threat at the moment, she allowed herself to look at his face.

"Bowie!" she called and ran toward him, her pistol hanging from her right hand. "Bowie, you're safe."

Grinning, Bowie lifted her in his arms and swung her around with her skirts flying. He stepped on an icy patch, lost his footing, and they both fell laughing to the hard ground.

When Erin's hand struck the rigid dirt, her finger compressed the trigger, and the gun fired. All the people in camp dropped to the ground and drew their weapons.

Silence befell the camp, and several men peeked up from their prone positions to see who had fired the shot. Erin's shocked expression faded when she scrambled to her feet to see if anyone had been hurt. All around her, people began to stand up and smile sheepishly. She turned to face Bowie, expecting him to be furious with her for her carelessness.

Bowie got up and brushed the ice off his breeches. He motioned for Sidney to run a short distance up the road to see if the British had heard the report of the pistol. Sidney, an uneducated but intelligent man, understood and hurried away.

Bowie and the other men prepared to defend themselves in case Sidney returned with bad news. After about fifteen minutes Bowie saw Sidney approaching. From the look on his face, Bowie knew that the soldiers had marched on.

At first Bowie had been angry, but as he saw that the British weren't alerted and all the men were fine, he began to laugh. "I stroll into camp, and you're the only one who draws a weapon." He looked at the men. "You trust this woman to protect you, eh? Well, it appears that she is prepared to accept the job."

"Fine shot, miss," said Sidney as he joined the group. "Ball sailed right over me head."

"Oh, I'm so sorry. I forgot that I cocked the pistol when I thought we might be under attack," Erin apologized, feel-

ing the color warm her cheeks. "I'm really sorry. I could
have injured you."

"If I'd a-been standing up, you coulda killed me," Sidney
said with a laugh. "I won't never sneak up on you again,
Missy."

"Enough said. Erin, I presume you'll be more careful
with your weapon if you insist upon carrying it," Bowie said
and glanced at the group of men gathering around the fire.
"I'd like some stew, and then we must go. Everything
looked fine at the hideout, and I want to head back there
as soon as we've eaten."

'Lasses handed Bowie and Sidney their bowls of stew and
cups of coffee. The rest of the group began to break camp.
Bowie watched with interest as Erin reloaded her pistol. Apparently unaware that she was being watched, she slid the
weapon into the boot and then tugged at the leather. Bowie
grinned as he glimpsed a short length of her leg. Beneath
her brown woolen gown she wore a pair of boy's breeches
and thick cotton stockings.

When she looked at him questioningly, he looked away
to hide the amusement on his face. He found Nero scowling
and shrugged. Bowie knew the black man would shoot any
man in his stockings if he dared to touch Erin without the
blessing of marriage vows.

Sidney took his and Bowie's bowls and cups to the creek.
While he was gone, Bowie took a moment to warm his feet
and hands before someone doused the fire. When steam
began to rise from the leather soles of his shoes, Bowie went
back to work. He helped put away dishes and the blankets
on which the men had been sitting, and then helped Erin
mount her horse.

"Easy, Fancy, easy girl," Erin said softly.

"Why would you name a horse Fancy?" he asked and
swung himself into his saddle.

Erin patted her horse's flank and cooed to her. When the
animal calmed down, Erin looked up at Bowie on his tall,
black horse. "I call her Fancy because she's a fancy lady.
Don't you think that's so?"

"Maybe." Bowie flicked his reins and called to the group. "Let's hurry. When we get a little closer, we'll send another scout to make sure we don't ride into an ambush."

The ride didn't seem to take very long, and Erin was eager to begin her journey. As they neared the hiding place, she remembered that when she started up the route, Bowie would return to his ship. Loneliness settled over her, and she became quiet.

"What's wrong, Erin?" Bowie asked as he stared at her frowning face. "Have I done something wrong? Or are you upset about the gun firing?"

"Wrong?" Erin repeated and met his gaze. "Nothing. It's nothing. I was just thinking of the road ahead."

"Changing your mind about going on this journey, I hope." Bowie rode closer to her so they could talk quietly without everyone else hearing them. "It's not too late, you know."

Erin stretched, feeling the cold and dampness intrude on her comfort. "I wouldn't think of turning back."

"I wish you would. You know, this is going to be a tough journey, even though the sleet and snow have stopped. You could still freeze or come down with pneumonia." Bowie came near to giving up. He knew how determined she was to make this trip, but he felt he must try once more to dissuade her.

"Don't you worry about me." Erin attempted to look courageous, although she didn't necessarily feel that way. The bleak forest ahead would dampen anyone's spirits, she told herself sternly, and diverted her thoughts to her timetable. She could be in the outskirts of Charlotte within two weeks. General Daniel Morgan, Colonel William Washington, and Andrew Pickens were heading toward Charlotte and would arrive there about the same time as Erin's group. General Greene, who was near Charlotte, would be easy to find, and his men, like most of the Continental Army, were in dire need of the clothing, shoes, and ammunition she would carry.

She planned to reach General Francis Marion's headquarters between the Great Pee Dee and the Little Pee Dee rivers by the next day. In his encampment she and her men could rest without much danger of being discovered by the British. The day after, the little group would move on toward Charlotte.

Bowie worried about her. Women didn't belong in the wild areas outside of Charleston and certainly not in a military capacity, but it seemed he had no choice. Erin, he'd discovered, could be as stubborn as the most contrary mule ever to pull a plow through a furrow. And he had to get back to his ship. He was scheduled to sail in two days, and the ammunition he would buy on this trip was crucial to a Patriot victory.

Riding silently as they approached the hidden wagons, Erin cast a furtive glance at Bowie. He'd said nothing since she told him not to worry about her. She hoped he wouldn't, because she didn't want to burden anybody, least of all him.

He held up his hand, and the riders stopped. At his signal Sidney dismounted, handed his reins to Jimbo, and moved ahead through the brush and naked trees. Several minutes later Erin heard another low whistle and turned to Bowie. She watched as he pursed his lips and responded with a series of sharp sounds.

"Let's go." Bowie led them off the almost nonexistent trail through the brush and bushes to the point where the wagons were waiting. "All right, everybody, listen. We've got several wagons more than we anticipated, but we've also got more men." He glanced at Erin and 'Lasses. "And women. So we'll have two people per wagon."

Erin smiled in anticipation of setting off. In spite of the fact that leaving Bowie cast a gloom over the day, she was ready to go. The men set about loading the gear they'd brought with them while Erin and 'Lasses started a fire and put the coffeepots on.

Bowie draped a quilt across his arm and walked over to Erin. "Let's walk a little ways off. I want to talk where we won't be overheard."

Erin nodded and followed him through prickly briers and

shrubs until they came to a large deadfall. Bowie looked around and saw that they were alone and far enough away to talk openly. He placed the quilt on the ground, and they sat down.

"What did you want to talk about?" Erin asked, settling with her feet tucked beneath her. The pistols, tucked inside her father's boots, made her legs uncomfortable pressed between her body and the ground, so she adjusted enough to lessen the weight on them. Shifting slightly, she twisted to look at Bowie.

"Look, Erin, I realize I can't talk you out of this, but I can give you some advice." He glanced down at her, wondering if she'd ever take advice from him. "Be careful. When I saw you draw your pistol this afternoon, I was damned proud of you. The rest of that motley crew with their rocks and sticks would have been taken if Sidney and I had been British soldiers. You made the difference. Remember, they're farmers, not soldiers."

Unable to suppress a grin, Erin looked down and folded her hands neatly in her lap. "Thank you. I wanted to be prepared."

"And you should be. Take no chances," Bowie continued and picked up a twig. Snapping it between his fingers, he gazed down at her.

She looked up to see why he'd stopped talking and found her lips very close to his. His eyes, as blue as the sky over the juncture of the Ashley and Cooper rivers on a sunny summer afternoon, seemed to make her a part of him. She felt as if she knew what he wanted to say but couldn't. Erin experienced the same kind of reaction as he, and she could no more express those feelings aloud than he could.

"Erin," he whispered and tilted her chin until her lips met his.

Somewhere above them Erin's heart soared as if it had wings of its own. Neither could say the words, but she instinctively felt that he loved her, and she was beginning to recognize that emotion in herself. Her hands flew around his neck and urged him to deepen the kiss.

She felt as though her very life force were being drained from her, and she didn't care. All that mattered to her was Bowie's lips caressing hers as his hands massaged her back through the thick fur cloak. Despite the frigid temperature, she wanted to fling off the coat and feel Bowie's body next to hers.

Shocked by her thoughts, she drew away and peered into Bowie's eyes. What must he think of her? Did all the women he knew succumb so easily to his charms? Erin thought they must; she didn't know how a woman could resist.

When Erin pulled back, Bowie was surprised. Her body had lain pliant against his while he kissed her, and her response had been as eager as his. But then whatever troubled her seemed to disappear because she closed the distance between them and clung to him as tightly as ever a woman had.

Before he realized what he was doing, he pushed her down onto the quilt and lay beside her, never breaking the kiss. Erin didn't stop him when he slid his hand inside her cloak to draw her closer. Never had he wanted a woman as badly as he wanted Erin. From the moment he'd met her, he'd known that someday they would make love.

Make love? Bowie raised himself and looked down at her. Her eyes opened lazily, and she gazed at him in surprise. Her eyes, as clear and glittering as the green sea outside Charleston Harbor, had a puzzled expression with their corners crinkled in a small frown as if she was disappointed.

"Come, Erin. We must rejoin the others before they come searching for us." Bowie didn't wait for her to reply. He stood immediately and pulled her up after him. The color in her cheeks, he realized, resulted from an insult she perceived because he'd stopped kissing her. "Erin, my darling, the time is wrong. Both of us . . . I mean, we're too . . . you're not like other women I've known, and I—"

"I understand," she said and pulled her cloak close about her. Other women. Not like other women. Erin turned and started walking back toward the fire.

"Wait, Erin, don't misunderstand. It's just that I . . . I

mean that we . . . oh, hell, I don't even know what I mean. How can I expect you to understand?" Bowie caught up with her. "Look, we'll talk about this when you get back from Charlotte. I want you to travel carefully. Stay off the main roads and try to avoid the British at all costs. You'd probably be better off traveling at night."

"I'm quite capable of making such decisions on my own, but thank you for your advice." Erin strode into camp and glanced around. Every person's gaze was on her. "Mount up. It's time to go."

CHAPTER
9

THINKING BACK, ERIN REALIZED SHE DIDN'T WANT TO be angry with Bowie, but she didn't understand what had happened between them. His kisses had been so insistent, so passionate, that Erin simply couldn't fathom why he had pulled away so suddenly. She tried to reconstruct the minutes preceding the strange event but couldn't think of anything that would have caused him to stop. Was it her? Was she too young and inexperienced for a man like Bowie Gallagher?

She allowed herself a few moments of regret, then shook off those thoughts. She had to stop thinking of Bowie and what hadn't happened between them. Her men, as she liked to think of them, would be tired and hungry soon, and they had to find a place to stop that afforded some protection from the elements and from the British who might be moving about in the area.

In the dim light she spotted an old, rutted road almost covered over by leaves. If she hadn't been looking carefully, she would have missed it, though she knew it was there.

"Turn off here, Jimbo," she commanded and pointed in the direction of the road.

He pulled the reins, and the mules plodded toward the side road without hestitating. Erin had held the reins for a while but was secretly glad when Jimbo offered to drive her wagon. This had been an extremely tiring day. They rode only a short distance farther before they came to a small clearing surrounding a ramshackle cabin with a large hole in its roof. Nobody lived there anymore, Erin decided, and told Jimbo to stop. "Send some of the men back to throw leaves and brush over the road. We don't want to leave fresh tracks for the British to follow."

Jimbo jumped from the wagon, helped her down, and then ran off to issue orders to several men at the back of the group. Erin watched for a moment, then went to the cabin door.

Hanging from its hinges, the door provided little protection. The windows were shutterless and had no glass panes. Erin peeked inside and found a thick layer of dust on the few pieces of furniture that remained in the cabin.

"Missy?" 'Lasses called from the doorway.

"Yes? Come in." Erin moved to the fireplace and glanced over her shoulder at 'Lasses. "You know, even though the roof is rotted, the walls will provide some shelter from the wind for us. We can hang a blanket over one corner so you and I can sleep in privacy while the men sleep out here."

"Them men can sleep in the yard. It ain't fitten for men to stay in a room with a unmarried lady." 'Lasses looked at the room and nodded. "It'll be good to cook over a fire in a fireplace, instead of like we done this mornin' on the open fire. Them men can eat in here."

"What nonsense, 'Lasses. We'll all sleep in here and stay warmer." Erin shook her head at the idea of asking the men to sleep outside. "Now, let's get the fire started. I'm hungry."

"I'll start the fire, but you ain't sleepin' in no house with a bunch of men you don't even know, and that's that."

Erin stared after 'Lasses as she headed out the door. There would be time later to resolve the issue of sleeping quarters. Everyone seemed to be busy except Erin. She hurried out to her wagon and helped to remove the dishes and cooking utensils, along with her own toilet articles.

Jimbo brought in an armload of wood and arranged it in the fireplace. "Missy, don't worry about a thing. We'll make sure we have enough wood to keep you warm for the night."

Watching him leave, Erin wondered if 'Lasses had spoken to him about sleeping arrangements, but decided that the black woman wouldn't do that without permission. She sat down on a log and warmed her hands. The men clearly expected her to remain apart from them, as if she weren't a real part of the group. "Why?" she whispered.

"Why whut?" 'Lasses entered with another box of goods. "This is the last of the stuff we need for tonight."

" 'Lasses, why do the men treat me as though I'm different? I mean, I'm the leader of this expedition, and they treat me as if I'm a passenger."

"Missy, you is a lady. Most of them ain't never had no associations with a lady like you. They believes you is to be treated like a lady, and as long as I'se with you, you *is* gonna be treated like a lady," 'Lasses stated emphatically as she began to unload the box.

" 'Lasses, do you mean they'll never accept me as a part of this group?" Erin asked, feeling a little disappointed. Her bottom was bruised, her legs were aching, and her feet and hands were freezing as she imagined theirs must be. Yet they treated her as if she were apart from them.

"That's the way it has to be," came the reply as 'Lasses stacked the bowls on a wide board by the fireplace.

"That's not the way it has to be," Erin retorted and jumped up. She marched out the door and surveyed the area. Some of the men were chopping wood, others were caring for the animals, and still others were covering the wagons with brush and limbs to disguise them if the British came within sighting distance. She spotted Jimbo examining the wheel of a wagon and strode to his side. "Jimbo, as soon as the men finish what they're doing, bring them into the cabin. We're going to have a meeting."

"Yes, Missy. We should be finished in a few minutes." Jimbo rubbed his fingers along a crack in the wheel. "Looks like we may need a new wheel for this wagon pretty soon."

"How long do you think it'll last?" Erin bent down and looked more closely at the wheel. She could hardly see the crack.

"Maybe until we get where we're going, maybe not. Hard to tell." Jimbo continued to run his hands around the wheel. "Nothing for you to worry about, miss."

Erin turned and stalked back into the cabin. Even Jimbo seemed to think she was along for the ride, a nice outing for the little lady. She'd have to find a way to exert her authority, to make these men realize that she intended to take care of herself and them as well.

She darted out of the cabin and down a path that led into the woods. Needing time to think, she decided that a walk would do her good. Not only would it stretch her taut muscles, but it would give her some exercise to keep her occupied while she worked on a solution to her problem.

Bowie liked the feeling of being afloat again. His men knew exactly what to do, but he enjoyed doing some of the manual work himself. He stood beside the tall mast and listened to the briskly flapping sails. The sound was more dear to him than a woman's skirts, he decided and chuckled. *Not all women.* He'd found that one woman stood above the rest in his regard, and he wasn't sure whether he liked it or not.

The air off the ocean lifted a cold mist from the Atlantic and threw it in his face, as if to jar him back to reality. Erin Banning seemed to be different from other women. Her values were unlike those of most Colonial women, Whig or Tory. Erin seemed to see through a situation and recognize its importance—or lack of it. She possessed none of the attitudes that made other women so distasteful to him. Erin seemed to think for herself, and Bowie found that quality very attractive.

Thinking of Erin, Bowie suddenly wished he'd gone along with her, especially on this first trip. Though he thoroughly hoped this would be her first and last, he feared it wouldn't be because she was so damnably stubborn. Since he'd met Jimbo and Phillip, Bowie felt a little better about her going along, but he knew the few men with her would be no protection against Tarleton's butchers. For that matter, Bowie would have been little help.

Still, he wished he'd left Sidney in charge of this voyage and gone along with Erin.

Erin thought about Bowie, about his strength and daring, his courage and convictions. According to her father, Bowie had known the heavy influence of a Loyalist father. He'd come a long way since then. After he'd left them this afternoon, Erin felt a chill that had nothing to do with the weather but had everything to do with Bowie.

"What's wrong with you?" she asked herself and picked up a twig. Twirling it between her cold hands, she tried to analyze her feelings for Bowie, but her emotions were too new, and she was too inexperienced in her relationships with men. She missed his laughter and the way his brows knit together when he was vexed with her. Without him this journey seemed dull and lifeless. She could imagine him sitting so straight and tall in the saddle, handsome and confident. She fixed her eyes on a big holly tree and remembered the holly basket she'd used to attract Bowie's attention when she had something to report. She wished he were here now.

What would Chauncey Farthingale do? She could almost see him sitting primly beside her, fussing about the dirt staining his ridiculous pink satin breeches.

Oh, why couldn't she stop thinking about Bowie? She wondered if this constant connection could be what love was all about. Could she be falling in love?

Erin smiled, then glanced around to see if anyone might have seen her, but she was alone. "In love. How ridiculous can you be, Erin?" she questioned herself and sat on a log. "You've known the man but a few days. Now, stop daydreaming and think about how to make these men realize you're a part of this effort."

Tilting her head slightly, she looked through skeletal tree branches to the brilliant sapphire sky. The warming sun pulsed like a white-hot heart above her, lending the first heat she'd felt all day. The frigid temperature had been rising all afternoon, and tomorrow promised to be a beautiful day.

It'll be a bad day for traveling, though, she thought. All the sleet and snow will melt, and the wheels of the wagons will bog down in the muck and mud.

"That's the answer," she whispered. "Muck and mud. The men won't expect me to be willing to get dirty. When the wheels bog down in the mire, I'll get out and walk, maybe lead the mules instead of driving them."

That ought to convince them, she concluded, along with the fact that she would accept no more comfort than the trip afforded the men. She would be their equal—nothing less, nothing more.

With that thought Erin hurried back to the camp. Despite the heat from the sun, her hands were freezing, and she longed to curl them around a cup of hot coffee.

" 'Lasses, how long till supper's ready?" Erin asked as she burst through the door. "I could eat a saddled horse."

Erin stopped. Bowie had said that. She'd known the man no more than two weeks and was already quoting him. As far as she knew, she'd never done that with anybody except her father and not often at that. Why was Bowie so different? Why did his words stick in her brain when other men's passed through and disappeared without consequence?

This was a question she couldn't answer, not now anyway. Feeling the warmth of color in her cheeks, she wanted to do something to take her mind off Bowie Gallagher and bustled over to help 'Lasses finish her preparations for supper. She picked up a spoon and started to stir the stew.

'Lasses eyed Erin suspiciously and took the spoon out of her hand. "Supper's bout ready. Where you been? You been gone from this shack for most an hour. Git from outa here. Set yourself down and act like a lady. I ain't raised you to act like no field hand, and that's what you been doin' the last two weeks ever since that Mr. Gallagher come strollin' in one night. I've a mighty urge to take a broomstick to your backside and straighten you out."

Erin grinned. 'Lasses had lapsed into one of her stock sermons on ladylike behavior. True enough, Erin had displayed few of the graces a woman should possess if she intended to marry well and be respected in Charleston society, but she had gained something else: her freedom. The men of Charleston, the few who would be left after this devastating war, wouldn't look longingly at a woman who took to the trail with a bunch of men she hardly knew. Erin's reputation would be ruined if anybody ever found out about her secret trip—or trips—and she prayed that this wouldn't be her last.

Bowie swore. He couldn't get Erin Banning out of his mind. He couldn't think; he couldn't act; he couldn't eat; he couldn't captain his ship. Damn her for wriggling into my heart!

He had never intended to love a woman. Bowie had nothing against women, but he'd seen what a difference of opinion could do to a home, to the children, to a marriage. His mother, strong and courageous in her own right, had stood up for her convictions one evening at supper, and his father had slapped her. The sound of Douglas Gallagher's hand still rang in Bowie's ears.

In that moment of contact Bowie decided two things: to leave home and never to marry. He didn't want to see himself ever treat a woman that way, but his temper was as volatile as his father's, and Bowie knew the possibility existed. He'd come close to shaking Erin Banning just a few days ago when she'd refused to accept the possibility of danger to herself on this mission.

Never before had he felt that way about a woman—or anyone, for that matter. But he found that he cared about Erin. His opinions about women were well established, but he discovered that none of them applied to his relationship with Erin.

Damn her for being so brave and determined! Those traits set her apart and attracted him to her. He moved over to his desk and sat down, burying his head in his hands. It would serve her right if Tarleton— God! What was he thinking? If Tarleton caught her, he'd kill her. If Tarleton touched Erin, Bowie would kill him. He jumped to his feet so quickly that his chair toppled over behind him. He went to the cabinet and removed a bottle of brandy and a glass. Starting to pour the shimmering liquid, he saw Erin's lovely face swimming before his eyes, taunting him with her stubbornness and strong will. With all his strength, he flung the glass at the wall just as Sidney opened the door.

Sidney leaped back outside, then peered in, glancing around to see what had happened. "Is it safe to come in?"

Bowie motioned for him to enter and took a long drink from the bottle. Slumping into another chair, Bowie leaned back and propped his feet on the pillar supporting the deck above. He pushed slightly and tilted the chair back on two legs while watching Sidney ease into the room.

"Mate, are you drunk or just gettin' that way?" Sidney crossed the room and took a glass from the cabinet. He held it for Bowie to fill.

"You can stay, but keep your tongue to yourself. I don't want any of your philosophizing." Bowie slammed the bottle on the table. "Fill your own damn glass. I don't care if I never see Erin Banning again. She's nothing but trouble wrapped in ribbons and curls."

After the men finished their supper, Erin stood. "Men, I want to talk to you."

"Go ahead, Missy, we've our bellies full and don't care to move around much," Jimbo said and rubbed his rounded stomach.

"Good," Erin began and inhaled deeply. She still didn't know exactly how she could convince these men of her intentions to be treated equally, but she'd give it her best. "Men, from this moment you must call me Erin. I'm no different from any of you. I don't want to be treated any different. Though I'm a woman, I'm a part of this group and expect no special treatment."

"Beggin' yer pardon, Miss Banning," Jimbo said, rising from his chair. "We can't do that. Mr. Gallagher said we was to take care of you or he'd hang our hides from his mast and let the sea gulls pluck our eyes out."

Erin closed her eyes for a moment as the image stirred the contents of her stomach. "Jimbo, be seated. You work for me. My father and Mr. Gallagher are partners. On this journey I'm your boss."

Jimbo stood taller, almost defiantly. "Yes, miss, that's true, and we ain't disputin' yer word, but just to be honest and all, Bowie Gallagher meant ever word he said, and you can't say nothin' to ease the thought of us hanging from a ship's mast."

"That's absurd. He didn't mean that." Erin silently cursed Bowie for making her job even harder than she thought it would be. "From this moment my name is Erin. I expect to be treated with the same courtesy you afford each other and nothing more."

"But—" Jimbo began.

Erin held up her hand to stop him and continued talking. "If I hear any disagreement, I'll . . . I'll turn over a wagon, tie you to the wheel, and leave you for the wolves to eat."

Eyes widened all around her. She narrowed her gaze and looked at each man individually, scowling as she scanned the room. "To begin with, we'll all sleep in the cabin, except for the lookouts, of course. I'll partition off a section for 'Lasses and myself."

"Naw, Missy, we'll sleep under the wagons. Don't you worry your purty—"

"Jimbo, if I hear you say Missy one more time, I swear I'll leave you tied to a wagon wheel." Erin glared at him until he sat back in his seat. She wasn't sure whether her words meant anything to the men or not; surely they must know an empty threat when they heard one. Still, they all looked at one another uneasily and nodded.

Until that moment she hadn't ventured a glance at 'Lasses. One glimpse of her face told Erin that the men would be much easier to convince than the servant.

Cleaning her place at the long plank table, Erin avoided the men's eyes. She moved quickly about, acting busy as if she had a purpose. When they regained their composure, each of them did the same. After she washed her bowl, she found a couple of thin blankets, strung a length of rope to cordon off one corner of the room, and hung the blankets across the rope.

She turned once more to the men. "We leave at first light. Get some sleep. Jimbo, assign guard duty for tonight. Give each man a two-hour shift so that everybody gets a chance to sleep and doesn't get too cold."

Jimbo appointed two men to take the first watch, and two for each succeeding shift. All together, eight men were required to guard the encampment during the night. After settling who would be on guard when, Jimbo and the selected men walked around the property and set up perimeters. Each man who returned with Jimbo knew which man to replace at what hour and where to go.

Satisfied that the arrangements for their safety were in good hands, Erin and 'Lasses disappeared behind the blanket partition for the night. They threw heavy fur skins on the floor and settled under warm blankets. Erin could tell that 'Lasses wasn't happy with the situation, but Erin didn't really care. 'Lasses had been angry before this and would undoubtedly be angry again in the future.

Bowie tossed and turned on his bed in spite of the calm sea he thought would feel like a cradle to a small baby. Erin clouded all his thoughts, and his concern for her refused to allow him a moment's respite. When he closed his eyes, her face automatically appeared. During the night he got up and drank another glass of whiskey, but the solace and comfort he usually found in the brew eluded him.

Finally he rose and walked up the steps to the deck. Resting his arms on the railing, he peered across the sea and tried unsuccessfully to get Erin out of his mind. He scuffed his foot on the wooden deck and started to walk. Maybe exercise would provide him with some respite.

From bow to stern and back again, Bowie walked like a man possessed. He found no enjoyment in walking, no sweet serenity that would allow him to nod off pleasantly when he returned to his cabin.

"Say, mate, you're gonna wear holes in the deck if you keep that up." Sidney Sterne peeked around the mast and grinned. "Not to mention keeping the rest of us blokes awake."

"The rest of you be damned," Bowie retorted and shook his head wearily. "The only time I have trouble sleeping is when I'm on land. Why am I so awake now?"

"Looks to me like a case of weddin' jitters," Sidney answered and strode to his friend's side.

"Wedding? What an absurd thing to say. I'm not getting married, as I've told you countless times before." Saying the words didn't make Bowie feel any better, but the familiar affirmation did help some. "I think you've been sucking a rum bottle too long."

"Now, there's a pleasant occupation," Sidney agreed. "Maybe it'll cure what ails you."

Bowie glared at his friend. "I tried that."

"This is serious, mate." Sidney propped his elbows on the railing and shook his head sadly. "I never thought I'd see the day—or night."

Waiting for Sidney to complete the thought, Bowie stared across the gentle Atlantic. "Well? Are you going to say what you think or not? If not, it'll be the first time."

Sidney straightened and gazed at Bowie. "Well, mate, I never thought I'd ever see Bowie Gallagher fall in love."

"If you persist in prattling like a madman, I'll hang you from the crow's nest until you—"

"Hey, mate, just makin' an observation. Don't be jumpin' down the throat of the doctor what diagnoses the disease." Sidney laughed and clapped Bowie on the shoulder. "I'd say it ain't fatal, mate."

For a moment Bowie stared at Sidney, disbelieving what he said. Bowie Gallagher in love? Never. He grinned and caught Sidney playfully around the neck. "Oh, it just might be fatal this time. The patient's doctor may die."

"Hold on, there—"

"Quiet!" Bowie interrupted Sidney and pointed off the starboard side. "Lights. A ship. Sound the alarm."

Within minutes every man stood ready at his duty station ready for battle if need be. The *Midnight Star* was as fast or faster than any ship in His Majesty's fleet, but Bowie didn't like to run under full sail at night, particularly around the reefs that bordered the islands.

Observing the ship, he could tell that it was headed toward the *Midnight Star* at a fast clip. With the momentum of the war swinging toward the Americans, many privateers' ships were being seized by the British, especially if the cargo indicated that they were being used to help the Patriots.

The muskets and ammunition in his hold were enough to convict him of treason and to cause the seizure of the *Midnight Star*. Bowie felt bile rise in him as he considered losing his ship to the British. He wouldn't do it. Glancing at the full moon, he cursed and called for Sidney.

Running across the deck, Sidney answered, "Aye, aye, Captain. Here I am."

"Sidney. Extinguish all lights. Tell the crew to prepare for diversionary measures." Bowie gripped the starboard railing so tightly his fingers cramped, and finally turned to face his friend. "I won't let the *Midnight Star* be captured and her men conscripted into British service."

"Aye, mate, on that we agree." Sidney hurried away, calling orders to the sailors.

Tension mounted as the sails were raised full, and the *Midnight Star* lunged forward as she caught the wind. Sailing in darkness, Bowie watched for a reaction from the other ship. Her approach seemed slower, perhaps because of the increased speed of his own vessel. Sidney had passed the word among the men, and the ship began to respond to Bowie's orders.

Unable to stand and watch, Bowie took the wheel. Calling orders in a clipped tone, he never removed his hands from the wheel—nor his gaze from his pursuer. The other ship's speed increased.

Amazed, Bowie spun the wheel and prayed that the moon would find its way behind a cloud soon. Without the silver glow of moonlight bathing the sails in light, the *Midnight Star* would have a chance to lose its British nemesis. Otherwise, it looked like the faster ship would win—and the British ship was faster.

Bowie spun the wheel again, and the *Midnight Star* lurched forward in a zigzag pattern that took him off course, but he couldn't be concerned with that. Escape was his only objective.

"Sir!" Sidney called from the crow's nest.

Venturing a look up, Bowie saw that his friend was climbing down the mast. "What is it?"

"We'll never outrun 'em." Sidney reached the deck and raced over to Bowie. "We gotta stand and fight."

Stand and fight. The words echoed in Bowie's head over and over. "No," he said finally. "No. If we fire on them, we'll be unable to sail again. Any man who's close enough to see the name of this ship will pass the word, and every British ship will make a target of the *Midnight Sun.* We'll have to outsmart them."

Sidney nodded and climbed back up the mast. Bowie glanced up to make sure his friend was secure before spinning the wheel. The main sail took a few seconds but caught the wind again and stiffened.

The British ship came closer. Bowie felt fear rising in him, a fear he'd never known before. Within minutes his ship might be blasted into bits—or captured. Pain tore through him as he considered the *Midnight Star* sailing under another captain, one who had no real love for its timbers and canvas.

"Sidney, get down here," Bowie called and waited as his friend made his way down again. When he reached him, Bowie began to relate his plan. "From the crow's nest, you can see the dark shapes of coral reefs in the water, can't you?"

"Not so good at night, but fine in the daytime," Sidney answered, puzzled.

"We're going to head into the reefs," Bowie announced and didn't wait for an answer. "You go back up. We'll slow down and pick our way through the reefs. It's our only hope."

Bowie sent the word out to his men. Several stationed themselves at the bow as lookouts while Sidney climbed back to the crow's nest. Sailing under one small sail, Bowie guided the *Midnight Star* into the labyrinth of reefs off the southern coast of Florida. Knowing that missed directions could destroy the ship, he listened carefully to his men, particularly to Sidney.

Noting that the British ship had slowed considerably before reaching the first reef, Bowie smiled. At least they couldn't sail any faster than the *Midnight Star* now, and the distance between the ships seemed to be growing.

Soon, however, Bowie's hopes faded. High above, the moon refused to cooperate. First it hid behind a silken cloud that filtered its light and then behind a thick storm cloud that obliterated its incandescence completely.

Bowie had no choice. He called for the sail to be furled and the anchor dropped. They'd have to stand and fight. He waited on the deck, pistol in hand. The British ship should reach them in a few minutes—unless they'd been forced to stop.

Rain began to pelt the crew as they stood in ready on the deck. Bowie cursed silently, knowing that a rain-slicked deck would prevent effective combat.

The first boom sounded. And a second. The British ship was firing at the *Midnight Star*. Bowie had no real effective cannon to return the fire from that distance. He'd installed two three-inch cannons early in the war, but they'd be no match for the big guns of the British fleet. Either the British were too far away or their aim was poor. Several times the sound of cannon blasts echoed across the water, but the *Midnight Star* remained untouched.

Sidney came down to stand beside Bowie. "Mate, from what I could observe, they're too far away to do any damage. Looks like they've stationed themselves outside the reef."

Bowie wiped the rain from his face and grinned. "I hope so."

He watched the flash of fire from the distance and came to agree with Sidney. The British captain was obviously afraid to sail into the reefs. A bolt of lightning confirmed his belief. Bowie grinned like a foolish boy with a stick of candy. "You know, Sidney, I think you should go back into the crow's nest. At the first sign of light, whether moonlight or daylight, we'll make a run for it."

With all the sails furled, the *Midnight Star* made a poor target. The British had no object light enough to see without the help of the moonlight. Bowie could barely see their sails in the distance when lightning flashed, and it looked as though they were getting further away.

"I think they're gone, Sid," Bowie called. He knew they weren't safe, not yet, but they were safer than they had been in hours.

After a few more minutes the rain began to let up. Bowie ordered his men to their posts in case the moon showed itself again. To be sure, he wanted to extricate himself from the reefs as soon as possible and slip away from the British ship.

When the moon slid free from the clouds, Sidney began to call directions. The men raised the anchor and unfurled the forward sail. With a steady hand Bowie threaded his way back out of the reefs and ordered all the sails to be unfurled. When the British took notice, Bowie wanted to be as far away as possible.

From across the Atlantic the wind caressed his skin as it had a thousand times, but Bowie didn't stop to enjoy the feeling. He paced back and forth, peering at the moon, at the stars, wondering if Erin was looking at the same sky.

From her makeshift bed Erin could see the sky through the remnants of a window. She gazed at the stars—midnight stars, when they were their brightest—and sighed. Somewhere Bowie lay sound asleep, untroubled by the danger of attack because he was safely away from America. His ship would never be identified as the enemy because he flew a British flag when he was under full sail.

Erin didn't lie awake because of the danger she might be in, but because Bowie's image refused to let her sleep. Scowling at his vision for torturing her when she needed to rest, she couldn't forget how strong his face was, how commanding.

She had the feeling that their first meeting had been ordained, but she couldn't fathom the reason. What did fate have in mind for them? What part would they play together in this war that neither could have done separately?

Filled with questions that had no immediate answers, Erin turned on her side. Cold air slipped between her and her covers, so she pulled them closer around her face. From here she could still see the sky with its brilliant gold moon rising above the branches to sail proudly across the midnight sky. With that sight in her eyes she forced her eyes closed and tried to fall asleep.

Each time the guard changed, Erin awoke shivering with cold. The simple noises of two men leaving to take the place of two others comforted her and broke the monotony of the snoring of the other men. When the last guards entered the cabin to lie down, 'Lasses rose and pulled on her homespun dress. Breakfast had to be made for twelve people.

Erin waited for 'Lasses to leave the confines of the enclosed area before rising. In the semidarkness Erin dressed quickly and hurried out to put more wood on the fire. She wanted to be done with most of the morning duties before she woke the men, but Jimbo had already risen.

"Mornin' Miss . . . um, Erin." He hurried out the door without waiting for her reply.

Grinning, Erin puttered around, helping 'Lasses with breakfast and packing up some of the utensils that wouldn't be needed. When the smell of coffee reached the men, they began to get up one by one. By this time Jimbo had returned and sent two of them to replace the men standing guard.

Cold and hungry, the men gathered around to eat biscuits and honey and to laugh and talk for a few peaceful minutes before the realities of their venture intruded. When everybody had eaten, Erin gave instructions to break camp. As soon as the first rays of sunlight peeked through the trees, everyone was assembled for final instructions.

Jimbo divided the men and assigned wagons. Once again he paired himself with Erin. Her wagon held less than the others, but 'Lasses and Nero rode with her, making up for the shortage of cargo. One man rode ahead of the group, and another followed them in case some British soldiers were riding their way.

All along the road Jimbo regaled Erin with stories of when he was a boy in backcountry South Carolina. She hardly listened since her mind was involved in other thoughts, but she occasionally nodded or made some remark that indicated she was interested in what he had to say. The cold air found ways to reach her through the cracks in the wagon bed, through little folds in the skins covering her, in tiny open places between her face and hood, but she persevered.

Erin's gaze searched the forest ahead. She knew they were nearing Georgetown and that the British held that city. Their plan was simple: they were going to bypass Georgetown altogether by heading up the Santee River for a few miles and then going northeast.

Exerting extreme caution, they reached the vicinity of General Francis Marion's encampment between the Great Pee Dee and the Little Pee Dee rivers almost a week after they left Bowie. With the wagons heavily loaded and traveling prudently, the trip took longer than usual, but eventually bringing the goods safely to General Nathanael Greene at his headquarters farther up the Pee Dee River was the main objective.

The sentries spotted them quickly, Erin guessed. She began to hear low whistles and calls that sounded like birds, but she knew they weren't—not this close to Marion's encampment. She stopped her wagons at the edge of the swamp and waited. Without the help of General Marion's men, she knew they couldn't proceed any farther.

Before long a lone man rode toward them. Jimbo reached uneasily for his gun, but Erin stayed his hands. "No. Any sign of aggression, and we won't be admitted to Marion's encampment even if this man knows who I am."

A few moments later he reached them and called, "Where you folks headed on such a cold day?"

Erin identified the man as Elijah Forbes, a friend of her father's from the old days of the wagon road, and knew the heavily bearded man must recognize her although he made no sign. "I am Erin Banning, Mr. Forbes, here on my father's business."

"And what might that be, Miss Banning?" he asked, never taking his gaze from her face.

"I have supplies for General Greene. My men and I need safety for the night." Erin's patience was nearing an end. This man knew her and knew her father well. Why was he keeping them waiting? "My father is ill, and I am here in his stead. I demand to be taken to General Marion's camp at once."

Elijah Forbes glanced at the group of travelers and then back at Erin. "What makes you think I would know the whereabouts of General Marion?"

"Elijah Forbes, you know who I am and what I'm doing here. Are you refusing to conduct us to General Marion's camp?" Erin glared at the obstinate man, knowing that he didn't really understand why she had arrived instead of her father. "I insist on seeing the Swamp Fox at once."

"Swamp Fox, eh?" Forbes chuckled and glanced toward the swamp. "Lots of swamp foxes out there."

"Mr. Forbes, I believe you are purposely being contrary because I'm a woman. If you don't conduct us immediately—"

"Follow me, Miss Banning."

Jimbo helped Erin down from the wagon and assisted her into the saddle of one of the horses brought along for the scouts. She asked Phillip Hunter, her father's assistant, to remain with the wagons. Jimbo came along with her.

Elijah Forbes turned his horse and trotted ahead of the

small group. Never looking back, he picked his way through
the quagmire to the Great Pee Dee River. They rode to the
place where Elijah crossed the river. Erin hesitated because
she knew she would get wet trying to cross, but she couldn't
afford to refuse. With a glance at Jimbo she urged her horse
into the water.

After crossing the bank, they rode silently on until they
came through the cypress trees to the encampment. During
the trek, Erin desperately tried to conceal the shivers that
racked her body because of her wet feet and legs. She
seethed, though she realized the need for great precaution.
General Marion and his campsite had to be protected at all
costs.

When they reached the camp, several men appeared,
seemingly from nowhere, with guns trained on the small
band. Erin knew this to be policy and waited while a decision was made about her. Trembling with cold, she remained on her horse until a young man came out to look
at her.

"Miss Banning?" he asked finally. "I'm Major Dunn, Andrew Dunn."

"Yes, Major Dunn," she answered simply, afraid that if
she said more her teeth would begin to chatter and never
stop.

After gazing at her another moment, he called, "Forbes,
find clothing for Miss Banning and her companion. Bring
it to my tent. Sergeant," he said to another man standing
near Erin, "help Miss Banning from her horse and bring
her into my tent."

Erin thought for sure her dress would be frozen, but she
found that it was merely cold. She entered the tent gratefully
and accepted a cup of hot coffee from the sergeant.

After a moment Major Dunn came in. "I apologize for
the reception you encountered, but we have knowledge that
Cornwallis and Tarleton are moving northward. We don't
know exactly where Tarleton is, but Cornwallis is in the vicinity, probably heading north to engage General Greene
and the main Continental Army."

"Oh, dear." Erin dropped into a seat and sighed. "We're heading north as well. How far ahead of us is Lord Cornwallis?"

"I believe you may be ahead of him, though not by far." Major Dunn sat in a chair opposite her. "The route will be dangerous, far more dangerous than when you left Charleston."

"Major Dunn, where is General Marion?" Erin asked, believing that the Swamp Fox was the only man who could advise her under the circumstances.

"I'm afraid I can't say, Miss Banning." Major Dunn rose and opened the tent flap. Glancing back over his shoulder, he grinned. "Cornwallis would give his estates for that knowledge. I can't tell you because there's a chance you'll be captured, and after all, I mean . . . you're a woman and might be forced to talk."

Erin bristled at his reference to her gender. "I suppose if I were a man, you'd tell me."

"You'd have a better chance of finding out," Major Dunn admitted. "I recommend that you leave your goods here and return to Charleston. The road ahead is too dangerous for a woman."

Erin rose, mentally cursing her small stature, and strode from the tent. "Major Dunn, I'm afraid we've taken too much of your time. We'll be on our way."

"But, Miss Banning, won't you stay to warm yourself, to change into something dry?" he asked as he followed her out of the tent.

She motioned for Jimbo to assist her onto her horse. Once in her saddle, she towered over Major Andrew Dunn, looked down, and smiled. "Major Dunn, we have no need of your clothing nor of your fire. Don't concern yourself with our safety. Our men need the goods we're carrying. We shall deliver them safely to General Greene."

Elijah Forbes reappeared and led them out of the swamp and across the river. When Erin and Jimbo had changed into dry clothing, she climbed onto the seat of her wagon. "Goodbye, Mr. Forbes."

"God speed, Miss Banning," he replied and started to ride away. "Uh, Miss Banning, I know your father well. I'm sorry to hear he's ill."

"Thank you, Mr. Forbes. I'll tell my father you asked after his health." She nodded to Jimbo, who flicked the reins, and added under her breath, "Be careful, Mr. Forbes. I'll see you again soon."

Bowie listened to the bow of the *Midnight Star* as it bumped gently against the wharf, and finally went ashore. Though he usually enjoyed a few days leisure while he purchased the goods for the troops, this time was different. He hurried through the shops and stores, buying only necessities until he came to a store that displayed satin ribbon. One color caught his fancy—exactly the emerald green of Erin's eyes—and he bought it, all the while wondering why.

He almost left the store when he caught the fragrance of rosewater and turned around. A lady entering the shop smelled of the scent and reminded him again of Erin. Without stopping to consider why he was doing it, he asked the lady where she found the cologne. She directed him to a small ladies' shop down the street, and he hurried out.

Bowie wasn't one to buy gifts for women, but he couldn't resist this purchase. With his parcels in hand he rushed back to the ship to await the arrival of the goods for the Continental Army.

He could hardly wait to visit Erin, to see the expression on her face when he gave her the ribbon and cologne. He knew that the gifts were too personal for him to give a woman he hardly knew, but Erin wasn't like other women. He wanted to pamper her, to inundate her with lovely trinkets, to feel her soft lips touching his.

Stopping abruptly, he examined his thoughts. What was he doing? Erin wasn't some trollop from the wharves. She was a lady, the daughter of a planter, the daughter of his best friend and business partner. Swearing angrily to himself, Bowie vowed to respect her, to treat her as she deserved to be treated. From now on he'd keep his hands to himself and think of her as a friend, not as someone to satisfy his sexual demands.

He wondered how long he'd keep his promise and decided that he'd be strong, a man of his word, no matter how difficult the task became. Relieved that he'd settled his feelings for Erin, he sat on the edge of his bunk and closed his eyes. Her vision swam before him, delicate and lovely, her lips in a tender pout, just waiting for his kiss. Why did he keep imagining her this way?

In short, he concluded reluctantly, he couldn't wait to see her again.

CHAPTER
10

THE ARDUOUS TRIP TO GREENE'S HEADQUARTERS TOOK a great deal out of Erin, much more than she anticipated. Her bones ached from the chilly rain; her nose ran from the cold she'd caught; and her heart beat fast from thinking about Bowie. Luckily she encountered no problems more severe than those.

Erin felt almost giddy with her success. Against seemingly insurmountable odds, she'd managed to bring the wagons safely to General Greene. She could hardly wait to tell Bowie and her father. Prouder than she'd ever been, she looked for General Greene to tell him she was leaving.

Before she left Greene, he passed on some wonderful news. General Daniel Morgan, assisted by Colonel William Washington and Andrew Pickens, had soundly defeated Tarleton's stronger force at the Cowpens. Greene himself left to consult with Morgan on the day Erin and her group left to return to Charleston.

Elated by the information, the group made their way south without encountering so much as an antagonistic squirrel. After stopping at Bluffwood to relate the details of her journey to her father, Erin went into town to await Bowie's arrival. She could hardly wait to tell him of her victory, along with the news of Morgan's battle at the Cowpens.

Several days passed, and Erin began to wonder if something had happened to Bowie. When he'd left her that day on the trail, he'd told her he'd be back before the end of

January. Today was February first, and she'd heard nothing from him. What if he'd been captured? Slipping in and out of the coastline around Charleston on a ship was a dangerous occupation, though he'd downplayed the peril. Where could he be?

Several more days passed before she spotted Bowie, gaily attired in his pink satin breeches, walking down South Bay Street. Unfortunately, Erin couldn't run out to greet him because Walter Martin was entertaining a guest in the parlor. Remembering their signal, she waited until darkness fell and changed the ribbons on the basket on the piazza. Since the first of February seemed a peculiar time to keep a basket of holly on the piazza, she decided that after Bowie responded this time, they'd have to decide on a new signal.

Around midnight Erin found herself pacing back and forth in front of a fire that lent no real warmth to her room. Knowing that Bowie was in town and that she couldn't see him irritated her. If Walter ever suspected that Chauncey was anything but the fop he presented himself to be, suspicions would be aroused, so Erin knew better than to risk sending Bowie a note.

She decided that she'd try to lock the door, though the lock had stubbornly refused to work properly for the past several weeks. At times the key wouldn't even turn the tumblers, but she had to try for her own peace of mind. Fidgeting with a key that refused to turn, she vowed to hire a locksmith to repair the lock before she left Charleston again.

Bowie gazed at Erin from across the garden. He watched her shadow cross back and forth in front of the window several times while he hid behind the bushes in her garden. When he was sure no one was watching, he scaled the live oak tree outside her room. He planned to climb onto the roof and enter through her window when the silence indicated that everyone was abed.

Briskly rubbing his hands together, he blew on them to get warm. If he had to wait long, he'd freeze in the wind blowing off the bay. He couldn't delay his entrance too much longer. Not only was he cold, but he also wanted to see Erin badly.

Since her return, Erin had found Walter as pesky as a dogfish, always around when one was fishing for sea trout or flounder. As she paced the floor, she heard a noise outside her window and hurried over to see what was going on. Looking down at South Bay, she could see nothing out of the ordinary, but she raised the window anyway. Walter hadn't come in yet, but she expected him at any time. She hoped he wasn't in a drunken stupor, as he had been for several nights.

Cold air flowed over her as she hung her head out the window to try to see better. The streets were empty, and Erin peered across the harbor. British ships floated there like sharks waiting for their prey. The moon slid behind a cloud, and she could hardly see, so she drew her head back, shivering from the cold.

"Erin," Bowie called softly as he realized she hadn't seen him. Warily he slid onto the roof and began his ascent. "Erin, wait."

Pausing, she glanced back out the window. The wind was teasing her, making her believe she heard her name. Still, she looked until her eyes adjusted to the darkness again.

"Oh, no," Bowie whispered as he felt himself begin to slide. "Grab my hand."

Stunned, Erin reached out and caught Bowie's hand. "What in the world are you doing out there?"

"Just help me get inside, and I'll answer all your questions. It's freezing out here!" Bowie stuck one leg through the window and pulled himself the rest of the way. He paused only seconds, then took Erin in his arms and kissed her hungrily. He'd waited for this moment ever since he'd left her that day on the trail.

"I missed you," he whispered against her hair and held her tightly. She felt so right, so warm and comfortable in his arms, that he was reluctant to release her.

Her heart pounding, Erin smiled wanly as she stepped

back and looked into his eyes, eyes as blue as the midnight
sky filled with the glint of midnight stars. "What . . . um,
how did you get onto my roof?"

Grinning, he drew her into his arms again. "I climbed
your tree. Don't tell me I'm the first to risk life and limb
climbing that tree to get your attention."

Giggling like a girl of ten, Erin nodded. "I'm afraid so.
If you'd bothered to ask, I could have told you to climb up
the front. The roof's flatter there over the piazza."

"You should have told me earlier," he quipped and
rubbed his shin, "before I scraped my leg."

Bowie's gaze devoured her. She was every bit as lovely
as he'd remembered, more so, in fact, than he'd allowed
himself to believe. Her petite frame supported generous
breasts above a tiny waist he could easily span with his
hands. Everything else about her seemed doll-like, though
he knew well the strength that lurked in her five-foot-tall
body.

Heat raced through his body, begging for the satisfaction
of touching her, of feeling the silk of her skin against his.
Bowie inhaled deeply, as if he were a drowning man sucking
in his last breath, his lungs bereft of air, air saturated with
the fragrance of rosewater.

Erin walked to the divan and sat, tucking her foot beneath her. "What are you doing up here at this time of
night?"

Rosewater? He felt his pocket for the gifts he'd bought
her. "Oh, this is for you."

He reached in his pocket and removed the bottle of cologne and the packet of ribbon. "I thought you might like
to have these. I found them on my last stop for supplies."

Erin took the cologne and ribbon from him, surprised
that he'd thought of her while out of the country. "For me?
How very thoughtful."

She got up and placed the cologne on her dressing table.
After a moment she tied her hair back with the ribbon and
turned to him. "How does it look? I'll have to do something
more formal with it later, but for now I'll wear it like this."

He thoroughly approved. Against her curls the emerald ribbons complemented the color of her eyes and, if anything, made them more intense. "Lovely. Just as I'd imagined."

Erin felt the color rise in her cheeks and turned away. Without looking at him again, she returned to the divan and dropped down, feeling suddenly warm and happy.

Bowie strode to the door, listened for a few moments, and then tried to lock it. Finally giving up, he sat beside her and whispered, "Don't worry. I'm not here to seduce you and then flee."

"Well, what *are* you doing here?" she repeated. A warmth began to spread throughout her that had nothing to do with the fire crackling merrily in the fireplace.

"I came to see you, silly girl." Bowie rested his arm on the back of the divan and watched her cover her ankle primly. The thin dressing gown rising and falling over her breasts seemed to irritate him unreasonably, though he knew that the soft fabric would tear easily if he chose to do so. He averted his eyes. If he continued to look at her, he'd get himself into trouble. "Didn't you change the ribbons on the basket?"

"Yes," she answered, a little puzzled. "But I just did that this evening. How did you know?"

"I saw you do it," he admitted and allowed his arm to slide slightly closer to her. Just let your arm rest on her shoulders, he told himself. That'll be enough.

Erin squirmed in her seat and looked up at him. "But you'd already gone by. I saw you."

Bowie didn't want to tell her that he'd walked by a dozen times since he'd arrived, hoping to catch a glimpse of her. "I came back. What did you want to tell me?"

"Oh," Erin said and nodded. Feeling the enthusiasm and excitement rise in her, she beamed at him. "We were victorious. We arrived at General Greene's headquarters without encountering any real problems."

"I'm happy to hear that," Bowie conceded, even though he wasn't too happy about her feat. One victory would only whet her appetite for another. "Tell me all about it."

"You don't sound too excited," she complained. Why wasn't he as delighted as she was about her triumph? "I think we really accomplished something. Most of us were newcomers to the task. You must admit we did well."

"I said I was happy. Do you want me to stand on your roof and announce your conquest to the citizenry of Charleston?" Bowie realized he sounded brusque, but he feared that she would demand to go again, and he didn't know if he could stand the ordeal.

Erin couldn't really complain about his response. After all, he didn't feel the exhilaration of the success as acutely as she. He hadn't been happy to see her go.

For a few minutes she told him quietly about the journey, about the condescension she felt in Marion's camp when she spoke with Major Dunn. "He is really arrogant."

"I don't know him. Go on." Bowie let his hand slip farther down the back of the sofa until he felt the warmth of Erin's skin through her wrapper.

Erin felt Bowie's hand come to rest on her shoulder. Even though she often wore dresses that exposed her entire shoulders, she knew her cheeks glowed with color from shyness. No man had ever seen her in her dressing gown, except Bowie, who had seen her not once but twice. Without appearing obvious, she knew of no way to relieve the situation. Did he know how her heart hammered in her chest when he touched her?

No, she surmised. Bowie Gallagher was a cosmopolitan man who'd undoubtedly known the pleasures of many women. He cared little for the pounding of her heart. Erin felt herself leaning toward him, all the while wondering what motivated her to commit such a brazen act.

Silently hearing the speech 'Lasses had made many times about forward women, Erin smiled. What would 'Lasses say if she viewed this scene? Though 'Lasses hadn't disciplined Erin for a long time, she could still feel the sting of the hickory that had done much to teach her ladylike behavior and good manners.

"What's so amusing?" Bowie's forehead wrinkled as he

watched the grin on Erin's face. "What are you thinking
about that's taken you away from me so suddenly?"

Embarrassed for being caught daydreaming, Erin shook
her head and smiled. "I was wondering what 'Lasses would
do if she saw me . . . I mean, with you here, in my dressing
gown."

Bowie chuckled. "I'll have you know I'm not wearing
your dressing gown, but if you'll take it off, I'll be glad to
try it on."

"Oh, silly, you know what I mean." Erin glared at him,
but she couldn't be angry. His words were deliciously
naughty. No man had ever spoken to her in such a way, and
she found it thrilling.

"Yes, I know. My old mammy would probably whip the
hide off me for saying such a thing," Bowie agreed. Then
silence hung between them like the fog that rolled off the
river in the early morning hours, dense and pregnant. He
couldn't think of anything witty to say.

"Maybe I'll tell her when I see her," Erin quipped to
break the disturbing silence. "You'd better tread carefully."

The smile left Bowie's face as he cupped his hand over
her shoulder. The contact seemed to burn through his skin,
race through his veins, and kindle a fire in his loins, the likes
of which he'd never experienced. He opened his mouth to
reply to her jest and found himself staring into her eyes.

Almost immediately he leaned over to kiss her. The magnetism he felt overpowered his normal caution, and he
swept her into his embrace before he could stop himself. Her
lips were soft and pliant, yielding beneath the pressure of
his and parting slightly to tantalize him further.

Erin felt her breath whoosh from her lungs as if it were
sucked away by a whirlwind. Bowie's tongue gently probed
the inner recesses of her mouth, teasing and taunting until
she felt she could stand no more. She slipped her arms
around his neck and turned slightly to accommodate his caresses as his hands massaged her back through the thin fabric of her wrapper. Untutored as she was in lovemaking, she

tentatively stroked his cheek and his neck, hoping to return the pleasure his touch brought her.

"Erin," he whispered, nibbling on her ear and circling her delicate body with his arms.

Her petite frame seemed too tiny to be that of a full-grown woman, but the firm breasts pressed against his chest said otherwise. Erin's caress told him that she moved instinctively rather than from experience, but her gentle touch aroused him far more than the most knowledgeable woman he'd known.

Bowie sensed a passion in her that lay beneath the surface of her composure, waiting to be awakened and explored, and he wanted to be the one to awaken and explore that scintillating experience with her. He tried to tell himself that his excitement stemmed from her victory, from the joy that he saw in her emerald eyes, that her heightened emotions were the result of her new confidence, but his need refused to allow him to lie to himself. He simply wanted her more than he'd ever wanted another woman.

Magic sizzled in the air as he cuddled her close, wondering whether to continue or run. "Erin, stop. We can't do this. You don't know what you're doing."

He was right. Erin didn't know exactly. All she knew was that she'd never felt this way before and might never feel this way again. Her heart sang; her blood hummed through her veins; and her heart banged a faster and faster pace like a drum. Suddenly she knew what he meant—but she didn't care. She wanted to feel him close to her, all of him taut against her body.

"This is madness." Bowie sprang to his feet. "You sit right there and . . . shhh!"

From downstairs the sound of the front door opening and closing reverberated through the house. Erin jumped up and stared wild-eyed at Bowie. "What shall we do?"

Bowie felt a surge of protectiveness. If Walter Martin entered Erin's room, Bowie would have to kill him. But the death of a British official would cause an investigation that might implicate Erin and Arlen.

Bowie refused to precipitate such an inquiry. He raised the sash as quietly as possible and slid through the window to wait. Hugging himself, he peered at Erin as she turned to the door.

Erin couldn't face Walter, not tonight. Everything in her life had changed. Bowie meant more to her now than simply a business partner, though she couldn't really define his role in her life yet. Glancing at the door, she made her decision. Instead of lowering the sash, she climbed through the window to join Bowie on the roof of the piazza.

"What are you doing? You'll freeze to death out here!" Bowie exclaimed. He closed the window and wrapped his arms around her. Bowie should have never agreed to Erin's return to Charleston. Except for a few slaves, she was alone with Walter Martin. Even though the war forced a relaxation of society's rules, he now realized that she wasn't safe with Walter—and Bowie wondered about himself. "If you hurry, you have time to go back inside before Walter gets upstairs. Go!"

Snuggling more deeply into the warmth of his arms, Erin shook her head. "I couldn't do it. I'm afraid that if Walter came in and stared at me as he did the other night, I'd go mad."

"Mad is better than dead," Bowie chided her gently. He shifted so that his body protected her from the piercing wind and placed his cloak over both of them as best he could. "I hope he's tired tonight."

"Me, too," Erin whispered.

An attack of guilt plagued Bowie as they waited. He should have repaired her lock, or at least he should have sent someone to do it. He mentally surveyed the room. Had they left evidence that would arouse Walter's suspicions?

Bowie didn't think so. They'd sat on the divan in front of the fire. Walter would probably enter the room, glance around for Erin, and leave. When Bowie considered her actions, he decided that she'd done the right thing. If she'd stayed in the room, Walter might have lingered.

"Where is he? He must be upstairs by now," Erin murmured to Bowie and slid her arms around him. As cold as she was, she felt her blood racing through her veins like molten lava, and she looked up at him. What was he thinking as he held her so close in this frightening moment in such a ridiculous place?

Feeling her gaze upon him, Bowie glanced down at Erin. Her firm breasts were pressed against him, much as they had been when he'd almost broken his promise to himself earlier. Now he made himself another promise: he'd make sure the damn lock was repaired.

With Walter becoming more infatuated with Erin, Bowie felt that she needed protection. Hell, he thought, she's probably safer on the trail than in her own home. He had to find a way to keep her out of Charleston, if possible.

"Can you see anything?" she whispered.

Bowie peered through the window and watched as the door opened slowly. Damn Walter for being the cad he is, Bowie thought, and drew Erin closer in his arms. He put his finger over her mouth to assure her silence.

What was Walter doing? Instead of glancing in and seeing that Erin wasn't there, he'd begun looking in drawers. What could he be looking for? An intense cold clutched at Bowie's heart as he realized that Walter must be suspicious. He'd have no other reason for snooping in Erin's private things.

Stroking Erin's hair, Bowie wondered how she'd react to such an invasion. It was bad enough that the British had invaded and now occupied her city and home, but to encroach on her personal privacy in such a manner was inexcusable, even for the British.

Acutely feeling the pain she would feel when she discovered Walter's trespass, Bowie lifted her chin and gazed at her. From the crinkles around the corners of her emerald eyes, he could tell she sensed his anger. He tried to smile reassuringly but knew he failed.

The fragrance of rosewater wafted to his nostrils, and desire stirred deep inside him for this courageous young woman. She seemed to flinch at nothing. Despite temperatures low enough to freeze the lakes of fire in hell, she crouched with him, silently waiting for Walter to leave.

Erin knew that Bowie was upset. Walter must have come into her room, if she could judge by Bowie's reaction. What was happening? Was Walter waiting for her to return? There must be something else, something that disturbed Bowie and tensed his muscles until he almost crushed her.

Staring up at him, she tried to fathom the reason for his anger, but she couldn't read his face. Even his eyes, those startling blue eyes that looked like the harbor on a sunny day, seemed muted and cloudy. Why was he scowling like that as he glanced back through the window? Erin wanted to ask him questions, to rise enough to see over the window-sill, but he held her too tightly.

She surmised that Walter was indeed waiting for her, or else he would have left. How long would she and Bowie have to crouch here on the roof of the piazza? Looking at him, she tried to respond to his forced smile, but could do little more than he. They'd simply have to wait for Walter to leave.

Bowie had such a strong face, a countenance filled with confidence that inspired faith in people around him, or so Erin believed. She trusted him, and had from the moment she'd met him that night he'd brought her father home. Her hands, warm from being tucked around his waist, touched the cold strength of his cheek, and he glanced down at her.

Her warm hands startled Bowie, and he gazed at her. Was she trying to tell him something? He reveled in the tender touch and closed his hand over hers. From the point where her hand touched his face, minute sparks shot through his body, jolting him like tiny lightning bolts. Cold air burst through the opening she created between his cloak and his body.

Bowie glanced at Erin and desire swept over him, pure unadulterated passion unlike anything he'd ever known. With emerald eyes glittering in the soft light filtering from the moon through the naked limbs of the live oak, she gazed questioningly at him. Damn Walter to hell, Bowie thought, and pulled the cloak over his head.

In the darkness of the tent his cloak created, Bowie drew Erin closer. He thought he heard her sigh softly as she rested her cheek against his chest. Though he didn't want to disturb her, the pressure in his loins grew until he felt he could handle no more.

Erin wasn't surprised by his kiss. She'd expected it, longed for it, ever since they'd climbed onto the roof. Giving herself completely over to his caress, she allowed him to deepen the kiss, opening her mouth to invite his gentle plundering. She wrapped her arms around his neck and pulled him closer to her, wriggling to eliminate the minute distance that separated them.

His arms felt like steel bands around her body, binding her to him as if she were a part of him. With a motion as fluid as the tides, he drew her across his lap, never releasing her from his grasp. Her body trembled as his hand slid down her back to her waist and then edged up to rest beneath her breast.

Shivers of desire flew up and down her body as she writhed in the pleasure his touch elicited. Erin didn't know how to respond. She felt as free as a gull in her heart, while her body was caged like a canary by his arms. She wanted the moment never to end.

Erin couldn't tell how long they'd been on the roof, nor did she care, but the bells of St. Michael's announced the hour of midnight. The raw power of passion raged in her veins, demanding to be satisfied, though she hardly knew what was happening to her.

Bowie knew that this was neither the time nor the place to make love. When he and Erin reached that point in their relationship, he wanted it to be a special moment, not some stolen sordid affair.

Bowie released her and peeked through the window. Disgusted with himself, he wondered how he had allowed this to happen. In a matter of moments he would have torn her gown off and made love to her on the roof of her house. So much for promises.

CHAPTER
11

ONCE INSIDE HER ROOM, ERIN FELT THE STING OF COLOR in her cheeks. Never in her life had she allowed such liberties to be taken by a man. She knew she should feel as soiled and dirty as the women of the wharves, but somehow she didn't. Instead she felt free and excited. She felt the first stirrings of love.

Could it be love? Bowie didn't seem to experience the same emotions as she. He'd brought her back inside, mumbled something about business to attend to, and left the way he'd come. Erin didn't care. Her heart sang, and ripples of pleasure still racked her body as she curled up on the divan and remembered the urgency of his last kiss.

Instinctively she knew that Bowie did feel something more than friendship toward her. One day that feeling might turn to love for him, too. *Love*. Such a splendid word, she mused as she toyed with the soiled hem of her wrapper.

Hugging herself, she leapt up and danced around the room with a joy she couldn't really define. The night would be long indeed if she couldn't quell her excitement long enough to sleep. But with events occurring as rapidly as they had, she knew she must rest.

Within a few days she'd be on the road again.

One afternoon when she could remain in her house no longer, Erin visited with Lilly. While there, three soldiers stopped by to see her cousin.

William Fuller, blushing with pleasure, bent and kissed

Erin's hand. Then he took her arm and led her away from the others. "Miss Banning, I can't say how I've missed you."

Relieved that William hadn't been injured when Bowie stole the British goods she'd taken to General Greene, Erin sat on the pink brocade sofa and gushed. "Why, Captain Fuller, how delightful to see you again."

She couldn't mention the trip or ask the questions that kept coming to her mind, but she could try to obtain other information. "Have you been busy? I haven't seen you since Lilly's party."

"I've been sick. I must have eaten some bad oysters or something. Right after the party I became ill and have been unable to keep anything down for . . ." His voice dwindled off as he seemed to realize what disgusting things he was saying. "Oh, please forgive me. I never meant to mention such—"

"Think nothing of it," Erin interrupted. She cared little for his weak stomach but wanted him to believe she cared about him. "You poor dear. And with nobody to nurse you but men. How sad. I wish you would have sent me a note. My mammy has a wonderful cure for such . . . problems. I'd have brought it right over."

"Oh, no, Miss Banning, that wouldn't be right." He paused and wiped his brow. "What I mean is, it's kind of you to be concerned, but I would never ask a lady such as yourself to nurse . . . I mean, well, I just couldn't."

Privately Erin was glad. She didn't particularly like nursing sick people, but she would have if she'd been in Charleston. "You know, I might have been away. I had to take my dear sweet parents to our plantation. They're both so ill that they couldn't stand the hustle and bustle of city life any longer."

"I'm sad to hear of their illness." William Fuller sat beside her on the sofa and shyly took her hand. "Is there anything I can do?"

Erin looked down at her hands, as if to imply a deep sadness. "I'm afraid not. It's a cross I must bear alone and a trip I must make alone."

"Indeed not, Miss Banning. If I didn't have to leave Charleston soon, I'd be happy to escort you to your plantation. I couldn't stay, of course. My duties demand that I be at the ready."

Fluttering her eyelashes, Erin smiled and nodded. "You are kindness itself, Captain Fuller."

"William. You promised to call me William," he reminded her.

"Oh, yes. William," she repeated breathlessly and sighed.

Erin didn't know how long she could continue with this charade. She liked William Fuller more than any British soldier she'd ever known, especially Walter Martin, but she was a Patriot. She needed to know more about the journey William must take. "You mentioned that you must leave Charleston. Will you . . . You won't be in danger, will you . . . William?"

Beaming like a child with a cookie, William patted her hand. "Now, don't you worry your pretty self, Miss . . . Erin. I'll be back safely. This time there'll be plenty of us to guard . . . I mean, I won't be alone."

So, the British were sending more guards this time. How could she find out when they would be leaving? She leaned closer to William. "Captain Fuller . . . William . . . I'd like to invite you for supper one night. How long will you be gone?"

He glanced at the other soldiers and then at Erin. "Well, Erin, my dear, I'll be leaving in four days and returning within two weeks."

Erin calculated the time. Bowie could surprise the guards, rob them of their shipment, and she could take the goods from there to the north. She didn't know the exact whereabouts of General Greene, but she could take the goods to General Marion's encampment and leave them to be disbursed from there. She would be gone for about ten days.

"Well, William," she whispered and batted her eyes coquettishly, "I'm going to be at my parents' plantation for about three weeks. Could we . . . if you're agreeable, that is, would you come for supper then? You could stop by in about three weeks, and we'll set a definite time."

Erin paced back and forth in her morning room. For the past two days she'd awaited Bowie's visit, or rather Chauncey's, until she could hardly be civil to the servants. Her temper, never successfully hidden, now appeared with appalling frequency, and the servants stayed out of her way.

Even Walter seemed to sense her mood. He'd been gone for the better part of these two days and when at home had left her alone. Though she'd made sure her lock was fixed, her concerns had been unwarranted. He simply didn't have time for her now. Something had changed him; perhaps he was embarrassed because of his behavior.

"Well, he should be after entering my room uninvited and rifling through my personal belongings," she said out loud and peered out the window. Where could Bowie be? If he didn't appear soon, she'd go searching for him.

Bowie stopped and looked at the Banning house. He'd avoided it for the past two days, even though he knew Erin would be expecting him. After chastising himself for his behavior, he again promised to treat her with respect—from a distance. Though he'd longed to see her, he'd forced himself to occupy himself with other less interesting jobs. He had two reasons for staying away.

First, he felt that his presence endangered her. Walter Martin wasn't as dumb as Erin liked to pretend he was. Something had made Walter curious about Erin's habits, and Bowie knew it had to be related to the stolen shipment coming at a time when she left Charleston, along with other clues that Walter might have discovered.

Second, he couldn't face Erin. The other night he'd practically made love to her on her own roof—after he'd promised himself to treat her as she deserved to be treated. His behavior was abominable. For some reason he seemed to lose all control around Erin—when he most needed to keep his wits about him.

Even though he stayed away, Bowie wanted to see Erin. For that he also had two good reasons.

He'd heard of a shipment of British goods that he could capture if he was careful. That in itself would have been enough to bring him back to see Erin. He needed her help.

Then there was Erin herself. He couldn't sleep. He couldn't think. He couldn't enjoy himself with other women. He simply felt as though a part of himself had been stripped away.

He found himself standing on Oyster Point, watching her house and arguing with himself about whether or not to knock on her door. As Chauncey Farthingale, he could saunter up to her door, sashay in, and while away the afternoon in fits of giggles designed to disguise his discussion about the shipment he wanted to seize from the British soldiers.

Where was Bowie? Erin collapsed into a soft velvet wing chair and sighed. Why hadn't he come? Had he been captured? Any one of the men who'd helped her take the goods up the wagon road could have confessed if they were caught.

She considered each of them. None of them seemed to be the kind of man who would provide information to the British. Who then? Had Walter discovered something that had given him enough knowledge to have Bowie arrested?

Erin couldn't imagine that. Here in Charleston, Bowie was known as Chauncey Farthingale and as such would be the last man the British would believe to be a supply thief or spy. Bowie must be delayed for some other reason.

Erin stood and began to pace again. She glanced at the lovely carpet and decided that if she didn't stop pacing, she'd wear it thin in places. A noisy laughter from the street attracted her attention, and she ran to the window. Looking down on South Bay Street, she could see the back of a man preening and posing in peacock blue satin, with a froth of lace at his throat and wrists. He was waving gaily to a soldier who seemed to be hurrying down the street to escape being seen with the elegant fop.

Grinning, Erin raced downstairs. That man could be none other than Chauncey Farthingale. No other man in Charleston would be seen on the street wearing such fussy clothing.

By the time Chauncey reached her piazza, Erin was swinging the door open. Fighting gales of laughter, she composed herself and said, "Why, Mr. Farthingale, how delightful of you to call."

"My dearest Miss Banning, you can't imagine how I've longed to see you again. What a darling gown," Bowie gushed, once again posing and preening like the peacock whose colors he wore. "I simply must find out who makes your lovely—"

Rudely interrupting him, Erin grabbed his hand, jerked him inside, and slammed the door. Laughing so hard by now that tears threatened to flow, she flung herself into his arms and kissed him soundly. "Oh, you scoundrel. How could you stay away so long?"

Bowie took her hand and fairly danced into the parlor. "My dear, you can't know what I've gone through. Why, that scamp of a seamstress—"

"Forget Chauncey while we can," Erin interrupted again and pulled Bowie over to the sofa with her. "Make yourself comfortable on this lovely satin brocade sofa with me," she mocked and hugged him.

Taken aback by her enthusiastic greeting, Bowie allowed her to continue her embrace. When he could keep his hands away no longer, he tilted her chin upward and kissed her until she went limp in his arms. He held her back and gazed into her eyes, feeling all his resolve melt away. "There, now behave yourself like a proper lady instead of the hoyden you are."

"Hoyden?" she repeated and giggled. "You have the face to call me a hoyden? Why, you're—"

Bowie kissed her again. All the pressures he'd been facing for the past few days seemed to disappear when he was with her. "All right. You're a lady," he admitted and changed the tone of his voice back to that of Chauncey. "That's why you flung yourself at me instead of punching me. Am I correct, my dear Miss Banning?"

"You are quite correct, my dear Mr. Farthingale," she mimicked and leaned back in his arms. "What would my friend Mr. Gallagher think if he saw me in the arms of the elegant Mr. Farthingale, I wonder?"

Bowie reverted to his own voice. "I'd kill any man other than Mr. Farthingale for touching you." Surprised by his words, Bowie tried to cover his obvious jealousy with teasing. "But somehow I know that Mr. Farthingale isn't a threat."

Erin didn't miss the edge to Bowie's voice, nor the import of his words. Excited by them, she blushed and said, "Pray continue, Mr. Farthingale."

Glancing around, Bowie asked in a whisper, "Walter's out?"

Nodding, Erin murmured, "He's busy for the afternoon and evening. He won't be home until after midnight. Something about *supplies.*" She emphasized the last word and smiled. "I've news of a shipment."

Bowie grinned. "That's why I'm here. I heard there's to be a shipment of warm clothing and ammunition the day after tomorrow."

"That's what I've been dying to tell you for two days." Erin clasped her hands around his neck. "I could wring your silly neck, Chauncey or Bowie, whoever you are, for staying away so long."

With a questioning look Bowie teased in a high-pitched voice, "Oh, dear Miss Banning, please control yourself. I'd have been here sooner if possible."

Erin ignored his plea and continued. "I've arranged to go to Bluffwood. I'm leaving in the morning. When can we meet?"

For more than an hour Bowie and Erin discussed plans for their next venture. Along with the supplies he expected to seize from the British, Bowie had the stores he'd bought on his last voyage. They'd need every wagon they could find and many men to drive them.

"I've a bit of news you might find interesting." Bowie held her close, reluctant to let her go even for a moment.

"What's that?" she asked dreamily now that their business was concluded. "I'll tell Tupper that you'll stay for supper. Walter will be gone for the remainder of the evening."

Erin ran from the room and returned moments later. "Tupper is about to serve. Would you like to join me, Mr. Farthingale?"

"I'd be delighted, Miss Banning, if it won't be an imposition." Bowie took her arm and led her to the dining room. "I must say, you set a lovely table," he concluded after glancing at their supper.

"Well, Mr. Farthingale, my mother taught me that being a proper hostess is the most important duty of a lady." Erin sat down and placed her napkin in her lap.

Bowie walked to the other end of the table and did likewise. "Mayhap, I would disagree with that opinion, but I agree it's an asset."

Erin signaled to 'Lasses. As 'Lasses served their plates, the front door opened. Frantically Erin stared at the door to the dining room, praying that Walter hadn't returned. Through the open doorway, she saw him hand his hat to Nero. With a quick glance at Bowie to warn him, she called merrily, "Oh, Mr. Martin! Won't you join us?"

Walter spun around and looked at the two of them in surprise. "Why, greetings, Mr. Farthingale. Good evening, Miss Banning. If you'll give me a moment, I'll wash and return to join you."

He nodded and ran up the stairs. Erin turned to 'Lasses, who had frozen over Bowie's plate as she served soup. " 'Lasses, bring another place setting for Mr. Martin."

The moment Erin had prayed would never occur had arrived. With a pregnant glance at Bowie she prepared herself to spend the next hour with both Bowie and Walter.

When 'Lasses returned with silverware and plates, Erin whispered, " 'Lasses, serve the courses quickly. We don't want to linger at table."

Nodding, 'Lasses set a place for Walter and filled his bowl

with soup. Scurrying from the room, she grumbled and shook her head.

Walter returned to find Erin and Chauncey discussing the peculiar weather.

"Yes, one day is warm and the next is frigid. I do declare, one never knows quite how to dress," Chauncey said, almost whimpering.

Staring at Chauncey, Walter circled behind Erin and sat down at his place. "I'm sure you're right, *sir.*"

Erin noticed the emphasis on the word *sir* and almost giggled from the tension. Walter seemed to be as uncomfortable as she and Bowie were, except his reason was far different.

Undaunted, Chauncey continued "Why, Mr. Martin, I'm delighted you could join us. I do feel that we could become quite close friends."

Walter dropped his spoon and darted a glance at Erin as he muttered an apology. "I . . . I stay so busy, I have very little time for a social life."

Watching Walter squirm in his chair, Erin sipped her soup quietly. Chauncey, at the other end of the table, made a show of taking prim little tastes of the wonderful potato soup.

"Oh, I do say, this is a fine supper," Chauncey replied and arched his eyebrows thoughtfully. "I say, Mr. Martin, would you like to join me for a game of draughts later? I have a fine board in my room."

The spoon clattered from Walter's hand again, this time splashing soup on his clothes. "Oh, I seem to have soiled my shirt."

Chauncey jumped up and almost swooped down on Walter. "Here, dear sir, allow me to help you."

He dabbed at Walter's shirt with his napkin. Seemingly frantic, Walter glanced at Erin, almost imploring her to help him, but she was working too hard to cover the laughter that threatened to embarrass her further.

When he saw that Chauncey was about finished, Walter leapt from his chair toward Erin. He sidled over to her and took her hand as he eyed Chauncey warily. "You're most kind to invite me to dine with you, but I'm afraid I must return to my duties."

Walter almost ran from the room and up the stairs. Within two minutes he ran back down the stairs and out the front door without another word.

"Oh, my," Chauncey said and clapped his hands to his cheeks. "It seems that Mr. Martin is terribly upset about something."

"Why, I believe you're right." Erin giggled, picturing the frantic look on Walter's face when Bowie had come to wipe the soup off his shirt. "Strange man."

Bowie waited a few minutes to be sure Walter didn't return unexpectedly. "As I was about to say, I have good news."

"What?" Erin asked and dabbled at the corner of her mouth with her napkin.

"Morgan and Greene eluded Cornwallis successfully." Bowie grinned and nodded. "Fine work, eh? But there's some bad news, too."

"Oh, dear, what's that?" Erin asked and placed her fork across her plate.

"Major James Craig now occupies Wilmington." Bowie stood and walked to Erin's chair. "Let's go into the parlor. Does your father keep cigars around here?"

"Yes, I'll ask Nero to bring one for you." Erin found the servant and gave him instructions to bring a cigar. She returned to the parlor and found Bowie standing before the hearth. "He's coming."

In a few minutes, Nero entered carrying a box. He opened it and allowed Bowie to select his cigar.

When Nero left the room, Bowie took a candle from the mantel and lit his cigar. Puffing for a moment, he gazed at the fire. He felt terrible about Walter finding him here, but it hadn't been too bad. Walter couldn't have suspected anything or he would have remained. Nonetheless, Bowie vowed to be more careful the next time he called.

"Erin," he began and turned to face her. "We've got to

be careful. Walter isn't stupid, even though he's afraid of Chauncey Farthingale."

"I know. I was terrified the whole time he was here," Erin admitted. "I just knew he'd arrest you or . . . something worse."

Bowie held his cigar and stared at her. She didn't realize the danger she was in herself. He didn't want to frighten her unnecessarily, but she needed to be aware of the possibilities if Walter should discover their ruse. "I want you to be careful. Send me no more messages from here."

"But, Bowie, that's impossible. What if I hear—"

"No more. I won't endanger you further." He threw his cigar into the fire and sat down beside her. "Erin, you don't know the horrors of this war. This is a game to you, especially now when you're having so much fun at Walter's expense."

"I understand the ramifications of my actions," she retorted and jumped up. After pacing for a few seconds, she whirled and faced him. "I'm a soldier the same as you are. Neither of us wears a uniform, but we're both fighting for the same cause. I won't be treated like a child or a helpless woman because you feel some misplaced responsibility for my actions and my safety. We are partners—equal partners. When I hear something important, I'll come to your apartments."

"Misplaced responsibility? Under no circumstances will I allow you to put yourself in such danger." Bowie vaulted from the sofa and landed beside her. Shaking her gently, he felt the urge to rattle her brain. "Erin, this is serious. I *am* responsible for you. How can you say—"

Erin wrested free of his grip and strode behind the chair. "No. I refuse to let you feel responsible for me. I am an adult, a competent, capable woman who has successfully assumed a man's job. Like it or not, I'm your partner now. You have no more responsibility for me than you had for my father."

"But you're a woman. There is a difference, you know." Bowie walked toward her, his frustration demanding action.

"I am your partner, no less, no more." Erin strode from the room. When she reached the doorway, she turned and said, "Good night, Mr. Farthingale. Thank you for a pleasant evening."

Disappointed and angry, she ran up the stairs, taking them two at a time. When she reached her bedroom, she began to feel a little foolish for making such a dramatic exit, but Bowie had really made her angry. She had thought he recognized her intelligence and ability to act rationally in an emergency. She began to pace as she removed her gown, muttering to herself about the insensitivity of some men. After slipping into her wrapper, she flounced down at her dressing table and began to brush her hair. Pulling hard on a tangle, she winced in pain. After a while she heard the front door open and close.

"Wonderful, he's gone," she mumbled as she began to brush her long hair more carefully. "Doesn't pay to do this when I'm angry," she muttered.

Footsteps on the stairs startled her. "Must be Nero."

Without stopping, she continued to brush her hair until it gleamed. When the door opened, she spun on her seat, her mouth open in astonishment.

"Bowie!" she exclaimed and jumped up. "I thought you left."

"I started to, but I decided that this discussion wasn't finished just because you ran from it." Bowie closed the door behind him and started to walk toward her.

"I never did such a thing in my life. As far as I was concerned, we were through talking." Little shivers chased up and down her spine as he came closer and finally stopped when he was near enough for her to feel the gentle puffs of his breath on her cheeks.

"You may have been finished, but I wasn't." Bowie took her arms, holding her so that she couldn't run away this time.

"You're hurting me," she protested and wriggled to free herself from the man whose scowl frightened her as much as the possibility of an encounter with Tarleton himself.

"I'm not trying to hurt you, I'm trying to talk some sense into you." Bowie didn't release his grip immediately but pulled her closer and then wrapped his arms around her. He had to make her understand that one false move could jeopardize her life. Gazing down into deep green eyes glinting with gold that indicated the level of her anger, he opened his mouth to chastise her but found he couldn't speak.

Erin stopped struggling. His expression suddenly changed, softened, until he looked pleasant again. "What's . . . what's wrong?" she asked finally.

"I . . ." Bowie glanced at her mouth, full and sensual, open slightly and inviting.

He knew he had to escape, to get away from the spell cast by this delightful witch who had the prowess to make him forget everything except her. What power did she possess that lured him here?

Unable to resist any longer, Bowie bent down and kissed her. He clasped his arms around her in a caress, rather than the imprisoning state like before. Her slim body pressed against him as he felt the hostility leave her, and her mouth welcomed his kiss. Lifting her in his arms, he carried her to her bed and laid her across it.

Glancing down at her, Bowie felt a tightening in Chauncey's snug breeches and sat down beside her. When he lay down, his heart pounded in his chest like the strumming of the sails at full wind, and he knew she could hear it.

Making love to Erin would be the most pleasurable thing he'd done in a long time. He kissed her gently, enjoying the tender sigh that escaped from her lips as he pulled her into his arms again. Then he remembered Walter.

"What about the door?" he asked, looking down into her eyes.

"Lock it," she said dreamily, reaching up to kiss him again.

Bowie slid out of bed and crossed the room. He listened at the door and then locked it. Remembering the door to the morning room, he went over and locked it as well. Can't be too careful, he told himself and returned to Erin.

He hesitated, knowing that if he lay down again, he'd break his promise to himself. He saw the confusion in Erin's face as she watched him. Shrugging, he said, "Blast my promise to hell."

Removing his clothes, he silently cursed the tight-fitting breeches Chauncey Farthingale wore and wished for his own comfortable ones. Erin giggled as he worked hard to take off the breeches, and he cast a quelling glance at her.

Covering her mouth to hide her laughter, Erin felt giddy. Her nineteenth year had been a year of growth, and now she was about to take the final step in becoming a woman. A little frightened, a little eager, a little curious, she set about to take off her dressing gown.

Bowie was having so much trouble with his own clothes that she didn't want to waste any more time than was necessary, so she helped as much as she could. Naked, she settled back against her pillows and watched as he blew out the candles, leaving only the dim light from the fireplace.

Silhouetted against the glow of dying flames, Bowie's body aroused a passion in her she didn't realize she possessed. She longed to trace her fingers down the smooth planes of his chest to his narrow waist—and below to that place a lady would never mention, see, admit to knowing about, or even think about in the privacy of her room.

Try as she would, she couldn't get an inkling of how he looked below the waist, except for his long muscular legs. Frustrated that she could really see nothing because of the way he stood, she sighed and closed her eyes in anticipation of his kiss.

Bowie remained outside the covers for a few minutes, telling himself that he was giving her time to change her mind—but her mind seemed to be made up. He felt that he should talk with her, warn her about the step they were about to take.

"Erin, love, are you sure you want to do this?" he asked,

kissing her forehead. He prayed that she would say yes. He'd never wanted a woman as much as he wanted this one.

"Yes," she whispered.

"You know that once we do this, I mean when we . . . you'll never be the same. I mean, a woman's virginity is . . . Bowie stopped. He'd done a lot of things in his life that he was ashamed of, but he'd never taken advantage of a maiden. He sat up. "This is madness. We can't go on, Erin."

Her eyes sprang open. "What do you mean?"

"Erin, my darling, I want this as much as you think you want this." Bowie racked his brain for a way to tell her, to explain the consequences of this act. "What if you become pregnant? What of your future?"

"Pregnant?" Erin considered the point. She pictured herself hugging a small, wriggling creature that looked like Bowie. Startling blue eyes would stare at her from a tiny round face. A little fist would clench her finger, perhaps gnaw on it. She imagined the soft suckling that would occur when she fed the child, and a warmth spread all over her. Erin had never thought of having a child, but now she found that she really wanted one for the first time.

Bowie wished he could see what she was thinking. The slight furrows across her brow indicated that she was deep in thought. Was she changing her mind? Watching the changes that took place in her expression, he wondered what thoughts caused the little smile, the soft dreamy look, the quiet sigh.

Erin didn't know exactly what to say to him. Her mind was made up. She wanted him to make love to her; she accepted the consequences. How could she tell him? It wasn't exactly the sort of conversation she had every day. "Uh, Bowie, I—"

"Erin, I understand. We'll pretend this never happened." Bowie tried hard to disguise his disappointment. He shifted his weight to one knee and looked down at her. Beneath him, her bare breasts rose and fell as she breathed deeply. He looked at her face and didn't understand the puzzled expression. Why did she look so crestfallen?

She couldn't say the words; they refused to be voiced, no matter how hard she tried. Frustrated, she reached up and wrapped her arms around his neck, entwining her fingers to make sure he didn't move until he understood. Using the strength of his body for leverage, she pulled herself up and kissed him with every ounce of energy she possessed.

Bowie's eyes opened wide, and he stared at her. What was she doing? She couldn't intentionally be teasing him, because she wasn't that mean. He prized her arms from his neck and watched her lie back on the pillows, cursing himself all the while. "Erin, I don't think you understand. You can't do this to me and expect me to . . . to walk away. It just doesn't work that way. A man can't—"

"Don't talk, Bowie," she whispered and pulled him down beside her. "I can't talk . . . about this, but . . ."

Did he understand her? Erin searched his face for signs of comprehension and prayed that she wouldn't have to say or do any more. Color suffused her cheeks, and she knew she would simply die of humiliation if he didn't understand this time. She kissed him again, long and deep, thrusting her tongue in his mouth as he had in hers.

Bowie allowed her to kiss him, wondering if she didn't really understand the implications of her behavior. And then he didn't care. He wanted her, and he'd warned her. He could do no more except make this the most wonderful experience of her life.

He gathered her into his arms and began to shower her with tiny kisses, all up and down her neck, pausing briefly at the center where it joined with her chest. He moved to her earlobes and nibbled gently, touching his tongue to the tiny furrow that rimmed her ear. When she shivered in response, he continued his delicate assault.

Kissing her deeply, he slid beneath the bedclothes and pressed his body against hers. For a moment he felt her stiffen, but she gradually began to relax once again. The fragrance of her cologne mingled with the scent of the firewood and surrounded him with a pleasant aroma that intoxicated him. Bowie's blood raced in his veins, urging him on like the chant of a native dance.

Fire filled him with passion, and he kissed her breasts gently, feeling ecstatic when she moaned with pleasure at his gesture. Moving quickly, he planted butterfly-like kisses all over her breasts, pausing to tug gently on her large nipples, nibbling, teasing with his tongue.

Erin writhed beneath him, not understanding the flame that shot through her each time his lips or tongue touched her. Her body belonged to her no more; it was Bowie's to play like a fine instrument—and he played like a virtuoso.

She didn't realize what he was doing when he positioned himself above her, pausing to look into her eyes.

Cuddling her and kissing her, wanting to make this wonderful, Bowie took a moment to whisper, "Trust me, Erin. I won't hurt you."

Erin tried to smile, but her senses were so heightened that she couldn't even command the muscles in her own face. Then she felt the quick stab of pain as he plunged his tongue into her mouth simultaneously with the moment he entered her. Bowie hesitated, covering her face with kisses, cooing tender words in her ears, never stopping his fondling while he waited for her to catch her breath. When the pain lessened, she responded by returning his kiss.

Her blood sang in her veins, keeping time with Bowie's caresses. Erin felt as free as the birds that flew over the bay, rising and soaring on unseen bursts of wind. She'd never felt this way before—wild and willful as she tried to encourage Bowie to continue.

Erin's body writhed with Bowie's in a harmony all their own. When she felt she could stand no more, that her entire body would explode into a million tiny fragments of pleasure, he slowed his pace. Wondering why, she glanced up at him, afraid that he would stop.

From the expression on his face, Erin realized that he derived as much pleasure from this moment as she did. Relaxing, she mimicked his movements, matching his rhythm as best she could. And then it happened. Somewhere deep inside her the explosion materialized, and a wild shudder shook her entire body.

Bowie smiled. The groan that escaped Erin's lips told him she had achieved that precious moment of ecstasy, and he quickened his pace again. Feeling the beginning of his own rapture, he slowed to enjoy it fully. When it came, Bowie felt as though his entire body had been flared with passion that left him drained and breathless.

Lying beside her and gasping for air like a drowning man, he tried to put the experience into perspective. He'd never before reached gratification with such explosive power. Bowie cuddled Erin in his arms and clung to her, to the woman who could mysteriously command a performance that he didn't know he was capable of. Kissing her, he felt the stirring in his loins again and drew away. Why was this time different?

Erin smiled. Tingling from the ends of her hair to her toenails, she sighed happily. Bowie must love her. He couldn't have done what he'd done if he didn't.

And somewhere deep in the recesses of her body, had the first stirring of life occurred? Closing her eyes, she imagined Bowie holding their child, and in that moment she prayed that her dream would come true.

CHAPTER
12

ERIN LOOKED AT HERSELF IN THE GLASS PANELS BESIDE the door. Could she tell the difference in her face? Would anyone else notice the change?

Probably not. Her parents were the same as when she'd left them, except that her father's cold seemed to be better. Her mother didn't seem to notice that she'd been gone.

Erin studied her face again. She was a woman now in every sense of the word. She belonged to someone, truly belonged, even though the vows of marriage had not been said.

Any minute now Bowie would ride up and take her in his arms again. What would her father think? She hadn't told him about the change in her status, of course, but she knew that he perceived a difference in her. Humming, she wiped the condensation from the window and turned to go back to the parlor. Her bags were packed and stood waiting in the cupboard beneath the stairs.

Though Bowie would probably spend the night here at Bluffwood, Erin could hardly stand still; she was so eager to get back to the trail. Erin wanted to see Bowie, too. Remembering the moment when she'd made her decision to make love to him, she smiled. She felt giddy all over again, nothing at all like the prim-looking young woman who stood at the door awaiting the arrival of a friend.

Erin had come to think of that strange emotion that made her heart pound and made her feel funny inside, all quivery and fluid, as love. She didn't know exactly what the word entailed, for she seldom heard it used, but she decided that she was in love with Bowie Gallagher.

How would love change her life? She couldn't tell yet. Bowie hadn't said he loved her, although she suspected he did, for after that very special moment when each cell in her body seemed to explode with pleasure, he'd experienced a similar feeling, she thought. His face had screwed into a frown and was quickly replaced by the most angelic expression she'd ever seen.

She wondered if he felt the same as she did. Did his pleasure equal hers? She thought it couldn't possibly. That first time would always be the best, the most special, the most earthshaking.

Erin wondered how Bowie would greet her. Would he take her in his arms and kiss her—or pretend that nothing had happened between them? Oh, but she wished he would hurry! Tonight, after all the servants were asleep, she planned to sneak into his room and . . .

Bowie spotted the white columns of Bluffwood and slowed his horse. Somewhere within the confines of that lovely mansion, Erin awaited him. How did she feel? Had she realized what she'd done? What they'd done?

Would she hate him now for robbing her of the most precious gift a woman gives a man? Would she hate him as much as he hated himself for taking it? For his weakness?

"Damn," he swore under his breath and urged his horse forward. He hated to face her and fully expected to meet Arlen with a Brown Bess in his hands.

Bowie didn't know how he really felt about the act of love he'd experienced with Erin. It was very different from the times before with other women. He couldn't really understand what had happened to cause the change. Maybe he was learning more about the act itself.

He didn't want to believe it, but somewhere deep inside a little voice kept saying that Erin was the catalyst that precipitated the vast difference in his experience. Without a doubt he cared for her, but Bowie wasn't the kind of man who needed a wife. He refused to admit that his parents' marriage—if that travesty of the institution could be called a marriage—affected his decision to avoid entanglements.

Bowie's chosen way of life was dangerous. Even after the war he wouldn't sit on the porch whittling animals from a piece of wood; he'd be back at sea, fighting the elements of nature. He couldn't be concerned about a wife waiting and worrying alone. He didn't want to be forced to return to a specific place called home. He no longer had a home, not since his father had ordered him to leave Edisto.

Home was an elusive place that few people ever found, or so Bowie thought. It had nothing to do with walls and a chimney. It had to do with the heart, and the heart couldn't be trusted. Even after years of marriage his parents hadn't discovered that they really had no home, but only a place to live and be unhappy.

Would life with Erin be like that? he wondered and concluded that it probably would be wonderful at first. Then the problems would begin. He grinned when he thought of her feisty spirit and the passion he'd discovered. Could spirit and passion overcome the nagging devils that intruded on a marriage and killed it before it could blossom into its special splendor?

Bowie was concentrating on his thoughts so hard that when he rode into the low-hanging limb, it caught him off-guard and toppled him to the ground. "Damn!" he shouted and scrambled to his feet.

His horse stood a few feet away and nickered. If Bowie didn't know better, he'd think the horse was laughing at him. "Damn you for the nag you are, riding right under that limb. I ought to . . ."

Realizing how ridiculous he must look, standing there cursing at his horse, Bowie found his hat and put it on. Climbing back into the saddle, he muttered, "If this happens again, you're bound for the wagon trains. You've got a nice job, not too much strain, so you'd better act accordingly."

Feeling a little foolish, Bowie glanced around to see if

anyone had seen him. Luckily, he could see no one, so he rode out of the woods as if nothing had happened.

Erin saw him coming. Fighting the urge to run out of the house, race down the slope, and fling herself into his arms, she merely left her bedroom and walked calmly down the stairs. Her carefully schooled demeanor masked a wild, fluttering heart and enough uncertainties to drive her to the brandy decanter—almost.

Like most youngsters, she'd tried her father's brandy once and found it so awful that she swore she'd never drink the stuff again. She couldn't understand what men could find remotely satisfying in the horrible drink and stinking cigars, but then there was a lot she didn't understand about men.

When she reached the bottom stair, she hesitated. Should she open the door herself or wait for one of the servants to do it? She bit her lip and fluctuated from one decision to the other, finally settling on the latter.

Erin didn't want Bowie to know how eager she was to see him again. She wanted time to gauge his response before she exposed herself to the possibility of being rebuffed.

She sat on a chair by the fireplace. "No, that looks too prim," she told herself and moved to a standing position by the hearth. Her deep green woolen gown hung gracefully around her, and Erin took one last peek at herself in the mirror. Her hair hung in curls down her back, tied by a single emerald satin ribbon—the one that Bowie had brought her. Would he remember?

Bowie expected Erin to answer his knock, but she didn't. A servant he hadn't seen before conducted him into the parlor, where Erin stood by the fire with her back to him. Her hair hung in a mass of auburn curls to her waist, and the picture took his breath away. When the servant announced him, Erin turned slightly and smiled. She was alone in the room.

She was wearing his ribbon. He returned her smile while

he waited for the servant to leave. "Good afternoon, Miss Banning."

Erin held her breath. She thought Sadie would never leave. Carefully monitoring her voice to disguise the tremble, she replied as formally as he. "Good afternoon, Mr. Gallagher. How nice to see you again. My parents were unable to join us."

For a moment Bowie was puzzled. Why was she acting so stiff? He turned and confirmed that the servant was gone, then faced Erin again. Now he could see the confusion in her face. She was trying desperately to hide her feelings as much as he was.

He took a hesitant step toward her and then broke into a run. Ignoring his vows to remain on friendly terms, he caught her when she dashed across the wide room and almost leapt into his arms.

The hunger that her kiss conveyed told him plainly that she hadn't regretted their act of love. His own response to her told him just as plainly that he'd never keep his vows where she was concerned. But as Bowie held her, relishing the knowledge that she invigorated his life by her presence, he wondered where the relationship would go, what possible meaning it could have in his life when he had vowed never to marry. As he'd so recently discovered, however, he was unable to keep his vows concerning Erin Banning.

After supper they sat in the parlor by the fire and talked. Erin peered across the distance and watched Bowie fidget with his fingers like a nervous child. He'd seemed distracted all during supper, but she couldn't discover why.

"Did the ambush go as you expected?" she asked, finally breaching the subject he seemed to want to avoid.

"What?" Bowie jerked to attention. He'd been lost in thought about Erin's passion, a passion that rose to the surface at the slightest touch. Her eyes glittered like emeralds flecked with gold. He considered the involuntary gasp he thought he heard every time he accidentally touched her. Now he was beginning to wonder if his touches were all accidental.

"I asked if the ambush went as you expected," Erin repeated and watched him shift in his chair.

Bowie didn't want to talk about it. As he'd expected, the British provided more guards—more alert guards—this time, and a skirmish had ensued. Bowie had lost a good man, but the British casualties were much higher. Still, he didn't like fighting.

He never could stand his parents' bickering at home and he hated the war, although he believed with all his heart in the rightness of the Patriots' position. Standing abruptly, he looked down at Erin. How much could he tell her? How much did she really want to know?

Pacing, he hesitated to tell her anything. She had assumed the responsibility of her part in this war with such alacrity that he didn't want to discourage her, although she had every right to know. He stood in front of her, gazing down into her expectant face, a face that made him want to forget everything and kiss her worries away.

"We expected extra guards, and they were expecting us. I don't know whether they just figured that since we'd stolen from them once, we'd try again or just got lucky." Bowie strode to the fireplace and leaned against the mantel.

Erin nodded grimly. She sensed that Bowie was uncertain about how much to tell her. After all, she was *just* a woman, as he'd said often enough. "Tell me . . . everything," she insisted, not quite sure that she really wanted to know.

"I lost a good man. A sailor. He'd been with me for years, ever since I first took to sea." Bowie turned and faced her, trying to gauge her reaction to the bad news.

Struggling to fight tears that threatened to flow, Erin dropped her face in her hands and closed her eyes. She was responsible, as responsible as if she'd pulled the trigger or lunged with the bayonet. William's eager face swam before her closed eyes. "What about William? Do you know if . . ."

Bowie had hoped she wouldn't ask about William. The young soldier was a nice enough boy but a lousy soldier. "He was injured."

Erin looked up at Bowie. She jumped to her feet and took

his hands. "Not dead? Just injured? Where is he now? Can we bring him here? Is someone caring for him?"

"We took him captive. I doubt whether he could have made it back to Charleston," Bowie admitted and slipped his arms around her shoulders. So much weight during this war, he mused, for such delicate bones.

"Will he . . . will he survive?" Erin asked finally. She gazed directly into Bowie's eyes. She wanted to see the expression on his face when he answered.

Bowie sighed and arched his eyebrows. Her eyes demanded honesty. "I don't know."

Erin leaned against him, taking what comfort he offered. "Can we bring him here?" she repeated.

"It could be dangerous. What if he—"

"Bowie, I'm responsible for his injury . . . for his life. Don't deny me this opportunity to help him. I can work it out safely." She wanted time to think about this, to think about what she was doing. Dear God, but she hated war and injury and death. Why wouldn't the British go home?

Hours later Erin lay awake, staring at the ceiling. The last sounds of life had died down some time ago, and she hesitated to get up. She intended to go to Bowie's room, to revive the wonderful feelings she'd put aside for the past few days.

She wondered if he was sleeping? Was he lying awake, too? Was he thinking of her?

There was but one way to find out. Erin slid out of bed and slipped on her wrapper. Taking a candle, she hurried out her door and down the hallway to Bowie's room.

Outside his door, she listened for sounds that would indicate whether or not he was sleeping. She could hear nothing.

What if he locked his door?" she thought and then glanced up and down the hallway. With shaking hands, she touched the cold brass doorknob and twisted. It gave easily, and she let herself in.

The bed was empty. She turned quickly, looking about

the room, and found him standing behind her with a poker in his hand. "Were you planning to kill me?"

Sighing with relief that he was awake, she placed the candle on a table. Their relationship was still too new for her to put her feelings into words. She couldn't say she'd come to make love to him, not yet. "I . . . I couldn't sleep."

The distance between them seemed like a chasm of monumental proportions to Bowie. He took her in his arms and clung to her as if she were his very lifeblood. "I'm glad you came," he whispered.

"I . . . I'm sorry if I disturbed you, but—"

"Don't talk," he interrupted and lifted her into his arms. Carrying her to the bed, he marveled that such a delicate, gently bred young woman would have the courage to enter his room, but he'd witnessed her courage in other situations and knew that she was not like other women.

Sunlight dappled the comforter as Erin stretched and yawned. "Oh, my goodness!" she exclaimed and looked at Bowie. His grin told her he'd been awake for a few minutes longer than she.

She jumped out of bed, slipped on her gown and wrapper, and peeked into the hallway. Wondering if anyone had discovered that she hadn't slept in her bed, she scurried down the corridor and into her own room, thanking the gods for hiding her secret rendezvous. Her parents were still unable to be about much because of their illnesses.

Within an hour's time she and Bowie were on horseback heading across the wide yard that surrounded Bluffwood toward the wagon camp. Out back, indigo fields were fallow and covered with frost, but the grass in the front looked like snow had fallen during the night.

"A heavy frost," she said and glanced at Bowie, wondering when she would find the courage to say the words she longed to say to him.

"Sure is. Almost like a snowfall." Bowie glanced at the plantation. Bluffwood was every bit as large as his parents' plantation and just as beautiful, but in a different way. He could feel at home here.

They rode in silence for a few minutes before he spoke again. "Look, Erin, I want you to be extra careful this trip. We've tweaked the noses of the British too often, and they're likely to be looking for revenge."

"I promise to be careful," Erin said as contritely as possible, knowing that arguing with him would be useless. After he'd told her about the ambush, she'd decided to double the guards and take extra precautions during the journey, but she let him continue to give her advice.

"You might double the guards at night. You've got enough men for that." Bowie glanced at her to see if she was listening. It wasn't like her to accept his advice without a fight. "Is something wrong?"

"Wrong? No, why do you ask?" Erin turned to face him. She thought that if she acceded to his wishes, she could avoid a confrontation with him, one she didn't feel like engaging in this morning. The day was too crisp and beautiful—and she felt wonderful and happy, almost glowing with joy.

He studied her. There seemed to be something different about her, something almost imperceptible. "I don't know. You just don't seem like yourself today."

Smiling, Erin nodded. "You're right. I'm not myself. I feel wonderful, free, and excited."

Bowie didn't know how to interpret her statement, but he knew she wasn't being coy or evasive. "All right. Tell me about the plans you've already made."

The smile faded from Erin's face. She hadn't wanted to tell him anything about her plans because she wanted him to feel like he was protecting her in some small way. "I decided last night when you told me about the problems you encountered that I would double the guard and that we would proceed with extraordinary caution, even though the trip would take longer."

"Then why didn't you stop me from rattling my head like that? We could have been talking about something else."

Bowie wasn't really irritated, but he was angry with himself for misjudging her again. She'd proven to be resourceful and intelligent; why couldn't he accept that and treat her as an equal? "Erin, honestly, next time don't let me go on like that. I . . . I know you deserve better. It's just that I'm not used to women who use their brains for anything other than selecting ribbons and geegaws for dresses."

Erin felt color sting her cheeks. He actually admitted that she was smart enough to plan her own safety measures. What a change from the night she'd told him she wanted to drive the supply wagon. Feeling a tender warmth deep inside, she smiled. "I can always use your advice, Bowie."

They reached the encampment and had no more time to discuss anything. All the men gathered around Erin as if they were eager to talk with her again and happy to see her pretty face, as if they acknowledged her as their leader. Bowie helped her dismount, and they walked among the men to one of the wagons.

Since the confrontation with the British, Bowie had refused to allow the men to have a fire. He hoped that Erin would have the good sense to do the same, but he knew she would. He lifted her into the wagon and watched as she transformed herself from a delicate young lady into the leader of the wagon train.

"Men," she said and smiled, a smile that touched her eyes with joy, "I'm glad to be back with you again. This trip won't be the pleasant jaunt we took before. This time we're in for some hard work, unpleasant living conditions, and a . . . a damn angry British Army."

The men chuckled, and Jimbo grinned. "Yeah, but they ain't got Miss Erin Banning for a leader."

Bowie stepped back and watched as Erin outlined her plan for their success. Marveling at how well she handled herself and fielded their questions, he smiled, knowing he'd discovered her. That made him as proud as if she belonged to him.

Belonged. He hadn't belonged anywhere or to anyone for a long time. Could Erin belong to him and he to her? Would it work, or would they come to hate each other as his parents did? Would his and Erin's home always be a home, or would it become a prison?

Funny, but he sort of liked the idea of coming home to Erin Banning more and more.

CHAPTER
13

With a blanket over his arm Bowie approached Erin. Her men were gathered around her, chattering about everything that had happened to them since they'd seen her last. Smiles of pleasure were on every face. He threaded his way among the men and caught the end of her remarks.

"So we'll be more careful than ever. Nobody outside of this little group is to be trusted. We can't know for sure who's with us and who's against us." Erin glanced at Bowie and, noticing the blanket, felt herself flush with color. "That's all for now. We'll be pulling out as soon as we get all our gear stored. Jimbo is my second in command. In my absence you will obey his orders. Should we become separated, our mission remains the same. Those of us who can do so will deliver our goods to the Continentals. Prepare for the worst."

"Let's go and talk," Bowie said and took her by the hand. As they walked across the clearing, he noticed Jimbo watching them. For some reason the crusty old soldier wore a grin that baffled Bowie. Sidney wore the same silly grin as Jimbo, except that Sidney had more teeth.

Talk? Erin wondered why they were going somewhere to talk when they could talk right there. But the blanket said more than Bowie's words.

They stepped across a narrow creek and a felled tree before he looked around and decided to stop. "This place is fine. I just wanted to get out of hearing distance of the men. 'Lasses, too."

Erin, too, wanted to get away from 'Lasses. The servant would scold Erin for going off with Bowie, but she didn't care, not today. Too soon they would be separated for several weeks, and Erin didn't know how she could ever stand the loneliness she felt every time she thought of leaving him.

Bowie excited her. Even the touch of his hand on hers sent tingles of power through her that she'd never known before. She felt grown and mature, giddy and girlish, playful and passionate, the way a woman should feel when she was with the man she loved.

Did Mama ever feel this way about Papa? she wondered as she sat on the blanket feeling the joy of being alive and free to choose her husband. Not so many years ago, husbands were chosen for women. Erin wondered if Papa would have selected Bowie for her. She wanted to think he would have, if circumstances were different. Husband? Was she thinking of Bowie as a husband when he'd never indicated that he loved her?

Settling on the blanket beside Erin, Bowie draped his arm across her comfortably and tried to decide what to say. He didn't really have anything particular in mind when he picked up the blanket, but now, with Erin so close and smelling so sweet, every rational thought fled his mind. He shifted slightly so that her body was nearer than when he'd sat down.

"Well, what did you want?" Erin asked, tucking her feet beneath her wide green skirt.

Bowie caught a glimpse of her big, bulky boots and stared. "Are those your boots?"

Erin grinned. "They're Papa's. My guns fit inside them better than in my own."

Sighing with relief, Bowie hugged her. "I'd lo—like you even with feet that big."

Love—he'd almost said *love*. What was wrong with him? He'd vowed never to fall in love, and here he was expressing that very emotion to Erin. Did he mean it or was it merely a slip? He didn't want to mislead her about his feelings, nor did he want to mislead himself. This was something Bowie would have to think about—long and hard—when he was alone and without Erin's influence.

Not that he thought she would try to influence him in any way. She'd accepted their lovemaking without stipulation, without any promises on his part. His admiration for her rose once again. Erin was like no other woman.

"Bowie?" Erin touched Bowie's hand. He looked as though his thoughts were miles away, and she wondered briefly if he was thinking of another woman, someone more sophisticated and experienced than she. With that thought came the image of Bowie with his arms around someone else, kissing someone else, and Erin felt a flash of jealousy, but she quickly overcame it. She hadn't any right to demand loyalty in him, and she didn't want him to know that she was jealous. She couldn't let him know she wondered about where he went and whom he was with when he left her. "Did you bring me all the way out here to ask about my boots?"

"What? Uh, no. Of course not." Bowie was caught daydreaming by her question. He grinned and kissed her forehead. "Your boots are lovely. Actually they're good for the trail. I presume you have your own boots inside those."

"Yes. My boots, the padding, and Papa's boots keep my feet very warm, although I'm pretty clumsy when I wear all that," she admitted, wondering where his questions were leading. Bowie wasn't the kind of man to bring her away from a job that was vital to the war effort merely to discuss her footwear.

"You have gloves and a muff?" he asked, feeling more like a mammy than Erin's lover. Why couldn't he say the things he really wanted to say to her? Maybe Erin's innocent smile melted the words before they left his mouth. Well, some things had to be said, and there was nobody to say them but him. He'd have to find a way to do it. "Erin, this isn't easy for me to say, but—"

"Then just say it. Don't waffle on about my boots when you have more important matters to discuss." Erin looked up at him, admiring his profile in the warm sunlight. His slightly patrician nose made him even more handsome in a strong, rugged way she hadn't noticed before. She'd always thought him handsome with great strength and character in his face, but now she really studied him. Any other combination of features would have lacked distinction. The slightly curling light brown hair, those wonderful sapphire eyes that pierced and probed when he caught a hint of something that interested him, his high, prominent cheekbones, all set him above the other men she knew.

She'd seen him angry, sad, anxious, loving, laughing— and she cherished every moment, every expression. This one, Erin decided, could be nothing but love. Shakespeare wrote of it, and she'd read enough of his sonnets to know what love should be like, but until recently she had never applied that emotion to any relationship she'd ever had.

"Erin," he said, still wondering how to explain the things that troubled him about their relationship. "Erin, my dear, you are an innocent, a lovely innocent, in the ways of the world. You've got to be careful how you share your . . ." Now he'd really tangled himself in his sails. How could he get out of this mess? Blunder on, old salt, he told himself. "How you share your love. You and I . . . What I mean to say is . . . You can't just go around and . . . Men can't be trusted."

Erin watched the emotions play across his face. He bit his lip; he scowled; his forehead wrinkled. He sounded like 'Lasses giving Erin a scolding for smiling at a strange man. She giggled at the thought. "Bowie, are you trying to give me a lesson in ladylike behavior?"

"Of course not," he denied, although that was exactly what he was doing. His shoulders sagged in the light of her perception. "That's not what I want to do at all. It's just that, well . . . well, damnation, Erin, you can't let men take advantage of you, and we certainly will do it given the opportunity."

Erin's face flamed. "How dare you accuse me of loose behavior? You well know that there was no man before you, yet you automatically assume that there will be a steady stream of others." She jumped to her feet, squared her shoulders, and placed her hands on her hips as she glared down at him.

"Wait a minute, I merely—"

"Hush up and let me finish," Erin commanded. "I don't know what your problem is, but you're either the most insecure man I've ever known or you think I'm some peabrained schoolgirl with nothing but feathers filling her head."

Bowie rose and put out his hand, only to have it slapped away by his furious companion. "That's not it at all, Erin, I'm just trying to warn you—"

"You're trying to run my life. I'm an adult, not a child you have to diaper, feed, and control, and you're not my father or my mammy." Erin grew angrier as she spoke, and she began pacing in front of him. "Leave. Go on before I say something I'll be ashamed of later."

Ashamed. Bowie felt ashamed. He'd meant to be helpful, but instead he'd allowed himself to become parental. "Look, Erin, I know you're an intelligent adult. It was never my intention to preach or—"

Erin glared at him. Why wouldn't he go away and leave her alone? She wanted to hate him, to loathe him. "That may not have been your intention, but that's what you did."

Feeling a little encouraged that she hadn't physically attacked him or stomped away, Bowie continued. "I wasn't trying to dictate your behavior—God knows I have no right—but trying to warn you against others."

"I know about men. I've dealt with them all of my life." Erin lifted her chin and gazed into the deepest blue eyes she'd ever seen. Why, oh why, did he have to be so handsome? Why did his eyes have to draw her like a magnet draws metal? Why had she given her heart to him? "And now I've dealt with the likes of you. There are no surprises left for me."

"Erin, I can't leave you like this. We've got to find common ground again. We've—"

"Common ground? Does that mean you want to make

love to me here on this blanket? Is that why you brought it?" Erin pointed to the wrinkled blanket where she'd been sitting so happily moments ago.

"That's not what I meant at all. You're being unfair." Bowie's frustration stemmed not from Erin's misunderstanding of his words but from his own mishandling of the entire matter.

Why was he such a fool around her? He would have been much better off kissing and cuddling her before sending her off to face the British Army alone. Damn, but he wished he could go along. Something was bound to happen; she would need him. But the Patriots also needed him, and before he could think of himself, he was honorbound to do his duty, and that duty took him to tropical ports for supplies that the men desperately needed.

Without further thought he grabbed her and drew her into his embrace. He expected a fight and wasn't disappointed. While he lowered his lips to hers, the little hellcat fought him with all she had. He could hardly hold her at first, but after a few moments her rigid muscles relaxed, and she leaned against him, accepting his kiss.

Erin wanted the kiss to last forever, to silence the voices that still raged in her head, but she knew it couldn't. When Bowie drew away, she lay her head on his shoulder in acceptance of his silent apology. She sensed what he meant to say, but that didn't make hearing it any easier. She'd done something that simply wasn't done; how could she expect any other reaction?

"Erin," he began again, this time choosing his words more carefully. "Please be careful. When you return, we need to talk about . . . about us. We're in a delicate situation, and we need to decide . . . something."

Erin warmed to his words. Us. He'd said us for the first time, perhaps including her in his future. That would have to be enough for now.

Bowie picked up the blanket, and they walked hand in hand back to the others. He'd nearly made a fatal mistake. Never again would he underestimate Erin. He should have known better this time. She would exercise care and caution during the trip—and in her relationships. Erin's intelligence would provide a barrier between her and harm—he hoped.

Erin couldn't look back. She knew that Bowie and his men hadn't left, that they were watching the little band as they rode north. She fought the urge to turn, to run back to Bowie for one last kiss, for one last caress before she started on this arduous journey.

With Lord Cornwallis and Tarleton so furious over the victory at the Cowpens and Morgan's escape, Erin would have to be extremely careful. Her band could light no fires, so the nights would be cold and damp.

The March winds tore through the trees and found ways to bring the chill air to Erin's skin. No matter how she tucked her cloak around her, no matter how tightly she wound her kerchief, no matter how low she crouched in the seat, the cold wind found her. But she wouldn't complain.

Her men, as she'd come to think of them, were not as well off as she. They didn't have cloaks as thick and warm as hers; their boots were often dappled with holes and tears; their caps left their ears exposed; and their breeches were more often made of homespun than wool.

She'd have to find warmer clothing for them. The men fighting for freedom needed warm clothing and good shoes, much as her own men did, perhaps even more. That was the reason she was risking her own life to drive this cursed wagon up this rutted road, bruising her backside and jostling about until she could hardly think.

Erin didn't really want to think. Her feelings for Bowie had been one-sided until today. Guilt beset her as she recalled with a flushed face the intimacy she'd allowed—no, invited—from him. What could she have been thinking of to have ventured so far from her own good sense, not to mention the thousands of sermons she'd endured from 'Lasses?

Glancing at the servant who rode in the bed of the wagon, Erin grimaced. The look on 'Lasses' face said that she was suspicious of Erin and Bowie. She'd have to be extremely careful how she acted around the woman who had reared her to be a lady.

What of Bowie? Erin wondered. How did he really feel about her? Was it possible that the exquisite moments they'd shared meant nothing to him, no more than if he didn't know her name, no more than if she'd been a woman from the wharves? Could he not feel the marvelous staccato pulse of blood racing through his veins? Could he ignore the exciting moments when they became one, in a powerful rage of passion that refused to be bridled?

Erin wanted to believe he could not. "Could it be the same with every coupling?"

"Whadya say, Missy?" Jimbo asked and peered at her beneath the rim of a worn hat.

"Say?" Erin's cheeks flamed with color. She hadn't realized she'd spoken aloud. How much had she said and how much had he heard? Grasping at anything to hide her embarrassment, she murmured, "The horses. What a fine couple of horses."

"Horses?" he asked and glanced at the animals pulling the wagon. "Them is mules as sure as I'm a settin' on this consarn hard wagon bench."

"Mules," she repeated and tried to smile. "I meant mules. I . . . I can't think what got into me." Erin had to do something to get her mind off Bowie. "Here, give me the reins a while."

Slowly he handed the worn leather to Erin. "Careful, Missy. Them mules ain't used to a lady's hand."

"They'll be fine." Erin liked the feeling of power over the mules. She had no power over anything else—or anybody else—but she enjoyed being a part of a team. "Jimbo, why don't you ride about and see if anybody needs anything?"

When Erin stopped, Jimbo jumped down and walked to the horse tied to the wagon's back gate. "I'll be quick about it, Missy."

"Erin," she called after him.

Alone except for 'Lasses, who sat in the back, Erin flicked

the reins and cooed to the mules. The wagon jolted as the mules began to plod down the wagon road.

If she followed this road far enough, she'd end up in Philadelphia. She'd ridden that far with her father more than once. The trips had been exciting to her as a child, much as they were now. During those fun excursions, she'd pretended she was a pioneer headed toward the unknown, toward danger, toward freedom.

Like all pioneers, Erin embraced that freedom wholeheartedly. She had fewer restrictions than most young women she knew, however, because of her mother's condition and her father's secret occupation; she had grown accustomed to making her own decisions and choosing her own path.

She had chosen her path, and it had led to intimacy with a man who was almost a stranger to her. It had led to falling in love with a man who might not share her feelings. Where else would such a wanton path lead her? she wondered.

Still cursing himself, Bowie had watched Erin ride away. He knew he should go with her. That feeling nagged him for the rest of the day. He decided that when he left Charleston within the next few days, he'd make a quick run. He wanted to be nearby in case Erin needed him.

With Sidney at his side, Bowie rode hard and fast toward the little cove where he hid his ship. After a few repairs he'd set sail. As much as he wanted to feel the rise and fall of the deck under his feet, he was reluctant to leave. Something about this journey bothered him, although he didn't know exactly what it was.

William Fuller lay in a cot on Bowie's ship, recovering from injuries received in the fray between the Patriots and the British soldiers guarding the since-pirated supplies. Bowie wanted to talk to the soldier about the mission, to see if the Patriots were riding into an ambush designed to capture the men transporting supplies to the Continental Army.

Bowie knew that his ability to operate in Charleston depended on his dual identity. If William Fuller suspected that Bowie Gallagher and Chauncey Farthingale were one and the same, then Erin's life would be in jeopardy, particularly since Walter Martin had found Chauncey dining with Erin. Bad company for a Loyalist to keep.

What was Erin doing now? Would she hate him forever or would she find the generosity within herself to forgive him? Erin Banning was an extraordinary woman; he hoped he hadn't destroyed the tenuous thread that bound them together.

Bowie looked around. He'd stayed with Erin so long that darkness would fall before he reached his ship. In the twilight Bowie could easily make out the road, but little else.

"Ho, sir," Sidney called in a low voice and grabbed Bowie's reins. "Riders coming."

Bowie didn't stop to listen. He turned his horse and rode into the dark shadows of the woods by the road. They didn't go too far because of the noise that would be caused by the dry leaves and twigs underfoot. Stopping by a large fir tree where they could hide, he slid from his horse's back and handed his reins to Sidney.

Stepping carefully, Bowie moved back toward the road to see who was traveling this late in the day and headed away from Charleston. When he came close to the road, he crouched on the ground beneath a scrubby bush and waited.

British troops, Bowie told himself as he spotted the red woolen coats in the growing darkness.

Erin! How far had she gone? Were these men following information that would lead them to Erin and her crew? Of course not, he chided himself. These men were no more than patrols that rode the outskirts of Charleston routinely.

He'd come farther than he thought. Darkness was falling, and he could hardly see the men, but he counted six. Undoubtedly a patrol, he reaffirmed to himself and allowed himself to breathe normally. Bowie waited until the men were past him, then returned to his horse and mounted. He waited for several minutes more.

He didn't want to risk making a noise that would attract

their attention. Though he felt that he and Sidney could easily defeat these few men, Bowie couldn't risk the encounter this close to his ship.

Pistols drawn, Sidney watched alongside Bowie. When the riders were past and out of hearing distance, Bowie and Sidney regained the road and continued toward the *Midnight Star.*

Above Erin the stars sparkled with an intensity rarely seen in Charleston. The cold clear night provided a panorama of constellations that would thrill even the most experienced astronomer. Rising about the treetops, the moon bathed her in a golden glow as she lay on her blanket and tugged her fur skins tighter about her to keep out the cold air.

Erin and 'Lasses were sleeping beneath one of the wagons on a bed of pine needles and leaves. They'd pulled off the main road and found a clearing large enough for all the wagons to fit. There'd been an inn here years ago when she'd traveled with her father, but now there was nothing more than a chimney standing vigilantly over a pile of blackened timbers.

Her dinner of cold bread, cheese, and coffee had formed a lump in her stomach that wouldn't dissolve. When she thought of the fine meals she could have been enjoying at home, Erin felt a little homesick. Thinking of roast duckling, fresh steamed oysters, and flummery reminded her of Bowie and the meal they'd shared on Christmas night.

Was that when she'd started falling in love with him? No. She wasn't in love. That couldn't be right. She wanted to think she was in love to excuse her behavior where he was concerned. She could never love a sea captain. Their lives were so uncertain, the time they were at sea too long. Erin needed someone more like herself—someone who would love Bluffwood as she did, someone who would be content to stay there and help her run the plantation. If she felt anything at all for him, it was nothing more than friendship resulting from their business dealings.

Erin Banning did not love Bowie Gallagher. She didn't.
She couldn't. She wouldn't.

When Bowie arrived at the *Midnight Star,* he inquired
about the health of his prisoner, William Fuller. Fuller was
not really a prisoner, but he was being held hostage because
that was the only way to save his life. Bowie had withheld
that information from Erin and was glad when she didn't
ask too many questions about the fray.

Without hesitating further, Bowie went to his cabin and
sat at his desk. He recorded a few notes in his journal and
then leaned his chair back with his feet propped on the desk.
Though he knew he'd be heading to sea within a few days,
Bowie didn't relish the idea.

He thought that Erin was vulnerable, more so this time
than before, and he ought to be there to help her. "Damn
this war and every British soldier in South Carolina!" Bowie
slapped his leg in disgust and then suddenly toppled back-
ward to the floor with a crash.

Scrambling to his feet, Bowie looked around in time to
see Sidney burst through the door, his pistol drawn and
cocked. "What is it, mate?"

Bowie dusted off his breeches and righted the chair before
he spoke. "Damn chair toppled over with me aboard."

Sidney grinned, even though he tried hard not to. "My
reckoning is that you should be picking your *ride* like you'd
pick one for a lady—if you can't ride no better'n that."

"And my reckoning is that if you don't want your neck
stretched, you'll be picking your words more carefully like
you'd pick for a lady, or the captain of this vessel will—"

"Mate, you sold me. I'll just be scuttlin' back to me cabin
for a bit of a nap." Still grinning broadly, Sidney backed
out the door and closed it behind him.

"Picking your ride," Bowie muttered and flopped across
his cot. "Got a lot of face saying something like that to me."

Lying back, he thought of Erin again. Unable to rest, he
jumped up and began to pace. He couldn't decide why he

felt so uneasy about this trip, but he did. Was he sending her into a greater danger than he'd believed?

"Damn this not knowing." Bowie strode across the floor, his boots thudding on the worn wood, swung the door open, and shouted, "Sidney! Get your worthless hide in here."

Whirling, he moved back to the center of the room and resumed his pacing. "Something's wrong. I can't figure it, but something is wrong. I feel it. I know it."

Sidney poked his head into the room and watched for a moment. "A body won't ever rest with you hollerin' like a hog on butcherin' day."

"Rest? Forget rest. I need to talk, and you're the only person I can talk to." Bowie dropped onto his cot again and motioned for Sidney to take the chair.

"And exactly what sort of talk were you thinkin' of? Is this to be a father-son sort of talk, or were you—"

"Blast you, Sidney." Bowie glared at his friend, but relaxed a little. "I feel something deep inside. I can't figure it out, but I think I sent Erin into a trap."

"Ah, it *is* to be a father-son talk." Sidney grinned and pulled the remains of a well-chewed cigar from his pocket. "Erin, is it? I'm a-thinkin' that Miss Banning is a capable lass that don't need no lookin' after from you."

Bowie shot Sidney a look that seemed to quell his humorous approach to the subject. Bowie propped himself up on one elbow and studied his friend. The man was about ten years older than Bowie, and much broader in the chest and hips. Bowie considered Sidney's appraisal of Erin for a moment.

"Well, sir, if you don't mind me a-sayin' so, Miss Banning is as bright as a copper kettle before it's been kissed by a fire." Sidney draped one leg across the arm of the chair and continued to chew on the stub of his cigar.

"Bright is one thing, Sid." Bowie stood up and paced a few times before continuing. "I think those British dogs set a trap for her. I think we should go after her."

"And just where might you be a-doin' that thinkin', sir?

In your head or in your loins?" Sidney removed his cigar and dropped it in the spittoon near the desk.

Bowie spun around and stared at his friend. "Just what is that supposed to mean? I think you've been spending too much time ashore, and it's addled your brain."

"Aye, I've been spendin' too much time ashore. And there's another sail stiff with that same wind, if ya' get my drift." Sidney propped his feet on the desk as Bowie had done earlier and grinned widely. "Now, don't mind me none, I ain't got nothin' agin' chasin' skirts, but—"

"Chasing skirts? Is that what you think I'm doing?" Bowie began to pace again. He knew that Sidney was wrong, but proving it to an old salt like him would be nearly impossible. Bowie slowly dropped back to his cot. "Sid, you know that's not true."

"Well, let's just say your loyalties are divided and leave it at that." Sidney lowered the front chair legs to the floor and stood up. "Will you be needin' me for anything else?"

Bowie glanced up with a puzzled look on his face. Sidney was as good as saying he was through talking. Bowie was by no means finished. "If you don't sit down and talk seriously with me, I'll have you strung up on the crow's nest to flap like a skull and crossbones in the wind."

Chuckling, Sidney sat back down and crossed his arms. "Carry on, sir."

Bowie jumped up and walked over to his desk. He sat on the edge and faced Sidney. "I've got a suspicion . . . and I'm serious about this . . . I'd almost wager the *Midnight Star* on it. I think the British set a trap for the men running supplies to the Continental Army. God knows Cornwallis is furious. Tarleton's so humiliated that he'll do anything to regain his stature. What do you think?"

Sidney seemed to study the problem for a few minutes. Bowie watched as the usually jolly face contorted into a scowl.

"Aye, that shark Tarleton would do something like that." Sidney scratched his coal-black beard and frowned again. "That man's a blood-thirsty one if ever I saw one. I'd hate to think of Miss Erin sailin' into waters infested with a shark like 'im. An' her without a harpoon."

Bowie grinned at the image. "Well, Erin's got Arlen's dueling pistols, but she won't be any match at all for that bastard Tarleton if he's as riled as I think he is."

"Are ye up for a little shark hunt? Is that what yer a-sayin' to me?" Sidney fingered the butt of his pistol thoughtfully. "Seems to me like the odds is a mite agin' us."

"To be honest, I don't know what to do." Bowie stood up and tucked his thumb into the waist of his breeches. "But I'll be damned if I'm going to let Erin walk into a trap while I do nothing about it."

CHAPTER
14

FROM A SENTRY POSTED ABOVE GEORGETOWN ERIN learned that Cornwallis might be headed that way. She didn't want to risk leading the British to Francis Marion's encampment, so she ordered the wagons to bypass the Pee Dee Rivers. She would simply have to find Greene or Light-Horse Harry Lee.

Unfortunately, that meant she'd be gone from Charleston—and Bowie—longer than she anticipated. It couldn't be helped. Riding horseback instead of on a wagon was much more pleasant. Erin took a turn as scout after her group passed Georgetown, and found it a delightful experience.

Using extraordinary precautions, she'd instructed the scouts to ride ahead for about thirty minutes and then report back. With the slow progress of the wagons, that meant that the scouts would be gone about fifty minutes. If they were gone longer than one hour, the wagon drivers stopped. If the scouts were gone for longer than an hour and a half, she would send someone searching for the missing men. When they made camp for the night or stopped for a meal, she insisted that their trail be covered with leaves to prevent someone from finding them inadvertently.

When they reached Charlotte almost two weeks later, Erin heard that the Articles of Confederation had been ratified and the Second Continental Congress became the United States Congress Assembled. Jubilant with the news, Erin sent Jimbo to pass the word on to the little group.

She also heard that Light-Horse Harry Lee and his men skirmished with Tarleton at Clapp's Mill, North Carolina. The innkeeper who told her about the skirmish said that both sides lost few men without a decisive victory.

Erin pushed her men northward toward the Dan River. After defeating Tarleton at the Cowpens, Morgan and his men had marched across North Carolina and crossed the Dan River where Greene had provided for boats and ferries in case they were needed for escape.

Loaded with casks of flour, rice, molasses, and salted meat, Erin knew that her group would be welcomed. The few boxes of clothing and shoes would be helpful, but the ammunition she carried was a necessity to the depleted resources of Greene's Continentals.

Tired almost beyond endurance, Erin nonetheless carried her share of the load. She drove the wagon, stood guard, or rode scout in a regular rotation. Her men, unaccustomed to being on the trail this long under such rigorous conditions, were tired, but Erin was tired into her joints, muscles, and bones.

Though she never complained, she often had to force a smile for one of the men who came to her for support. After a day of riding hard, she helped unload their food and utensils from the wagons. She still forbade a fire, but she helped 'Lasses prepare what scanty meals they could without heat.

Riding scout one March morning, Erin encountered a small group of Tories. She answered their questions quickly and without showing her fear, but Erin knew her chances of capture were great. She refused to give them her name. The other scout had ridden off the road to investigate suspicious sounds coming from the woods. She knew that from his position he could see her talking to the men, and she hoped he could hear.

When the leader of the group suggested that she should come with them, Erin rose taller in her saddle and glared at the man. Using her most withering glare and hostile tone, as loudly as possible, she demanded, "Are you threatening a lady? Have you sunk to that level?"

"No, miss, but we have orders to capture anyone we meet," replied the sergeant who seemed to be in charge. "Are you riding here alone? Where is your escort? Seems to me that a lady of your obvious stature would have—"

"I demand that you release me at once." Erin stared at him with such pugnacity that the man leaned away from her and averted his eyes. "I'm alone. My grandmother is ill, and I'm her only kin."

"I'm afraid you won't be seeing your grandmother this day. We can't let you pass," he said and watched her carefully. "Look around men," he called to the group of twelve or so men who were with him. "But don't scatter too far. Tarleton will want to interrogate this lady as soon as possible. He may even take you to see the earl himself."

Tarleton! Cornwallis! The names struck terror in Erin, but she refused to allow the man to see that she was afraid. "If you don't remove yourself from my path, I'll ride over you."

Her audacity did her no good. The man snatched her reins and led her toward the north. Within a few minutes the other men rejoined them.

His horse at full gallop, Bowie caught up with the wagons. "Jimbo, where's Erin?"

"She's riding scout this morning," Jimbo replied, grinning at the out-of-breath riders.

Sidney looked at Bowie and shook his head. "Right into the shark's teeth."

"What's your schedule?" Bowie asked and felt the strength of his body drain away as he thought of the predicaments in which Erin might be caught.

"She's to ride for thirty minutes and turn back," Jimbo replied. "She's been gone for fifty minutes. Our instructions are to stop if she hasn't returned in an hour."

"Go," Bowie called to Sidney and flicked the reins of his horse.

They rode north for about two miles before they met the man with whom Erin had been scouting. The man was riding at a gallop, but pulled up short when he saw Bowie and Sidney.

"Oh, thank the gods you've come! Them greenbacks have got Erin!" he exclaimed, his chest heaving and terror written across his face.

"Calm down. Now, what's this about Miss Banning?" Bowie asked, hoping that answering questions would put the man at ease.

Phillip inhaled deeply and looked from Bowie to Sidney. "Are you come to help us?"

"We've come after Miss Banning," Sidney answered and glanced at Bowie.

"How long ago was she captured? How many men? Were they well armed?" Questions tumbled from Bowie's mouth as the terror began to well in him. He refused to believe that Erin could be injured, but if he didn't hurry, she might be. "Come on, tell me."

Gazing fearfully at Bowie, Phillip said, "Well, I couldn't rightly count the men, sir. Could be as many as twenty. If there'd a-been less, I'd a rescued the lady myself."

Sidney realized that Bowie was about to ride off without obtaining the essential information that might save their lives. "Tell us all ye know, Phillip, or we'll feed ye to the sharks."

Phillip Hunter's eyes widened, and he looked from Bowie to Sidney. "You wouldn't . . . sir, he don't mean that, does he?"

"If you don't hurry and tell us what we need to know, I'll personally see to it that you're bound and dragged behind my ship until the sharks strip the last bit of flesh from your hide." Bowie could hardly sit still in his saddle. Erin was in grave danger, and this idiot was stalling.

"Well, sir, it happened along about thirty minutes ago. Them greenbacks said they was taking her to Tarleton. I heard them talking about a lot of men just up ahead at someplace called Guilford Courthouse. Cornwallis, too. There must be a right big bunch there." Phillip paused and sucked in a breath of air. "Them men was well armed from what

I could see. I'd say Erin—uh, Miss Banning—is in a lot of trouble."

With that information Bowie knew there was little he could do at that moment. He and Sidney would be killed long before Erin could be rescued. An all-out assault by two men on twenty was about as senseless, hopeless, and useless as trying to sail out of Charleston Harbor in broad daylight flying the United States flag.

Bowie and the two men returned sadly to the wagon train. Bowie knew the small band of men could do little to help Erin, so he discussed the possibilities with Sidney, Jimbo, and Phillip.

Sidney's cool thinking helped Bowie to settle down and work out a plan. Phillip seemed to be too afraid to lead the wagons on though he knew the wagon road. Jimbo was the logical choice for the leadership of the train since Erin had named him as her successor. Perhaps with Phillip's knowledge and Jimbo's good sense, they could succeed in finding Greene.

Bowie wanted to scout ahead first to find out where Tarleton and his men were camped. Knowing that Tarleton and Cornwallis were both within a few miles of the little group, Bowie was greatly disturbed. He instinctively felt that some grand battle would ensue before long, and he didn't want the wagons to blunder into the fray.

"Jimbo, who's the best scout of your band?" Bowie asked finally when a plan began to formulate in his mind.

"Sir, I'd say that would be me." Jimbo removed his hat and placed it over his heart as if to suggest honesty and humility. "I ain't meanin' to brag, but I've done a powerful lot a scoutin' in my day. Why, you know I lived up around the frontier for a long time, and I was called on to—"

Bowie held up his hand and shook his head. "You've got the job. But I don't want to take any chances. We need you to lead the wagons."

"Yes, sir, and I'm the man to do that, but I want to find the little missy before—"

"No, Jimbo. We're going to find out where Tarleton and

his men are. This scouting expedition is for that and nothing more. When we determine their location, we'll decide on a route that will take the supplies safely around them." Bowie felt a little sorry for the older man. Clearly Jimbo liked Erin a great deal and wanted her release almost as much as Bowie. "I'll go with you. Sidney, remain here and make sure nothing happens to these supplies."

With that Bowie and Jimbo mounted up and rode out of the camp. Darkness was about to fall, and Bowie counted that in his favor. The sun cast little light as it was about to set, but Bowie's eyes were accustomed to the dark. They rode in silence and then stopped a short while later.

"Jimbo, I think we'd better leave the road here. This is the spot where we encountered Phillip," Bowie explained and looked around for the best cover. "Let's ride out through the woods there. We'll parallel the road for a ways and then tie our horses and go on foot."

"Sounds like a plan I can live with, sir." Jimbo clucked softly to his horse and followed Bowie through the woods.

They rode for another two miles or so before Bowie held out his hand to stop Jimbo. "What do you think?" he whispered. "Should we go on foot from here?"

Jimbo seemed to think for a moment before he answered, "Yes, sir. I don't want to take a chance on being heard, and horses ain't concerned about where they put their hooves."

Erin rode into Tarleton's camp with her head high. She refused to look as scared as she felt. Her reins were held by the man who'd captured her, and she was surrounded by the other men. Escape seemed an impossibility—for the moment.

They stopped before one of the tents, and the officer helped her down from her horse. Erin glared at him as he jerked her arm and led her into the tent.

"Sir," he said and paused inside the entrance.

A red-haired man looked up at the two of them questioningly. "Yes?"

"I found this lady riding all alone—I thought—a few

miles from here." The officer inhaled deeply and smiled. "I thought you might want to interrogate her.

Tarleton rose and walked closer to Erin. "Who are you? Where were you going?"

"I don't see that it's any of your concern who I am and where I'm bound." Erin lifted her chin proudly. She wasn't going to be intimidated by this man in spite of his reputation.

Tarleton's smile looked unfriendly as he returned to his chair and threw a blanket on the ground. "Tie her. Leave her there."

The officer called for rope, and when it arrived, he tied her hands. Tarleton watched with interest. "Tie her feet, too."

"You, sir, deserve all the names people call you," Erin spat as Tarleton leaned back to watch the officer push her into a sitting position and tie her feet. She could see that the young officer was embarrassed but couldn't disobey his superior.

"I say, those are large boots for such a petite lady," Tarleton said and edged forward. "Look inside the boots."

Close to panic, Erin drew her feet closer to her body. "How dare you search a lady? That's unheard of, even for a man of your character."

"Search them," Tarleton insisted and watched as the officer pulled out both dueling pistols.

He handed them to Tarleton. "Looks like she's wearing two pairs of boots, sir."

"How interesting. What would we find if we searched further?" Tarleton grinned as he examined the two fine pistols. "Pretty well armed for a lady who's out for her morning ride, I'd say."

Erin hated Tarleton for his treatment of her. Fortunately, the young officer who tied and searched her didn't bother to look in her own boots—where her dagger was hidden. After finding the pistols, he'd stopped the search.

"Dismissed, Sergeant," Tarleton commanded and waited

for the other man to leave. "Now, miss, tell me who you are and why you're spying on me."

"I was not spying on you. As I told your sergeant, I am going to my grandmother's. She is ill," Erin lied again, staring straight into Tarleton's eyes and hoping he'd believe her because she didn't act the way a guilty person would act.

"Young lady, I'm not a patient man." Tarleton rose and hovered over her, his face inches from hers. He screamed the next words. "I suggest you cooperate, or else I shall become violent!"

Erin sat on the blanket, her hands and feet bound, and glared at the man with the shock of red hair falling across his forehead. Tarleton had shouted at her and threatened her, but she'd told him nothing but the same lie she told the men who captured her. She hadn't even told him her name.

A young boy entered the tent and handed Tarleton a letter. Figuring him to be nothing more than a messenger, Erin hardly looked at the boy, but he wore a Tory coat.

The sparsely furnished tent contained a cot, a low stool with a candle burning on it, a chair, and a makeshift desk. Erin saw nothing she could use as a weapon. Tarleton had taken her father's pistols, and with her hands tied behind her, she couldn't reach the dagger she'd concealed in her boot.

She hadn't heard any further commotion in Tarleton's camp, so she felt sure that Phillip had escaped being caught. Escape weighed heavily on her own mind. As soon as this despot left her alone for a moment, she'd break for the woods that bounded the encampment.

Briefly she thought about Bowie and where he was. Safely at sea, she assumed. He should have sailed two days after he left her just outside Charleston. Would she ever see Charleston again? she wondered, but didn't allow herself to dwell on the subject. She was a soldier like every American who carried a musket into combat, except that her duties were to provide supplies to the men.

When she'd asked for this job—no, demanded it—she'd

known the dangers. But I didn't count on this, she admitted to herself. The safety of Bluffwood seemed dear to her at that moment, and she wondered fleetingly what her father would say when he heard of her capture.

Sitting in this rough tent with nothing but a horse blanket to protect her from the cold ground, she remembered the last day she'd seen Bowie. They, too, had sat on a horse blanket, cuddling and kissing before the argument erupted. How senseless the disagreement seemed to her now. If she ever had the chance, she'd tell Bowie that she'd reacted unfairly. Deep down she knew what he was trying to get across to her—even if he didn't actually say it. Bowie simply didn't realize he loved her.

That thought gave her renewed courage. "How dare you treat a lady in such a manner? Release me at once."

Obviously ill at ease, the boy glanced at her and then at Tarleton. For a moment something akin to hatred contorted the young face, but it quickly passed.

Tarleton laughed. "Little chance of that, my dear. Now, tell me what you were doing out all alone today."

"I've told you and I refuse to tell you again. You may be deaf, but I'm not stupid, and telling the same story again and again is simply stupid." Erin tilted her chin higher in spite of the fear that rode her spine like a demon.

She wasn't prepared for Tarleton's next act. With all his force he slapped her across the face twice. Tears sprang to her eyes, but Erin willed them to evaporate rather than fall. Her lip began to swell, and she had the salty taste of blood in her mouth. Her next words were almost fatal. She glowered at him with all the malice she could muster and, with blood trickling from her mouth, said, "I see. You are unable to defeat American Patriots like Morgan, so you've declared war on an American woman."

The rage that filled his eyes frightened her far worse than anything she'd encountered thus far. His hands clenched and unclenched for a second before he struck her with his fist squarely on her jaw.

*   *   *

Thinking of Erin, Bowie walked as quietly as possible. He felt the responsibility for this dread moment acutely. Erin should never have gone along on this mission. Jimbo, while not the shrewd leader Erin was, could have managed the wagons. Erin's presence wasn't really a necessity as far as Bowie was concerned.

His mind drifted back to that last day when they'd argued because of his ridiculous refusal to admit that Erin knew her own mind. How could he presume to know what was in her mind when he didn't even know his own?

Mistakes, he mused. Our relationship's been one mistake after another. No, not mistakes. His thoughts drifted to those moments of exquisite passion, to tender kisses, to gentle touches that threatened to sear his skin. Passion that powerful couldn't be a mistake.

Jimbo caught Bowie's arm, and the two men stopped.

"Sounds like men ahead," Jimbo whispered and dropped to his knees.

Bowie did the same and listened intently. There, he heard it, too. Somewhere not too far ahead a group of men were camped. Here in the deep woods he couldn't even see the moon, much less depend on its light to guide him.

Jimbo crawled forward. Bowie felt the excitement rippling through him. Erin was nearby; he could almost feel her presence. What would he do if he found her? He and Jimbo couldn't attack the camp.

An aching in Bowie's chest surprised him, for he knew that it wasn't really physical. It was more of an emptiness; a bottomless chasm threatened to envelop him if he didn't find her, if she were dead. He refused to accept either concept as a possibility.

They found the edge of a clearing and stopped. A fire blazed in the center, and several men were huddled around it for warmth. There were two tents pitched nearby, and a makeshift corral for the horses stood at the north side of the encampment.

Bowie raised up a little and looked around. If he could determine which of the two tents Erin was in, maybe he

could sneak in and free her. It would be risky, but he was
willing to try. He signaled for Jimbo to go back to the clump
of bushes they'd passed and followed. From his vantage
point, about ten feet inside the edge of the forest, he would
maintain his vigil. First he'd send Jimbo back so that the
future of the wagon train wouldn't be jeopardized. For now
all Bowie could do was watch the tents.

When Erin came to, she was lying on a blanket, her body
racked with shivers. Tarleton was nowhere in sight. She
waited for a few moments, gingerly moving her jaw to see
if it was broken. Wincing in pain, she tried to sit but couldn't
maneuver well with her hands and feet tied. The lone candle
burned low on a stool a few feet away, and Erin tried to
wriggle over.

Her feet were asleep from lack of circulation, but she refused to let that stop her. When she reached the stool, she
curled her feet beneath her and sat up with her back to the
stool. Feeling the ropes with her fingers, she tried to find
a place where more rope than hand was exposed.

Then she held her hands close to the flame. The heat from
the small candle singed her skin, but the rope finally caught
fire. Biting her lip to keep from screaming, Erin pulled with
all her might while the fire burned through the rope. At last
it gave, and her hands were free.

She glanced at her burned hand but wasted no time on
self-pity. She removed the dagger from her boot and cut the
ropes binding her feet. Careful, Erin, she cautioned herself.
You can't escape until the feeling comes back into your feet.

Someone was coming! Erin couldn't run; she couldn't
even walk, but she refused to allow Tarleton to find her with
her hands and feet free. Lying down, she forced her way
under the back of the tent and lay there, hoping they'd think
she'd escaped.

Bowie felt helpless. He knew Erin was in one of those
tents. He'd seen Tarleton leave the larger one and guessed

that he might be holding her there. "Jimbo, I think I have this figured out."

"How's that?" Jimbo asked and moved slightly closer to Bowie. "I'm about ready to charge in there, sir. You can lie here if you want to, but I'm for rescuin' Missy."

Grabbing Jimbo's arm, Bowie shook his head vigorously. "Damnation, we're not going to do anything stupid. We're going to plan this carefully. I think—"

"Look, sir," Jimbo interrupted and pointed toward the tent.

Bowie watched a young private walk over to the tent, look all around, and then enter. A few seconds passed, and the man came out again with a puzzled look on his face. He looked not much more than sixteen years old, too young to fight in this war, and yet he wore the Tory green. He sauntered around, peering into the forest on either side of the tent.

"Something's wrong," Bowie observed and continued to watch. At any moment he expected the private to give the alarm that the prisoner had escaped, but he didn't. "From his actions I'd say that Erin isn't in the tent any longer. Why doesn't he call for a search?"

"I can't be knowin' what's in a British soldier's head, sir," Jimbo declared and watched intently. "But I'm thinkin' you're right. Somethin's amiss."

The boy walked over to a log near the tent and sat down. He continued to stare at the tent as if he expected someone to come out. Bowie wanted to leap from his hiding place and look into the tent to verify his suspicions, but he couldn't jeopardize his chances of saving Erin. After a few minutes Tarleton strode toward the tent. Suddenly alert, the private jumped to his feet and called out, "Sir, have you any instructions for this evening?"

Tarleton stopped and looked at the young Tory. "What are you doing here? Aren't you supposed to be resting for your turn at watch?"

"Um, well, yes, but I'm so excited I can hardly—"

"Then go and rest. This isn't a parlor game, Private. Tomorrow we'll need all our energies." Tarleton turned to enter the tent, but the young man stepped in his way. "Is there something else, Private?"

"Uh, do you want me to bring some food for the young . . . I mean, the prisoner before I turn in?" he asked, a frantic look drawing his face into a grimace.

"What I want, Private, is for you to step out of my way," Tarleton shoved the young Tory so hard that he fell back over the log. Tarleton hurried into the tent.

"Now, there's a real bastard," Bowie stated and shook his head. "It's a wonder his own troops don't—"

The young private stood and sidled off into the trees behind the tent as Tarleton emerged. "Sergeant! Major! Quickly. Organize a search. Rouse everyone. The prisoner's escaped. This captive is important."

"Hell, she's escaped!" Bowie scanned the forest, wondering in which direction she'd headed. He knew that he and Jimbo would be in danger when the search ensued. "Jimbo, go as fast as you can back toward our camp. Withdraw the wagons and men as far into the woods as possible. Make sure they can't be seen. If you have to, hide the wagons down a riverbank. We can worry about getting them out later. Be sure they're covered."

"Yes, sir," Jimbo answered and began to crawl in the direction of their camp.

"Jimbo, if you find Erin, you make damned sure Tarleton doesn't recapture her." Bowie waved Jimbo on.

Wondering what he could do to help Erin, Bowie slid farther under the protective covering of a clump of bushes. She must have gone out the back of the tent.

"Down the road here, men." Mounting the horse one of his men brought, Tarleton pointed in the direction of the wagon camp. "The rest of you, go that way."

Hoping that Jimbo would get there first, Bowie watched as some of the men mounted their horses and rode away. Well, that's a third of the men, he thought, praying the rest would stay in camp.

"You men, go north." Tarleton frantically scanned the

area. "And you, search the woods behind the tent." Tarleton galloped off toward the south.

Damn! Bowie swore to himself. Erin had to be back there somewhere. She couldn't have gone too far because too little time had elapsed. Tarleton hadn't been away from the tent more than ten minutes when he'd returned and discovered her missing.

Bowie thought of Erin. She had to be scared within an inch of madness. He wanted to hold her, to comfort her, to let her know he was out here and everything would work out fine, but he couldn't. He had to lie in the accursed bushes and wait.

If I ever find—when I find her, he corrected himself, I'll never let her out of my sight again. Was this love? he wondered. Could he be in love with Erin Banning?

Nonsense, he scolded himself. He was never going to fall in love. Even as the thought passed through his mind, Bowie knew it wasn't true. Marveling at the realization, he pictured Erin, brave and noble, beautiful and intelligent. If he truly was in love, he was glad she was the woman, a woman he'd never expected to find.

Bowie shook himself. He could act like a lovelorn fool later. Now he needed to find Erin.

What about that young private? Bowie wondered. That man had known Erin wasn't in the tent. He'd tried to conceal that knowledge from Tarleton as long as he could. Where had the young man gone?

Bowie squinted and looked at the log where he'd last seen the boy. He was no longer there, but Bowie hadn't noticed him joining the groups searching for Erin. Realizing that if Tarleton concluded, as Bowie had, that the boy had tried to help Erin, he was in as much danger as she was.

Unable to leave the boy to his own devices against Tarleton, Bowie decided he'd have to rescue both Erin and the boy. Watching as Tarleton's men fanned out behind the tent, Bowie crawled forward, closer to the camp.

Then he spotted the boy crouched behind a tree not far from one of the men searching the woods. Not hidden very well, the boy would be caught within seconds. Bowie acted as quickly as possible. He picked up an apple-sized stone and threw it. It landed about ten feet past the young man and diverted the soldier's attention.

Now if only he could find Erin. Bowie waited until the men had gone far enough into the woods—out of hearing distance. Watching the guard who remained in camp, Bowie crawled along the edge of the forest over to the spot where the boy was hiding. When Bowie got there, the boy's eyes were wide with fear. "Shhh. I'm not going to hurt you. Keep still."

The boy nodded, but the fear didn't leave his eyes. "Who are you, sir?" the boy whispered. "Are you one of those Patriots?"

Bowie studied the boy for a moment. "I am. What's your name, son?"

"Kenneth Lambert, sir." He looked at Bowie for a few seconds. "What's your name?"

Wary of answering until he was sure that the boy's loyalties had changed, Bowie grinned. "Let's find the prisoner."

"Yes, sir," Kenneth agreed. "I . . . I saw him hit her. Tarleton, I mean. He yelled at her and then hit her again. It made me sick."

Fury rose in Bowie. If he caught Tarleton . . .

"Sir?" Kenneth tugged on Bowie's sleeve. "Where are we going to look? I mean, with all these men around, don't you think we'd better—"

"I'm not leaving here without Erin," Bowie announced and looked at the young man. He had every right to be afraid. If Tarleton had hit Erin, what would he do to this boy who had tried to help her? "Look, you can try to escape if you want to, but I think we've got a better chance together. Let's go back to my hiding place."

Bowie led the way back to the bushes. Until he could decide where to look for Erin, he didn't plan to move. If he blundered into one of the soldiers—well, he just wouldn't think about that. Erin became the focus of his thoughts.

*   *   *

Erin watched the men run past her into the woods and was glad she'd remained so close to the tent. They hadn't thought to look there. Most prisoners would have sprinted for freedom at the first chance, but her cool head—and tingling feet—had saved her.

Her captors would be returning soon. She had to do something. Tarleton had sent riders to the north and south. Men combed the woods behind the tent. If she could make her way around the tent and cross the clearing without being seen, she'd be free.

Had anyone remained to guard the supplies? Surely—Tarleton wouldn't be stupid enough to leave his camp completely unguarded, she decided.

Her horse was probably gone, used by one of the soldiers to search for her. But she'd probably be better off without a horse, at least for now. The soldiers could spot her much more easily if she were riding.

With a sigh she crawled to the edge of the tent and looked around the corner. The camp seemed to be deserted, so she slithered around the corner and stopped when she reached the front of the tent.

Carefully scanning the clearing, she spotted a man slouched across the seat of a wagon with a musket in his hand. She'd have to find a way to get by him unnoticed. If she could reach that big log, she might have a chance.

Creeping along the ground, she finally attained her goal without being caught. The distance across the rest of the clearing was obscured from the view of the guard by the fire and a table. Her hands shaking, Erin decided to head for the table instead of straight for the woods. If he happened to get up for a stretch, the guard would see her in the open ground. This way she would be less exposed.

Sharp stones bruised her legs and arms as she crawled across the clearing to the table, but she never hesitated once she got started. If she expected to escape, she'd have to worry about the pain later. Now she had to move—and fast.

Bowie pulled Kenneth back into the bushes. "Look!" Bowie whispered. "It's Erin."

Kenneth looked over at the log near the tent where he'd posted himself earlier. "It really is. Do you want me to go and help her?"

Bowie grinned. "No, we'll wait here unless something happens."

Watching her, Bowie couldn't help noticing the gentle rise and fall of her hips as she crawled across the rocks. Not bad for a woman. She's really brave, he thought, and beautiful. He couldn't really see her face because of the way she was moving. Her head was tucked down, and she pulled herself along with her elbows and knees.

Erin heard the wagon creak and hurried the rest of the distance to the table. Peering from underneath the wooden bench, she saw the guard stand and glance around. When he looked at the table, she was sure he could see her, but he didn't move out of the wagon.

Breathing heavily, she waited until he settled back down. Erin looked back at the path she'd taken from the tent and marveled that she'd made it without being spotted. Then she saw the displaced rocks. Her trail was as clear as if she'd marked it intentionally.

Well, there's no helping that now, she mused and glanced at the guard again. He seemed to be fidgeting with his musket, so she began moving again. Wriggling like a snake, she started across the grass toward the woods. Once there, she'd head for the creek and throw any searchers off her path that way, then head for the wagon train.

She hesitated a second. Would the wagon train still be there when she escaped? Or would she be alone in these woods, so far from home without a way to return? Erin refused to think negative thoughts and continued to crawl. She could worry about that when she completed her escape.

Ahead, she spotted a clump of bushes and low cedar shrubs. That became her target. If she could reach that without being spotted, she would be free.

Bowie grinned. Erin had waited until the guard in the wagon sat back down and started working with his musket, hardly paying any attention to his surroundings. Now she was headed directly for the spot where he and Kenneth were hiding. His only regret was the obvious path she left through those stones, but that couldn't be helped.

If she could cross about fifteen feet of clear ground without being spotted, she'd be safe, Bowie decided. Once she gained the woods, nobody could see her easily. From the edge of the woods she'd have a distance of about ten more feet until she reached the clump of shrubs where he waited for her.

Bowie motioned for Kenneth to move farther back into the brush to allow room for Erin when she arrived. He could hear the sounds of men calling to one another and wondered if they were returning, but he knew he couldn't allow fear of discovery dictate his actions.

His chest burned painfully by the time Erin found shelter in the edge of the trees. Bowie realized he wasn't breathing and inhaled deeply. "Come on, darling, just a few more feet," he murmured, then glanced around.

Behind him, Kenneth was grinning. Bowie refused to acknowledge the questioning look and turned back to watch Erin's progress. She was almost there.

Her chest heaving, Erin smiled. With about five more feet to crawl, she felt like celebrating her victory over Tarleton, but she didn't. Thorns scraped her face and forearms, but she didn't care. Her injuries could be tended to later, when she found her way back to the wagon train. "Let it be there when I get there," she whispered but knew the chances were slim.

Her instructions had been explicit. If she didn't return, the train was to proceed without her. Jimbo would assume her position, and the goods would be delivered.

Her entire body ached, but Erin kept crawling. The bushes were almost within the reach of her hands when she spotted something moving in the bushes. God, had she come this far only to be caught and returned to captivity?

Bowie reached out of the bushes and caught her hands,

pulling her into the cover of the shrubs. He clapped a hand over her mouth to keep her from screaming, though he doubted that someone with as much presence of mind as Erin would resort to something so irrational, considering that she'd escaped from Tarleton.

"Erin," he whispered against the wonderful fragrance of her hair. "It's me."

Warmth spread through Erin like a flood of hot liquid. "Bowie?" she asked quietly. "What are you doing here?"

"I came—"

"Never mind," she interrupted and turned in his arms. "I love you."

CHAPTER
15

Bowie's kiss took Erin's breath away. She wriggled more deeply into his embrace, releasing all her fears, now that she was with him, in the form of passion. Now everything would be all right. They were together again.

Together? What was Bowie doing here? Why wasn't he halfway to the tropics for supplies? How had he found her?

When Bowie drew away, he peered at her intently and placed his fingers over her mouth to keep her from speaking. "Erin, we've got to get out of here. Those soldiers are going to be returning any minute, and they'll extend their search once they see your trail."

"I know. I saw that, but I couldn't do anything about it." Erin glanced back at the clearing and saw the smoothed places where her gown had dragged the stones out of place.

"Let's go." He took her hand and turned her around. "This is Kenneth Lambert."

"A Tory!" she spat. "What's he doing here?"

Bowie answered, "I think he's no longer a Tory."

"Bowie, he—"

"Let's get out of here," Bowie interrupted and pulled her along with him.

Kenneth brought up the rear as they crawled out of the bushes and moved as silently as possible away from the camp. When they were about fifteen feet from the shrubs, Bowie stood up, still holding Erin's hand. He, too, was scared. Having come so close to losing Erin had made him think of her in a different light.

223

Noises from nearby stopped Bowie's reverie. He'd been so happy about Erin's freedom that he'd nearly lost sight of their problem. He dragged her behind the closest tree and motioned for Kenneth to follow. He listened to the sounds of horses coming closer. "We've got to get out of here fast."

Pulling Erin along, Bowie shot out from behind the tree and headed for the sound of water. He didn't think the creek was really large enough to hide them, but it was better than being found here. At least they wouldn't leave any tracks in the creekbed.

Kenneth seemed to understand where they were headed. "The creek. I went down there for water this afternoon. It may be deep enough for us to hide in."

Bowie merely nodded and kept running. Out of breath, he knew that Erin must be exhausted, but he kept dragging her with him. Kenneth took her other hand and tried to help.

Erin glanced at the Tory who'd taken her hand. Who was he? Why was he with Bowie? Why was he helping them? Turning them in to Tarleton would most certainly gain the boy a promotion.

She forced herself to stop wondering about him and take care of the business at hand. Her lungs burned, her legs ached, her stomach rolled, but she kept running. Not long ago Erin had stood up to Tarleton and been beaten for it. Now fear wrapped itself around her heart and lungs like a cocoon of steel, stifling her and sending shivers of terror down her spine. Erin wouldn't give up now that she'd come this far. She ran harder, lifted her chin, and squared her shoulders. No Tory, not even Tarleton, could cause her to cringe in fear. She refused to succumb to intimidation.

The sound of water grew louder. Erin knew they were coming to the creek that she and her men had crossed earlier in the day. Bowie, she concluded, planned to use the creek to escape Tarleton, much as Erin had decided earlier. Feeling encouraged, she hurried along with the two men.

A glance at Kenneth told her that the boy must be younger than she, much too young to be fighting in this war.

In the darkness she couldn't see well enough to gauge his emotions, but he acted as though he were as scared as a jackrabbit. She wondered how he'd come to be with Tarleton—the most bloodthirsty of the British commanders.

Erin felt the ground giving way beneath her and grappled to regain her footing to no avail. In their haste they'd come to the creek bank more quickly than she'd thought possible. Now the three of them were sliding down a steep embankment toward the cold water. When Erin hit the surface of the water, it took her breath away.

Bowie and Kenneth landed near Erin, and Bowie grabbed her hand. "Hold on," he called.

Bowie never imagined the water would be this deep. Though it chilled him through to his bones, he floated gladly away from Tarleton's encampment. Kenneth seemed to be swimming without help, so Bowie concentrated on Erin. Her heavy cloak and gown would make staying afloat tedious since she was already worn out.

Finally Erin gasped for breath. The cold water soaked her clothing, and the current tried to drag her beneath the surface, but she kicked and fought to stay afloat. Her father's heavy boots were leaden on her feet, but she couldn't get them off without going under the water.

Thanking God for Bowie's strong hands, she clung to him and allowed the current to carry them where it would. Bowie reached out and grabbed a low-hanging tree limb, and they swung close to the bank. "Kenneth, over here."

Erin held out her hand and caught Kenneth's as the creek almost swept him past. He struggled to join them by the bank. He started to say something, but closed his mouth and pointed back upstream.

Bowie heard it, too. Horses. He pulled Erin back into the shadows and rushes. The riders were too close for them to do anything else. Kenneth lay against the bank by Erin, trembling.

Feeling sorry for the boy, Erin put her arms around him. She couldn't tell whether he was still scared or simply shivering from the cold. Looking around, she saw that they were in a good position to remain hidden. They'd come to a bend in the river as Bowie caught the limb and swung in an arc to the bank. From where they lay she couldn't see where they'd been.

Peering through the limbs, Bowie could watch for the soldiers. He felt almost positive that the riders wouldn't spot the three of them unless the moon cast plenty of light on them. He held Erin close, trying to protect her as well as he could from the British and from the elements, but he could really do little about either.

The moments dragged on as Erin awaited her fate. Shivering with cold, she wondered if she'd managed to get this far only to be hauled back to that tent and Tarleton's abuse. Then she heard the horses coming closer. In a few seconds the riders would come crashing right in front of her.

Biting her lip, Erin uttered a silent prayer for respite. She'd worked hard to do her part for the rebel cause; would she be repaid by being hung as a spy by a British officer who seemed insane? Moments would tell her fate.

Hugging Kenneth to bolster his spirits, Erin felt her own lifted. They were out of sight. The soldiers were likely to be as cold and wet as the escapees. She suddenly felt that their chances of true freedom were good.

Then the horses were passing them. Two, four, six, Erin mentally began to count but gave up. There must have been close to forty of them, and she shuddered to think what would have happened if any one of those men had looked to his left as he rode past.

They were gone. Bowie offered a prayer of thanks and continued to cling to Erin. He needed to decide what would be the better plan of action: to lie here and wait on the soldiers to return or to try to get out of the creek. In truth, he felt that lying in the creek until after the soldiers returned would be better because the three wet Patriots—he considered Kenneth a Patriot now—would leave an obvious trail when they climbed out of the creek.

Here they had cover from the low-hanging limbs and

rushes. He looked at Erin and whispered, "Do you think you can remain in the water until after they return?"

Erin knew she could. She could have withstood the fires of hell if they sheltered her from Tarleton's men. "Yes, but Kenneth seems to be freezing."

"Kenneth, are you going to be all right?" Bowie asked and tried to see the boy past Erin.

"Y-y-y-yes, sir. I th-th-think so," Kenneth answered through chattering teeth. "J-j-just don't make me go back w-w-with them."

"You're free now, son." Bowie paused. He'd never called anybody son. Bowie wasn't old enough to be the boy's father, but somehow it felt right to call him that. "You can do what you want to."

"C-c-can I stay with you and Mrs. . . . uh, I d-d-don't know your n-n-name."

Bowie glanced at Erin, wondering how she felt about having a son not quite two years younger than she. "My name's Bowie Gallagher."

"Mr. and Mrs. G-G-Gallagher," he said and sat up a little.

Erin felt herself blushing and for once was glad for the warmth of the color staining her cheeks. "Kenneth, Bowie and I aren't married."

"Yet," Bowie added and suddenly felt warm all over in spite of the cold water. "But if Miss Banning will accept, we will be soon."

"Bowie—are you . . ." Her voice dwindled into silence. Was Bowie . . . dare she hope he was asking her to marry him?

"Erin, I realize this isn't the time or the place I would have chosen to speak of such a tender feeling, but I fear this will have to do." Bowie kissed her forehead lightly. "I love you. I want to marry you, if you'll have me. I'm not nearly good enough for you, but if love counts for anything, I'm rich with nothing less than adoration for you."

"Bowie, that's a lovely proposal," Erin whispered, resting her head on his shoulder.

"Well, M-M-Miss Erin, are you going to m-m-marry him?" Kenneth asked, giggling and shivering at the same time.

"Stay out of this, boy. I'll make my own pitch." Bowie reached over and patted Kenneth's shoulder. "But if I think I need help, I'll come to you."

"You don't need help, Bowie," Erin began, feeling a little conspicuous for accepting his proposal in front of a stranger. "I love you."

"You'd better," he admonished and kissed her lingeringly. "Or I'd kidnap you and take you away to some deserted tropical island."

"And I'd chase you through British lines until you gave in." Erin laughed quietly, feeling a sense of peace settle over her.

The three of them talked quietly to pass the time and to keep their minds off the icy water in which they were sitting. Erin remembered that she didn't know how they'd acquired Kenneth, so she asked Bowie. "Tell me about our new friend."

Bowie explained how he'd seen Kenneth come to help Erin and then rescued him. "I knew he had to be a real Patriot in spite of his Tory green."

Erin peered through the darkness at the boy. "Were you the soldier who brought in the message for Tarleton while he was interrogating me?"

"Yes, Miss Banning." Kenneth averted his eyes. "I'm sorry. I heard how he hollered at you. And I saw him hit you, too."

"My God!" Bowie exclaimed. "I'd forgotten about that. What did Tarleton do?"

Erin explained how she'd been captured and taken to the camp. Wincing as she spoke, she told Bowie about the interrogation and abuse she'd suffered at Tarleton's hands. "But I didn't tell him anything. He doesn't even know my name. I refused to tell him."

Pure rage roared through Bowie like a hurricane on the high seas. Tarleton had no reason to suspect Erin of being anything but innocent. His assault seemed to be born of sadism rather than patriotism.

"He didn't really hit me hard until I mentioned General Morgan," Erin admitted and turned to Bowie. She could barely see his profile, but she felt the comfort of his arms around her. It was too bad Kenneth was with them at this moment, but she was glad he'd been rescued.

Erin's heart sang. Bowie had asked her to marry him, and she'd accepted. Conversation flowed around her while she took a moment to revel in her happiness. The past few months, even years, had offered her little in the way of happiness. She wasn't really *un*happy, but there'd been little cause for celebration. Grief had intruded frequently when she heard of the death of a friend. Anger had become a permanent state of mind for her since Clinton had occupied Charleston and left it in the care of Balfour and Rawdon, the British commandant. Tension had fairly sizzled in the Banning household ever since her father resumed his wagon route at the beginning of the war.

But now happiness enveloped her like a warm comfortable cloak. She could hardly be still with Bowie so close, but she didn't want to make a spectacle of herself in front of Kenneth. Erin grinned and blushed. She'd already made a fool of herself when she'd discovered Bowie hiding in the bushes back at Tarleton's camp, so why worry now?

Erin lifted her face to look at Bowie and took his chin in her hand. When he glanced down at her, she kissed him as passionately as she knew how. Behind her, she felt Kenneth moving away slightly, and she stopped. She was embarrassing the boy.

Bowie chuckled. He'd seen Kenneth scooting away from Erin. "Some day, boy, you'll have your own girl and you'll understand."

The sound of horses splashing up the creek prevented them from discussing romance any further. Almost without realizing what she was doing, Erin slid farther into Bowie's arms. She reached for Kenneth and drew him close again, feeling instinctively that he was more afraid than she was.

Once more the three huddled together in the creek, shivering and silent as Tarleton's men rode by. The chance of being caught was greater this time than when they'd hidden here before because the soldiers would have full view of the three without the bend of the creek sheltering them as it had from the north. They could do nothing but wait.

Erin lay her head on Bowie's shoulder, taking what comfort she could from his icy woolen cloak. Closing her eyes, she imagined Bowie's face as he had kissed her back in Charleston after the first time they'd made love. It helped to stop the shivers for a few moments and to distract her attention from the troop of soldiers riding by.

At last the hoofbeats faded away, but Erin couldn't move. The feeling that she was really free almost overwhelmed her, and she went limp in Bowie's arms.

After waiting quietly a little while longer, Bowie stood and helped Erin up. "Come, it's time to leave. We shouldn't be here if those men return."

"Mr. Gallagher," Kenneth said as he stood, "I don't think they'll be coming back."

"Why not?" Bowie asked. So far Tarleton had put everything he had into the search for Erin. Why should he stop now?

"Well, sir," Kenneth began and wrung out his green jacket. "While Miss Banning was there . . . I mean, when Tarleton was questioning her, he got a message from Lord Cornwallis."

"That message you brought in was from Cornwallis? What did it say?" Erin asked, looking with renewed interest at the boy.

"I don't rightly know, Miss Banning. I just know Colonel Tarleton was awful excited." Kenneth looked at his companions and trudged along through the icy water. "How much longer do you think we have to walk in the water?"

"Well, in view of the information you've given us, I believe we can safely leave the creek." Bowie decided that something big was about to happen. He couldn't tell what, but he knew that if Tarleton and Cornwallis were joining forces in the general vicinity of General Greene's troops, then a battle would ensue. "Let's hurry."

After walking in silence for almost an hour, Bowie stopped and let out a long, low whistle. They waited for a few moments and finally heard the answering call. The wagon train was still camped where he'd left it.

Feeling much better now that the protection of her own men was so close, Erin bristled. "I told them to go on. They should never have waited."

Bowie chuckled, glad to have the old feisty Erin back again. "Relax. I needed Jimbo to help me find you. He can't have been back too long."

"Why should he take orders from you? I'm—"

Bowie silenced her with a kiss. "I know who you are, and they do, too."

Erin turned around. Men were emerging from behind trees all around them. Jimbo rushed up, gave the boy in the Tory green a curious glance, and hugged Erin. "Missy, you're a sight. I told 'em you'd get away." He turned to Bowie. "How'd you manage without gettin' yourself killed?"

"Well, Jimbo—"

Erin cut Bowie off in midsentence. "I escaped myself. After I got away, I found Bowie and Kenneth . . . oh, this is Kenneth Lambert." Erin put her arm around the shivering boy. "He's a Tory who got converted."

"Well, we're glad you've come to yer senses, boy." Jimbo clapped Kenneth on the back.

"Jimbo, get some warm clothing for us. And some food." Erin looked through the crowd for 'Lasses, but didn't see her. "Where's 'Lasses?"

"Here I is." 'Lasses elbowed her way through the throng of men around Erin and scowled. "See? I done told you not to go runnin' off like a heathen. You ain't got no sense a'tall. I've a mind to turn you over my knee—"

" 'Lasses," Erin interrupted, laughing happily and hugging her servant. "I missed you, too."

"I tole you it wasn't fitten for you—" 'Lasses paused in

midsentence. "Well, I sees you ain't too bad off. I reckon I'll overlook this time."

Everybody laughed as the little group moved toward the hidden wagons. Some of the men brought Erin, Bowie, and Kenneth dry clothing and thick slices of bread and cheese.

Erin hesitated and looked around. "I think I'll change clothes first."

She and 'Lasses moved a discreet distance away from the men, and 'Lasses hooked a blanket across a limb to provide some privacy while Erin changed clothes. Alert for intruders, 'Lasses was silent for the few minutes it took for Erin to remove her wet gown and replace it with a dry one.

Erin finally broke the silence. " 'Lasses, Bowie asked me to marry him."

'Lasses abandoned her vigilance and looked at Erin. "That's a mighty fine man, but I can't reckon why he'd want to marry a woman as stubborn as you is. I ain't never knowed nobody like you."

Erin giggled and shivered. Her hair was wet, but she didn't care. She'd escaped from Tarleton. She'd said she would marry Bowie. Tonight, there was nobody in the world any happier than she.

CHAPTER
16

BEFORE DAWN ERIN WAS AWAKE AND ISSUING ORDERS. Bowie worked like the rest of the men without complaint. When the wagons were ready to move on, Erin, glad that Bowie didn't expect to usurp her authority, happily exchanged Jimbo for Bowie as her driver. Erin wanted to reach General Greene at Guilford Courthouse early. She and Bowie agreed that Cornwallis was probably ready to attack, and the Continental Army needed all the supplies they could muster.

'Lasses, sitting in the back of the wagon with young Kenneth, watched Erin and Bowie carefully. Erin realized that if anyone could detect a difference in her, it would be 'Lasses. And 'Lasses would see beyond the bruises that marked Erin's face. Having raised Erin from a baby, 'Lasses knew every nuance of Erin's personality. Though she knew that hiding the fact that she and Bowie were already lovers would be almost impossible, Erin tried anyway.

The expression on Bowie's face was one of amusement. During the early morning Erin felt that she needed an expert scout and consulted with Jimbo. "Who do you think are the best scouts in the group?"

Jimbo studied the question for a minute, scratching his beard thoughtfully. "I'd say—"

"Let me go, Erin," Bowie asked, turning to look at her. He grimaced. Every time he saw her face, he was reminded of how much he hated Tarleton. "I'm as good a scout as there is in the group."

"He's right, Missy," Jimbo agreed and nodded vigorously.

"No. That's out of the question," Erin blurted, feeling her cheeks burn with color. She couldn't face having Bowie out there in danger, possibly being captured by Tarleton and receiving treatment similar to what hers had been. "Who else?"

Bowie took her hand, understanding her reluctance to let him scout. "Erin, you need me to do this. Just because we . . . because of our relationship, you can't refuse to let me do a job you need done."

"No, Bowie. You can't do it. We have plenty of others who are—"

"Erin," he interrupted and kissed the back of her hand tenderly. "You wouldn't love me if I were a coward, the kind of man who shirks his duty, would you?"

"No, but this is unnecessary, and you—"

"It is necessary," he insisted gently and embraced her. "I have to do this, Erin."

"I suppose you're right," she agreed, clinging to him as if it were the last time she'd ever see him. Erin tried to smile, but her lower lip quivered. She knew she looked a mess with her lip swollen and her eye blackened. The bruise on her cheek gave evidence to the power of Tarleton's punch. Finally she whispered, "I love you. Be careful."

When Bowie rode away with Phillip Hunter, her father's assistant, tears filled Erin's eyes. For the past few years she'd always hated to see her father go, and now it was even more difficult to watch Bowie leave. She refused to let her men see her cry, so she sniffled and blotted the tears as best she could without appearing to be doing so.

Jimbo rode alongside her in Bowie's place and attempted to be cheerful. Perhaps, Erin thought, he realized what it meant for her to let Bowie go like that. She resolved to appear happier, even though her heart felt like lead.

Bowie and Phillip circled the area where Tarleton's men had been camped—far enough away to keep from being captured. Guilford Courthouse was past the next ridge, and Bowie wanted to arrive as quickly as possible. Maybe General Greene would send an escort to bring in the supplies.

Bowie held up his hand for Phillip to stop. "Do you hear horses?" he asked in a whisper.

Phillip nodded, and the two of them rode into the forest to see who was approaching. They didn't have long to wait. A troop of men escorting empty wagons passed by.

"Looks like Carolina militia," Bowie commented as he watched.

"You're right. What'll we do?"

"I think we'll go and talk to them," Bowie announced and flicked his reins. "Go carefully."

Their horses trotted back to the hard road surface. By now the troop had passed. Bowie urged his horse into a gallop, and they soon caught up with the rear guard. "Ho, friend," Bowie called and waved when the riders turned around with their pistols drawn.

When Bowie and Phillip reached the guard, the man clad in a fringed hunting coat asked, "Who are you and where are you going?"

Bowie felt a little uneasy. Some Tories couldn't afford the green coats that gave them away. Had he and Phillip blundered into a Tory band that was joining Tarleton? He answered evasively. "We're friends."

"Friends of the Patriots or friends of the British?" the guard probed.

By this time a young major joined them. "What's the trouble?"

"Trying to find out who these men are, Major."

The major looked at Bowie and Phillip. He hesitated and gazed at Bowie. "Have I seen you somewhere before?"

Studying the major, Bowie thought he might have seen his face, but it still didn't help to answer his question. Were these men Whigs or Tories? "I was reared on Edisto."

"Gallagher?" The major's frown deepened. "A Tory! Arrest them. I know your father—Tory through and through."

Bowie grinned and nodded. "That he is, Major. But I'm Patriot through and through."

"Uh, that's right, sir," Phillip added. "Work for Arlen Banning."

"Banning? From Charleston? My name's Drake Hastings." The major relaxed a little. "I know Mr. Banning's daughter."

"Erin?" Bowie asked and looked at the major with renewed interest. "How do you know her?"

Drake smiled. "She's my wife's cousin."

How could that be? He'd met Erin's cousin, and Lilly was as Tory as a woman could be. Bowie stared at the major for a moment, unwilling to believe him. Maybe it was a trap. "Lilly's husband? Are you Lilly's husband?"

Laughing, Drake shook his head. "No. I've heard that one's a Tory, but I'm not married to her."

Somewhere in the back of his mind, Bowie recalled hearing Arlen say something about a niece in the upcountry. Maybe Erin had mentioned her, too. "I'm afraid I don't remember the name. I may have heard Arlen speak of her, but—"

"Since we live in upper Ninety-Six District, you probably haven't met her. Noelle Arledge Hastings is my wife's name." Drake held out his hand. "And you're Bowie Gallagher."

Bowie stared at Hastings. "How do you know my name?"

"Unfortunately, and I apologize for feeling this way, I know your father." Drake Hastings looked away for a moment and then faced Bowie again. "You see, I was a Tory spy."

"Was?" Bowie asked and glanced at Phillip to see if he knew anything that would help them.

"Was." Drake nodded. "Don't get excited. I'd had my fill of slaughter and butchery. I was assigned to Tarleton. One day I met Dan Morgan. That changed my life. Through him I obtained information that I leaked to Tarleton. That led to the Battle of Cowpens."

"You were there?" Bowie asked, thoroughly confused. "Whose side were you on?"

"I fought for General Morgan. I've abandoned my green jacket and taken this fringed jacket of a militia man. Morgan kept me with him and promoted me to major. Tell me about the Bannings, unless you wish to question me further."

Although Bowie didn't want to question Drake Hastings openly, Bowie decided to try to find out if he was telling the truth by talking in a friendly manner, as if he believed Hastings. "Erin was captured by Tarleton—"

"By God, that bastard! He did the same thing to Noelle." Drake's grimace revealed pain as he obviously recalled his wife's experience. He straightened in the saddle and tried to smile. "She's a feisty one. Won't stay at home and mind the house. She rode to Cowpens to warn us that Tarleton was on the way. She thought I was a double-spy and wanted to tell Dan about me."

Bowie chuckled with Drake. If anyone could, Bowie could relate to the story of a woman who refused to stay home and mind the house. "I think that runs in the family. My Erin's just down the road, taking her father's place."

"Erin? Here?" Drake looked over his shoulder at his men. "Let's go."

As they rode, Bowie related the story of Erin's capture and his own suspicion that Cornwallis was about to attack. "We're scouting for a wagon train of supplies headed for General Greene's men."

"We're scouting for food. General Morgan . . . you know, he's a sick man. He's being sent home to recover." Drake rode to Bowie's side. "What's this about supply wagons?"

"Follow us," Bowie said and rode to the front of the troop. "We were looking for a military escort since there are so many British soldiers and Tories in the area."

"Well, since you're looking for an escort, and we're looking for food, we'll join up and come in together." Major Drake Hastings grinned. "Sounds like a fine day starting out. I hope it ends as pleasantly."

"Do you know anything about this battle? We think it's going to start anytime," Bowie asked.

"Don't know much. General Greene asked General Morgan to take some of the men and command them, but Morgan's not fit to command anybody. He's got piles. And sciatica," Drake added.

They soon reached the wagon train. Bowie noted that Erin was driving her wagon as expertly as any of the men. When she saw them approach, her eyes lit with happiness that made Bowie warm all over. "Erin, my dear, do you remember—"

"Drake Hastings, is that you?" Erin grinned and took his hand. "Of course, I remember, Bowie. He escorted my cousin to Charleston after her father died."

"I'm not sure whether you know it or not, Miss Banning, but your cousin and I are married," Drake explained. "I do thank you for your hospitality. I hope we can come again under more pleasant circumstances. But for now we need to ride."

"Yes, Noelle wrote of your marriage. Drake, this is Kenneth Lambert. Until last night, he was a Tory," Erin told Drake and smiled. "He was going to try to help me, but I'd escaped. Bowie saved him from Tarleton's wrath."

"Intelligent decision, son," Drake said with a grin. "I know how difficult that kind of decision can be, since I had to make it myself."

After introductions were made to the rest of the men, the group moved as quickly as possible toward Guilford Courthouse. From a distance they could hear the rumble of artillery and musketfire.

To Erin it sounded like the world was about to end. She watched Bowie carefully as he and Drake Hastings led the wagoners toward the back of General Greene's troops. When they reached a place well behind the lines, Bowie talked for several minutes with Drake and a group of officers while the wagons were unloaded.

Bowie returned to Erin. "I think we need to leave as soon as possible. I don't want to go toward Charleston right now.

When this battle is over, there's a chance we could be over-run by Cornwallis's cavalry and infantry. Drake agrees."

"Is Cornwallis winning?" Erin asked, remembering Tarleton's intensity and hatefulness.

"Nobody knows yet." Bowie turned to Jimbo and talked with him for a moment, discussing the possibility of other routes.

"Bowie," Erin interrupted and placed her hand on his arm. "Why not go to my cousin's? To Noelle's. She'll be glad to have us, I'm sure."

"Erin, we can't go visiting when—"

"Bowie, I'm not talking about a visit. She lives down past the Cowpens. Southwest of here. There's not much going on there, is there? In the upper Ninety-Six District." Erin tried to look very businesslike but couldn't keep the smile from creeping into her voice. "Maybe we could find a preacher there."

Bowie grinned. "What do you think, Jimbo? Should we head for your neck of the woods?"

"Sir, I have to admit I'd like to see the missus again." Jimbo grinned and shifted uneasily in his saddle. "And if you're goin' lookin' for a preacher, maybe I can help. I know one in the neighborhood."

The wagons started to roll. Happily Erin rode beside Bowie on the wagon seat. In less than a week, they'd be mar-ried. They plodded along, and it seemed to Erin that the time was moving as slowly as the medicine 'Lasses dosed her with each spring. The horrible-tasting liquid seemed to stick in her throat and take forever to reach her stomach. Just the thought of it made Erin's stomach lurch and turn.

"What's wrong?" Bowie asked, looking worried. "Are you ill?"

"Ill?" Erin repeated. Every hole and rut the wagon rolled into caused her stomach to twist. She felt that any minute her breakfast of cold bread would come back up. "No, I'm fine," she lied and hoped the road would smooth out soon. "I'm glad that Noelle married that nice Mr. Hastings. He's a fun person."

"I liked him, too." Bowie kept watching her as they rode. Once he touched her forehead and muttered, "No fever."

Erin ignored that remark and tried to act normal. It was the excitement of being so close to a real battle that had her stomach churning, she told herself.

When they camped for the night, she felt a little better. She helped 'Lasses prepare supper. This was going to be the first hot meal they'd had in days. With so many of the British engaged in North Carolina, she and Bowie agreed a fire would be safe.

Several of Jimbo's men scoured the area for meat while Erin and 'Lasses cut the last of their vegetables for stew. Kenneth helped one of the men search for firewood and then started the fire. Bowie and Jimbo watched the women and talked quietly about plans for the future of the wagon train. Erin listened to their conversation and occasionally added her own comments. In reality she had no say in those matters. As an agent of her father, she could voice her opinion, but Bowie's word would be final.

She was glad when they decided to take the wagons back to the hiding place near Bluffwood and then decide what was to become of them. The men brought in several rabbits and gave them to 'Lasses to cut up for stew. Erin rested and tried to make a few plans for herself and for her men.

Bowie was certain the war couldn't go on much past the end of the year. The British would make the sea lanes more difficult to pass, as he'd seen recently when he'd almost lost the *Midnight Star,* so he felt that he couldn't really do much more blockade running. The wagons would have to depend on what could be stolen from the British or from farms.

He watched Erin. She was resting against a tree across the clearing. Bowie rose and went over to her. "Would you like to take a walk before supper?"

"Oh, could we?" Erin asked and took Bowie's hand.

He pulled her to her feet. "We can't go far, but we can stretch our legs."

Erin took his arm, and they strolled out of the clearing. She noticed that 'Lasses watched carefully, but Erin didn't care. She and Bowie would be married in a few days, and 'Lasses couldn't say anything. "I can't wait to see Noelle. She's so sweet. I just know you'll love her."

"Well, since she's already married, I doubt—"

"And you're almost married," Erin retorted, squeezing his hand.

"Drake told me she'd been captured by Tarleton. Did you know about that?" Bowie asked and looked down at her. "Can we sit here for a few minutes? I forgot to bring a blanket, but you can sit on my coat."

As he spread his coat, Erin shivered, remembering her experience with Tarleton. "He didn't . . . Tarleton didn't hurt her, did he?"

Bowie stopped and placed both hands on her shoulders. She looked so frail and pale that he wondered again if she might be ill, if her pallor might be the result of the beating she received at Tarleton's hands. Fury raged in Bowie, and a muscle twitched in his clenched jaw. "Not badly."

Erin dropped down on Bowie's coat and curled her feet beneath her. "I'm glad. I . . . I'd hate for her to be injured or . . . worse."

Bowie gathered her in his arms and held her close. He'd wanted to do it all day, but with 'Lasses' sharp eyes trained on them, he'd behaved as decorously as possible. Now he gave in to his desires and kissed her gently. They lay back for a few minutes and watched the sun set. "Erin, it's time to go back."

"I know," she admitted, "but I don't like the idea."

When they reached the campsite, 'Lasses glared at Bowie and Erin, but Erin ignored the servant. The stew was ready, and several of the men were already eating. The smell was tempting, but Erin's stomach still felt queasy, and she ate little. Everyone was so tired that after they finished their meals, they quickly scrubbed their tin plates and handed them to 'Lasses. She packed the plates and utensils away before dragging Erin off to bed.

Erin would have liked to sleep with Bowie, to spend the whole night with him. She knew that 'Lasses would never stand for that, so the two women hung their blankets for a shelter and went to bed.

Dawn found Erin bustling about the campsite. She fried salt pork and made gravy for the biscuits 'Lasses made. All the men gathered around when the smells of breakfast began to wake them up.

Bowie tasted the food and grinned at Erin, noticing that the bruise on her face had turned slightly greenish yellow. Her smile seemed brighter, and her eyes were more alert. Knowing those to be signs of improvement, he felt better, ate his breakfast, and even whistled while he washed his plate.

When the wagons were ready to go, he lifted Erin into the seat and joined her. Bowie looked up at the clear blue sky and commented, "It's going to be a wonderful day."

Erin agreed. When she had awakened, she'd felt much better. Her mood had improved drastically, and her stomach wasn't the least bit queasy. As they rode along, she hummed a merry tune, and Bowie joined her. She looked back with a smile for 'Lasses and found the servant staring from one to the other of them.

Who cares? Erin thought. In just a few more days, I'll be Mrs. Bowie Gallagher. Happiness seemed to tinge the atmosphere with extra sunlight, and the rays warmed her as she rode.

Spring would be here soon, in just a day or two. Maybe she and Bowie would be married on the first day of spring. With that thought Erin looked shyly up at Bowie. How would their relationship change after marriage? Would he ignore her as many men ignored their wives? Could their relationship stay the same, with lots of laughing and teasing, lots of passion? Erin hoped it would.

"What are you thinking about?" Bowie asked, gazing down at her. Her expression was almost angelic, her cheeks tinted with a delicate blush. He decided that few angels would have the exquisite coloring of Erin Banning. Auburn hair gleaming almost like gold in the sunlight, green eyes as vibrant and sparkling as the Atlantic on a summer day, lips like the first strawberries of summer were all imprinted on his eyelids so that he could never shut his eyes without seeing her face. Looking at her now, he hoped that the dark circles and shadows didn't become a permanent part of the image emblazoned in his memory.

Embarrassed by his question, Erin looked down at her hands and locked her fingers together. "Oh, nothing . . . and everything. Life and living. Love."

Bowie's eyebrows rose in question. "Are you having second thoughts about marrying a seafaring scoundrel like me?"

"Oh, Bowie, you won't be gone for many months at a time, will you? I mean, after we're married, you won't . . . I mean, some husbands . . . forget they're married." Erin lowered her eyes momentarily and then gazed deeply into his. The blue of the sky had somehow translated itself, mirrored itself in his eyes. The wind ruffled his light brown hair, and he grinned boyishly.

"I'll love ye till the day we die, me darlin', and that's a promise." He was deliberately teasing her but meant every word. He, too, had wondered if their relationship would change quickly. Many of his friends and acquaintances were perfectly content to remain away from their wives as long as possible. Bowie believed that would never happen with Erin.

He reached down and kissed the top of her head. From behind him he could hear 'Lasses making noises to catch his attention. Clearly she didn't want him too close to Erin until after the ceremony. He turned, glanced at the servant, and winked. Her eyes widened and she scowled at him, but Bowie didn't care. This day was too marvelous for a frown to upset him.

With a grin for Kenneth, Bowie turned his attention back to Erin. They talked for a while about inconsequential things. "Erin," he said finally, "where would you like to live after we're married?"

Erin turned to look at him. She'd never considered where

they'd live. "I . . . I don't know. I just expected . . . I don't really know what I expected."

Bowie grinned. "I know what you mean. I never thought of it until just now."

"Where do you want to live?" Erin asked and looked up at him. She knew that he hadn't been home to Edisto in quite a while. Would he want to go there after they were married? From her father Erin understood that Bowie didn't get along with his own father very well.

"I don't know," he answered simply. He'd like to take Erin home, home to Edisto Glade, a paradise surrounded by the ocean and replete with lush green growth, abundant wildlife, and stunning sunsets. "I want you to meet my mother. My . . . my father may object, but I don't care. I'm going to take you there and show you the most beautiful place on earth."

Erin saw the pride written across his face and wanted to go there, to be with him in a place he loved that much. "I want to meet her, too. She must be very special."

Bowie agreed with her, and they were quiet for a few moments. He'd thought when he left that he could stay away forever, but he knew now that wasn't possible. Somehow, when the war ended, if not before, he'd have to go and make peace with his father. This war had split families and friends, spawned hatred where once there had been love. Bowie hoped the fight was worth the cost.

Before long they made camp for the night, and once again Erin and Bowie took a walk. This time Bowie remembered to bring a blanket. A short distance from the camp they spread the blanket and sat down.

"Erin," he said after a few minutes, "tell me about your mother."

Erin closed her eyes. She'd carried the weight of her mother's illness for years. Could she share it with Bowie now? She wanted to but hesitated. Then she decided that if she and Bowie were to have a chance of happiness, she'd have to be completely honest. "She fell. For a few days she was unconscious. We didn't know whether she'd live or die."

"That must have been hard on you. How old were you then?" Bowie put his arms around her and pulled her close, trying to comfort her as best he knew how.

"I was twelve." Erin snuggled against him and slid her arms around his waist. "She was never smart, but she was beautiful. She *is* beautiful. Almost childlike. I've pretty much mothered her ever since."

"What a terrible thing for a child to face." Bowie kissed her on her forehead. "Seems like we've both got problems with our parents."

"Yes." Erin smiled, thinking of her mother's silliness. "I wonder what she'll say when she finds out we're married."

"Do you think she'll object?" Bowie asked, suddenly uncomfortable with his entrance into this family. Arlen had been like a father to him, but having a mother-in-law who might object had never occurred to him.

"I doubt it. Even if she does, she won't remember that she did." Erin thought of her father. "But I bet Papa will be happy."

Bowie grinned. "I think so, too. And I know my mother will love you. I guess if half of our parents are happy, what do we care about the other half?"

With Erin pressed against him, Bowie felt his passions begin to rise. He kissed her forehead, her cheeks, her eyelids, and then her mouth. Feeling an urgency that superseded everything else, Bowie drew her closer to him until they were lying side by side.

He couldn't make love to her here in the woods where anyone might happen upon them, but he wanted to do just that. Since the moment he'd seen her crawling across the clearing at Tarleton's camp, the thought of making love to her had never been far from his mind. Now, lying with her in his arms, his need became acute. Aching with want, Bowie stood up.

"What's wrong?" Erin asked, rising to a sitting position.
Bowie turned away from her. He didn't want her to see

the evidence of his desire. "I think it's time we returned. 'Lasses will be out looking for us."

Erin giggled. "So she will. I suppose you're right."

Bowie helped her up, and they walked slowly back to camp. He felt foolish for allowing his emotions to take hold of him that way, but there was nothing to be done about it. He'd simply have to be more careful until after they married, but then they'd have a lifetime to look back on this and laugh. He knew that the rest of the journey wouldn't be easy. For the next few days 'Lasses would be watching Erin like a lioness.

CHAPTER
17

LUCKILY JIMBO KNEW THE WAY TO TYGER REST, THE
Arledge plantation on the Middle Tyger River. It had been
so long since Erin had visited with her cousin that the little
group would have been hopelessly lost if they'd counted on
her to give directions. When they reached the road that led
to the plantation, Erin and Bowie left the wagon with Jimbo
and rode the rest of the way on horseback.

Bowie's horse, Bahama, was high-spirited and eager to
gallop, but Erin's mount, Honey, trotted along at a decorous
pace as befitted a horse bearing a lady. When they came
through the narrow lane lined with boxwoods and crape
myrtles, Erin felt the excitement course through her.

A tall black man ran out to meet them. He held a musket
in his hand and refused to move until they'd introduced
themselves.

"Please tell my cousin—"

"Erin!" came a feminine squeal from a window on the
top floor of the house. "Is that really you? Lard, bring them
in at once."

The servant she addressed as Lard lowered the musket
and took their reins. Bowie dismounted and helped Erin
down. Hand in hand, they walked across the yard and onto
the wide porch. By this time Noelle had raced down the
stairs and swung open the door.

"Erin Banning, it *is* you! Come in, come in!" Noelle Arledge Hastings threw her arms around Erin and smiled at

247

Bowie. Noelle held the door for them to enter the keeping room. "What brings you to Tyger Rest?"

Erin giggled and hugged her cousin again. "Noelle, I'm so happy to see you. We saw Drake two days ago. He sends you his love."

Noelle beamed and blushed. "Can you believe it? I'm married."

Bowie stood behind Erin, smiling at the two giggling girls. He noticed that the shape of their faces was similar, but little else. Noelle's eyes were blue, almost sapphire; Erin's were deep and glittering green. Noelle's hair looked as if it had been kissed by the sun's golden rays; Erin's looked like copper gleaming in the same sunlight.

"This is Bowie Gallagher," Erin said and took his hand once again. "We're going to be married."

Noelle hugged first Erin and then Bowie. "When?"

Bowie laughed. "As soon as we can find a preacher."

"If I send Lard after him, Caleb York will come tomorrow." Noelle pulled Erin toward the sofa. "Sit down. I'll send Lard right now."

"Oh, Noelle," Erin called, and Noelle turned around. Erin smiled. "The rest of our group is coming soon. They're in wagons, so it'll take a few minutes. You'd better warn Lard. I wouldn't want him to shoot any of them."

"I'll do it." Noelle whirled and hurried out the door.

Bowie slipped his arm around Erin as he watched Noelle leave. "She's a pretty girl, but not as lovely as you."

Erin laughed and kissed him lightly. "You'd better say that, or you'll be in big trouble."

"Jealous, are you?" Bowie teased, feeling free and relaxed for the first time in days. He felt safe here among the back-woods of South Carolina.

"Not in the least," Erin denied and kissed him again. "I'm just warning you, that's all."

Bowie looked around. The room was neat and clean but smelled strongly of smoke. There was no fire in the fireplace. "Do you smell smoke?"

Erin sniffed the air. The odor of smoke clung to the room,

but it wasn't a fireplace scent. "The smell must be from when the Indians tried to burn this place down."

"Indians? When?" Bowie asked and stood up. He strode to the window and looked out. Beside the porch a tall cedar tree shaded the house, but part of the tree was burned and scarred.

"Last fall. That was why Drake brought Noelle to my house." Erin giggled. "He wanted to let her stay with us because she'd be safer there. Little did he know that Walter Martin lived with us. Noelle could never pretend to be loyal to the king or take that silly oath, so Drake brought her back here."

Bowie sat back down beside Erin. "This is a nice place. Quiet and out of the way. How many slaves does she own?"

"I don't really know. There used to be nine, but some of them were killed when the Indians raided." Erin shook her head slowly, knowing that if her own slaves were killed, she'd mourn for them like family.

"Looks like a lot of work goes into running this place. Who does it?" Bowie asked.

"I do a lot of it," Noelle answered as she came back through the door. "There's Lard and Mandy. Drake gets home when he can. With the war going on, we don't have too much to do."

"It must be hard," Erin replied, wondering how she could ever manage without the help of her own slaves.

Noelle smiled shyly. "I sort of like it. Without a lot of slaves, life is less complicated. Lard and I can manage most of the chores when Drake isn't here. Mandy handles the inside work. Was Drake . . . he hasn't been hurt or anything, has he? I haven't seen him in almost two months."

Erin knew exactly what Noelle was experiencing. Having been separated from Bowie on several occasions, Erin was familiar with the loneliness and worry that accompanied those times. "He was fine. He's been promoted to major, did you know?"

Nodding, Noelle replied, "Yes. I had a letter from him. One of the soldiers brought it when he returned from Virginia. Drake formally joined Dan Morgan at the Cowpens. Since then he's been riding with Morgan and the Continentals."

"Not anymore," Bowie said. "Morgan's been furloughed because of his health. He's returning to Virginia to recuperate."

"Well, where's Drake, then?" Noelle edged forward on her seat. "Is he . . . in danger?"

Bowie looked at Erin and decided he would be the best one to answer Noelle's questions concerning Drake's safety and whereabouts. Bowie ran his fingers through his hair and sighed. "When we left, he was with General Greene's men at Guilford Courthouse, and there was a fierce battle going on. We don't know how involved Drake became, but when we met him, he was searching for food."

"For the army?" Noelle asked and rose. She strode to the fireplace and gazed into the ashes. "Maybe he's safe. He doesn't know yet . . . maybe, he'll never know. I'm going to have a baby."

Erin jumped up and embraced her cousin. "Noelle, how wonderful! Of course he'll know. He'll probably be home soon. I know he wanted to come—he said he'd be here as soon as he could get a leave."

Noelle looked at Erin and smiled a tremulous smile. "Do you really think so?"

Bowie stood and patted Noelle's back. "He'll be home soon, very soon."

"Well, then, I'd better get this place cleaned up." Noelle smiled at her guests. "How long can you stay with us?"

"Just a few days," Bowie answered and sat back on the sofa. "We'll be giving our men a few days to see their families. Many of them are from around here."

A commotion arose in the yard, and all three went to the window to see. Erin waved at her odd group. "There they are. Our crusaders."

Erin, Bowie, and Noelle went out onto the porch. Noelle called, "Here we are. Put the animals in the barn. Lard, help them."

'Lasses got out of the wagon and strutted over to the porch. "How you, Miss Noelle?"

Noelle hugged her and grinned. "I'm fine. Guess what? I'm going to have a baby."

'Lasses held Noelle at arm's length and peered at her stomach. "Looks like you is for sure. This a happy day!"

Giggling, Noelle hugged 'Lasses again. "Tomorrow will be even happier. The preacher is going to be here to marry Erin and Bowie. Go out to the kitchen and find Mandy. I know she'll be glad to see you. You can sleep in her cabin."

Noelle led Erin and Bowie back into the keeping room. "Did you have any trouble getting here? I mean, I know you were at Guilford Courthouse, but what were you doing there?"

Erin explained about her father's injury and the resulting decision to allow her to lead the wagons. "The first time I had no trouble at all, but the second trip was horrible."

"What happened? Tell me everything," Noelle said and sat across from Erin and Bowie. "Did you encounter British soldiers?"

"We certainly did," Bowie answered. "Look at Erin's face. Those bruises are faint now, but they were dark and ugly a few days ago."

Noelle leaned forward. "I assumed you'd fallen. What happened?"

"I ran into Tarleton." Erin closed her eyes briefly but managed to smile. "I escaped. I know he's furious."

Noelle shook her head. "I'll wager he is. He found me, too. That man is a sadist if ever I met one. What did he do?"

Erin smiled mischievously. "Well, I refused to talk. I wouldn't give him my name or anything. That made him furious. Then I mentioned the magic name, and he went wild."

"What magic name?" Noelle asked and clasped her hands together around her stomach.

"Morgan," Erin answered and burst into laughter. "It wasn't funny at the time. I mean, Tarleton really hit me hard. I guess my goading was more than he could stand after losing so many men, cannon, and ammunition. But it was almost worth the bruises to see the look on that man's face when I said Morgan's name."

Noelle nodded. "I wish I could have been there. I'm probably the reason he was so angry with you because he let me go. Drake intervened and said we were betrothed." Noelle laughed. "At that time, marrying a British officer was the furthest thing from my mind."

"You didn't know he was working for Morgan?" Erin asked and curled her hand in Bowie's. "At least I've never had any doubts about whose side Bowie is on."

"At that time I had nothing but doubts," Noelle admitted and then added, "I think most of my doubts were feasible, considering that he'd just walked into Tarleton's camp, into the tent, and told Tarleton to let me go. I figured anyone with that much influence must be British for sure."

Mandy announced that supper was ready. Erin, Bowie, Jimbo, Kenneth, Sidney, Phillip, and Noelle ate in the dining room while the others ate in the kitchen. After eating food prepared on the trail, Erin savored every bite of the chicken and dumplings. Afterward, Mandy surprised them with thick slices of apple pie.

"That was a fine supper," Bowie said and stretched.

"It sure was, ma'am," Jimbo said to Noelle. "I didn't want to interrupt you folks before, but I wanted to tell you that I knew your pappy. Charles Arledge was a fine man."

"Thank you, Jimbo. I miss him a great deal." Noelle smiled and led the party back to the keeping room. "Bowie, will you light a fire? Spring may be here tomorrow, but there's a chill in the air tonight."

Bowie lay new logs in the fireplace and lit the kindling. Soon the dry wood caught and began to crackle and pop. Lard came to the door of the keeping room, and Noelle went to speak with him while everyone else settled down. Bowie and Sidney sat at the Queen Anne tip top-table and played draughts while Erin took a seat near the fire.

"Wonderful," Noelle announced. "Caleb York will be

here tomorrow. Erin, come with me. We'll plan your wedding."

Erin and Noelle consulted with Mandy and 'Lasses about food and accommodations. Then they went into Noelle's bedroom to decide what Erin would wear. Noelle brought out a sapphire gown.

"That's the gown I gave you last fall, isn't it?" Erin asked, fingering the fine silk.

"Yes. It's the nicest dress I have, and I've worn it only once." Noelle held it up to Erin. "I thought this dress was lovely on you then and couldn't understand why you gave it to me. Now I'm giving it back to you. You can wear it tomorrow."

Erin held the dress close. "I gave it to you because it's prettier on you. But I'll wear it tomorrow anyway." She looked down at her travel-worn homespun. "I think it'll be better than this, don't you?"

Forgetting that a war raged outside the house, the two girls set about planning the wedding. When bedtime came, Noelle said Erin could sleep with her. Bowie could sleep in the small bedroom upstairs, and the rest of the men could sleep in the dormitory or old slave cabins that had stood empty since the Cherokee raid.

Noelle asked Lard to fill the bathing tub with water. Within a few minutes Erin was submerged in warm, soapy water. "Oh, this is luxury. I've been on the road for too long."

Bowie waited in the keeping room. He wanted to spend a few minutes with Erin before retiring. All evening, especially since Noelle had announced that the preacher was coming, he'd been nervous.

Erin slipped out of Noelle's room and closed the door. She found Bowie standing before the fireplace. "Oh, I didn't know you were still up."

Bowie spun around. Erin slipped on her wrapper and crossed the room. To Bowie, she'd never looked lovelier. Her hair hung like a cloud around her head, and her eyes glittered. There was something about her face, something indefinable, that appealed to him. It was as if she had some secret knowledge, some wonderful feeling, something that nobody else knew about. "Tell me why you look so happy."

Smiling, Erin stood on her tiptoes and kissed him. "Because we're getting married tomorrow, silly goose."

Bowie studied her for a few moments. That might be it, but he thought it was more. He led her to the sofa. "Let's sit here for a minute. I wish there were curtains. I can just imagine 'Lasses standing out there in the cold, watching us."

Erin laughed at his silly imagination but glanced at the windows anyway. "I doubt she'd brave the cold just to spy on us."

With her sitting so near, smelling so sweet, Bowie could hardly think. He wanted to forget about the promise of tomorrow and make her his today. Vivid in his memory were the moments he'd first made love to her, her innocent wide-eyed pleasure, his own gratification. Bowie kissed her, unable to keep the distance between them any longer.

Turning slightly to accommodate his kiss, Erin gave herself over to his expertise. Bowie's kisses were more intoxicating than the most powerful wine and much more exhilarating. Tomorrow his kisses would belong to her forever, and she could get drunk on them every night for the rest of her life.

Bowie pulled away, hating the distance that separated them. "I think we'd better stop or . . ."

Inhaling deeply, Erin nodded. "Good night," she whispered. She rose and ran back to Noelle's bedroom.

Erin's wedding day, the first day of spring, dawned as crystal clear as the tropical sea. Late in the afternoon 'Lasses brought in biscuits and molasses, but Erin couldn't eat. She paced back and forth while Noelle giggled and shook her head.

"What's so funny?" Erin asked, hating the churlish tone of her voice.

"You are, goose. You're acting like a chicken that knows

it's going to be Sunday dinner." Noelle sat back in the chair and arranged a little bouquet of wild azaleas Kenneth had picked. "This soft pink will be perfect with your dress."

Noelle arranged Erin's hair. She brushed until it shone, then wound it into a high chignon. Pinning in a spray of the azaleas, she stopped for a moment and looked at Erin. Noelle hugged her cousin and continued.

"What was that hug for?" Erin asked.

Noelle sat on the chair with Erin and looked in the mirror. "I'm so happy for you. I know you and Bowie are perfect for each other. I just wish Drake could be here."

Erin felt her cousin's sadness as if it were her own. "I'm sorry, Noelle. I wish he could be, too."

"Our wedding was sweet, but we didn't have any guests. Just Mandy and Lard." Noelle sighed and smiled as she remembered. "We were so happy just to have found each other."

Erin could understand Noelle's feelings. Bowie and Erin would never have met if he hadn't brought her father home. Fate sometimes stepped in to bring two people together who were meant to be together.

"Do you hear that?" Erin asked, listening intently to the sound of music filtering through from the other room.

"It's Papa's fiddle," Noelle explained. "Kenneth has agreed to play for you."

"Oh, how wonderful!" Erin turned and enjoyed the lilting sounds for a few moments. "I love music."

"We'll have dancing later, after your vows are said." Noelle hugged Erin again and sighed. "If only Drake could be here, the day would be perfect."

"Oh, Noelle," Erin whispered and clung to her cousin. "I'm scared."

Noelle laughed. "Wasn't it you who told me last fall that you admired a woman who'd kissed a man? Surely you've kissed Bowie. I can tell you that the relationship between a man and a woman is so special, so . . . private. I just know you'll be happy."

Inside Erin quivered, but she lifted her chin and tried to smile again. "I know. I'm just a little nervous, I suppose."

"Erin, my sweet, all brides are nervous. Don't worry. Everything will work out beautifully." Noelle stood and looked at the door. "I think it's time we met our guests."

Erin rose and walked with Noelle to the door. "Go ahead. I'll wait."

Noelle opened the door, left the bedroom, and closed the door behind her. Erin hesitated for a few moments, but the door opened slowly again. Thinking Noelle had returned, Erin asked, "Did you forget—"

"Oh!" Erin clapped her hand over her mouth as Drake Hastings stepped into the room. "Noelle just went out—"

"I saw her." Drake took Erin's hand. "I know Noelle will stand with you, but I want a part in this wedding, too. As I'm the nearest of kin here, though we're stretching the term a bit, could I escort you to the minister and your waiting husband-to-be?"

"Thank you, Drake. I would be proud to walk with you. I'm proud to call you cousin." Erin placed her hand atop Drake's arm and walked through the door with him.

As they strolled between the people waiting for the vows to be said, the satin underskirt of Erin's dress whispered softly, the only sound in the room. Bowie, looking handsome in the best frock coat and breeches Noelle could find, stood by the minister. Noelle smiled through tears of joy as Drake and Erin reached the small knot of people by the fireplace.

Erin's hand shook as Drake released her and moved to Noelle's side. She'd never been more frightened. Marriage was a step she'd seldom allowed herself to consider taking because of the lack of suitable men in Charleston since the war. Now a man had found her, a wonderful, strong, passionate man, a man she loved more than life.

Bowie looked down at his bride. He sensed that she was afraid and took her hand. Standing together, hand in hand, they listened to Caleb York. When the minister finished, Bowie couldn't remember all the words he'd heard, but Erin belonged to him now, forever. They were one in the sight of God and man, and nothing could separate them.

The crowd thronged around them, clapping him on the back, shaking his hand, hugging Erin. Noelle and Drake disappeared momentarily, but they returned and joined the well-wishers. Bowie shook Jimbo's hand and saw tears in the man's eyes.

"That's as purty a weddin' as ever I seed." He mopped at the tears and pumped Bowie's hand. "And shore 'nuff the purtiest bride."

"I agree wholeheartedly." Bowie grinned and turned to Drake. "I'm glad you managed to get here. I hadn't told Noelle you were going to try, because I didn't want to disappoint her."

"Thank you. And congratulations." Drake handed Bowie a cup of cider. "Sorry I can't offer you anything stronger, but this is good."

They stepped into the dining room and sat down to smoke a church warden pipe and talk while Erin and Noelle fussed with their guests. Bowie noted that Drake hadn't mentioned the battle and hesitated to bring up the subject, but he wanted to know the outcome. "What can you tell me about Guilford Courthouse?"

Drake shook his head slightly from side to side and took the white kaolin pipe from Bowie. He sucked briefly on the clay stem. "Cornwallis is claiming victory although he suffered much higher casualties. He's now running for the sea. Wilmington, we believe."

"What's he doing in North Carolina anyway? I'd heard his instructions from Clinton were to hold Charleston and South Carolina at all costs," Bowie said and watched Drake carefully as he broke off the end of the kaolin pipe and passed it back to him. If anyone in the Patriot force could know about Cornwallis, then Drake would, having been a soldier in the British Army until recently.

"I don't know. He should have stayed where he was. General Greene seems to think that South Carolina is vulnerable since Cornwallis left. Tarleton's with him, too."

Drake shook his head slightly. "Who knows what Cornwallis will do next?"

Noelle came in and took Drake's hand. "Come on. We've cleared the furniture to make room for dancing. You can smoke that silly pipe later. Since our wedding feast was so quiet and private, I want to dance and dance."

Bowie followed them into the keeping room and took Erin's hand. "Will you dance with me?"

"Yes," she whispered and took her place beside him. The touch of his hand sent tingles through her. Erin knew she was blushing as the others watched her and Bowie dance, but she didn't care. This was her night, the most special night in her life.

They danced for more than an hour, but Erin's men were leaving early the following morning to visit their kin, so the party ended early. Erin walked up the narrow stairs while Bowie remained for a drink with Drake. Silently she thanked Bowie for being so thoughtful.

Noelle brought up a pretty white batiste nightgown and handed it to Erin. "Here, you need something pretty. I have another." She looked at the green ribbon tying back Erin's hair. "This nightgown has blue ribbons, but it'll still be lovely, even with your green ribbon."

"Noelle," Erin began and sat down on the narrow bed. "Thank you for everything you've done. You've made this a very special day for us."

"Nonsense. You'd have done the same for me," Noelle contended and fingered the pearls Irene Brooks had given her moments before she died. "Besides, I loved doing it. Someone very dear tried to make my wedding, when I was engaged to John, just as special." Thinking of Irene clouded Noelle's eyes with tears. In time they could have been as close as mother and daughter. Noelle thought of John Brooks. He'd been so kind, so gentle. She hadn't loved him, even though they'd been engaged. It seemed so odd that she was now so happily married to John and Irene's nephew. Noelle looked at her cousin and smiled.

"You've been through so much, yet you're so happy,"

Erin said and took Noelle's hand. "I admire you very much."

"I had to learn not to wallow in sadness and grief. These times are too hard." Noelle's eyes glistened with unshed tears. "We have to make our joy whenever and wherever we can. Now I have Drake and this little one."

Erin smiled as Noelle patted her stomach. "Go to your husband. I know he won't be home long."

When Bowie came up the stairs a little while later, the room was bathed in the soft glow of a single candle, and Erin sat at a little dressing table. "I'm sorry. I thought you were . . . I can wait a while longer."

"No," she said and sprang to her feet. Erin had wanted to appear calm and reserved, like a proper bride, but she couldn't. She ran across the tiny room and threw herself into Bowie's arms.

Bowie closed the door behind him and wrapped his arms around her. He lifted her slight weight and carried her to the narrow bed. "I'm sorry this isn't the place I would have chosen to take a wedding trip in normal times."

Quivering inside, Erin tried to smile. "We can travel after the war. For now this will be fine."

Bowie placed her on the bed and covered her up. He began to remove his clothes. He felt shy all of a sudden but couldn't say why. He'd undressed in front of many women, even Erin. Somehow the wedding vows and the fact that this was their wedding night made him slightly nervous. He hung his clothes on the nail next to Erin's clothes and climbed into bed.

Breathing heavily, Erin whispered, "Aren't you going to blow out the candle?"

"If you insist." Bowie started to get out of bed.

"No." Blushing, she caught his arm and held him. "I want to . . . I mean, whatever you want."

Bowie slid back down beside her. "I love you, Erin. I never thought I'd say that to a woman . . . any woman."

Erin could feel his breath warm on her face, and she looked into the shadows of his face. His eyes, dark glittering sapphire, almost matched the gown she'd been married in, and she felt a warmth begin to spread through her. It had started when they danced and continued now. Her body, clad in the thinnest of batiste gowns, responded to his touch.

She wriggled into his arms, fluttering her hands across his chest and encircling his neck. Though Erin didn't know exactly what to do, she understood that her fingertips brought a gasp from him. Trembling with timidity, she wound her hands in his light brown curls, drew his head down, and kissed him. She wanted this night to be one he would never forget, as special to him as it would be to her.

Bowie fought hard to restrain himself. Tonight was a special night for Erin. He wanted it to be the most memorable night of her life. Her fingers entwined in his hair, her lips open and willing, her fragrance so soft and enticing, it sent shivers of desire down his spine. He wondered how long he could remain in control if she kept up her gentle ministrations.

It was time he took over. Bowie drew his body alongside hers and cradled her in his arms. Deepening their kiss until he felt her arch against him, he allowed his hands to massage the muscles of her back and play in her silken hair. Her wide-eyed gaze shattered his composure, and for a few moments he allowed passion to assume command of his body.

Willfully he resumed control of himself. This night, of all nights, he wanted to restrain his emotions until he was assured that Erin's desires were satisfied. He would begin a long period of teaching her to make love, a time that would thrill him and gratify her.

When Erin's fingers playfully brushed across his nipples, he decided that he had a willing and apt pupil. Delighted with his bride's initiative, he kissed her gently, then placed many little butterfly kisses over her face and neck. He moved his hand slowly down her body until he reached her breasts. Through the thin fabric of her gown, he played with her nipples until they were as hard as the tiny pebbles on the beach.

Bowie could stand the gown no more. He wanted nothing

between them, nothing but love. With a deft motion he took the hem of the gown and drew it up until he pulled it over her shoulders and threw it across the room. Lying down beside her again, he shifted until his mouth caught her nipple and began to tease and touch it, gently at first with his open lips and then with his tongue. The tiny bud of her nipple hardened quickly as his tongue caressed it, tracing tiny circles, nibbling with his teeth until she moaned with desire.

Erin thought she could stand no more. Instead of climbing atop her and taking her quickly as she'd thought he would on their wedding night, he seemed to be enjoying himself with this slow teasing that sent quivers of pleasure through her body. His fingers played across her stomach, barely touching her, and then down her legs, sending fire and sparks from each point of contact.

Pressing her hands against his chest, she began to trace tiny circles in the thatch of hair that gave evidence of his masculinity. She trailed her fingers down the dark line that led from his navel to the apex of his legs. When her hand touched the firmness of his manhood, she drew back in surprise. She hadn't expected anything so hard and large so soon.

Bowie could stand no more. Erin's fingertips on his masculinity set his body quivering with passion. Groaning, he drew himself over her and eased his way between her pliant legs. Holding back for a few moments longer, he fondled her legs, then caressed that tiny part of her that could send her body into spasms—and did.

When his lips covered hers in a kiss that promised fireworks, she arched her body toward him. The hair on his legs prickled her a little, and she purposely rubbed against them as he slid inside her. Nothing in life prepared her for the ecstasy she felt now, the uncontrollable passion that unleashed itself in that moment. Waves of sensation flooded over her in a moment of spontaneous fusion with his body.

He was lying on top of her, moving gently, when Erin opened her eyes to the smoldering sapphire of his gaze.

What had happened? Why was he still there? she wondered, vaguely feeling that she'd done something wrong.

And then she felt it, the warmth and strength of him still inside her. Gasping for breath, she marveled that he'd given her such pleasure and gained nothing in return. Her entire body felt spent, and she knew that nothing would ever equal the moment she'd experienced.

He began to move again, slowly, tantalizingly, and Erin felt something deep inside respond. Could she find that delicious desire again so soon? Yes, she could. A smoldering coal flamed to life, and she began to match his rhythm. The crescendo began all over again, rushing forward in wild dissonance that caused ripples of pleasure to radiate throughout her body.

Bowie moaned with pleasure. Erin's hips ground against his own, and her breasts pressed against his chest. Catching her nipple in his mouth, he sucked gently and felt the pressure building in his loins. He'd held back long enough. With Erin's body writhing beneath him, he allowed himself to reach that precipice from which there was no return. All around him the air sizzled with his passion, and he clung to Erin as she fell with him over that vast escarpment of rapture.

Moments later, lying beside her once again, Bowie kissed the tip of her nose. Bowie Gallagher, he told himself wryly, you've met your match. . . .

CHAPTER
18

WAVING GOODBYE TO NOELLE AND DRAKE, ERIN AND Bowie rode down the road that led from Tyger Rest. 'Lasses sat in back, her vigilance somewhat relaxed since the wedding. Kenneth, happy to be considered a member of this party, dangled his feet off the back of the wagon.

Jimbo and the men had returned after being gone for a week. Bowie, Drake, and the men had spent a few days gathering food for the South Carolina Irregulars. Without doubt, General Greene would make a renewed effort to regain control of South Carolina now that Cornwallis and Tarleton seemed to have abandoned it.

Camden lay between Tyger Rest and Charleston, so Bowie suggested trying to search the upcountry for supplies that could be needed in the upcoming weeks. They could take the supplies to General Greene, who Drake felt would march toward Camden. With Sumter, Marion, and Lee all headed toward South Carolina with Greene, Drake and Bowie believed that Camden, under British control for almost eight months since Gates had abandoned it, would be the logical focal point of the campaign.

Now, almost three weeks since the wedding, the group of wagoners was on its way. Though she'd enjoyed the time she'd spent with Noelle, Erin was glad to be getting away. She'd felt ill off and on since the wedding. "It must be the difference in the food," she told herself when she vomited one morning after breakfast.

She didn't tell Bowie because he was already concerned

that she looked pale. Laughing at his worry, she'd told him it was because she'd been indoors too long.

He didn't believe her, she realized, but she didn't want him distressed over nothing. Erin was strong and healthy, and this malady, like the cold she'd had last winter, would pass quickly. 'Lasses occasionally eyed her suspiciously but said nothing.

Erin knew that admitting she felt bad would only encourage both of them to worry, so she tried very hard to smile often and was as cheerful as she could be. This morning she felt fine. Shifting easily in the seat of her wagon, she tucked her arm in Bowie's and lay her head on his shoulder.

Smiling down at his bride, Bowie marveled at the way she'd adjusted to marriage and to the marriage bed. Her hunger there more than made up for her loss of appetite. At first he'd attributed her listlessness to exuberant intimacy, but now he was worried. She tried hard to hide her weariness from him, but he'd known the tireless girl too long to believe her ruse.

Instead of insisting that she didn't feel well, Bowie went along with her game—but just until they reached Charleston where he would speak with Dr. Rutledge. Now, with her head on his shoulder, he decided to make camp early tonight. The sun was hardly above the horizon, and she already looked tired.

Time passed quickly on the trail. At noon they stopped and ate the meal Mandy had packed for them. She'd surprised them by including a basket of apples for them to munch on while they rode.

When they made camp for the night, Erin came to life. She issued orders and organized the watches without hesitating for a moment. Then she scurried about, helping to gather firewood. She and Kenneth seemed to enjoy the exercise.

Erin made a tent of two blankets. With the weather warming up, she needed less to cover her and more to protect her privacy—since her marriage. She and Bowie slept in each other's arms all night. Some nights they made love;

some nights they did not, but they were always cuddled together when morning came.

As they followed the road to the northeast, Erin crooked her arm through Bowie's. "Why do you and Drake think that Greene is heading toward Camden?"

Bowie looked at Erin. She'd never asked him why he thought anything. When he told her what he thought, she accepted it. Maybe she was becoming more interested in the war itself or perhaps trying to understand the strategy. "Well, Lord Rawdon has about eight thousand men divided among ten garrisons in South Carolina. Some are regular British soldiers, but a great many of them are Tories. We believe that Greene is counting on some of those Tories to change sides if South Carolina begins to fall back into the hands of the Patriots."

"Would you trust them?" Erin asked, thinking of Kenneth. She did trust the boy, but what of people who had firm beliefs, those who really wanted to remain a part of the British Empire?

"I don't know, Erin. I'm just a soldier of sorts, and I leave the thinking about such subjects to Greene and Washington. They're more familiar with the state of our defense." Bowie grinned at her and shook his head slightly. "I'm glad I don't have to make the kind of decisions they must."

"Well, why Camden?" she insisted, leaning her head against him. They were stopped near Turkey Creek to water the horses and take their noon meal. She raised her head and looked about. "Can we walk a little? My legs are cramping."

"Of course." Bowie jumped from the wagon and helped her down. "I guess there are a lot of reasons Greene might head toward Camden. The biggest militarily, I suppose, is the fact that they can restock their supplies and reach that fort sooner than anyplace else. But, even more important, Greene and Washington want Camden back because it will improve the morale of our men—and women."

"How?" Erin walked down by the creek and watched the water as it cascaded over smooth rocks on its way to join the Pacolet River. "Do you mean because it was such a blow to the people when Gates abandoned Camden?"

"I think so. We're almost certain that Cornwallis is going to head toward Virginia soon." Bowie stopped and picked up a handful of pebbles. One by one he began tossing them into the creek. "Erin, I don't know how much longer I can stay out of the fighting."

"Fighting!" Erin exclaimed and turned to look him full in the face. "You mean you're thinking about joining the army?"

"Not exactly." Bowie wished he hadn't said anything. He didn't want to make Erin worry, but she had a right to know his innermost thoughts. "What I mean is that my usefulness as a blockade runner is about over for right now. The British are guarding the coast more fiercely than ever. I can still sail out and bring back supplies, but the time it takes becomes greater each trip."

"What difference does that make?" Erin felt panic begin to rise in her. What would she do if Bowie joined the army? How could she face each day, knowing that he was battling for his life in some swamp? "Bowie, you can't do it."

"Erin, we've talked about courage and bravery before. You've never shirked a job because it was dangerous. Hell, you've even managed to tweak Tarleton's nose." Bowie placed his hands on her shoulders and tried to smile reassuringly. "You can't expect me to do any less, can you?"

"Yes. We're married now. You . . . you can continue sailing, and I'll take the loaded wagons to the army, but you can't fight. Not with guns and . . . oh, no, please say you won't."

"Erin, my darling, the sea's almost as dangerous. I never mentioned the close call we had on our last trip." Bowie embraced her and held her against his body. He could feel the tension making her muscles rigid against his hands. He wanted to reassure her, but there was no way short of lying, and he wasn't prepared to lie to her. "Look, I just wanted you to know what I'm thinking about. Nothing is certain at this point."

They continued walking, but Erin knew Bowie would be fighting soon. Even though she trembled when she thought about it, she didn't want Bowie to know how scared she really was. If he went into battle, she wanted him to go knowing that she believed in him completely.

The little band of wagoners ran into the lead scouts of Greene's army and settled down to await the arrival of the main force. Bowie and Erin sat beneath a tree on the bank of the Wateree River and talked about life.

"Bowie, when this is all over, what will happen?" Erin asked, twirling a dandelion between her thumb and forefinger.

"What do you mean?" Bowie propped his chin on one elbow and looked at her profile. He never seemed to tire of watching her. "One thing it means is that I'll never again have to make love to you under a wagon on the hard ground."

Erin laughed and turned to face him. "You are a naughty, naughty boy, Bowie Gallagher."

Bowie drank in her fragrance and the lilt of her laughter. He couldn't remember when he'd heard her giggle so freely. "And you, Mrs. Gallagher, are just as naughty."

She leaned back in his arms to be closer to him. She simply couldn't keep her hands off him. "I guess sleeping under a wagon is one thing I won't miss. But, I mean, how will the losers and winners come together again? Will the Whigs still hate the Tories? Or will we all forget that we were enemies? Will we be able to forgive our friends and neighbors—our relatives—for choosing the other side?"

"God, Erin, I don't know. We'll have to find ways of living together again, or the war will never really end." Bowie drew her close and cuddled her against his chest. "We'll just have to live each day and pray that each successive day becomes easier."

"Human nature may prevent that, though," Erin said thoughtfully. "Like when children play and one side defeats the other. The winners like to gloat, and the losers can be rather bitter."

"That's true, but we'll simply have to overcome that, Erin. Best friends may never be best friends again. Brothers may never again feel any closeness." Bowie kissed the top of her head and hugged her. "But all that won't change the way I feel about you."

When they'd unloaded the wagons, Bowie said they had to move on. Erin was glad. She felt so tired, more tired than she'd ever felt in her life. For two days the empty wagons rolled southeast toward Charleston.

As they neared the usual hiding place, Bowie became thoughtful. "Erin, we may never have to make one of these trips again."

"Oh, Bowie, do you think the war's that close to ending?" Erin slid forward on the seat and gripped his arm. "Will life return to normal?"

"I don't know about normal, but I think the war's ending." Bowie glanced at the wild azaleas and dogwood trees, pregnant with fragrant blossoms. "This is so beautiful, so peaceful. You'd never know that a war was going on all around us."

Erin agreed. They were getting close to Bluffwood, and she was excited about seeing her parents again. "I can hardly wait to see Papa. He'll be so happy to hear that we're married."

"Do you really think so?" Bowie asked. He hoped she was right. Arlen was a good friend, but Bowie knew that where a man's daughter—his only daughter—was concerned, men were sometimes irrational.

"He'll be thrilled. I know he loves you." Erin crossed her arms and hummed. She was in love and in love with being in love.

Back at the old wagon hideout Bowie stopped and jumped down from his wagon. He called Jimbo over, and they talked for several minutes before they called over several other men.

Erin didn't know what was going on. She was ready to

mount her horse and ride for home. 'Lasses, too, looked eager to get to Bluffwood.

Bowie came back to the wagon. "Erin, we think we won't be needing the wagons again, at least not for a while. We're sending out scouts to find a safer place to leave them."

"But, Bowie, this place has always been safe," Erin protested. Every moment away from home seemed to tick away like hours.

"I realize that, but we want a foolproof place, if we can find one." Bowie strode away to help in the search.

After an hour passed, the men started filtering back into the clearing. Erin watched the direction Bowie had gone, but didn't see him approaching. She began to wonder if something had happened to him but finally saw him striding through the woods.

Bowie found Jimbo, and they talked animatedly for a few moments. Then Bowie walked over to Erin. "I found a good spot. It's a ravine, not too deep, but deep and narrow enough to roll the wagons into. If we need them, we can always pull them out again."

Erin nodded absently. She still didn't understand why they were using another place. "What about the animals?"

"We're taking many of them to Bluffwood. Phillip will take some to his farm. The rest will be divided among the men." Bowie watched the men pushing the wagons down the trail he'd just traversed.

"What happens if you need them again? The animals, I mean. And the men," Erin asked and shifted uncomfortably on the hard wagon seat.

"Phillip will gather as many of the men as he can. We'll just have to do with what animals we can recover. We can't leave them here indefinitely." Bowie went back to oversee the operation.

Within two hours there were but three wagons remaining in the clearing. 'Lasses and Kenneth sat in one with Kenneth at the reins. Phillip and another man were driving off with a second wagon. Jimbo took the third, its bed filled with men from the upcountry.

Erin, Bowie, and Sidney sat on horseback, calling good-byes to their men. Feeling the tears sting her eyes, Erin blinked hard. She didn't want to cry. "For goodness' sake," she murmured. "You didn't cry when Tarleton beat you. Why are you being such a baby now?"

Bowie glanced at her. He heard her talking to herself and wondered if she didn't feel well. When he saw the tears in her eyes, he smiled and moved his horse closer to her. He leaned over and whispered, "I know exactly how you feel."

Nodding, Erin pretended to agree, but she didn't. Nobody could know how she really felt. Bowie, and other men, were free to pursue whatever careers they chose. Erin, because of the special circumstances, had been given that privilege for only a short while.

And now everything was changing. Once again she'd be relegated to the duties of the wife, or daughter, of a plantation owner. Her moments of freedom were no longer available to her. While Erin's tears were shed in part because of the friendships she'd made with her men and her sadness at watching them ride away from her—possibly forever—a great part of her sorrow resulted from the loss of her job.

When, or if, the wagoners were needed again, her father would probably be well enough to lead them. Erin's knowledge would no longer be necessary. Like any substitute, she had little real claim to the position.

Erin dabbed at her eyes with her lace handkerchief. Bowie would be hurt if he knew why she was crying. She wasn't being fair to him. He expected his bride to be happy, and really she was, but watching her men leave was like driving a stake through her heart.

They reached Bluffwood more quickly than she thought they would. As she'd expected, her father greeted them in the parlor. When she saw him, she ran across the room to his chair and hugged him. "Papa! I'm so glad to see you! Is your leg healed?"

"Oh, stop making such a fuss," Arlen complained and winked at Bowie over Erin's head. "You'd think I'd been close to death. You know I'm too ornery to die."

"Sir, I'm happy to see you up and about," Bowie said and held out his hand in greeting. "I can't deny that I've been worried about you."

"Come in. You must tell me everything. I apologize for not rising, but this leg is still giving me some problems." Arlen held up his cane and shook his head sadly. "I fear I'm lamed for life."

Erin glanced at Bowie. He was studying her, as if waiting for her to tell her father about their marriage. It was her place to tell him, but she felt like tiny moths were fluttering in her stomach.

She sat down on the sofa next to her father's chair and indicated that Bowie should join her. "First, Papa, I want you to meet Kenneth Lambert. He . . . well, I'll tell you how we met him later. Now"—she inhaled deeply and took Bowie's hand for support—"I have to tell you . . . well, sir, Bowie and I were married last month at Noelle's."

Arlen's face turned white as he looked from one to the other of them. "Married," he echoed simply.

"Yes, sir," Bowie replied and slipped his arm around Erin's shoulders. "Arlen, I realize I should have asked for her hand in the accepted way, but circumstances were . . . hell, I love her and she loves me. I hope you understand and will forgive us for overstepping your authority in this matter."

Arlen gazed at his daughter's face for a moment and then looked back at Bowie. "I've called you son for a long time. I never thought it would come true." Arlen's green eyes glittered with tears. "Now you truly are my son. You have my blessing and—"

"Papa," Erin interrupted and knelt beside her father. "I'm glad you feel this way. If you didn't, I would have been so sorry, but I love Bowie."

"Thank you, sir." Bowie beamed and joined Erin at Arlen's knees.

Hugging both of them, Arlen shook his head. When they looked up at him, he grinned and mopped his tearful eyes.

"Son, you've got a stubborn woman on your hands. I've never been able to do anything with her. I wish you luck."

"Papa!" Erin exclaimed. "What an ugly thing to say!"

"It's no more than I would have said to him if he'd asked me for your hand." Arlen chuckled and patted Erin's shoulder. "I believe in being honest."

By this time 'Lasses had told all the other servants about the wedding, and they were gathered outside the parlor door, watching to see what Arlen would say. He looked up at them and grinned. "Come in and meet my son-in-law. He has the dubious pleasure of being married to my willful daughter. Annabell, we'll be having a feast tonight to celebrate Erin's marriage."

From that moment the house buzzed with activity. Erin sought the quiet of her room while Bowie talked with Arlen. She had avoided mentioning her capture and hoped Bowie would as well, though she doubted he would.

She walked the short distance to her mother's room down the hall. Erin wanted to tell her mother about the wedding. Bowie could meet Vevila Banning later. Tapping lightly on the door, Erin opened it slowly. "Mama?" she called in a low tone and poked her head in to see if her mother was awake.

"Erin, is that you?" Vevila Banning asked and sat up in bed.

"Yes, Mama, it's me. May I come in?" Erin asked, steeling herself for her mother's reaction to the news.

"Yes, darling, yes." Vevila rose from the bed, walked to her mirror, and patted her coppery curls. "I don't recall seeing you this morning when I went downstairs."

"Mama, I've been . . ." Erin's voice dwindled away. How much should she tell her mother? Not much. It wouldn't do for Vevila to know enough to land Erin, Bowie, and her father in jail. Erin sat down on her mother's divan.

Vevila sat in her favorite rocker and began rocking absently.

"Mother, I want to tell you something. I hope you'll be as happy as I am." Erin placed her hands in her lap, knowing that in spite of her other deficiencies, her mother would demand ladylike behavior and manners. "Mother, I'm married."

"That's nice, dear. Are you and Mr. Perkins going to live at Crestwood?" Vevila asked and sat down to brush her hair.

Erin grimaced. Her mother thought Erin had married Thaddeus Perkins, a man she'd grown up with. Thad had been killed during the siege of Charleston last year, but he and Erin had never really been close enough to consider marriage. This was going to be more difficult than she thought. "No, Mother. I'm married to Bowie Gallagher, not Thad Perkins."

Vevila swung around and stared at Erin. "Not married to Mr. Perkins? Erin, what are you saying?"

"I'm saying that Thad is dead, Mother." Erin tried to think of a way to help her mother understand all this new information, but the outlook was grim. "Mother, I married Bowie Gallagher, a friend of Papa's."

"Erin, that's quite impossible. I don't know any Mr. Gallagher, and I'm not sure that Mr. Banning would allow such a marriage. Mr. Perkins is much more suited to your temperament." Vevila turned to her mirror and began brushing her hair again. "I won't hear anything else about any Mr. Gallagher. And it's quite forward of you to call Mr. Perkins by his first name. You know that's a sign of bad breeding. When I think of the time I spent . . ."

"Yes, Mother," Erin said and left the room. She'd have to ask her father what to do. She went downstairs and found her father and husband still in the parlor.

Arlen took one look at Erin's face and shook his head sadly. "You tried to tell your mother?"

"Yes, Papa. She thinks I'm married to Thad Perkins." Erin dropped onto the sofa beside Bowie and rested her head on his shoulder. "She wouldn't hear anything about Bowie."

"Don't worry, little one. She'll be fine." Arlen reached over and patted his daughter's knee.

*   *   *

The warm spring days passed slowly at Bluffwood, although Erin enjoyed showing the true beauty of the place to Bowie. They walked in the warm sunlight, rode horseback across the gently sloped meadows, rowed the small boat through the myriad tributaries that surrounded the plantation, laughed, and loved. For Erin it was the most wonderful time of her life.

Occasionally a soldier stopped by to eat. Then Erin, Bowie, and Arlen would gather around and listen eagerly to the news. They learned that the Patriots had besieged Augusta with a wooden tower called a Maham, mounted a six pounder on it, and succeeded in taking the strongest fortification.

General Greene had given ground at Hobkirk's Mill just above Camden, but the British under Lord Rawdon had suffered severe losses and were forced to retreat toward Charleston. On May 10, 1781, the British abandoned Camden. The following day the British post at Orangeburg surrendered to General Sumter, who was called the Gamecock. On the fifteenth, Fort Granby surrendered to Henry Lee.

These events made for a jolly household. Erin and Bowie settled into a seductively easy routine in which they didn't really have to think about the tomorrows they might have to face. Bowie, under Arlen's direction, took over the running of the plantation. Arlen beamed with pride at his courageous, lovely daughter and his son-in-law.

Some days Erin felt tired, but that long period of feeling bad had passed except for occasional bouts of leg cramps. Erin was so happy, and she was gaining back some of the weight she'd lost on the arduous trail. She established a routine and went about her normal chores, planning menus, seeing to the daily household assignments, settling squabbles among the servants, and spending time with Bowie.

To Bowie, she looked the picture of health again. He watched as she cuddled a litter of newborn kittens and noticed the new fullness of her breasts. Her cheeks had taken on the soft peach tone of a tropical sunset. He complimented her on her appearance more than once, and every time he saw her, Bowie fell in love with her all over again. He didn't know how he ever got along without her—and hoped he'd never have to again.

One morning Bowie left to take Arlen on a tour of Bluffwood's fields. They took a buggy after breakfast, viewed the sturdy plants of the kitchen garden, and watched several slaves picking early vegetables. The peas were ready to be harvested, along with onions, cabbages, radishes, and greens. Afterward, they traveled over the rest of the plantation and were gone until almost noon.

When Bowie returned, Erin wasn't in the parlor. He ran up the stairs to tell her about the progress of the rice and indigo planting—and found her lying on the floor, trying to rise. "Erin, my darling, what happened?"

Erin allowed him to pick her up and place her on the bed. She looked up at him through clouded eyes. "I don't know. I was walking and then I woke up on the floor. I recall feeling a little dizzy but thought it due to some . . ."

Bowie heard nothing else. He raced across the floor and jerked the bellpull four or five times. He knew that downstairs bells would be jangling in the kitchen and servants' quarters. Nero was the first to reach the room.

Almost dragging him into the room, for Bowie didn't want to take his eyes off Erin, he directed, "Nero, find a doctor. Miss Erin's ill."

Nero's eyes widened, but he didn't linger. He raced for the stairs and met Annabell, 'Lasses, and three other servants. "Miss Erin sick," Nero told them. "I'se goin' fer the doctor."

'Lasses grabbed his hand. "No. Not yet. Lemme see what's goin' on."

"But Mr. Bowie say go," Nero repeated.

"Hold on, Nero," Bowie called from the doorway. "Let's wait until 'Lasses talks to her."

'Lasses strode to the door, gazed at Bowie, and said, "Mr. Bowie, you go on and git yosef a cup of that scuppernong wine and set down in the parlor. I call you if'n I need you."

Bowie turned and watched 'Lasses close the door in his
face. He and the servants walked slowly down the stairs.
He could tell that they were as concerned as he about Erin's
condition.

He found Arlen in the parlor and poured a drink. "Arlen,
I don't know what to do. I just found Erin on the floor. She
fainted."

Arlen leapt to his feet, grimaced in pain, and almost tumbled to the floor. He grabbed the chair arm, caught himself,
and picked up his cane. "Hellfire and tarnation," he muttered. "Let's go."

" 'Lasses is with her. She said—"

"Damn that woman! She can't keep me from my daughter's bedside." Arlen hobbled to the door and called, "Nero,
go for the doctor."

Nero shook his head and strode off muttering, "One say
go. One say don't. 'Nother one say go. What a body to do?"

"Go on. Get Dr.—Hell, who can we get out here?" Arlen
paused and looked at Bowie. "There isn't a doctor near here
that I know of, not since the war started. They're all with
the army or in Charleston."

"We'll take her to Charleston." Bowie took the stairs two
at a time and met 'Lasses coming out of Erin's room.

"Out of my way, woman!" Arlen shouted and limped past
the servant.

"Hold on, Mr. Arlen," 'Lasses said and caught his arm.
"She don't be needin' no doctor."

Bowie glared at 'Lasses and ran into Erin's room. He
knelt beside the bed and took her hand.

"Bowie," she whispered and smiled like the old Erin.
"We're going to have a baby."

"Baby?" Bowie echoed and looked down her slender
body to her stomach. "Are you sure?"

"As sure as a woman can be," Erin admitted and smiled
shyly. "Are you happy or sad about becoming a father?"

"Whooeee," he sang out and danced around the room.

Arlen chose that moment to walk through the door. He
looked first at Erin lying on her bed with a comforter pulled

up to her chin and then at Bowie who stopped spinning and grinned boyishly. Arlen looked back at Erin. "Can you explain to me what is going on here?"

"I'm going to have a baby, Papa," Erin answered simply, her own face mimicking the silly grin on Bowie's.

Bluffwood changed drastically. Everybody deferred to Erin's every whim until she could stand no more. "Bowie, I want to go to Charleston. I need to see Dr. Rutledge, to confirm that everything . . . that the baby is well."

Bowie blew out the candles and slid into bed with her. "Erin, my love, whatever you want to do, we'll do."

She snuggled into his embrace and kissed his cheek. "You're such a sweet husband."

Kissing her lightly, Bowie felt the stirrings of passion and backed away. "Good night, my darling."

Erin gazed at his silhouette against the light coming through the window. "Good night? You mean you're not going to—I mean, I wanted to . . ."

"But, Erin, you're pregnant. We can't do anything to harm this baby." Bowie patted the gentle slope of her stomach.

Feeling the frustration rise in her, Erin reminded him of his promise. "You said whatever I want to do, we'll do."

"Yes, but—"

"Bowie Gallagher, are you telling me you don't love my body since you found out I was pregnant?" Erin turned over and buried her head in her pillow. "You hate me because my body's ugly."

"Ugly? You're more beautiful than ever." Bowie rubbed her back tenderly and tried to turn her to face him, but she stiffened her body. "For God's sake, Erin, what do I have to do to prove that I still love you?"

Smiling in the darkness, Erin turned slightly and kissed his cheek. She slid her arms around his neck and laced her fingers together. "Love me."

Bowie gave up. He kissed her lightly, then more insistently. He'd never wanted her so badly before, but he'd tried to keep from thinking about her body. Now he played his fingers across her stomach and pulled off her gown. "You, my dear, are a very bad girl."

"I hope you like bad girls," she answered breathlessly. Then she added, "One bad girl."

Bowie buried his face in her hair, then nibbled her earlobe. He found her breasts firm and taut as he caught a nipple between his thumb and forefinger, and then covered her breast with kisses. Bowie felt as if he were in heaven, soaring among the stars. "When I named my ship the *Midnight Star*," he said kissing her lips hungrily, "I never knew I was naming her after you."

Erin's body felt weightless. The heaviness that had made her so tired of late vanished, and she floated somewhere above the earth. The stars were like flowers she could gather and frolic with as Bowie sent her reeling from constellation to constellation by tormenting her so deliciously with his tongue.

Never had Erin felt so wild and free. She grasped his hair with her hands and pulled his face toward hers. When he slid inside her, Erin gasped at his enormous proportions, but he waited until she grew accustomed to him and then began to rock above her, tantalizing and teasing. Erin locked her fingers together behind his neck and used him for leverage as she tried to match his rhythm.

Bowie endeavored to be gentle, but the power of his desire overcame him, along with Erin's seductive motion. He could hardly hold himself above her as their pace increased until Bowie felt he would explode with the intensity of his passion. Beneath him, Erin's head thrashed back and forth on the pillow as she reached her stunning gratification and Bowie denied himself no longer.

"Bowie, love me. Love me," she whimpered and opened her eyes dreamily. "You won't stop loving me when I'm fat and ugly, will you?"

"I'll always love you, my dearest," he whispered in return. "More than anybody or anything on earth. You'll always have me."

"Even more than the *Midnight Star?*" she asked and turned slightly in his embrace and trailed her fingers down his chest to his abdomen.

Bowie kissed her forehead, her cheeks, and finally her lips. He marveled that even after making love, her caresses still intoxicated him and he mumbled, "Even more than the *Midnight Star,* for you are my midnight star."

Erin smiled slightly and clung to him, suddenly afraid. "Bowie, promise me you won't leave me."

"Leave you? Why should I leave you?" he asked and kissed her forehead. "You're stuck with me, like it or not."

"You said you might have to join the fighting. Promise me you won't." Erin felt tears sting her eyes. "I couldn't bear for you to leave me alone."

"I won't. Don't worry about something like that." Bowie held her close and wondered what had put such a thought in her head while they were making love.

"Promise me," she insisted as a tear rolled down her cheek and dripped onto Bowie's chest.

He wiped away her tears. "I promise, sweet. I promise."

CHAPTER
19

ERIN AND BOWIE RETURNED TO CHARLESTON SO SHE could consult with Dr. Rutledge. Once again posing as Chauncey Farthingale, Bowie moved into the Bannings' town house with Erin. He sent Nero immediately for Dr. Rutledge.

Smiling at Bowie's concern, Erin puttered around the house and garnered the news from Tupper. "Tupper, tell me what's happened in the time that I've been gone."

"Well, Miss Erin," she began and wiped her hands on her apron. "That Mr. Martin been awful nosy. He done poked around in ever room of this house. I don't know whut he lookin' for, but he sho been lookin' hard."

"I suspected as much," Erin answered, remembering how Walter had pilfered through her things before she left. "Has he asked about me?"

"He asks ever day or two."

"What have you told him?" Erin needed to know before she had to face Walter's questions.

"I done tole him you was at your plantation wif yo mama and papa who sick." Tupper kneaded her dough and rolled it out on the big wooden dough board.

Erin grinned and hugged the cook. "Nobody makes biscuits as good as you do."

Walter wasn't home, so Erin could easily move Bowie's— or Chauncey's—clothes into her room without worrying about being questioned. Bowie had gone to his apartment to retrieve some of his more flamboyant costumes while

Erin made room for them. Before she finished, Dr. Rutledge came in.

"How good to see you, Doctor."

He kissed Erin on the cheek and then held her at arm's length. "You look beautiful. What's wrong? Nero says you're ill."

Color bloomed in Erin's cheeks. "Not ill, precisely. I'm going to have a baby."

"What wonderful news!" Dr. Rutledge kissed her cheek again and hugged her to him. "I delivered you, and now—"

"Good afternoon."

Erin spun around at the sound of a man's voice and found herself staring into Walter Martin's face. "Uh, hello, Walter. How nice to see you."

He strode into the room, took Erin's hand, and kissed it lingeringly. "Why, you look stunning, Miss Banning."

Glancing at Dr. Rutledge, Erin withdrew her hand and sat on her favorite chair. "Mrs., uh, Farthingale. I'm now Mrs. Farthingale, Mr. Martin."

Walter threw back his head in laughter. "I've always known you had a sense of humor." He turned to Dr. Rutledge. "Have you met the elegant Mr. Farthingale? He's a—"

"I'm afraid I wasn't joking, Mr. Martin," Erin interrupted in an insistent voice. "And if you can't speak kindly of my husband, please don't speak of him at all. He's quite sensitive, you know."

Staring blankly at her, Walter sank into the chair opposite her. "You're serious. You're really serious. Please forgive me, Miss—er, Mrs. Farthingale. I had no idea you'd . . . I mean, I knew you entertained him on occasion, but . . . You have my best wishes."

Erin could hardly keep from laughing but smiled sweetly. "Thank you, Mr. Martin. I'll be happy to convey your good wishes to Mr. Farthingale when he returns."

"Please do," Walter said and stood. With his head erect he strode from the room.

Dr. Rutledge waited until Walter's door slammed upstairs before turning to Erin. "Farthingale? That fop is actually Bowie Gallagher?" Dr. Rutledge laughed heartily when Erin nodded. When he quelled his laughter, he shook his head gently and asked, "My dear, have you had any problems? Do you know how far along you are?"

Erin rose, walked to the harpsichord, and trailed her fingers along a few keys. "Not really. I'm tired more frequently. And I fainted."

Nodding, Dr. Rutledge came to her side. "Erin, you must rest. I want you to do nothing more strenuous than writing menus. Please remember this for your child's sake as well as your own."

"Is there anything else?" Erin tried to smile at her old friend but couldn't quite manage.

He looked at her eyes and shook his head. "Rest. Eat properly."

Erin sat down, and the doctor felt her pulse. "I promise to behave."

When Dr. Rutledge was gone, Erin returned to her task. She wanted all of Bowie's things to be stored by the time he arrived. Living with Walter would be difficult, she mused as she hung "Chauncey's" pink satin breeches and frock coat.

Walter Martin was seldom at home, and Bowie knew his presence made Walter uneasy. He ate dinner with Erin and Bowie less and less frequently. By the first of July they saw him so rarely that they were surprised when he came home at all.

Bowie surmised that Walter's schedule was dictated as much by business as conditions at home. In the middle of July the Patriots forced the British to retreat from Monck's Corner. The rear guard of the fleeing British Army was attacked by Marion's advance troops at Quinby's Creek and the Cooper River. The British troops were busy trying to find food and housing for all the people coming into Charleston.

Erin's stomach swelled until she was seldom comfortable.

She tried to exercise moderately and eat well, but life in Charleston wasn't easy for anyone—least of all a pregnant woman. Being so obviously pregnant, she couldn't walk about Charleston, so she confined herself to her garden.

From there she could see the British ships in the harbor and grew angry every time she looked over Oyster Point. One day soon, she told herself, they'll be gone.

When Bowie came in one afternoon, Erin saw that something was troubling him. "What's wrong?" she asked and settled herself in her rocking chair.

Bowie paced back and forth for a few minutes. Then abruptly he turned to face her. "Erin, I've got to go. I can't remain here as the elegant Mr. Farthingale any longer."

Erin sprang to her feet, grasping the back of the rocker for support as astonishment registered across her blanched face. "Go? Where? Bowie, what do you mean?"

"I want to join Marion's men," he began and watched her lower herself slowly back into her chair. "We've got the British on the run, Erin. Marion needs every man."

"You promised me," she said slowly and evenly. "You promised you'd never leave me."

Bowie strode to the fireplace and propped his arm on the mantel. He'd promised, he knew, but he had to find a way to convince Erin that he had no choice but to join up now. "Erin, my darling, I won't be gone for long. The British will be sailing out of here in a matter of weeks, I'm sure. Then I'll be home again."

The air whooshed out of Erin's lungs, and she stared into the eyes that she loved more than her own life. "You're serious. You want to leave me."

"It's not that, Erin." Bowie had known she'd think he was leaving because of her swollen body. "I love every ounce of you. It's my child you carry. How could I not love you?"

Tears pooled in Erin's eyes and slid down her cheeks. She loved him so much. Could she let him go? "Please, Bowie, don't do this to me, not now. Wait until after the baby's born."

"Erin, I want my child to be born free of the oppression

we've lived with for the past few years." Bowie walked over to Erin and knelt before her. "Erin, every day I stay here I feel like less of a man. I'm becoming Chauncey Farthingale."

On the morning Bowie left, Erin clipped a small braid of her auburn hair and gave it to him for good luck. "I haven't a rabbit's foot to give you."

Bowie kissed the braid and then Erin. "This is much better than a rabbit's foot." He grinned and winked at her. "The rabbit still has all four feet, and you're my lucky charm."

She watched Chauncey ride out of town on his tall white horse, knowing that once he arrived at Bluffwood, he would be transformed into Bowie again. Erin walked back up the stairs, her steps echoing in the emptiness of her home. She resolved not to leave her morning room again until Bowie returned.

A few days after he left, Kenneth arrived. "Bowie . . . I mean Chauncey, sent me to stay with you."

Erin's life was immediately transformed. Kenneth's vitality seemed to put the life back in her, and her days were considerably shortened by his exuberance. He walked with her in the garden and even persuaded her to walk out by Oyster Point in the evenings when the streets were no longer crowded. The salt air and exercise made Erin feel much better. When she saw Bowie again, she'd thank him for sending Kenneth to keep her company.

August came to an end. Bowie hadn't returned, and Erin didn't know for sure whether he'd reached Marion's men. All she knew was that he'd gotten out of Charleston and arrived safely at Bluffwood.

One afternoon while she and Kenneth were sitting in the garden, she glanced at him and saw that he looked a little sad. "What's wrong? Are you feeling poorly?"

"No. I'm fine. It's nothing." Kenneth walked over to a low-hanging limb of a live oak and sat down on it, hanging his head glumly.

"Come on, tell me what's wrong. Are you homesick?" she asked, hoping he'd talk about his home or whatever was troubling him.

"Oh, no. You've been just fine to me. I haven't really got a home." He kicked at a grasshopper and sighed.

"Kenneth, that's not true. You've always got a home with us. Bowie and I love you. We think of you as, well, as our son." Erin pushed herself up and went to stand beside him. She put her arm around his shoulder. "What's troubling you?"

Kenneth looked up and tried to smile. "I want . . . I think I want to go with Bowie."

"Kenneth!" Erin exclaimed and sat down again. "You can't do that. You're too young. You could be killed. I thought you were through with war and fighting."

"I was. I mean, I was through fighting for the Tories." Kenneth closed his eyes briefly and then gazed at her. "I feel like a . . . a sissy sitting here while all the men are out fighting the damn British."

Erin laughed. When Kenneth looked at her with a puzzled expression, she said, "Come over here." She patted the bench and waited for him to comply. When he was seated, she put her arm around him and hugged him. "You know, Bowie said exactly the same thing. That's why he finally left. But he left you here to be with me in case something happened and I had to leave Charleston in a hurry."

Kenneth eyed her suspiciously. "You're not making that up, are you?"

"No, of course not." Erin now knew why Bowie had sent Kenneth to her. The boy wanted to fight the British. Bowie knew she'd talk Kenneth out of it. "What would I do if something awful happened here? Where could I go?" Erin patted her distended stomach.

Kenneth lifted his chin and smiled. "Oh, I'm here to protect you."

"That's right." Erin felt as if she'd conquered the British herself. "Let's go back inside. I'm tired."

*   *   *

For the next few days Kenneth hovered around Erin as if she was about to deliver. If she had calculated correctly, her baby would be born sometime in November. She prayed that Bowie would be home by then.

Erin felt instinctively that something was wrong. She hadn't heard from Bowie since he'd left. From the gossip she could glean from Lilly, Marion's men had attacked the British at Parker's Ferry, crossing on the Edisto River. Was that why Bowie had left? she wondered. Did he feel that his home was in danger? She had no answers.

One hot night as she lay in bed, unable to sleep, she heard a sound. "Bowie," she whispered and sat up. Pulling on her wrapper, she hurried to the window and looked out.

"Are you coming out, or may I come in?" Bowie asked and stepped through the open window.

"Bowie!" she exclaimed and flung her arms about him. "You're safe. You're home."

Kissing her as if he'd never be able to do so again, Bowie lifted her and carried her back to bed and lay down beside her. "It looks as if you've grown a bit since I left." The baby chose that moment to kick, and Bowie felt it. "Must be a boy. He's strong."

"What'll you do if she's a girl?" Erin asked and hugged him with all her might. She planted kisses all over his face. "Oh, I missed you. Where have you been? Why didn't you send me a message?"

"Hold on. I can only answer one question at a time. Now, what'll I do if *he's* a girl? Hmmm. Build a tower to keep out all the boys." Bowie grinned. "Is Walter home?"

"No. He's been with Stuart for a few weeks." Erin giggled. "He never thought he'd have to fight. I don't know what he's doing, though. He may be a supply officer."

"That's where we're going. Marion wants to join Greene and push the British the rest of the way out of South Carolina." Bowie propped himself up on one elbow and looked down at her. He memorized every nuance of her face. That was what kept him going.

Erin froze. She stared at him in disbelief. "You're leaving again? You can't. You mustn't."

"Erin, I can help make a difference. You once said that to me." He quoted her own words to her and then gazed into her eyes, trying to determine her true feelings. "You wanted to make a difference in this war. Would you deny me that right?"

"Yes!" she cried and clung to him. "Yes, I deny you that right. I love you and I need you."

"What'll I tell my child? That I couldn't go to war to fight for the independence of our country because his mother wanted me to stay at home and help her make diapers?" Bowie rose and strode across the room. He'd known that Erin would react this way. In her condition he couldn't blame her, but he couldn't stay here, either. "Erin, don't make this time we have together into a night of pain and sorrow. Let's make it special."

Erin knew he was right. She could no more deny him the right to fight for freedom than she had allowed him to deny her that same right almost nine months ago. In about two months their child would be born. He or she would have a father to be proud of. No matter what happened, Erin couldn't take that away from Bowie. "I'm sorry. It's just that I get so emotional so easily these days. I know you're right. I'm being selfish."

Bowie returned to the bed and gathered her into his arms. He lifted her and carried her to her rocking chair and sat down. For a long time they sat there silently rocking and clinging to each other.

Finally Erin broke the silence. "How long can you stay?"

"Until just before dawn." Bowie had hoped she wouldn't think to ask that question so soon, but he couldn't lie to her.

"Are you hungry?" Erin asked and looked at him carefully. There was a hardness about his face, a tension she hadn't seen before. "I'll go get something for you."

She hurried downstairs, put a biscuit on a plate, and poured a cup of milk. Thinking quickly, Erin grabbed a tray, some jam and butter, and a piece of chicken left from dinner. It looked like pitifully little for a hungry man, but it was probably more than he'd eaten for days.

While he ate, she sat across from him, watching and listening. At first he didn't say much, but the words finally began to flow.

Then he told her of the battle he'd fought with Marion and his men. "You wouldn't believe him in battle. He looks ten feet tall. His men never question an order he issues. It's a privilege to serve with him."

Erin could easily have done without him. Marion, while a hero to most of South Carolina, symbolized the loneliness she'd suffered the past weeks. Now she could look forward to more of the same. As she moved the tray and settled herself back in his lap, she almost wished there was something she could do. "Bowie, do you think I could gather my men together and take another load—"

"Erin Edana Banning Gallagher, if you step one foot out of this city, I'll . . . I'll personally tie you to this bed when I get you back here and won't let you go until this child is born and the war is over." Bowie leaned away from her and gazed into her eyes. "Erin, I want you to promise me you won't do anything foolish."

She sighed and rested her head on his shoulder. "I promise."

Before dawn Bowie rose and slipped on his clothes. He'd said goodbye to Erin before they went to sleep during the night. Looking down at her, he felt filled with love and adoration for his courageous wife. Soon, he promised himself, very soon this war would be over, and they would live together and rear their child properly.

He turned to leave, then faced her again. He couldn't resist one last look. Her tiny frame, except for the large middle, lay absolutely still. On the white pillow her hair flared around her in a flame of color. Beneath those long lashes he knew were green eyes that were usually so alert and probing. Unable to leave without touching her, he tiptoed back to the bed and kissed her forehead lightly while laying his hand on her swollen stomach.

The baby kicked, and Erin shifted restlessly. "Just a little while, little one, and Papa will be back. Be good to your mama," he whispered and spun around to leave. He knew that if he looked down at this vision much longer, his resolve would abandon him.

Bowie slipped out the back door and walked down South Bay. He had rowed across to Charleston and hoped his little boat was still there and unnoticed. He found it, shoved off, and boarded.

Somewhere across the Ashley River and southwest of Charleston, he would catch up with Marion's men. Crossing the Ashley River would be the most difficult part of his journey. The British had lookouts posted, and Bowie was counting on the cloak of darkness to protect him.

The oarlocks squeaked as he maintained a regular rhythm, but other than that the river was quiet and as still as glass. He had to reach the far shore before the sun rose, or he'd be spotted for sure. That last moment with Erin had made him later than he'd planned, but he'd simply have to hurry to keep from being on the river at daylight.

When he reached the shore, he climbed out and hid his boat well. The undergrowth was thick, and he pulled several limbs across the boat to cover it. He studied his work and decided that unless someone knew it was there, it couldn't be easily seen. To make sure he could find the small craft should the need arise, he cut a straight line across a live oak limb that hung low over the river.

After making his way up the bank, he glanced back at the river. In the twilight the mist turned from gray to golden as the sun rose, and Bowie smiled. He'd beaten the British again.

Bowie hurried through dense undergrowth to the spot where Sidney was waiting with their horses. Bowie sat on a stump beside his friend and grinned.

"Well, mate, I reckon that grin would be meanin' you saw

her." Sidney sat up and said, "I expect she'll be doin' fine. That's a strong lass."

"She's fine. Doesn't much like my leaving again, though." Bowie remembered the panic in Erin's eyes when he'd told her he wasn't home to stay.

"Seems to me if she had any sense a'tall, she'd be glad to be rid of a bloke like you, always dallyin' around like a bad cold." Sidney pulled on his hat. "I s'pose we'll be movin' on shortly."

"As soon as you can stand." Bowie walked over to his horse and patted his neck. "I brought you a biscuit."

"A biscuit? That's all?" Sidney stood up and placed his hands on his hips. "I baby-sit that horse of yours, and all you can bring is a biscuit, mate? Much more of this, and I'm takin' back to the sea—with or without you."

Bowie laughed. "There's a piece of ham there, too."

Sidney took the linen cloth and opened it up. "Now, there's a good boy, lookin' after his best mate like this."

Bowie cleaned the campsite and made ready to go while Sidney ate his breakfast. They didn't linger too long because the British patrols would be by soon, and the two rebels wanted to be well away before that.

Once out of the district Bowie and Sidney rode hard. They could make good time on the road without much chance of being caught. Lord Rawdon's troops were so busy that he had little time and no men to patrol outside Charleston.

As Bowie rode, he thought of Erin and how his life had changed since he met her. "What a woman," he said and smiled with fondness at the memory of her.

Eyes narrowed, Sidney looked at him. "Talkin' to yerself, are ye now, mate?"

Bowie grinned sheepishly. "I suppose I am. Did you ever meet a woman like Erin before?"

Sidney shook his head. "No, and I hope I never do again. 'Twill be the undoin' of you."

"Now, what do you mean by that profound remark?" Bowie asked and shifted slightly in his saddle.

"Why, that if you meet another'n like Miss Erin, then she'll kill you for fallin' in love with another woman." Sidney laughed and urged his horse into a gallop with Bowie close behind.

They soon caught up with the trailing guard of Marion's troops. Bowie identified himself and Sidney, and they were allowed to rejoin their regiment.

Bowie thought of his child nestled in Erin's stomach and smiled. In a few months he'd be a father. For the next several hours he wondered what kind of father he would be. He wondered where they would live after the war ended.

He thought of Erin, his beautiful courageous bride, soon to be a mother. How daring she was! Unlike many women who sat at home worrying about the outcome of this or that battle, she'd set about a task to help win the war. He wondered how she would like settling down to a regular routine that involved no more danger than riding sidesaddle around the plantation grounds.

She'd love Edisto Glade with its sixteen hundred acres of formal gardens, riding trails, untamed woodlands, abundant wildlife, rice paddies, and indigo fields. His thoughts turned to his mother. She'd fall in love with Erin as he had. But what of his father? Would he hold on to his nasty grudge?

Bowie grinned. No, his father would succumb to Erin's charms as every man did. Erin, he felt sure, would be the key to reestablishing his relationship with his father.

CHAPTER
20

ERIN TOSSED AND TURNED RESTLESSLY. SOMEWHERE IN the woods Bowie was in danger. She knew he was.

Awakening, she sat up in bed and glanced about. He was gone, as he told her he would be. When Erin had argued about his leaving without saying goodbye, he'd told her he didn't want a tearful departure but would rather remember her as she'd been last night.

She lay back on the pillow and stared at the ceiling. When Bowie had come in, she'd thought he was home to stay. Now an uneasiness swept over her that she couldn't define. Erin rose and pulled on her wrapper.

With her stomach so swollen, she could hardly wear any of her clothes, even though they'd been let out three times. She felt so fat and ugly that she didn't want to be seen by anyone.

Kenneth did his best to entertain Erin for the next few days, but she could hardly smile. Her mind was out on the trail, where she knew Bowie would be heading. Just a few months ago she'd demanded a chance to do her part in this war; now she wished Bowie weren't so noble.

She seemed so listless that 'Lasses finally sent for Dr. Rutledge. When he arrived, Erin felt foolish. "Dr. Rutledge, I can't imagine why 'Lasses sent for you. I'm perfectly fine, as you well know."

"Yes, yes, I know, but I just want to make sure. She said you'd been moping around for several days." Dr. Rutledge felt her forehead and then her wrist. He sat down beside her on the sofa. "Erin, I know you're under a great deal of pressure, but you've got to stop worrying. It's unhealthy for you and your baby."

Erin gazed at him as if he'd said her face was green. "Stop worrying? How is that possible? My husband is out there somewhere fighting for his life—for our lives."

"You know you wouldn't have it any other way, Erin. You wouldn't ask a man to be less than he is." He patted her arm and felt her stomach. "That's a mighty strong baby. He'll be proud of his papa one of these days. And his mama, too."

Erin smiled a wavering smile. "Could I get you a piece of pie? Or some coffee?"

"No." Dr. Rutledge patted his own stomach. "I've eaten too many pieces of Tupper's pie. Now, Erin, stop worrying. I mean it. I don't want you to do anything more strenuous than lifting a fork. Today's the eighth. This baby will be here in about two months. It can't be jostled about. Promise me you'll behave yourself."

"I promise."

When the doctor was gone, Erin returned to the parlor. She couldn't shake the feeling that something terrible had happened.

All day she paced back and forth. She walked downstairs until the servants gathered at the parlor door to watch her. 'Lasses scolded Erin and demanded that she go to bed, but Erin couldn't lie down.

It was almost as though she needed to go somewhere, to be on the trail, to be ready in case something had gone wrong. Erin began to prepare. She couldn't say what she was preparing for, but she knew she had to be ready.

She took some clothing, her most comfortable, and tucked it into a valise. Making lists of things to do comforted her a little. At least she wasn't idle. She listed everything she'd take on the trail if she were to go out again. She catalogued the items she'd need from the kitchen and storerooms. She inventoried the blankets.

Kenneth followed her around, constantly asking questions she couldn't answer. He asked, "Why are you doing that?"

"I don't know," came the reply. Maybe just being busy kept her mind off the danger Bowie was in. Maybe she was preparing for an eventuality.

Bedtime came, and Erin found herself staring at the ceiling. She couldn't sleep, although she knew she desperately needed the rest. Finally she made herself a cup of warm milk, drank it, and dozed off into a fitful sleep.

Daylight came, and Erin felt horrible. Her eyelids were heavy and puffy. Her mouth felt like cotton. When 'Lasses came up with a cup of milk and hotcakes, Erin could hardly eat.

"If'n you don't eat ever bite of them hotcakes, I'se gonna send fer the doctor agin," 'Lasses declared and folded her arms across her chest.

"Now, 'Lasses, I'm not really hungry, and look at me. I've grown so fat now that I can't wear my clothes." Erin moved the tray. "Take it away."

'Lasses looked at Erin for a moment and then walked to the bellpull. She jerked it sharply.

"Why did you do that?" Erin asked and sat up. "Get this tray out of here."

"I'se sendin' Nero for the doctor."

"No, you're not. He's too busy to keep running over here every day because you're so nervous about this baby. Now, just go downstairs and tell Nero the ring was a mistake." Erin folded her hands primly across her lap.

"No'm, I ain't. Either you gonna eat, or the doctor gonna come." 'Lasses glared at Erin.

"You're the stubbornest woman I ever chanced to meet." Erin picked up her fork and stabbed a piece of hotcake. She made a big show of chewing and swallowing. "Go on. I'll eat them."

"I ain't leavin' till that plate's clean." 'Lasses settled herself in the rocking chair and watched Erin.

Erin ate until she thought her stomach would burst.

When 'Lasses cleared away the dishes and tray, Erin turned over and fell asleep.

When she awoke, it was dusk. "Goodness. I've slept all day. I won't sleep a wink tonight."

She climbed out of bed, slipped into her dressing gown, and went downstairs. Kenneth was sitting at the table, eating his supper. Erin smiled and tousled his hair. "What's for supper?"

"Vegetable soup," he answered between spoonfuls.

Tupper came in with a bowl for Erin as she sat down. "Thank you, Tupper."

Erin and Kenneth ate in silence for a few minutes before Kenneth's stare caught her attention. "What's wrong?"

"I don't know." Kenneth put down his spoon. "It's just kinda quiet here in Charleston. Like lots of soldiers are gone."

Erin thought back. Kenneth was right. Evidently Stuart had ordered some of the troops garrisoned in Charleston to move out. "I wonder where they are."

"I don't know, but I don't like it. Not with Bowie out there fighting." Kenneth picked up his spoon and began to eat again.

Kenneth's words merely echoed Erin's thoughts. Concern for Bowie had nagged her for days, but she couldn't do anything about it. She didn't know where he was or who he was fighting. Lack of knowledge ate away at her. If she knew where he was, Erin would have packed up and rode after him.

Erin returned to her room and put on a dress that fit. She felt foolish wearing a dressing gown in the parlor, even though she and Kenneth were alone. She tried to divert his attention, to ease the creases across his brow, by playing the harpsichord.

For some reason her usually deft fingers refused to cooperate, and instead of beautiful music, the notes came out as sloppy, haphazard, and unrelated. Erin gave up. She sat on the sofa and watched Kenneth light a fire.

"It isn't really that cold, you know," he said as he held the taper to the kindling. "I just want something to do."

Erin smiled and nodded. "I know what you mean." She picked up a baby dress she'd been working on and stitched quietly for a few minutes. She pricked her finger, and a tiny dot of blood appeared on the white dress. "I may as well quit. I'm doing more harm than good."

Putting the gown down, she watched Kenneth.

"I wish there was something we could do," he said and started to pace. "Next time Bowie comes home, I'm going with him."

There was nothing Erin could say to stop him. Kenneth was an orphan who was sixteen years old, almost seventeen. She had no right to keep him here with her, but she had to try. "Kenneth, don't do anything rash. This war's about over. We'll look back in a few years and laugh about this night."

"You might, but I won't." Kenneth hung his head for a moment before looking at her again. "You did something for the cause. You saw a need and filled it."

"You did, too," she reminded him gently.

"No, I didn't." He jumped up and walked to the window. "I did the wrong thing. I fought for the wrong side."

Erin tried to think of a way to deny his words but couldn't. "Look, Kenneth, you're young. We all make mistakes when we're young. Nobody will fault you for that."

"I feel like a traitor." Kenneth sank into the chair by the harpsichord and pounded his fist on the keys. "I'm so dumb. It's no wonder Bowie wouldn't let me go with him."

"Kenneth!" Erin exclaimed. She scrambled to her feet and waddled over to him. "You're wrong. That's not why he wouldn't let you go. He knew I'd need you."

"Sure. After the war when somebody asks me what I did, I can say I was a lady's companion." Kenneth pounded the keys again, and the dissonance echoed through the house. "It's not fair."

In that moment Erin realized she was being unfair. I

Kenneth felt that strongly, she couldn't stand in his way. "When Bowie returns, you may go with him."

The grin that lit Kenneth's face tore at Erin's heart. She was sending two men she loved off to war, or would be soon. She put her arm around him and smiled. "In the meantime, is being a companion that bad? I'm sorry if I've been so cross lately, but you know how worried I am."

'Lasses came into the room. "Miss Erin, Mr. Sidney here. He at the back door and won't come to the front of the house."

Erin whirled around. "Sidney? Bring him to the library. Come on, Kenneth."

She grabbed the boy's hand and almost dragged him to the library. The room, comfortable in deep green draperies, carpets, and leather furniture, was one of Erin's favorite rooms. She settled into her father's chair as Sidney came in. Greeting him with a smile, she opened her mouth to welcome him, but he never allowed her the chance.

"Miss Erin, Bowie's been captured," he said quietly.

"What?" Erin rose from the chair so quickly that it overturned behind her. "Where? When? Is he injured?"

Sidney gazed at her and shook his head. "I'll tell you everything, but I need some help. I'm going to try to get him back. I'll need any guns and ammunition you have around here."

Erin jerked the bellpull. 'Lasses returned with a puzzled look on her face. " 'Lasses, tell Nero to bring all Papa's guns and ammunition. Take the lists I made yesterday and load those items in boxes. I'm taking a trip."

"No'm, you ain't. The doctor done said you was—"

"I don't have time to argue! Go! Kenneth, get ready to leave." Erin turned to Sidney. "While they're preparing to leave, tell me what happened."

"Well, ma'am, me and the mate, eh, Bowie, was with Marion's men. We joined up with Greene." Sidney sat on the edge of a chair, as if he was ready to run at any moment.

"Never mind. You can tell me while we're on the trail.

I'll see that everything is prepared properly." Erin started to leave the room, but Sidney caught her hand.

"I can't let you go, ma'am. Bowie Gallagher would skin me alive if he knew I was here." His gaze implored her to reconsider.

"Either you take me with you, or I'll go alone," Erin insisted and left the room. She hurried up the stairs to her room and removed the packed valise from the armoire.

By the time she reached the library again, Kenneth was standing there with a box that contained several pistols along with powder, thin cloth cut in little circles, and balls. Nero brought in two muskets.

"Sidney, how are we going to get this stuff out of Charleston?" she asked when she surveyed the growing mound of supplies.

"Boat, ma'am. I've got a skiff waiting." Sidney picked up a box of utensils and food supplies. "Let's be headin' out."

" 'Lasses, you stay here and keep everything—"

"If I don't go, you don't go." 'Lasses piled a cloth sack on top of one of the boxes and picked it up. "You tries to leave without me, and I'll tie you down."

Erin sighed, knowing there would be no way to escape 'Lasses' vigilant watch. Nero refused to be left behind, too. The group of five slipped out the back door, each carrying a load of goods. Erin bore her own valise, which she'd thankfully packed with few items.

When they reached the hidden boat, Sidney looked up and down the coast for British troops while the goods were loaded and the passengers arranged themselves. He climbed aboard and Kenneth shoved off, jumping on at the last minute.

Erin wished he'd oiled the oarlocks to keep them from screeching. She was sure that everywhere in Charleston British soldiers were waking up and coming to see what made such a racket. In her opinion Sidney couldn't row fast enough. The river was fairly calm and the breeze cool as they crossed the Ashley and slid into the little cove where Bowie kept the boat hidden.

Praying that he'd hurry, Erin watched as Sidney methodically hid the boat among the rushes and limbs that Bowie had covered it with just a few days earlier.

Knowing that British sentries were stationed nearby, the little group walked about a mile in silence. From there, they could whisper among themselves, according to Sidney, but spoke only when necessary. They finally arrived at a spot with dense vegetation, which Sidney revealed to be hand-placed carefully to disguise a hidden wagon. He told them to load it while he went for the horses.

When Sidney returned, everyone was sitting in the wagon. Kenneth jumped out and helped Sidney hitch the horses to the single tree.

Erin sat on the wagon seat waiting for the reins. "Hurry, Sidney, hurry."

"Erin, I think you should sit in the back. Use some of them blankets to cushion you. I'd hate like hell . . . pardon, to jostle that baby." Sidney jumped into the wagon and sat down beside her.

She took the reins from his hands and grinned at him. "I'm sitting on two folded blankets. You just tell me which way to go."

They rode as quietly as possible for a few miles until they reached an area seldom patrolled by the British. Sidney watched and listened carefully. "I think we're pretty safe. Stuart had a lot of his men up at Eutaw Springs yesterday."

"Yesterday?" Erin asked and looked at Sidney.

"Well, bein' as how it's after midnight, I reckon it was two days ago," Sidney admitted.

"We knew it. Miss Erin and I knew it. We were awful caught up all day." Kenneth beamed with pleasure. He was active again. "We were ready to roll then if we'd known where to go."

Erin listened as Kenneth bragged about his foresight. She didn't know if it was really foresight or intuition or simple fear, but she did know that both of them had been upset all day.

The miles didn't pass swiftly enough for Erin. She wanted

to abandon the wagon and gallop off in search of Bowie. "Where are they taking him?" she asked finally.

"From what I could see, they was headed back to Charleston, but they had a bunch of men walkin' and some wagons and stuff." Sidney shook his head. "We should meet them sometime tonight or early tomorrow."

Glad that she'd slept all day yesterday, Erin nodded to the people in the wagon bed. "You all can rest, but I need you, Sidney."

For a few miles they kept to the main road. Sidney had said that Stuart's men would be coming this way soon. "Sidney, How are we ever going to rescue him?"

Bowie rode along, well guarded in every direction. He'd fought as hard as he could, but the British kept coming. Greene's men were tired and hungry—some were ill—while the British were well rested.

He'd seen many of his friends killed or wounded. Somehow he and Sidney got separated, and Bowie was glad. He'd been fighting hand to hand with bayonets and killed several Tories. Feeling sick all over, he'd continued to fight, blood all over his clothing and hands. His ammunition was gone, lost when a bayonet sliced across his shoulder and cut the leather strap that held his powder and balls.

Bowie had fought like a madman until he found himself alone in the midst of a British regiment. Knowing that he might die quickly during this battle, he'd thrusted and parried until his entire body ached. The smell of death made him retch, but he continued to fight until he slid on bloodied grass to the ground and dropped his weapon. A soldier poised to slice through him with his bayonet.

"Stop!" he heard nearby.

Bowie didn't take his eyes off the bayonet pointed at his heart, although he wanted to see who'd saved his life—momentarily, at least.

The soldier held his position. "Why should I not kill this rebel who's killed so many of us?"

"Because he's more important as a prisoner." Walter

Martin leveled a pistol at Bowie's head. "I thought that was you, Mr. Farthingale-Gallagher."

Staring, Bowie waited for Walter to continue. Bowie didn't know how much Walter knew or where he obtained his information, but he had a feeling that it saved his life. "What do you want from me?"

"Well, Mr. Gallagher, I believe Colonel Stuart might be interested in your company." Walter motioned for Bowie to stand. "Come with me. Remember, I won't hesitate to kill you, and I'll take your still-bloody heart home to that treasonous wife of yours. Then I'll kill her, too."

Bowie obviously couldn't take a chance with Erin's life. Walter sounded demented enough to do something like that, so Bowie walked along without making any threatening moves. As Stuart was busy preparing for the retreat back to Charleston, Bowie didn't have to meet him right away.

He prayed that Erin wouldn't hear of this until after he'd had a chance to escape. When I escape, he told himself, I'll kill that bastard Martin before I leave.

Erin considered her options. She could hope that Bowie wouldn't be well guarded. There were only five in her group, not nearly enough to attack the troops they would encounter. "Sidney, it's the only way," she insisted.

"Ma'am, I'm already riskin' my hide bringin' you along. I don't want to—"

"You don't have any choice. There's no safe way to do this." Erin made up her mind and wouldn't budge from her decision.

"Ma'am, this ain't no game. These men're some of the meanest I ever had the misfortune to clap eyes on." Sidney tried without success to dissuade Erin from her plan. "Me mate's like as not to be free already. We ain't gonna risk you till we know there ain't no other way."

"Nonsense. This is the safest way." Erin stared straight ahead. Though she spoke with confidence, she trembled inside. Remembering her treatment at Tarleton's hands, she wondered how she would be received by Stuart's men. She'd risk anything to free Bowie, she decided. Besides, nobody would recognize her. Tarleton's men were in Virginia fighting with Cornwallis.

Erin couldn't think about being captured herself, or her confidence would waver. She thought of every explanation she could give to the British for her being out alone at night in her condition. She'd have to find a way to make them believe her. Who would doubt a pregnant woman?

Bowie watched, his hands and feet bound, as Stuart's men made camp. Martin moved Bowie to a tent to await the arrival of Colonel Stuart. In the meantime, Martin questioned Bowie without success.

"Tell me, or I'll beat it out of you," Walter Martin threatened and stepped menacingly close.

Bowie refused to be intimidated by this man. He'd known Walter far too long to be impressed by this sudden display of confident behavior. He knew Walter for what he really was: a flunky.

Bowie considered Walter's reasons for not letting the soldier complete his job. Perhaps Walter saw a promotion, fame, or monetary gain for capturing someone he thought was a spy. But Walter probably didn't know what Bowie's role had been before he joined Marion's men, and Bowie wasn't about to enlighten him.

Walter's face hovered near Bowie's. Bowie half-smiled then spat in Walter's face.

Fury registered across Walter's countenance, and he smashed Bowie's face with the butt of his pistol. "Now, answer my questions."

Bowie refused to speak at all. His jaw ached worse than anything he'd ever felt, but he wouldn't give Walter the satisfaction of knowing that. Bowie spat again. This time blood from a loosened tooth splattered all over Walter's face.

Walter cracked Bowie across the skull with the butt of his pistol, and Bowie slumped to the ground.

*   *   *

Erin sensed that they were getting near the British encampment. She checked her boot for the small dagger she always carried while on the trail and found comfort in its cold steel. "Sidney, stop."

When the wagon stopped, she waited for him to help her down, and they walked a short distance away from the others. "I'm going to have a hard time with 'Lasses. You've got to help me convince her to stay with you. I can't be worried about getting her to safety while I'm looking for Bowie."

"I agree with that, Erin, but I don't agree with your strategy." Sidney touched her arm. "Don't do this. I regret that I ever came lookin' to you for guns."

"Sidney, you did the right thing. This is the only way we can keep Bowie from being killed or sent to a prison ship." Erin shuddered when she recalled the reports of men dying in their own excrement, of rats gnawing off fingers and toes of the prisoners. She refused to expose Bowie to that while she still breathed. "Bring me my horse and leave one nearby in case the British take this one."

Erin let him help her into the saddle. When 'Lasses started to get out of the wagon, Sidney stopped her.

"Git yosef outa here. You ain't gonna let . . ."

Erin rode out of hearing distance. Trembling with fear, she headed straight for the British encampment. The moon rose high above her, indicating that it was well past midnight, and Erin was glad. Most of the men would be worn out from fighting and marching. By now they'd be asleep.

Passing the first sentry, she heard a low call, then a second. Pretty soon she found the way blocked by men carrying muskets that were trained right on her.

"Halt!" one of them, a sergeant, called.

Tears, real enough when she thought of Bowie's predicament, flooded her eyes. "Please help me! Don't let them catch me!"

"Who, ma'am?" the sergeant asked, peering into the darkness behind her.

"Rebels. They . . . they burned my house . . . they killed—

oh, I can't talk about it!" she cried in false anguish. "Help me, please!"

The sergeant took the reins from her and led her into the camp. He stopped near two tents and helped her down. Handing the reins to a private, he told her to wait.

Erin nodded in compliance, and he walked a short distance away. She stepped sideways and peered through a gap in the tent. There were several men gathered there, but Bowie wasn't among them. What if he wasn't in one of the tents? God, let me find him, she prayed.

She stumbled forward toward the second tent. The young man holding her horse hurried after her. "Ma'am, you can't go in there."

"Help me!" she cried. "I'm going to faint."

Erin started to sway. She knew that Bowie must be in the tent, but she couldn't see. "Get a doctor—please!"

Bowie heard Erin outside the tent. He peeked at Walter through eyelids that were narrow slits. He must have heard the commotion, too, because he was looking at the entrance to the tent.

When Erin fell through the wall of the tent, it caught Walter off-guard. But Erin fell right into his arms and noticed Bowie lying on the floor with blood caking his face.

"So, Little Miss Standoffish is here." Walter's arms snaked around her, just below the breast. "How convenient."

Erin pretended to faint and fell to the floor. Beneath the cover of her gown, she reached into her boot and retrieved her knife. When Walter bent down to help her, she stabbed him in the stomach. Blood spurted over her, but she wasted no time. Pulling the dagger from Walter's stomach, she grimaced and retched. Walter wasn't dead, but he was incapacitated. She dragged herself to Bowie's side, knowing that they'd have no more than a few minutes to escape. If she stopped to think what she'd just done, she'd probably go into shock.

As she cut the ropes on his wrists, Bowie sat up. "What in hell are—"

"Hush and help me." Erin finished cutting the ropes that bound his wrists and started on the ones on his legs.

The young private who'd been holding her horse peeked in. Bowie jerked on the boy's coat and pulled him into the tent. After knocking him unconscious with one punch, Bowie jumped to his feet and pulled Erin up with him. "Let's go."

He opened the tent and helped Erin into the saddle. Several soldiers who'd been sleeping half rose to watch them. The commotion roused several others before Bowie could mount, but he managed to pull himself into the saddle behind her and rode out of the camp through the woods.

"We'll head for the swamp." Bowie urged the horse into a gallop in spite of the tree branches that cut across their faces as they rode. "We haven't time to waste," he called as an explanation.

Erin didn't care. Bowie was free. She'd carried off her scheme. Erin's body was jolted awkwardly as the horse sped along. She ached all over from the strain but refused to ask him to slow down. They had to move quickly or risk being recaptured. She took comfort in knowing that the soldiers would be following her and Bowie, thereby allowing Sidney, Kenneth, 'Lasses, and Nero to escape another way.

Bowie drove the horse as hard as it would go. In the distance he could hear the sounds of pursuit, but realized he couldn't go any faster with himself and Erin on one horse—especially in her condition. They reached a point where Bowie knew they'd be caught if they didn't do something drastic.

"Erin, are you in good health? I mean, how much of this can you take?" he asked, wondering if recapture would be easier on her than this headlong flight through the swamp.

"I'll be fine. Keep going." Erin didn't take time to consider how she really felt. She, too, knew that the soldiers were catching up.

Bowie stopped the horse by a huge live oak. "Here, let me help you."

He dismounted and lifted Erin from the saddle. He placed her on a low-hanging limb and tied up the horse. "Sit here a minute."

Climbing up beside her, he looked up into the tree, realizing he never would have expected to be in this situation with a pregnant wife! "Can you climb a little higher if I help you?"

"Yes. I can do anything you ask." Erin took his hand and held on as he moved up limb by limb and pulled her carefully after him.

When they'd reached a place high enough to provide some cover in the darkness, he settled her close to the trunk and made sure she wouldn't topple out of the tree. "I'm going to chase off the horse."

He scrambled back down the tree, untied the horse and rode him a short distance away. Hesitating because of Erin's condition, he decided that this was the only way to keep from being caught. He broke off a limb and swatted the horse's rump as hard as he could.

The horse reared and raced off through the woods. Bowie hurried back to the tree where Erin was perched and climbed up beside her, hoping he wasn't making a mistake. Erin's pregnancy would make walking more difficult, but he had to take a chance.

"What about your tracks?" she asked, remembering her own trail when Tarleton had kidnapped her.

"The horses will distort it so badly, they'll never be able to find us." He slid onto the limb with her and curled his arms around her to protect her. "Don't worry. They'll never see us."

Erin knew he spoke the truth. The soldiers would be in such a hurry, they'd never look up into the trees. As she watched, the shapes of men on horses approached. She closed her eyes and uttered a silent prayer for safety.

Bowie looked down at the soldiers as they rode beneath the tree. None of them bothered to look up, and Bowie felt safe for a while. When they were gone, he whispered, "We'll have to wait here a while to see if they come back this way. If we walk through here now, we'll leave tracks."

Erin nodded and settled comfortably against Bowie. Only then could she give voice to her fears. "All the way here from Charleston I worried that you'd be dead when I arrived. I was so scared."

"You?" Bowie kissed the top of her head, cherishing the feeling of her in his arms again. "How do you think I felt when I heard your voice?"

Erin looked up at the silhouette of his face. "I should think you'd be happy."

"Happy?" Bowie repeated in surprise. "How can a man be happy when his pregnant wife, who also happens to be a Partisan spy and supplier, walks into the middle of a British encampment? I thought they would hang us together, and it would all be my fault."

"But if I hadn't come into the camp, I couldn't have rescued you," Erin reminded him gently. "I love you and didn't want you to hang any more than you want that for me."

"I suppose we're stuck with each other, heroics and all," Bowie concluded. "Shhh! I think they're coming back."

The soldiers returned, more slowly than the first time they'd ridden past. This time they were searching all around, but they never looked up. When they'd gone, Erin said, "Bowie, we can reach the Santee River before sunup if we head north."

"What'll we do then?" Bowie looked at her but could hardly see her in the faint moonlight.

"We can cross the river or find a boat maybe." Erin didn't really have a plan, but she knew the river offered more safety than the road.

"All right." Bowie started to climb down and took great care to help Erin. "I think it was easier going up."

"You're right," Erin agreed and tried to keep from falling. "This is the first time I ever climbed a tree."

Bowie stopped and hugged her. "I hope you don't do it again until after the baby comes—if you *ever* do it again."

CHAPTER
21

BOWIE AND ERIN WALKED IN THE MOONLIGHT THROUGH
the shallow leaves and pine needles that carpeted the low-
country forest floor. They took care to avoid areas where
the ground was wet and mushy. "This could be dangerous,"
Bowie said. "We can't see the snakes or other predators."

"Snakes?" Erin hadn't given them a thought when she
suggested walking toward the river. "Do you think we
should wait until daylight?"

"No. I believe the British will come after us." Bowie
helped Erin to climb across a deadfall. "Walter Martin told
Stuart that I was a spy or some such, so I think we'd better
keep moving."

Erin tried hard not to depend on Bowie too much. He
was having almost as difficult a time as she. "Those walks
Kenneth and I took late at night are paying off. I'm not the
least bit tired."

Bowie looked at her, though he couldn't see her face well
enough to tell if she was lying to make him feel better. He
knew that a woman in her condition shouldn't be out under
these circumstances and hoped that her bravery wouldn't
severely affect her health. They walked slowly, hand in
hand, stepping carefully.

After a while Bowie decided they should rest. "We can
wait here for a few minutes." He removed his cloak and laid
it on the ground for Erin to sit on. She sat beside him, resting
her head on his shoulder, and he watched the direction from

308

which they'd come. "How'd you know that I'd been captured?"

Erin didn't know exactly how to answer that question. "I had a feeling deep inside. Kenneth did, too. We were both restless and unable to say why. Neither of us could sleep on the eighth."

That was when Bowie had been captured. "It's probably just your condition plus the fact that you were worried about me."

Raising up to look at him, she answered, "Kenneth isn't carrying your child."

"He was probably sensing your state." Bowie knew the feeling Erin described. He'd felt it when he'd left her the last trip up the wagon road. Luckily, he'd trusted his feelings enough to go after her.

"When Sidney came, I was packed, had a list of food and utensils prepared, and was ready to go." Erin sighed. "I knew I'd have to be ready to go if I had the chance. I'd have left before he arrived, but I didn't know which way to go."

Bowie hugged her close and rubbed her stomach. "Regardless of why you came, I was glad to see you." Then he looked sternly at her and added, "Except that you promised me you wouldn't do anything like this."

"Like you promised me you wouldn't leave me again?" Erin reminded him.

"Sounds like both of us broke a promise," Bowie conceded. Then he started to think of the future. "I think we've got a real problem. We can't return to Charleston. I don't think Bluffwood is safe. In fact, we may have to take your parents away with us."

"Where can we go?" Erin lay down because her stomach was cramping a little.

"The only place I can think of is Edisto Glade. We can go there for a while, but I don't even think that's safe for long because of my father." Bowie silently cursed his father for being a Tory. "Mother may hide us until the baby comes. Then we'll sail to one of the tropical islands. We do still have the *Midnight Star*."

The *Midnight Star,* Erin's thoughts echoed. It sounded like a beautiful ship. She wondered if she'd like sailing on a large ship or if she'd become sick as so many people did.

Erin's body was beginning to feel the strain of their arduous journey, but she refused to burden Bowie with her problems since she'd struck out on this trip without his consent. Deep down in her back, she felt a constant nagging pain.

By the time the sun rose, Erin and Bowie reached the Santee River. They would follow the Santee until they reached the great bend where the Cooper River forked off. The Cooper River would take them directly to Charleston if they could find a boat.

They walked along the bank of the river for miles, it seemed to Erin, before they found a small rowboat. It didn't look too sturdy, and she thought it might sink with their weight.

Bowie helped Erin into the boat. It didn't have an oar, but he found a long straight limb to help guide them. While Erin lay back in the boat to rest, Bowie kept them from crashing into rocks or low-hanging limbs.

Erin didn't mention food, though she was hungry. She realized that Bowie hadn't eaten, either, and to talk about it would make the problem worse. She eased herself into another position, musing that a woman in the family way shouldn't try to ride in a rickety rowboat.

The river moved faster, and Bowie had to work hard to guide the little boat. At one point Erin felt sure they'd be thrown against the rocks that lined the banks, but Bowie diverted the boat in time to prevent a mishap.

Water occasionally splashed into the boat, and Erin's dress was soon drenched and leaden. The warm sun did little to help. It made the dress seem more like a steamy tent than a garment. Mosquitoes and gnats lit on her damp skin and bit into her tender flesh, making her swat at them constantly. She tried very hard to look happy when Bowie glanced her way, but she thought she must be failing miserably because he hadn't spoken in some time.

By afternoon they reached the Cooper River. Bowie felt

much more at ease. He'd been worried about Erin all night and all day. She'd looked so pale at first, and now the sun had burned her face and hands. He knew she'd be sore by nightfall, but there was nothing he could do to help. To her credit, he thought, she was not a complainer.

He admired her more and more. Watching her as she lay dozing in front of him, he decided that she never seemed to be scared of anything. That a woman in Erin's condition would ride directly into an enemy camp made his chest swell with pride.

Night began to fall, and Bowie searched for a place to tie up. Though he would have preferred to continue their voyage, he didn't know the river well enough to try. In the morning Erin could point out the tributary that led to Bluffwood.

When he started to despair of finding a sheltered place, he spotted a small cover and guided the boat in. The trees hung low enough to hide them from anybody passing in boats or on shore. The rope, though worn, would keep them from drifting during the night.

"Erin," he said and shook her awake. "Let's put one cloak beneath us and one over us like a tent."

"It's too hot to be covered." Erin wiped the moisture from her forehead. "And the bottom of this boat is hard. Let's use both of our cloaks to cushion us."

"What about snakes?" Bowie reminded her. "One could very easily fall into the boat."

Erin sat up and looked around. "Let's tie up somewhere without trees overhead."

"We need the shelter," Bowie told her and threw his wrap over a limb. It wasn't really large enough to make a satisfactory tent, but it was the best he could do. "I'm sorry we don't have anything to eat."

"I'm not very hungry," Erin lied, remembering that Bowie had once told her he could eat a horse.

"Try to rest." He slid into the bottom of the boat beside her and tried to cushion her body as well as possible. "Do you remember when we were talking about never having to sleep under a wagon again?"

"Yes, why?" she asked and shifted slightly to give him more room.

"I'd trade a wagon for this boat anytime." He chuckled and squeezed her against him as he listened to the sound of bullfrogs and crickets. The forest and swamp around them sounded alive, seemed to press closer as he lay there listening. "Although I don't really care where I am as long as we're together."

"I agree with that wholeheartedly." Erin's eyelids slowly closed.

Bowie heard her breathing slowly and knew she was asleep. He couldn't very well sleep since somebody had to watch for soldiers, but he could cuddle her and make her journey easier whenever possible. He noted that she still hadn't complained. "What a woman," he murmured.

When Erin awoke, the sun was up. She looked at Bowie, who was still sleeping. "Bowie, wake up. Shouldn't we be leaving?"

Bowie's eyes flew open. He'd promised himself he wouldn't fall asleep, but he had.

He pulled his cloak from the limb, untied the boat, and pushed away from the shore. Within minutes they were floating aimlessly down the Cooper River toward Charleston.

Erin sat in her end of the boat and watched for a familiar landmark. When she saw the old Sullivan plantation, she grinned at Bowie. "Next tributary."

The entrance to the tributary was narrow and hard to navigate, but Bowie was a sailor and handled it smoothly. They floated along, carried by the current, for more than an hour before Erin began to sit more erect and glance around furtively.

"There. Turn there." Erin pointed to an even narrower creek, and Bowie managed to stop the boat before it floated past the inlet. "Bluffwood's not far now."

When they reached the dock, Bowie tied the rowboat to an iron ring and helped Erin climb up the little ladder. Bowie looked at her as she tried to walk and realized that her muscles must be cramped, and she'd never be able to traverse the distance to the house. Following her quickly, Bowie took her arm, and they walked over to the bellpull. The bell sang out, and Erin sat down to wait.

A few minutes passed before they saw someone coming from the house. Bowie waved when he saw Toby and ran to meet him. "Go get a wagon or buggy for Miss Erin."

Toby's head bobbed up and down, and he ran back toward the house. Before long Bowie heard the slave yell, "It's Miss Erin and Mr. Bowie."

When Toby returned with the wagon, Arlen was sitting on the seat with him. Arlen climbed down and hobbled over to them. "What's wrong?"

Bowie explained about his capture and Erin's daring rescue. He continued telling Arlen about the night in the woods and the remainder of the trip in the boat. "As you can see, Erin's exhausted and sunburned."

Bowie lifted Erin into the wagon and in minutes helped her out at the house. He carried her up the stairs and laid her across her bed. "Stay here."

Running back down the stairs, he called for Toby. When the man appeared, Bowie instructed him to prepare a warm bath for Miss Erin and have the cook heat some soup or stew. He then went into the parlor to speak to Arlen alone.

"I believe the Tories will come here for us. Although Erin stabbed that jackass Walter Martin, she didn't kill him, not outright anyway. He'll tell Stuart where to look for us."

"You'll be safe here. We can hide you." Arlen lifted his cane and thwacked it across a table. "Thunder and tarnation! I'll kill any Tory who sets foot in here. It was bad enough having to put up with that British idiot in Charleston."

"Arlen, we can't stay here," Bowie began as he sat down. "I want to take Erin where I know she'll be safe, where the British can't reach her, where they have no authority."

"Where's that?" Arlen asked and fell back into his chair.

"The tropical islands. We can sail on the *Midnight Star* until we find a place to remain until the war's over." Bowie didn't like to say what he had to say next. "I think you and Mrs. Banning should go with us."

"But why?" Arlen asked, eyeing Bowie suspiciously. "Is something wrong with Erin?"

"No, it's not that. I think the British will take their vengeance here." Bowie hooked one of his legs across the arm of his chair and slumped back. "And I don't want Erin to worry about you."

Within minutes the matter was settled. Erin, Bowie, Arlen and Vevila Banning and their servants would leave for the *Midnight Star.* Bowie wanted to take Erin there as soon as she bathed and ate and slept for a little while. She'd have plenty of time to rest later.

Once aboard the *Midnight Star,* they'd set sail for Edisto. Bowie felt that his mother would take them in for a while, at least until Erin gave birth.

Erin collapsed across her bed, allowing the soft feather mattress to comfort her as she drifted off to sleep. Her body ached so much she didn't know what part hurt the most. After a short while Annabell came up with Toby and plenty of hot water. They filled a bathing tub, and Toby left.

Annabell helped Erin undress and climb into the tub. "Ah, Annabell," Erin cooed as she settled in the water that came above her hips. "This is heaven."

"And you need a little bit a heaven, dearie," Annabell answered and beamed. "You're a wee one to be so brave. And you'll be havin' a wee one a your own soon."

Erin closed her eyes and leaned back. A wee one of her own. For the first time she allowed those words to flow over her and warm every part of her. All along she'd been so afraid that something would happen, that the child would cease to move.

She thought of the close call Bowie had had. Tears stung her eyes, but she didn't let them fall. Erin Banning Gallagher wasn't one to immerse herself in sorrow or agony for a past event that had turned out well.

The British soldiers were cruel and vicious. She knew that Bluffwood was in danger, along with its inhabitants, both black and white. Bowie had said they would leave here soon. Erin opened her eyes and took a long look at a room she'd adored for almost nineteen years.

The muted colors had been chosen because the soft pastels made her feel so feminine. Bowie must feel out of place in such a room. The ruffles and ribbons would have to be removed. A deeper tone of carpet would soon center the floor. The bed hangings, now a soft peach, would be replaced by a hunter's green with wine-colored markings.

Erin accepted her own proposed changes. She was a different woman, and the girlish colors were unsuitable now. She thought of the nursery down the hall that had been used but once. Her baby would soon lie in the old mahogany cradle.

As if in response to her thoughts, the baby kicked sharply, perhaps to make her think of him. What would she call him or her? She didn't know the names of Bowie's ancestors, but she knew her own. If she had a boy, she'd use one of her own family names and one of Bowie's. That thought pleased her immensely.

She looked around and found that she was alone. Annabell must have gone back downstairs. Erin hurried to wash in the rapidly cooling water, knowing she didn't have a lot of time since Bowie wanted to leave soon.

Bowie hesitated outside the door. Annabell had said that Erin was bathing, but that had been some time ago. He turned the doorknob carefully, opened the door, and peeked into the room. Erin was rising from the tub. He stepped inside the room as she turned around.

"Oh!" Erin pulled the towels in front of her. "I didn't expect you back so soon."

The look of abject embarrassment touched him. He knew that Erin thought her body was ugly to him now that she was swollen with child. He locked the door behind him and crossed the room. Without speaking, he lifted her from the water and carried her to the bed.

Her damp skin glistened when he unwound the towel from around her and threw it across the room. He cooed love words in her ear and clung to her. Kissing her gently, he laid her back in the welcoming softness of the feather mattress. Now that she was totally naked, he caressed the soft skin of her distended stomach and tenderly fondled her sensitive breasts.

Moaning, Erin caught his head in her hands. "Bowie, we can't . . ."

"I know, my darling," he whispered but didn't stop caressing her. "I love you. I adore you. I worship you and every ounce of your beautiful body. You've never been lovelier to me."

His words flowed over Erin like a warm summer tide. She relaxed and enjoyed his loving touch. Her head was cradled in a soft pillow, and Bowie played lightly with her naked body. All the tension seemed to stream from her and be swept away by the same tide of warmth that stemmed from Bowie's caresses.

Her body responded to his every touch. She writhed beneath his pliant fingers as they played across her breasts, stomach, and abdomen. Her mind soared free, floating on unseen currents of love that spanned a brilliant sky. Cradled in the cloudlike softness of her mattress, Erin felt lighter than air. All the pregnant heaviness left her under his gentle, loving touch.

His kisses became more urgent, more involving. Erin's arms went around his neck, and she clung to him with a ferocity she'd never experienced while his fingers found the tiny moist spot that emitted such wild emotions and sensations.

Gasping for breath, she covered his face with kisses and trailed her fingers all along his taut muscles. She knew that the moment would end soon, that all of this would result in a cold awakening, but she didn't care. She felt so alive with an awareness she hadn't known for some time that she felt she would burst into a billowing flame.

Erin was in ecstasy as his kisses fluttered over her. Lying there, she let him cover her entire body with those delicious kisses that set her on fire. She couldn't stand much more. Her body became rigid with a desire she could no longer control. Bowie's lips and tongue teased her until that flame consumed her, and Erin went limp from satiation.

Relaxed and contented, she opened her eyes briefly and saw Bowie's smile. She tried to return his gesture, but sleep claimed her.

Bowie rose. Maybe now Erin would realize that her body was as lovely to him as ever. He felt his own passion begin to ebb as he forced himself to think of other things. There would be a time when their bodies could be joined again, but not now.

The Gallaghers, the Bannings, and the house servants were crowded—along with the mahogany cradle that Erin had refused to leave without—into two small boats. 'Lasses and Nero were with Sidney and Kenneth somewhere, possibly at the ship. Erin wondered where they were, but it was useless to dwell on that facet of the rescue. The four of them were to flee as soon as they knew Erin had reached the camp, but she suspected that they had not.

Sidney would know a safe place to take them, Erin mused, and wondered why she hadn't instructed Sidney to take them to the *Midnight Star*. She couldn't have been thinking rationally at the time. Bowie's rescue had taken up all of her attention.

Now they were floating in the moonlight down the Cooper River toward a cove that would leave them close to the point where they could find Bowie's ship. They would cross a narrow neck of land, find another boat, and cross to one of the barrier islands where the *Midnight Star* awaited them—if she hadn't been discovered.

Behind them the sounds of soldiers broke the tranquility of the night. Bowie glanced at Erin, whose alert eyes told him she'd heard the noise, too. That could only mean that Walter had provided the army with information about Bluffwood.

Bowie rowed faster. He didn't doubt that the soldiers, once they discovered that the family had left, would pursue them. He called to Toby to row more quickly as well. From Bowie's vantage point, he could see Bluffwood fading in the distance. The others were seated with their backs to the plantation.

The moonlight wasn't strong enough for him to see the soldiers, but he knew they were there. Now they were lighting torches, perhaps to see better, to look through the barns and outbuildings for the people they'd expected to find. Little dots of flame moved jerkily around the house and other buildings.

Bowie grinned, knowing he'd outsmarted the British once again. The soldiers would find no one. Then his grin faded. They weren't searching. The torches were flung into the air and through windows. Bluffwood was burning!

He hadn't realized he'd stopped rowing until Erin touched his arm. Bowie couldn't look at her face. She hadn't yet seen the orange glow growing behind her, and he didn't want her to see it at all. He began rowing again, furiously this time.

Erin gazed at Bowie. Something was wrong. Then she saw it in his eyes. The reflection of flames. She spun around. "No!" she cried and stood up.

"Erin!" Bowie dropped the oars and grabbed her to keep her from falling overboard. He held her for a few moments to comfort her as well as he could, but he knew the soldiers would be after them soon. "Arlen, take her."

Tears were flowing from Arlen's eyes as he helped Bowie to get Erin back in her seat. Bowie started to row again, and Arlen held Erin close. Vevila, if she noticed the fire at all, didn't seem disturbed.

Bowie gritted his teeth and swore silently that the British may have won this time, but they'd never hurt Erin again. He calmed down slightly and once again began to row rhythmically. They soon reached the cove and beached the little boats.

Carrying Erin ashore, Bowie felt the tension in her body. For the moment she felt defeated, he knew, but that wouldn't last long. Erin would bounce back and find a way to get even.

Arlen and Toby helped the others ashore. The trek across the narrow neck of land wouldn't take long, but it was difficult. Thick undergrowth, spiny palmettos, and vines plotted to trip up the little troop, but Bowie managed to get them across without any trouble. When they reached the Atlantic shore on the other side, the major problems would begin.

Bowie had hoped Sidney would be here. As his assistant, Sidney should have known that Bowie would arrive at this place as soon as humanly possible. Disappointed, he organized the loading of the boat.

A movement behind a dune startled Bowie. He knew that this shoreline was patrolled, but he hadn't expected to find anyone on the beach at this hour. Drawing his pistol carefully, Bowie watched the spot where he'd noticed the movement.

"Say, mate, ye know where a body can catch a rig leavin' this cursed place?" came a voice over the dune.

Bowie grinned broadly. This was the first good news he'd had in days. "I know a mate that had better be in this boat before it shoves off."

Erin looked at Bowie. The voice was Sidney's. She couldn't mistake it. That must mean that 'Lasses, Nero, and Kenneth were around. She scanned the beach for them but saw nothing. Then they began to walk over the dunes.

When they reached her, she hugged them all at once. Tears flowed freely for she thought she'd never see them again. They all began to chatter at once.

"Erin, we must leave," Bowie insisted tenderly. "Everybody into the boat."

When they were all loaded in the bigger boat, Sidney, Nero, Bowie, and Toby began to row. Traversing the distance across the ocean between the shore and the small island made them susceptible to a British attack from land. Once they reached the island, they would be safe in the time it took them to set sail, but the Carolina shore was patrolled regularly by British ships looking for privateers.

The morose group was silent as they rode the swells of the Atlantic toward the island. Bowie's heart felt leaden. If only he could have gotten Erin away before she saw the flames, she wouldn't have known about the destruction of Bluffwood until after the end of the war. By that time she'd be more able to tolerate the loss. In her present condition every emotion she experienced was multiplied a thousand times by every ounce of weight she'd gained.

The men let the little boat glide into the cove where the *Midnight Star* awaited them. They reached shore without incident and began to disembark. Sidney went ahead to search the ship.

"We're all here, mate," he called from the deck.

Several heads appeared above the railing, and Bowie grinned. "Now, how did you manage that?"

"I sent word before I reached Miss Erin's house in Charleston. I figured if we got you free, we'd have to be leavin' at a right smart clip." Sidney returned and helped to get everyone on the ship.

Bowie took Erin to his cabin and settled her on his cot. "I'm sorry this isn't more comfortable. It just never seemed to matter before."

"It's wonderful," Erin whispered, relaxing with the gentle rocking motion of the boat.

Bowie made sure that everyone from Bluffwood had accommodations while Sidney and the crew prepared to set sail. Within a few minutes of the time they'd arrived, the *Midnight Star* sailed into the Atlantic under a single small sail that would take them slowly south without catching the attention of the British ships.

The trip to Edisto would take but a short time, and the crew knew their duties well. Bowie sat watching Erin as she slept peacefully for the first time in days.

*   *   *

When they reached Edisto, Bowie's mother, Emily Gallagher, met them at the wharf. Bowie hugged her briefly and then introduced her. "Mother, this is my wife, Erin, who, as you can well see, carries our child. We need shelter. I'll explain later."

"You have nothing to explain." Emily embraced Erin and looked at her through teary eyes. "You are just the thing for this wayward boy of mine."

After the introductions were over, Emily assumed command. She directed her servants to see to quarters for everyone and took Erin and the Bannings with her. All along the way she questioned Bowie about his journeys and adventures. By the time they reached the house, she looked admiringly at Erin. "My dear, you really are perfect for my son."

Bowie glanced around for his father. "Where is he, Mother?"

Emily grinned and said, "Why, he's tied up at the moment, dear."

"Mother," Bowie began and eyed his mother suspiciously. "Where is he?"

"Well, if you must know, I'll tell you." Emily settled herself on the sofa beside Erin. "When Hamlet told me he'd spotted the *Midnight Star,* I began to ply Mr. Gallagher with brandy. When he was sufficiently . . . comfortable . . . I asked Hamlet to bring a length of rope. We then tied Mr. Gallagher to his chair in the library."

Bowie laughed out loud. "Mother, you should be ashamed!"

"Well, I'm not. He's the one who should be ashamed." Emily ordered food for everyone. "We'll just keep him tied until he changes his attitude."

The days melted into weeks of comfort and safety at Edisto Glade. Erin came to love it almost as much as she loved Bluffwood. She hadn't met Mr. Gallagher yet, but Bowie had seen him and had told her that there was no changing the old Tory.

Erin's body swelled still more. Her back ached, her muscles cramped, but she kept silent. The plantation midwife had visited several times and pronounced Erin in perfect health.

In the middle of October, however, Erin started to experience more frequent stomach cramps. She didn't mention it at first because she thought they were normal. Then one evening as they were sitting by the fire, a strong cramp seized her, and she doubled over with pain.

Bowie leapt to his feet, picked Erin up, and carried her to their room. Emily sent for the midwife. Vevila smiled sweetly. Arlen began to pace the floor.

When the midwife arrived, she insisted that Bowie could not remain in the room with Erin. Swearing vengeance on the woman, Bowie sidled down the stairs to join Arlen. By this time Sidney and Kenneth had heard of the commotion and hurried into the parlor.

The motley crew of four began to pace, to mutter, to mumble, to drink, and to curse. Bowie felt himself seized with panic. Erin shouldn't deliver for another month at least. He knew she was in danger, as was his child, but there was nothing he could do to help this time. There was no war camp for him to charge into and save her, no soldiers to kill, no battle to fight except the one within his heart and mind.

Vevila sat on the sofa and watched the men pace. She seemed unaffected by the melee around her. After a while she wandered off. Bowie knew he should go after her but couldn't bring himself to be absent from the parlor should he be needed. Besides, he reasoned, Vevila would be safe here.

The pacing and muttering continued. Arlen, because of his injured leg, finally sat down and cursed. "Damn. I'm denied the only release offered a man when his child is having a child."

Bowie wanted to laugh; he wanted to cry; he wanted to be with Erin. The agonized expression she wore as he'd carried her upstairs ate at his heart, and he swore she'd never have to go through this again.

Upstairs, Erin breathed easily for a few minutes before the racking pain invaded her body again. Time held no meaning for her. The pains seemed to last hours, while the moments of respite were fleeting. Bathed in perspiration, she tossed and turned and writhed beneath the sadistic taskmaster called birthing.

She tried to concentrate on the moments of joy she'd shared with Bowie but couldn't. She wanted to see him, but the midwife denied her that right. Erin tried to smile at Emily, to reassure her, but couldn't. Erin felt helpless, a victim of excruciating pain and worry. Her baby wasn't due for another month. She sensed that this early birth signaled trouble, the problems she'd imagined early in the pregnancy.

No, Erin scolded herself, she wouldn't give in to supposition and fears.

The pain intensified. Erin knew the moment of truth had come.

Bowie covered his ears. He couldn't stand Erin's screams of pain. Tears flowed freely from his eyes, and he sought to drown his agony in brandy. Hamlet brought another bottle. Bowie poured himself a drink and passed the bottle to Arlen. When Arlen handed the bottle back to Bowie, he glanced at Sidney. His glass was still full. Kenneth simply watched the others drink.

Bowie attempted a grin and handed his own glass to Kenneth. "Here. Tonight, you are a man. Our equal as we all share in Erin's agony."

When Kenneth began to sip the brandy, Bowie turned up the bottle and swilled down almost half its contents. If he couldn't shut out Erin's pain, he would drown it.

Somewhere in the house another sound caught his attention, and his mind went fleetingly to Vevila. Where was she? What was she doing? The sound came from the back of the house, from the room where his father was imprisoned. What could Vevila be doing back there?

Suddenly Bowie became sober. What could Vevila be

doing back there? She could be releasing Douglas Gallagher!

Bowie sprang to his feet. "Sidney, grab a pistol and come with me."

Bowie raced down the hall to the room where his father was kept. He found Vevila smiling as sweetly as ever.

She patted his shoulder. "My dear Mr. Gallagher, did you know there was a nice man tied up in here?"

Not taking time to answer, Bowie fled the room. He checked the library, the smoking room, the gun room and found them all empty. He glanced at the wall where his father's guns were stored. Two were missing.

Seizing one of them, he prayed that Sidney had taken the other two. A scream split the tense atmosphere. *Erin.* Bowie almost fell over his feet as he ran from the room and up the stairs. The door to his bedroom, his and Erin's, stood ajar.

The silence in the room confirmed his worst suspicions. Douglas Gallagher had found Erin. Bowie eased into the room and found his father holding one of the pistols.

"Ah, my son, the spy." Douglas motioned for Bowie to move against the wall. "If you don't want your wife dead, then—"

A tiny cry pierced the hushed room. Bowie wasn't looking at his father anymore. The midwife, her arms covered in blood, lifted a tiny wriggling infant into her arms. She swaddled the baby in a pure white cloth and turned to face the two men.

"Your daughter," she said to Bowie and then looked at Douglas Gallagher. "Your granddaughter, sir."

Arlen, Sidney, and Kenneth burst into the room. Douglas lowered his pistol and stared at the tiny bundle. Bowie hurried across the room, cognizant only of his wife and daughter. The midwife wiped the baby's face and handed the blanketed bundle to Bowie.

He slumped down onto the bed so Erin could see. "It's a girl. We have a baby girl."

Erin smiled wanly and peeked at the little form that had caused such a silence in the room with a single faint wail.

The midwife made sure that Erin was modestly covered and then stepped back. Emily, Douglas, Arlen, Sidney, and Kenneth surged forward to see. Bowie looked up at the small knot of people and at the black faces gathered at the door. "A girl. We have a girl," he called, and the whispers spread through the hallway to all the servants.

Douglas sat down on the bed beside his son. He looked at the cherubic face of his granddaughter, at the shimmer of gold that covered her head, at the brilliant blue of her eyes. He looked from Bowie to Erin.

Bowie glanced at his father. In the excitement of the moment Bowie had forgotten the tense situation. The pistol was lying beside Douglas as he reached to take his granddaughter from his son's hands. Downstairs the clock struck midnight, and everyone looked around and grinned.

"What are you going to call my lovely granddaughter?" Douglas asked with tears in his eyes.

Vevila shuffled up to the group and peered over Kenneth's shoulder. "What a lovely baby. This one was born with stars in her eyes."

"I love you, Erin. This is the greatest gift you could have ever given me." Bowie looked down at his child, who had transformed a tyrant into a sobbing man. He glanced at the crowd and at Erin. He knew she would agree with his choice of names. "Her name is Star. She's our Midnight Star."

If you enjoyed CRIMSON SUNRISE and MIDNIGHT STAR, you'll look forward to reading the third book in *The Charleston Women* trilogy, CAROLINA MOON, coming soon from Diamond Books.

Turn the page for a sample of this glorious new novel by Kristie Knight—CAROLINA MOON.

CAROLINA MOON

BOOK III in *The Charleston Women* Trilogy

CHAPTER
1

Charleston, South Carolina
October 1781

Lilly Arledge strode to her window and stared out into the night. Lifting the sash, she stepped through the opening onto her piazza and inhaled the cool salt air. The crisp breeze ruffled the hem of her silk gown, and she hugged herself to keep warm as she watched the mist rolling across the juncture of the Ashley and Cooper rivers into Charleston Harbor to envelope King George's ships in a veil of gray.

Tonight felt almost springlike. She could almost catch the delicate fragrance of Carolina jasmine and oleander if she closed her eyes and imagined hard enough. She looked at the large vines that grew to the height of her piazza and smiled with pride. Her plants were among the largest in all of Charleston. She bent down, reached between the wrought-iron rails, and broke a stem with lush green leaves. Sniffing gently, she closed her eyes and recalled the scent of jasmine for a moment, shutting out her problems—the gathering crowd downstairs, the War for Independence that had gone on for so many years, and, most of all, her father. But she couldn't remain in her fantasy world for long.

She glanced down at the street. Below her, carriages lined up outside her gate, and guests clad in gaily colored silks and satins poured from them into the twilight. Some of them called greetings to one another, but no one seemed to notice

Lilly as she kept her silent vigil above them. From the look of my guests, she thought, you'd never know a war was going on. The War for Independence seemed far away as she prepared for her father's party.

A man emerged from a carriage and waited for the second occupant. As both men walked toward the lower piazza, the first man, a stranger, glanced up to where Lilly stood. In the dim light filtering through the palmetto fronds and live oaks, he gazed at her for a long moment. Lilly knew she should step back into her room, but she didn't want to appear rude. He was with one of her good friends, Gregory Weston.

The stranger smiled and touched his hand to his forehead in greeting before catching up with Gregory. Lilly felt a blush sting her cheeks and shrank back into the cool anonymity of the shadows. As she stepped back through the window, she thought tonight might not be such a trial after all.

She knew her father would be angry with her if she delayed her entrance any longer, but Lilly didn't hurry. She wasn't too happy with him, either. Twirling the jasmine stem between her fingers, she looked for a hairpin. In the springtime she would have worn the fragrant yellow blossoms so that when the evening became tedious, she could inhale their scent and hide in her private world of dreams. Tonight she sprinkled a bit of perfume over the leaves and pinned them in place. Tartuffe, Lilly's cat, leapt into her lap and purred, rubbing against the bodice of her gown. Lilly felt the prick of a claw on her thigh and jerked the cat's paw free.

"Ouch! Tartuffe, you naughty boy. You'll ruin my gown." But she couldn't be angry with her friend for too long. Lilly stroked the white cat's fur and scratched between its ears. "Now, run along and chase mice."

She watched the cat prance independently across the floor, grinned in spite of the pick in her skirt, and pinned the stem in place. She stood and tilted her chin jauntily to one side. "You'll do," she whispered to herself.

By now her father would be enraged over her lateness. The bells of St. Michael's were tolling the hour of eight, and she should have been downstairs thirty minutes ago. He controlled most of her life, but these few stolen moments were her form of revenge. These people were not her guests but his. The gown she wore was his choice and not hers. This evening, like so many others orchestrated by her father, promised to be a long, tiring event—except for the presence of the gallant stranger who might provide some entertainment. He certainly didn't look like most of her father's associates.

She shook the fine yellow silk of her skirt to make sure it hung gracefully over her petticoats and swished out of her dressing room. Hesitating a moment to gain her composure, Lilly placed her hand on the banister and inhaled deeply. From now until the early hours of the morning she would have to smile sweetly and dance with many British soldiers she hardly knew. Since her mother was dead, Lilly served as her father's hostess. He seemed to notice her only on evenings like this.

Jonathan Arledge, her father, worked very closely with the British authorities. The British occupying force required great amounts of food, and her father was getting rich procuring supplies for them from the outlying parishes. Lilly was forced to assist, but she couldn't stop her feelings of shame.

She could delay her entrance no longer without incurring Jonathan Arledge's wrath. Forcing a smile to her lips, she tugged at her low-cut bodice, trying to make the almost indecent gown presentable, and started down the stairs. Jedediah was opening the door to admit more guests as Lilly reached the foyer.

"Lilly, how lovely you look." Marigold O'Grady linked her arm with Lilly's and peeked into the parlor. "A room full of men—looks like a girl's idea of heaven!"

"Ugh," Lilly groaned and wrinkled her nose. Mari had pointedly refused to acknowledge the presence of several Charleston matrons scattered among the male guests. "Not

one interesting person in the lot. Except you, of course."
Knowing that her friend would make too much of the incident, Lilly failed to mention having seen the handsome
stranger earlier.

"Love the saints, my prayers have been answered." Marigold gripped Lilly's arm and pointed across the parlor to
a tall man standing near the harpsichord. "Who is that
Greek god?"

Lilly looked at the man and shook her head. He was the
man she'd seen from her piazza. "He's certainly very handsome, but I don't know who he is. And he's wearing far too
many clothes to be a Greek god."

"You're the hostess. Go introduce yourself and then introduce me." Marigold nudged Lilly forward. "It looks like
he's with Gregory Weston."

Marigold was right, although Lilly didn't confirm her
friend's conclusion. Gregory and the stranger were engrossed in their conversation and didn't appear to notice the
girls' approach. Lilly could hardly keep from staring. The
man wore no uniform, and she was glad. British soldiers
kept trying to impress her by regaling her with accounts of
their heroism in battle. Though the Arledge household—including Lilly—remained loyal to King George, Lilly hated
to be reminded of war every time a man spoke to her. They
seemed to have completely forgotten all other topics.

As she made her way across the parlor with Marigold,
Lilly paused here and there to welcome her father's guests.
With their arms linked, Lilly did all she could to restrain
her best friend, who seemed to want to rush past everyone
else to reach the handsome stranger.

Gregory Weston spotted Lilly crossing the room and gestured to the man standing with him. "Ah, here's our hostess. Miss Arledge, may I present Ethan Kendall. Ethan,
Lilly Arledge, the loveliest of Charleston's young ladies."

Before Lilly could reply, Marigold elbowed her way between Lilly and Gregory. "Shame on you, Gregory, for not
introducing me. I'm Marigold O'Grady. Call me Mari. Everyone does."

Ethan barely glanced at Mari but gazed at Lilly with a warm smile. "So nice to meet you . . . both."

Lilly felt herself grow warm under Ethan's gaze. Her eyes met his, and she smiled genuinely for the first time this evening. His eyes seemed to devour her, to lock out everything else. His grin deepened, and he cocked his head to one side. Lilly felt as if he'd come just to see *her*. Something about him made her feel important for the first time in her life. But then, she admonished herself, he probably made every girl he met feel important.

The foursome talked a few minutes before Lilly excused herself to make sure all her guests were comfortable. Her gaze kept drifting back to Ethan Kendall, and she found that he, too, was watching her. Color suffused her cheeks as she strode back to the kitchen to check on the preparations for supper.

Zipporah, Lilly's mammy, stepped from the dining room and nodded. "Supper 'bout ready. Go on back to yo comp'ny."

"Thank you, Zip. We're ready to eat." Lilly smiled at the older woman. She leaned close and whispered, "I'd like to be in bed by midnight. Do you think there's a possibility?"

A roar of laughter burst from the parlor, and Zipporah shook her head. "Sound like a rowdy bunch of geese. Them folks ain't gonna leave afore mornin', don't you know? I bet they be powerful hungry, too."

Lilly laughed and hugged the servant. "Oh, well, I can hope, can't I? Have Jedediah announce supper."

Returning to her guests, Lilly hesitated at the double doors to the parlor and studied Ethan Kendall. She wondered what he was doing here, why his gaze followed her as she walked from one cluster of people to another.

"Lilly!" her father called over the din of the crowd. "Come here."

She could no longer waste time wondering about Ethan Kendall. Her father sounded angry, and she knew better than to keep him waiting when he was upset.

*   *   *

Ethan Kendall watched his lovely hostess as she crossed
the room to her father. The yellow gown drifted around her
like the froth that rode the waves along the beach, making
her appear to float as she strolled gracefully to the hearth,
where a small knot of men stood talking. Her hair, braided
and pinned securely to the nape of her neck, shone like
chestnuts in the soft glow of candlelight. He wondered how
it would look hanging free down her back, blowing gently
with the breeze that blew off the rivers.

Her eyes were the rich, glittering color of brandy. Ethan
felt drawn to her and walked across the room, nearer to the
hearth so he could see her lovely face better. A wisp of hair
slipped free of its confinement and caressed her cheek. Without seeming to think about it, she brushed it back with her
small hand. He wanted to reach out and touch her; she
looked so soft and gentle.

As Ethan watched, Jonathan Arledge snatched his
daughter's hand and jerked her to one side. Ethan couldn't
hear the conversation, but he was surprised by the violence
of the act that took place in full view of the people assembled
in the parlor. He noted the color that rose in Lilly's cheeks,
and suddenly he felt protective. He'd heard of Jonathan's
temper, but hadn't really believed the tales until now—and,
beyond that, couldn't believe that the man would inflict his
foul temper on his daughter.

He studied Lilly's reaction. Rather than cower before her
father's anger, she lifted her chin and listened as he berated
her for some grievance of which he alone was aware. Ethan
sensed a detachment in her, as if she were oblivious to the
verbal abuse her father inflicted. In that instant Ethan understood that Lilly would do her father's will with dignity—
as it seemed she always had—but something didn't quite fit.
Her eyes were alert and challenging—not the cowed gaze
of a dutiful daughter who never risked disobedience. She
possessed spunk.

With her chin tilted high, she turned and strode away
from her father. To leave the room, she had to walk past
Ethan. For a moment he looked down at her as she glanced

up to see who stood in her way, but he moved quickly to one side. He didn't want to add to her troubles, but he decided to ask Greg if he knew anything about the relationship.

For a few seconds she gazed at him and then murmured, "Excuse me, please, Mr. Kendall."

"Certainly, Miss Arledge." He smiled, hoping to bring the light back into her eyes. "We didn't have much of a chance to talk earlier, but I know your cousin, Mrs. Gallagher."

Lilly had started to move past him, but when he mentioned her cousin, she stopped. "Erin? Is she well? I haven't seen her since . . . since her marriage."

"She's well, I understand. They're expecting a baby soon." Ethan smiled. He'd seen Erin a week ago. She and Bowie were still hiding from the British.

Lilly smiled and nodded, wondering whom Ethan had spoken with who seemed to know so much about her cousin. "She'll be a good mother. I wish I could see her. Do you . . . do you know where she is?"

He'd hoped to avoid lying to Lilly, but now she'd asked a question he'd pledged not to answer. "No. They haven't been seen in some time around Charleston."

He admired Erin and Bowie a great deal. Both of them had fought for the Patriot cause, risking their lives to assure that the Continental Army received supplies that were vital to the winning of this war. Ethan wanted to play as important a role as Bowie, to contribute to the victory. But Ethan hadn't yet found his place. He knew he could have a significant impact on the outcome of this war if only he could discover his fated role.

Ethan wasn't afraid to fight. He'd fought since he turned eighteen. He'd been in Charleston when the first British ships arrived in June of 1776. He'd seen action at Port Royal Island in 1779. He'd fought at Flat Rock, Thicketty Fort, and at the Battle the Blackstocks before joining Light-Horse Harry Lee in December 1780 soon after General Greene took over the Southern Department of the Continental

Army. Ethan was proud of his record, even prouder of his new assignment. He'd been sent to Charleston to infiltrate the British Army, the occupying force.

He looked at Lilly and smiled. What part would she play, if any? Many women were finding ways to serve during this seemingly never-ending war. Jonathan Arledge was a loyalist. Ethan guessed that Jonathan's loyalty to the British was solely a financial one. He believed that the British would win and he wanted to reap the benefits of remaining loyal to the winning side. Ethan prayed that Jonathan was wrong.

But he wondered where Lilly stood. Did she believe as her father did? If she'd remained loyal, he instinctively believed her reasons would be heartfelt. Almost all young women he knew had taken the same side as their parents, and Ethan felt that Lilly was probably no exception. He would have to be careful.

Ethan smiled down at her. He understood the pain of the experience he'd witnessed between her and her father. His own father had been abusive to a degree. With a desire to divert her attention from her father, Ethan asked, "Have you known Greg for very long?"

Glad for a moment's distraction before she would have to move on to other, more probing guests, she tried to smile back at him. "Since my early childhood. Greg, Mari, and I grew up together. We played together as children. And you—how long have you known him?"

"Not nearly so long," Ethan answered truthfully. "I met him in school. We've been friends since we were about fourteen years old."

"He's a fine man and a fine soldier." Lilly glanced at her friend, who was deep in conversation with Mari.

Ethan never doubted her words for a moment. Greg was the kind of man who attacked a task wholeheartedly or not at all. He, too, held strong beliefs about this war. Wondering how close Lilly and Greg were, if there was any feeling beyond friendship, Ethan looked down at her speculatively.

Lilly gazed at Ethan. He was staring at her in the same way other men did—a way that made her feel uncomfortable. The corners of her mouth tilted into a smile. She had smiled the same way at other parties or suppers when she wasn't particularly interested in the guests. Her smile faded. He had seemed so intriguing to her, so exciting, but maybe her assessment was wrong.

She lifted her chin and eyed him casually. "I'm sorry, Mr. Kendall, but I have other guests who need attention. Perhaps we can speak again some time."

Without waiting for his acknowledgment, she moved away from him. Glancing quickly about, she spotted Mari and strode toward her. Mari and Gregory were still deep in conversation and didn't notice Lilly's approach. "Hello, you two. Are you having a nice evening?"

Before either of them could reply, Jedediah announced dinner. As usual, she sat at the opposite end of the table from her father. Silently she thanked whoever wrote the rules of good manners for dictating that host and hostess should be separated by such a distance. She didn't want to sit near her father if possible. Then, to her dismay, she found the place cards rearranged. Ethan Kendall was seated to her right and Gregory Weston to her left. Mari sat beside Gregory while a woman Lilly didn't know took the chair on the other side of Ethan.

At first Lilly thought that Ethan might have rearranged the place cards but decided that he wouldn't have done such a thing. So far he'd shown no particular interest in Lilly, except for that moment when their eyes met, that moment when the real Lilly flickered to life for the briefest span of time.

Studying her carefully, Ethan held the chair for Lilly before sitting beside her. He smiled at the woman on his left, but then turned to face Lilly. She seemed to observe him briefly before turning to Gregory to ask about his mother. Ethan watched the interplay between them without participating. The two had been friends for a long time, Gregory had said, and Lilly had confirmed it.

He allowed his thoughts to drift. Earlier in the evening

Ethan had seen her standing on her piazza, a vision in soft yellow as she stood looking across the rivers. He'd been enchanted. He'd watched her from the window of the carriage for a few seconds before he climbed out. She hadn't noticed him, not until she finally glanced down at the street as he stepped from the carriage, and a smile had lifted her lips. She'd been lovely, almost as if a promise had been spoken between them. But her reception had been cool. Ethan had seen nothing of that promise when they met in person. Could he have been mistaken? Could her smile have been for Gregory?

The muscles in Ethan's jaw twitched as he observed the easy flow of conversation and laughter between the two of them. Glancing at Mari, he ate an oyster. She'd pursued him relentlessly, practically throwing herself at him. He already knew that she could never mean anything to him, however. Her head was stuffed with silly fripperies and flirtatious banter. The most serious thought Mari would ever consider for any length of time would concern her attire or hair.

Ethan never wasted time on such women. He studied Lilly. More beautiful than Mari, he doubted that Lilly would spend the hours most women did on their appearance, yet she didn't seem to be interested in news of the war, either. He felt that she was a devout Loyalist, was almost certain because of the way she talked, but she seemed to freeze up around the soldiers except for Gregory. Getting to know her would be entertaining, he thought and raised an eyebrow as he considered how to approach her without causing a stir.

"Well, it gave me quite a turn, I assure you," Lilly said and sipped her wine. "I never expected to find a cow in my garden."

Gregory and Mari laughed. Ethan grinned to cover his embarrassment at not paying attention to the conversation. He hoped nobody asked his opinion on the subject, but he didn't escape quite so easily.

"And, you, Ethan, what do you think of Lilly's discovering a cow in her garden?" Mari asked, batting her eyes playfully.

Ethan cursed his lack of attention but grinned again and tried to bluff. "I suppose that finding a cow in your garden is better than finding a cow in your bedchamber."

Poor Gregory nearly choked with laughter as he apparently tried to keep from spitting wine on his hostess. Resolving to pay closer attention to the conversation, Ethan sipped his wine and continued to eat. His comment must have been adequate since nobody asked him what he meant.

"You're quite right, Mr. Kendall." Lilly patted the corner of her mouth with a damask napkin and placed it back in her lap. "I'm sure I don't know what I would have done with a cow in my bedchamber, and beyond that, I don't know how a cow could get there. But I don't know how she got in the garden, either."

"What did you do with her?" Mari asked.

"I led her to the stable." Lilly placed her fork across her plate and gazed at her friend. With a slight lift of her eyebrows to include the listeners in her confidence, she whispered, "I decided that if someone missed her, he could come looking for her."

"And has anyone come?" Gregory inquired, leaning forward slightly.

"No, she's still there." Lilly laughed and shook her head. "Applejack milks her twice a day. For the first time since the occupation, we have plenty of fresh milk."

Conversation lapsed into a discussion of shortages caused by the war, and, with a sniff of jasmine fragrance, Lilly allowed her thoughts to drift. Her gaze moved to Ethan. Why was he here? He must be a Loyalist or he wouldn't be bold enough to walk into this party, let alone be so friendly with Gregory and the other British officers.

But he spoke of her cousin Erin as if he knew her well. Lilly puzzled over this enigma. She'd never discover the truth by thinking about it, but she liked challenges, and in that moment she made the mystery of Ethan Kendall her new project. She'd unshroud the story of his presence. Besides, he intrigued her.

She picked up the thread of conversation as Ethan said, "It's a lovely old place on Goose Creek." His voice lowered to a softer, more loving tone as he apparently recalled a favorite place. He darted a glance at Lilly, hoping she would forgive him for not telling the complete truth. He was proud of Carolina Moon but didn't want to risk having this group connect him with the Patriots. "My family's been there since before my birth."

"It sounds wonderful." Lilly smiled, not knowing exactly how to respond to a man who so obviously wasn't ashamed to show his emotions. Her eyes met his, and she noticed them for the first time. They were as green as the Atlantic and glinted with gold like the sun's summer rays off the water. With a slight catch in her voice she whispered, "I'd love to see it some day."

Ethan gazed at her. Her voice had changed. In that short time span, was it possible that her opinion of him had changed? Something in her tone, the soft throaty whisper, said much more than her words. "And so you shall. After all this strife is over, I'll take you there."

A wisp of mahogany-colored hair again fluttered across her cheek, and she absently brushed it away. Her fingers were long and tapered, and the graceful movement added to the aura of natural beauty that he kept seeing even when he turned away. But her eyes were spectacular. Wide open and the color of roasted chestnuts, they studied him with vitality and honesty. Nothing of the coquette abided within her, or if it did, she kept it well hidden from him.

Color suffused her cheeks as she realized that she'd allowed herself to reveal far too much to this stranger. She knew nothing about him except that a hank of his tawny hair refused to be bound by the tie in back. He'd mentioned Erin and attended this party with Gregory, but many people knew both Erin and Gregory—people on both sides of this horrible war. She watched him for a moment; he seemed more complex than most of the men she knew—and definitely more interesting.

Ethan turned to answer a question asked by the woman at his right. Greg and Mari were debating the merits of some soldier's feats. Smiling vacantly, Lilly withdrew into herself as she did so frequently these days.

The flames on the candles danced as the breeze wafted through the sheer draperies from the fully open windows. Lilly looked toward the harbor, which she could barely see because of the houses that stood between the Arledge house and the water. Dark clouds gathered on the horizon, and a storm seemed to be approaching. Lilly loved storms. They made her feel alive, vibrant. The hint of the coming disturbance lifted her spirits, and she grinned wickedly to Ethan, Greg, and Mari. "Jedediah, lower the windows a little. I'm afraid the wind will blow the biscuits off the platter."

The butler stared at her for a moment as if to determine whether or not she was serious, but the next puff of wind blew out several candles, and he scurried to lower the windows. The room grew quiet. As he pulled them down, a soft whisper came from the inner recesses of the walls where the weights slid up to allow the sash to be moved downward.

"Well, these are light biscuits, but not quite that light," Mari observed as she broke the crust on one. With her mouth full she added, "Good, though."

Lilly allowed herself to sink back into her personal world as the chatter resumed around the table. She found the normal sounds of routine relaxing. The windows, like most in Charleston, could be raised completely into the upper story to allow people to walk from the interior of the house to the piazza and gardens. On warm summer nights all of the windows were opened to allow the breeze off the ocean to blow through the house, chasing away the heat of the day. Now the window allowed a fresh breeze to cool the night. Lilly longed to walk outside where she could feel the approaching storm. Instead, she was forced to signal for the next course.

After a custard for dessert, everyone moved into the ballroom. A string quartet played softly as several couples meandered to the dance floor. Lilly watched as they lined up. She didn't enjoy dancing with the soldiers because they were quite often too ardent for her. Several of them had already proposed to her, and she'd turned them down. She refused to be a pawn in her father's devious tricks and, as a result, rarely accepted any invitations from the soldiers he invited to parties or suppers.

"Miss Arledge, may I have this dance?" Ethan bowed from the waist.

"How kind of you to ask, Mr. Kendall."

They joined the other couples on the polished hardwood floor. Lilly curtsied, and Ethan bowed. She laid her hand on his arm, and for a few moments they executed the steps without speaking. Lilly didn't know what to say to him. His touch seemed to chase all rational thought from her mind. "Mr. Kendall, have you been in Charleston for long?"

Ethan accomplished the next few steps before responding. He didn't know how to answer her truthfully without breaking a confidence that might jeopardize the Patriot efforts. "Miss Arledge, I've lived northwest of here all my life."

"I understand that, but—"

Lilly had no time to ask how he knew Erin. The dance ended, and Ethan walked her back to Mari and Gregory. Immediately Gregory asked her to dance, and she allowed him to lead her to the floor. Over his shoulder she watched as Ethan and Mari began to dance. Though she wanted to remain with Ethan—to find out how he knew Erin, what he was doing at this party—she managed to enjoy herself. She'd much rather dance with Greg than those other soldiers her father insisted on pairing her with.

Living with Jonathan Arledge was a constant fight. He insisted on her being friendly with the British soldiers he brought home. Lilly, basically a shy person, hated being pushed by her father into friendships that would always be one-sided. Though she heartily believed in the British cause, she refused to consort with the soldiers—particularly on the level her father was aiming for. She sometimes sensed that he wanted her to be . . . well . . . loose. As a result, she shied away from men almost completely—or had until tonight.

The ballroom was lit with fat white candles nested in jasmine bowers, and the scent of jasmine and candle wax filled the room. Lilly smiled. She loved the fragrance. Every year she dried the flowers and crushed the petals to save the scent for winter. At times when the weather became intolerable, she'd toss them onto a burning log, and the room would smell like summer again.

The music stopped while the musicians prepared for the next dance, and she walked with Gregory to the edge of the dance floor. She sat beside Mari and watched as couples began to whirl about the room to the next melody. Ethan and Gregory left to find the punch bowl.

"Lilly, I want to tell you that Ethan Kendall is the most exciting thing to happen in Charleston since the day we sat on the roof and watched the bombs flying through the air from the British ships." Mari leaned close and tugged on Lilly's arm. "More exciting."

Lilly smiled at her friend's obvious joy with the newcomer, who now headed back toward them with Greg trailing behind carrying two punch cups. But Lilly's thoughts ran deeper. She studied him. As he skirted the dance floor, he paused to speak here and there, occasionally a smile breaking across his face. Yet he seemed a bit reserved, aloof, as if he were above all that was happening. Intrigued, she kept a secret eye on him while she pretended to watch the dancers as they passed and called greetings to her.

Ethan listened to the chatter of a matron who appeared to be intent on keeping him from returning to Lilly and Mari. He listened as she pointed out the merits of her daughter, who more closely resembled the horse he rode than the human race. He smiled and nodded, hoping the old baggage would tire of prattling on. When it seemed she would never stop, he became almost desperate in his attempt to escape.

Desperate situations called for desperate measures, he thought, and wondered what could end this tirade. By now his arms were tiring from holding the two cups of punch he was carrying to Lilly and Mari. Punch. That was the answer to his dilemma. Nodding in agreement with the matron's faulty assessment of her daughter's virtues, he admitted, "I've seen none who compares to her in Charleston."

The matron beamed and turned to nod reassuringly to her coltish offspring. When the woman moved, Ethan seized the opportunity and adjusted his position so that her action caused him to spill a few drops of punch onto the sleeve of her gown. "Oh, I am sorry. How clumsy of me," he groveled. "I can't seem to do anything right. Here take my handkerchief."

He handed the embroidered linen to the woman and stepped back. She dabbed at the garnet-colored liquid and muttered something. Ethan repressed his smile. His assessment had been right. Her dress was more valuable to her than marrying off her daughter.

"I do apologize." Ethan attempted to help and jiggled the cups again. This time the punch fell harmlessly to the floor, but the matron stepped back out of his way. He felt horrible about using such a ruse to escape her grasp, but he didn't want to stay long enough to have to turn down the inevitable offer to drop by for supper. "Goodness!" he cried, an anguished look wrinkling his face into a mixture of a scowl and a grin. "Do let me carry this punch to the ladies for whom it was intended before I inundate you with it. Simply too careless of me," he muttered as he stepped around the woman and her still speechless daughter.

By the time he reached Lilly, he was grinning broadly. His good manners, ground into him by a mammy who threatened to restrict his riding, abandoned him as he handed Lilly and Mari their drinks. With a twinkle in his eye he shook his head briefly and inhaled deeply. "Your good friend"—He glanced back at the woman—"the old woman with the—"

Lilly interrupted. "Are you referring to Mrs. Montaigne?

One of our most outstanding matrons? A pillar of society? One of the most vigorous workers for the Loyalist cause?"

Ethan sobered somewhat and peered down at Lilly. At the corners of her eyes, those wonderful warm brown eyes whose sparkle beckoned like a campfire on a cold night, he noticed tiny wrinkles. She was teasing him. Her laughter welled up and spilled forth like a hundred tinkling bells, ebullient and carefree on a spring morning. The sound surrounded him and wrapped him in a cloak of pure happiness.

Ethan gazed down into her eyes once again and felt a catch around his heart. He hadn't felt like this since the war began.

THE TENDER TEXAN

by Jodi Thomas

Anna Meyer dared to walk into a campsite full of Texan cattlemen...and offer one hundred dollars to the man who'd help her forge a frontier home-stead. Chance Wyatt accepted her offer, and agreed to settle down and build a home with the lovely stranger. They vowed to live together for one year only. But the challenges of the savage land drew them closer together and although the boy in him never considered the possibility of love, the man in him could not deny the passion . . .

__THE TENDER TEXAN 1-55773-546-8/$4.95
(August 1991)